# PRAISE FOR CA

## *Love, Comme*

"Yardley brings humor and humanity into the cutthroat world of online influencers, showing the realm's pleasures and pressures. Both protagonists are delightfully flawed, and Yardley seamlessly weaves their backstories and details of their Asian American heritage into the fast-paced narrative. This smart, sexy tale of fame and friendship is a charmer."

—*Publishers Weekly* (starred review)

"A fun, lively romance mines the insecurities common in people transitioning to adulthood."

—*Kirkus Reviews*

"Cathy Yardley is the queen of modern love stories. Her books are clever and swoony and unputdownable!"

—Penny Reid, *New York Times* bestselling author

"*Love, Comment, Subscribe* is so. Much. Fun. Cathy Yardley wrote this modern romance with just the perfect amount of humor and heartwarming moments that I was all in for Lily and Tobin's collab, both in business and in love."

—Tif Marcelo, *USA Today* bestselling author of *It Takes Heart*

## *Gouda Friends*

"It's palpable how much Tam and Josh care for each other . . . Yardley's fans will gobble up this gentle but steamy romance."

—*Publishers Weekly*

"Yardley's prose is summery and light—you'll get swept up as Tam and Josh breezily fall right back into place as the lovably cheesy duo known as Jam. A mouthwatering romance."

—*Kirkus Reviews*

# ROLE
# *Playing*

# OTHER TITLES BY CATHY YARDLEY

## Ponto Beach Reunion

*Love, Comment, Subscribe*
*Gouda Friends*
*Ex Appeal*

## Smartypants Romance

*Prose Before Bros, Green Valley Librarian book 1*

## Fandom Hearts

*Level Up*
*Hooked*
*One True Pairing*
*Game of Hearts*
*What Happens at Con*
*Ms. Behave*
*Playing Doctor*
*Ship of Fools*

## Stand-Alone Novels

*The Surfer Solution*
*Guilty Pleasures*
*Jack & Jilted*
*Baby, It's Cold Outside*

# ROLE Playing

CATHY YARDLEY

Montlake

This is a work of fiction. Names, characters, organizations, places, events, and incidents are either products of the author's imagination or are used fictitiously. Otherwise, any resemblance to actual persons, living or dead, is purely coincidental.



Published by Montlake, Seattle

www.apub.com



ISBN-13: 9781662503979 (paperback)
ISBN-13: 9781662503986 (digital)

Cover design by Faceout Studio, Amanda Hudson
Cover illustration by Leni Kauffman

Printed in the United States of America

*To my mother . . . I finally get it. This raising kids shit?*
*Is hard. Thank you for not giving up.*
*To my father . . . I miss you,*
*and I hope you've found peace.*
*And finally, to my son. You are a weird, amazing,*
*hysterically funny, brilliant person who has flourished*
*in spite of my awkward parenting skills.*
*I can't wait to see where life takes you.*

# CHAPTER 1

## OBVIOUSLY NOT FINE

*Stay calm. It'll all be fine.*

If there was one place Maggie Le did not want to be, it was pushing a wobbly shopping cart through the narrow aisles of Tasty Great, the primary supermarket in the town of Fool's Falls, eastern Washington State, population five thousand. Unfortunately, it was the only place to get food, and after eating tuna straight out of the can with a few farting squirts of mustard from a bottle that was more air than condiment, she had finally conceded that her cupboards were truly bare.

Still, it was fine. She'd get in, stock up, and get out with a minimum of interaction. Some pleasantries to the checkout lady. Comments on the weather.

She could do this. Or, more to the point, her best friend, Rosita, had told her she *had* to do this when she'd left her a voice mail asking if flour had an expiration date.

She dragged her feet, frowning at the articles on various shelves. She would admit to feeling a little *off* the past few weeks. She wanted to blame it on being busy. She'd just finished edits on a nonfiction book for a business publisher that was a regular client, then done some sample edits for possible future jobs. She'd done some administrative stuff—spreadsheets and money tracking—then lined up a few more projects, including editing a horror novel at the end of the month. For a freelancer, busy meant money, and that was always good, even if it meant she overbooked occasionally.

Because she worked from home, she was used to setting her own schedule. In the past few weeks she'd started to abandon her circadian rhythms. She found herself working whenever she felt like it, getting up when she felt like it, sleeping when she had to. Which meant, for the past week, she had found herself asleep in the recliner more than once, sending a response email at three in the morning (her client later replied, "Why were you up at three a.m.?" which, okay, *rude*), and eating what was left in the house when she felt like it.

Some people might think this erratic, possibly a cause for concern. She preferred to think of it as not giving a single, solitary fuck.

Which, she supposed, might also be considered just the teeniest bit aggressive.

To frame it more positively, she saw it as *freeing*. That was the whole point of working from home and living alone. She could dance buck naked in her living room at four in the morning if she wanted to, music blaring. She could sleep twenty hours on her kitchen floor. Granted, her forty-eight-year-old body would probably make its displeasure known if she did either, but the point was, she *could*. She had absolute autonomy, no one to witness, no one else's opinion weighing in. As long as she was finishing milestones on time and meeting deadlines, and most importantly paying her bills, she was as free as the proverbial bird.

But she *did* need to eat. She was down to expired cans of light fruit cocktail, a tin of Spam, and condiments. Hence, going to town.

She navigated her way through the store, feeling a little disoriented. She hadn't bought groceries for one person in decades, she realized. She wasn't even sure what she wanted, as opposed to what her son would eat and what she could easily cook in large quantities. She just knew that she wanted this whole thing over with.

*If I load up,* she reasoned, *that will pare down the number of times I have to go to town.* She had an outdoor freezer as well as her refrigerator, and she was used to stocking up her pantry.

Her friend Mac would say that she'd graduated from introvert to hair-shirt-wearing hermit. Then again, Mac lived way out in Toronto. And she'd never actually *met* Mac in real life, although they'd been Twitter besties for the better part of fifteen years. They'd connected over a shared love of *Robotech*, both revealing that they'd written fanfic for the animated show years before the proliferation of fan fiction sites.

For all she knew, Mac actually lived in a cave with good Wi-Fi, so maybe Mac wouldn't judge.

After several agonizing minutes, she got an industrial-size box of chicken-flavored ramen, a big jug of soy sauce, and a bottle of fish sauce that ought to last her for a few months at least. Since she was in the store's "ethnic" section (such as it was), she tossed in cans of refried beans and salsa after it. Then she maneuvered to the pasta aisle and loaded up on pasta, tomato sauce, and parmesan in the plastic jars.

"Maggie? Is that you?"

She stiffened.

*Oh, God, no.*

She turned to find a woman with stick-straight toffee-brown hair and big hazel eyes smiling at her. Her face was a wide oval, wearing a casual amount of makeup, with smile lines at the corners of her eyes and her lips. She wore a pair of jeans and an aqua sweater with a camouflage-pattern hunter's jacket over it, a nod to the cooler October weather.

"How *are* you?" the woman said, and to Maggie's horror, she looked like she was going in for a hug. "I've been worried about you!"

Maggie made a little "eep" noise and instinctively took a step back.

*God damn it!* She'd deliberately rushed so she didn't shop on the weekend, a time when she'd be more likely to run into one of the few people she knew, even after living ten years in this town. So of course, today would be the one day she ran into . . .

"Hi, Deb," Maggie said, her voice sounding rusty to her own ears. It occurred to her that she didn't talk to clients often . . . her communication was purely online. She also tended to text if not messaging or emailing. She might not have spoken to anyone this week.

Okay. Maybe longer.

Deb looked amused. "How're you holding up?" she asked. "It must be so strange, Kit moving away so far. Of course, we always knew he'd be going off to college, but Seattle's so far away!"

Maggie felt like her chest was caving in on itself. She nodded curtly.

Deb either didn't notice, or did a good job pretending. "Harrison misses him something fierce," she continued, referring to her own son, "but at least they can still text and play video games online or whatever. When did you drop him off at U Dub?"

"Two weeks ago," Maggie croaked, then cleared her throat. "I drove him over, got him settled in the dorms."

Deb tutted. "Empty nest. And you're all alone on that big property! Not even a dog!"

*Shut up shut up shut up.*

"I'm fine," Maggie said instead.

"Oh, you poor thing," Deb instantly crooned. "You must be lonely. I know I would be if Harrison left town! Especially since the divorce . . ."

"I've been divorced for five years," Maggie snapped before she could stop herself.

Deb pulled away for a second, her expression sad. "*My* divorce," she clarified.

*Oh, shit. Right.*

Maggie vaguely remembered that Deb had gotten divorced, what, a year ago? Guilt pummeled her. "Sorry," she mumbled.

"That's fine," Deb responded, with a cheery smile. Deb was nothing if not cheery, Maggie remembered. Kit and Harrison had been best friends from grade school on, and while Maggie was hardly what anyone would call social, she'd still interacted with Deb—waving hi when one or the other dropped their kid at the respective best friend's house, talking to her while volunteering for whatever school functions Maggie couldn't weasel out of. "My point was, even though Harrison moved out after graduation, he's constantly over, raiding the fridge. Doing his laundry." She laughed. "It's like he still lives there!"

Maggie frowned, then remembered what Kit had told her: Harrison had moved in with his girlfriend right after school ended. The two of them eighteen years old. *Dear God.* "How is Harrison doing, anyway?" Maggie asked.

Deb shrugged. "Harrison's still working over at the hardware store, but he's saving up money to go to truck-driving school . . . or at least, he should be," Deb said. "Until the latest game console comes out, and then he buys *that*. But that's Anna's problem now, right?"

Anna. Harrison's girlfriend, she presumed. "And Anna's doing all right?"

"Well, she's not pregnant, thank God," Deb said, and Maggie choked. "So I'm counting it as a win. What are you doing with yourself these days?"

"Working," Maggie said. "Really busy."

"Oh, sweetie," Deb cooed. Then Deb's eyes traveled over her, and Maggie suddenly got a sense of what she must look like from the outside. She was wearing a fleece sweat jacket, stained with something she'd eaten, over an old Siouxsie and the Banshees T-shirt, thin and frayed. Her jeans had holes in the knees, not out of any fashion sense but because they were her oldest pair and the damned things had finally worn out. She was wearing knockoff UGGs that had mud on them. She wasn't sure she'd combed her wavy hair, which was down past her shoulder blades, and she certainly wasn't wearing any makeup, since she never did.

She probably looked like a natural disaster survivor.

"You know what you need?" Deb said, her voice determined. "You need to get out."

"I am out," Maggie protested. "Look. Here I am, out at the store."

Deb laughed, a trilling sound. Maggie felt herself scowl at it and then forced herself to pull it together. The last thing she needed was for Harrison to get back to Kit, claiming that his mother had been a bitch to Harrison's mother at the Tasty Great.

"No, silly," Deb said. Another quick once-over of Maggie's clothes and hair, and her smile was even brighter, if a bit forced. "If you have a reason to leave the house, you'll feel better. I mean, who doesn't love a reason to dress up a little, am I right?"

Maggie suppressed a shudder.

"I don't like leaving the house, though. In fact, I'll do a lot to actively avoid leaving the house. Case in point." She gestured to the industrial-size box of ramen.

"I know! You could come to book club tomorrow! I'm hosting, and you know where I live."

Maggie balked. "Oh, I don't . . . I haven't even read . . . whatever book you're reading," she tried.

"Nobody reads the book," Deb said with a laugh. "It's just an excuse to have a potluck, day drink, and gossip."

"Wow. That sounds . . ." *Like hell on earth!* "I mean, I wouldn't even know anyone."

"You'd know *me*," Deb said. "That's it, I'm not taking no for an answer. You can't let yourself just be miserable, alone in your house! We single girls need to stick together, now that our kids are grown!" She let out that trilling laugh again.

Maggie grimaced. "I really don't think so."

*I would rather eat my own intestines than cross your threshold.*

"Well, if you change your mind, it starts at two. You might want to grab something to bring—again, we're always up for desserts. Or booze!" Deb then moved in, giving her a quick and unwelcome hug. It made Maggie almost sad that she'd showered that morning . . . a four-day-long unbathed Maggie would've probably made Deb reconsider her book club invitation. Then Deb waved, pushing her own cart in the direction of the bakery section.

Maggie wanted to scream. Deb meant well, honestly. She was a raging extrovert, and she was convinced that she could solve problems with a casserole brigade and a metric ton of sunshine. The problem was Maggie was not the type to make friends. She knew she was isolated. She had been since childhood, growing up in her grandparents' house. She'd certainly been isolated in her marriage, for a variety of reasons.

Quite frankly, she took care of herself. Anyone who told her it wasn't healthy wasn't anyone she wanted to hang out with.

She moved more quickly, afraid Deb might do something rash, like invite her to lunch. She loaded up her cart haphazardly, adding a case of replacement tuna, boxes of mac and cheese, frozen vegetables, diet soda. A bag of clementines, a nod to health that was quickly negated when she added a few tubs of Chocolate Brownie Thunder ice cream. Then she fled.

There was no way in hell she was going to that book club. If she played her cards right, she might not leave the house until after Halloween. That was, what, three weeks away? She could definitely make it that long. Hell, maybe she'd see if she could order some staples to be delivered, price be damned . . . although she lived far enough away that grocery delivery likely wasn't an option.

She'd just avoid Deb. Avoid going outside. Keep her head down, do her work, text Kit and Mac. Pay her bills.

And it would all be fine.

# CHAPTER 2

## HEROIC SAFE MODE

"Aiden Stephen Bishop, are you even listening to me?"

Aiden winced as his mother middle-named him. "Sorry, Ma," he said quickly.

"You picked up the wrong kind of bran flakes," she sniped as she unloaded the groceries he was depositing on her worn Formica kitchen counters. She'd stopped dyeing her hair the past year, and it was now worn in a short, serviceable gray haircut that was getting a little shaggy. He'd have to remember to ask if she wanted to schedule going down to the salon. "And canola oil? I wanted vegetable oil!"

He fought against a sigh, then plastered a smile on his face. "Sorry," he repeated.

*In my defense, you just wrote "oil," and they're basically the same thing.*

"This is why I should have gone with you," she said, conveniently ignoring the fact that she'd been exhausted when he had offered to take her. She huffed impatiently, putting away some apples and bananas. He hoped she'd actually eat them this time, rather than let them go bad. She was still grumbling when she went off to the bathroom.

While she was out of the room, he rushed to store the rest of the groceries he'd brought in from his truck. He'd discovered that she still tried to put things up on the top shelves, which lately had become a recipe for disaster. Partially because she'd wear her house slippers on the step stool, which . . . well, often made her slip. And the longer she raised her hands over her head, the more likely she was to get dizzy and pass out. She'd already fallen twice this year, one time resulting in cutting her forehead and bleeding badly. He wanted to prevent that if he could.

When he had finally gotten all the food in its respective and easily accessible spots, he glanced around, making sure that he hadn't missed anything. His mother's kitchen was the kitchen he grew up in, and it hadn't changed much. The linoleum floor was worn, especially under the dragging feet of the kitchen table. The counters were meticulously scrubbed clean, faded in specific circles to the right of the stove top and the left of the sink. The fridge was new—he'd bought it a year ago, not long after his father died. He opened up the door, doing a spot check. Sure enough, there was what looked like a cucumber that had gone squishy. Grimacing, he tossed it in the trash . . . then took the trash outside for good measure.

He hadn't regretted moving home to Fool's Falls when his dad fell ill two years ago. He'd owned a damned hospice business when he lived in Seattle, and he'd been a nurse for years before that . . . he had more than enough experience to do whatever was needed. No matter how his father might've felt about Aiden's career, they'd gotten a bit closer that last year. Or at least, they'd come to some kind of peace.

Alas, the same could not be said of his mother. Before going back in the house, he pulled out his phone, shooting a quick text to his best friend and ex–business partner, Malcolm.

AIDEN: Fifty years old and I'm still being treated like I'm fifteen. Remind me again why I'm still here in the Falls?

MALCOLM: Because you're a good son. Possibly too good. She driving you up a wall again?

AIDEN: Only always.

MALCOLM: You got this. We still on for Thursday? This week's been brutal, and I could use a little online time to blow off steam.

AIDEN: Yeah. Was thinking the Castle Run?

MALCOLM: That's a good one. Let's hope everybody's up for it.

Aiden grinned at the phone. Sometimes he thought if it weren't for his online gaming guild, he'd lose his mind.

He came back into his mother's house to start dinner. "I was thinking of making black-and-blue salad this week," he said, keeping his voice upbeat. "What do you think? Grilled steak, and I picked up some salad and blue cheese."

"Steak's expensive," she scolded.

"It was on sale." Actually, it wasn't, but he'd paid for it. She didn't need to know that.

She sighed. "Why haven't you fixed my car yet?" she pressed. "If I had my car, I could've driven myself!"

He felt his shoulders tense. "I'm waiting on some parts," he said.

"Parts? What parts?"

"The . . . carb manifold," he said. That was a thing, wasn't it? "And the timing belt's not right. I had to send the old one back."

"Did you order it online?" she asked, then started shaking her head before he could even answer. "That's the damned problem. You should've gone to O'Reilly's and then gotten the right thing."

"You're probably right," he said, trying to soothe her.

"It's like your father always said," his mother added sagely. "You order online, you get those cheap pieces of crap from China. No wonder you got the wrong size! Probably would've snapped the first time you used it, for pity's sake."

"Mom," Aiden reprimanded her, and grimaced. Yes, his father's sentiments were well known, and shared by his mother, and if he was honest, a good population of the town. "Not okay."

His mother was sullen, but she fell silent. "Davy would've had the car fixed by now."

He forced his face to stay placid at the mention of his younger brother. "He probably would," he finally said, with forced cheer. "But he's running all those car dealerships, so maybe he'd be too busy."

Davy was certainly too busy to leave Spokane and come back to Fool's Falls, despite Aiden's repeated requests. He'd come back sporadically as their father battled with cancer, but Aiden knew seeing their once larger-than-life father reduced to the frail shell he was before he passed was too much. He also knew that, despite being their mother's favorite, dealing with the increasing acidity of their mother's tongue since their father's death was more than Davy was equipped to deal with. Here it was October, and he hadn't seen Davy in person since Easter.

And that was to say nothing of *the Issue.*

His mother walked over to her coffee machine, pouring herself an earthenware mug. Aiden shuddered to think what cup she was on by now. She drank almost a pot of the highest-octane stuff she could manage every day. "Still, he couldn't be slower than you've been," she grumbled.

Time to pull out his ace in the hole. "I could always drop it by Dominic's," he said, referring to the mechanic in town.

She reared back. "Are you kidding? I'm on a fixed income! That bastard would bleed me dry!"

His father's words, again. "I'll get on it," he said.

What he didn't say, and perhaps should have, was: *I haven't fixed the car because the problem isn't with the engine. The problem is you backed into a large light pole, bumped into two parked cars, and sideswiped a delivery truck.*

Three separate incidents. Three strikes, and please God, she needed to be out.

He'd finally pulled her spark plugs and made up a car problem. He wished he could be more honest, but she wouldn't listen, and he hadn't come up with a way to make her.

He'd tried discussing the matter with Davy, but Davy had been dodging his calls. Lord knows, neither of them wanted to tell their mother that she shouldn't be driving anymore. She was seventy-six years old and still sharp, or mostly sharp. He'd surreptitiously done tests to see how her memory was doing, her cognitive function. But especially since their father's death, she'd just gotten more acerbic. He knew why. He tried to grant her understanding and respect her independence . . . no matter how hard and painful it sometimes was to see her struggling. To bear the brunt of her anger. But there they were.

"So," she said, "Jason's wedding is coming up in December. Though why they're doing it right before Christmas, I will never know. Who the hell is going to want to drive to Coeur d'Alene in the snow?"

"Maybe there won't be as much snow," he said. "But if there is, I guess it'll just be a smaller wedding."

"They're getting married at some swanky resort," she said, her pursed lips saying just what she thought about *that* idea. "Did you get your invitation?"

"Yes," he said. "But I don't think I'm going to go."

It was the wrong thing to say. His mother's eyes widened, and her nostrils flared.

He sighed. This was going to suck.

"What do you mean, you're not going to go?" she snapped. "You *have* to go!"

*Stay calm. Be cool.*

"Do I, though?" he said. "Jason's twenty years younger than me, and we've never been all that close."

"He's your aunt's youngest, and the whole family is going to be there!"

"Yeah, well," he tried to joke, "the whole family and I have never been all that close either."

Wrong move, part two. His mother slammed the mug on the kitchen table, ignoring the slosh over the wood. "You are going," she growled, "and that is *final*."

As if he were twelve again, and not a grown man. Anger snapped like sparks from a fire, but he steadfastly ignored it.

"Davy's going to be there," he pointed out. "And you'll be there. I am assuming that it's enough representation from our branch of the family. Besides, if Davy's going to be there and he brings *her*, it's going to be . . . awkward."

He hated bringing it up. *Hated* it. But it was the truth.

"That's precisely why you have to go," she said. "Sheryl's going to be there with your brother, and the whole family is still gossiping about the three of you. They still think there's bad blood between you all. You need to put that to rest, once and for all."

"And how am I supposed to do that?" he said, his temper finally slipping the leash a little bit. "I've done everything but put up a billboard saying 'I don't care that my brother married my ex-girlfriend' for nearly twenty years! How will me being at the wedding change what countless family gatherings hasn't?"

"Yes, but you've never had a date or girlfriend since Sheryl," she pointed out. "So you're going to go to the wedding. And you're going to bring a date."

He wanted to shout. He wanted to punch a hole in the drywall.

He did neither.

Then his mother smiled, and he immediately braced for impact, because it was one of her crafty smiles. The one that usually preceded a gut punch.

"Of course, you should be done fixing my car by then," she said, drawing out each syllable. "I could always drive. All the way to Idaho. In the snow, in December," she said, her voice sly. "Or you could drive me."

She knew, or at least strongly suspected, what he was doing with the car. Damn it. "Mom, you shouldn't be driving," he finally said.

"I am a grown woman, and I am fine . . ."

"Remember when you passed out?" he asked. "And fell? Right here, in the kitchen."

She scowled. "Are you going to stop throwing that in my face?"

"Imagine passing out at the wheel," he continued relentlessly. "At least it's a good car, so you wouldn't necessarily get crumpled like a tin can. But let's say you plow into a crowd. Or hit someone in a parking lot. Or hit a bunch of kids. How are you going to feel then?"

"Don't you do that," she shot back. "That's not going to happen."

He took a deep breath. He should've known. She wasn't ready to hear it, no matter how much she *needed* to hear it. And it wasn't the only issue that they needed to discuss. His father had had a will, thankfully, but his mother didn't, and there were things she needed to take care of—things that, as someone who'd spent his career taking care of elder patients, he knew would be best. Durable power of attorney. Living will. Decisions about medical care. Hell, what would they do if she couldn't take care of herself anymore? She barely tolerated him in the house at this point.

"I'll . . . drive you to the wedding," he said, feeling outflanked.

She smiled. "*And* you'll bring a date."

"I'll get a date," he agreed, countermaneuvering, "*if* . . . you agree to talk to Davy and me about those issues you keep avoiding. Your driving.

The paperwork stuff." He paused for a beat. "Medical decisions, Mom. It's important."

She grimaced, and he wondered what he'd do next if she said no.

"Fine," she finally grumbled, wiping up the spilled coffee with a napkin from the holder on the table. "Go, cook that steak-salad thing you're talking about. And tell me you got a loaf of bread. I'm not one of those crazy keto people, you know."

He felt his shoulders retreat from their pinched position by his ears. It was a small victory, but these days, he'd take the W where he could find it. All he had to do was go to his cousin's wedding, and . . .

Find a date.

*Crap.*

# CHAPTER 3

## PRISONS ARE A GYMNASIUM

That night, after the Great Grocery Store Debacle, Maggie indulged in a bowl of instant ramen with Spam and soy sauce eggs and watched the first episode of a series that Mac had recommended. It was times like this that she missed California. She'd grown up in a small town, Mount Tonne, in Northern Cal. Still, it had been half an hour to Napa and not that much farther to Berkeley and San Francisco. Whenever she felt the urge, she could get real tonkotsu ramen, or Ethiopian food, or authentic chiles rellenos, and she had missed the convenience and diversity of cuisine since she moved to Eastern Washington. It had been easier when they'd lived on the west side, closer to Seattle, but once they moved to the Falls, those choices evaporated.

She did like food. Probably a little too well, especially toward the crumbling last few years of her marriage, when she had scrambled for the quickest legal endorphin sources possible. But the budding foodie she'd been in Napa had gotten squashed somewhere along the way. Her ex-husband, Trev, wasn't really into what he called "fancy" food, and she'd found herself going along to get along.

Story of her marriage, really.

She glanced at her phone. When it was eight thirty, she dialed her son, Kit. She doubted he'd answer. It was eight o'clock on a Friday, after all. Honestly, he *shouldn't* be answering . . .

"Hi, Mom," he said, and she could hear the eye roll in his voice. "You okay?"

She winced. "Yeah, yeah, I'm fine," she said, hating that it was his first question. "Wanted to hear the same about you."

"Yes, I have successfully survived my first two weeks of school."

"I honestly didn't think you'd pick up," she admitted sheepishly. "I was going to leave a message."

"You could've texted me."

"I hate texting," she answered, "and you know that."

He snickered. "Okay, boomer."

She huffed, but it was all for show. Then, suddenly, she froze as a thought hit her. "Oh, shit. Is your roomie there? Other people? Am I totally embarrassing you or seeming like one of those helicopter parents or making you look like some freak with mommy issues?"

He burst out laughing, even though that wasn't her purpose at all. "You're fine. My roomie went to a party, or to rush something, I don't remember."

Maggie fought her instinctive recoiling from the term "rush." She didn't understand Greek life at all, but then, she hadn't rushed in her brief college experience in Berkeley. But maybe it was a good thing? Something Kit ought to pursue? "Why didn't you go too?"

"Other than the fact that I wasn't asked?" Kit replied, with a wry tone. "I don't think that I'm the frat type. And I didn't feel like going to somewhere random on campus, like a café or something. And certainly not a party where I don't know anybody."

She bit her lip. She wouldn't, either, but she'd at least managed to make friends in college—sort of. "Yeah, but you will," she said. "Anybody seem nice in your classes? Or maybe in your dorm? It takes a while. Just, you know, say hi, be personable. Make a friend."

"Do you even know me?" he asked, with a chuckle.

"You hung out with Harrison every chance you got," she protested. "And you were the one who went up to him, not the other way around."

"I was eight," Kit said, his voice dry as the Sahara. "It was before I hit puberty and became emo and antisocial. He was grandfathered in before the cutoff."

She got up, pacing the kitchen. The TV was still on in the background, some cooking show, but the sound was muted. "I just don't want you to be lonely," she admitted. "You're my kid. And yeah, I know I can be . . . overprotective . . ."

She scowled when his laughter exploded through the phone speaker. "You think?"

"Hey, I'm trying!"

"I know, Mom," Kit said. "I know this is hard for you. I appreciate everything you've done to help me get here. I don't want you to think I don't."

He sounded so grown up, she thought. And hated what he'd gone through to sound this way.

"Besides, you can't point fingers at me," Kit pointed out. "It's not like you're Ms. Congeniality either. You're more antisocial than I am."

"I am not," she lied.

"I will text Aunt Rosita, and she will back me up," Kit scoffed.

"Aunt Rosita is proof that I'm social! She's been my best friend since high school!"

"Yes, but she's all the way in California, and you haven't been back there in ages," he countered. "Besides, calling her once a month or whatever hardly counts."

Maggie scowled, even though he couldn't see it. "I have other friends."

"Your only other friend is someone you've never met, that you DM on Twitter, who for all you know is an octogenarian war criminal in hiding who happens to like *Robotech* as much as you do."

"And is a Sagittarius," Maggie tacked on. "Her Twitter name is Macross Sagittarius."

"Ah, yes. Her zodiac sign helps," Kit said sarcastically. "Mom, we're a lot of things, but social we're not."

But he *could* be. It would be healthier if he was, ultimately—not like "big man on campus" or a party animal, but just having a support network.

She wanted to push the issue. She hated the idea of him isolated, feeling lost on that huge campus. Her brain conjured up images of him wandering like a stereotypical freshman in an eighties comedy or something, but with more disastrous effects . . . the guy who was the butt of jokes, the isolated, shy "loser." He might not have had a lot of friends in high school, but the ones he had loved him and thought he was hysterical—which, when given the opportunity to warm up, he really was. He'd even dated, although she didn't know how far that went, nor did she want to (beyond a painful talk about sex that had proved embarrassing and largely unnecessary, and her putting a box of condoms in his bathroom "just in case"). He was a slow starter, but very charismatic once you got past the Wall of Shy.

But that wasn't something she could just tell him. And she also knew she was hearing her ex-husband's words in her head.

*You spoil him.*

*He needs to learn how to deal with things on his own.*

*He needs to toughen up, goddamn it.*

*If he's going to cry like a baby because somebody tells him to stop fucking up, then we're failing him.*

*You think I'm the only person that's going to be hard on him?*

She closed her eyes. Not now. She wasn't going to walk down that toxic old memory path now.

"How did you do this week?" Kit asked. "What did you do?"

"Oh, you know. The usual," Maggie said, with a wave of her hand. "Lots of work. I went grocery shopping. Texted Mac. Called you."

He let out an impatient breath. "Tell me you're not going to go all Howard Hughes in that house."

"I'll stop short of peeing in jars," she assured him, with a sarcastic edge of her own. "Besides, again—this is not different than before you went to school. I wasn't waiting for you to go off to college to suddenly party my ass off, kiddo."

"I just don't want you to go full hermit."

"Kit, what do I keep telling you?" she said, gently but firmly. "*I'm* the parent. *You're* the child. Relax."

He waited a beat. "Okay. I'm playing the no-hypocrisy card."

"Wait, what?"

"You want *me* to get friends, but *you* won't get friends?" He paused a beat. "That's not exactly fair, is it?"

"Mac's my friend," she protested.

"Harrison's my friend," Kit countered. "Maybe I won't make any IRL friends. Maybe I'll only leave my room for classes and eating, and not talk to anybody I don't have to. I mean, it works for you, doesn't it?"

She tried desperately to see a loophole in his argument, but ever since Trev left, she'd largely abandoned "do as I say, not as I do" edicts because she hated how unfair they were. God knows, she'd gotten enough of them from Nana Birdie and Papa Chris growing up, and Trev had a stance that when you were an adult, you could do what you wanted—but as a child, you did what you were told. It was how he'd been raised and a big part of why he'd left his large and overbearing family behind in California. Trev's family had been well meaning but intrusive. His parents had wanted him to go to college rather than working the manual-labor jobs he'd chosen, first in construction, then in logging. His grandparents had wanted him to take over their hardware store, but he hadn't wanted that either. Also, as much as they'd been friends with Maggie's grandparents, they hadn't been thrilled when he'd started seeing Maggie. She often wondered if marrying her, as well as moving out of state, was a "fuck you" to them, since both had managed to get Trev cut off from his family completely. Kit had never even gotten to know his paternal grandparents. It was funny, then, that Trev had gotten just as autocratic when he'd become a parent.

Long story short, she wanted to teach Kit about parity, and while it wasn't always feasible, she tried desperately not to simply impose her will on him.

On the plus side, it made their bond closer. He knew that when she told him to do something, it was because she had a damned good reason for it, not because she was being tyrannical or impulsive.

On the minus, it did mean he'd developed arguing skills a trial lawyer would envy and thought that everything was open to debate. She'd made a tactical error on that one, one that Trev would probably rub her nose in like a puppy with shit if he were still in the state and they were still communicating.

"What if I did something social?" she said. He laughed again. "Okay, now that's getting insulting."

"First of all, What's social in Fool's Falls?" he asked. "And secondly, What's social in the Falls that you're actually interested in going to?"

"As it happens, I bumped into Deb at Tasty Great when I went food shopping, and she invited me to her book club tomorrow. I thought I'd drop by."

"You're going . . . to a book club? By choice? With *Ms. Deb*?" The incredulity was palpable. "No way."

"Yes way," she said, even as her stomach fell a little at the thought that she would have to do the thing. "So, what about you? What are you going to do?"

His following pause was long, and she realized he was nervous.

"How about you go to a club meeting too?" she said. "Something you're interested in. They've got to have something. Game design. Asian heritage . . ."

"Mom, I'm a quarter Asian," he countered quickly. "I don't even really look Asian. I seriously don't think going to a club where they think I'm a fetishist is going to help."

She winced. "Okay, maybe not," she agreed. "But they've got to have something. If I go to book club, you've got to at least try to go to something. Agreed?"

He paused again, then sighed heavily. "Pics or it didn't happen," he finally said.

"I will selfie as proof," she said, feeling a little victorious. "Now, what are you going to do?"

"Harrison and I are going to do a dungeon run on *DeathCharm Vengeance* tonight, I think," he said.

"Okay, tell him I said hi. And make sure you get some sleep, okay?"

"Tomorrow's Saturday, and sleep's for the weak," he said, and she could hear the smile in his voice. "Love you, Mom."

The sudden slash of missing him was like one of those cuts with a sharp kitchen knife, where you don't even know how deep it is until it starts bleeding . . . where it doesn't hurt until it stings like fuck.

"Love you, too, sweetie," she said, then hung up as tears welled.

Well, this was stupid, she told herself, wiping at her eyes. She'd always scoffed at parents who talked about empty nest and how it hurt. She had made the primary aim of her life getting Kit off to school, or trade school, or whatever it took to make him a healthy, relatively happy, as-well-adjusted-as-could-be-expected adult human. But even as she felt thrilled that he was finally on his way, she missed him, so much.

And now she was committed to going to the book club, she realized with horror. And taking a selfie.

This was going to suck; she just knew it. But if it would help Kit . . .

Well. *Needs fucking must.*

# CHAPTER 4

## BECAUSE DESTINY SAYS SO

She was here because she *had* to be here. It would help Kit. That was the important thing. All she had to do was get a . . . *selfie*, she admonished herself with a cringe. Just provide Kit with some proof that she had made the effort, gone to Deb's book club, interacted with other humans. Made a stab at friendship.

She had texted Deb, letting her know she'd be coming. She'd made a pan of chicken enchiladas—the toss-together-casserole kind, emphasizing convenience over authenticity, with cream of mushroom soup and canned chicken and a fuck-ton of shredded cheese. She was freshly showered, and her hair was combed, although frizzy from a hasty dry. Her jeans were intact. She'd drawn the line at wearing a bra, confident that her cable-knit sweater and her (now clean) fleece jacket would cover anything potentially egregious. Not that showing a nipple bump was going to kill anybody, but still, she could almost hear her Nana Birdie shrieking at the mere thought. Her grandmother had tried to instill a sense of southern social graces from the time Maggie had been unceremoniously dumped in her lap at age three.

Obviously, *that* hadn't quite worked.

Bracing herself, Maggie stepped into a house that was easily seventy-five degrees and a living room full of women that she barely knew. They smiled, but their eyes assessed her. She shifted nervously in response.

"Everybody, this is Maggie," Deb gushed, grabbing the enchiladas and ushering her over to the couch. "These smell amazing! Can I get you a drink? We've got margaritas!"

"Ah, no, thank you." The idea that she'd have to hang around until the alcohol wore off made her skin itch. Then she looked around and saw every one of the other five women had a salt-rimmed margarita glass in hand. "I'm a lightweight, and I'm driving," she clarified awkwardly.

"Maggie is Kit's mother," Deb added. "Remember? Harrison's best friend, Kit. He's just gone off to college, and she's all alone!"

The women all started cooing "ohhh" and nodding, like this explained the sudden presence of a teetotaling stranger. Maggie pushed herself to smile. It was probably a bit ghoulish, or at least forced, but hey, she was trying.

"This is Cordy," Deb continued, gesturing to a slightly older woman sitting on one of the couches, with short gray hair and bright, inquisitive blue eyes that seemed to pierce right into her. "We met at church group—that's where I met Klara, as well," she added, gesturing to a woman whose ashy blonde hair was going a barely perceptible gray. Klara held up her hand in a hesitant wave.

"Hi, I'm Patience," a stick-thin woman with voluminous blonde hair said, shaking her hand. She had hazel eyes like Deb's, and Maggie wondered briefly if they were related, until Patience confirmed, "I'm Deb's cousin."

"And I'm Lisa," a red-haired woman chimed in. "I live next door. I also own the little general store? Down Copperhead Trail?"

"Oh, yes," Maggie said. She went there very rarely—it was too expensive, albeit convenient. Also, she seemed to remember the woman being friendly and a little . . . well, nosy. She tended to share the business of everyone else in the small town, whether it was solicited or not.

"I used to get Kit those strawberry-shortcake ice cream pops there," she added.

Again: she was *trying*.

"Well, that's all of us," Deb said, with a grin. "Come on, come on. We were just going to eat!"

The group of them got up, putting their margaritas on the dining room table before heading en masse to the kitchen. She shuffled behind them, her brain working frantically. She really only needed a photo with Deb to prove to Kit she was social. Then, she could make up some excuse and go.

"Just you and your husband, then? Empty nesters?" Lisa, the inquisitive convenience store owner, said with a look of sympathy. "Clyde and I felt that way after Scott moved to Chewelah. I mean, it's not that far, but it felt like it, you know?"

Before Maggie could respond, Deb quickly piped up. "She's been divorced for a few years now. And she's in one of those houses in the Upper Falls. She's all by herself on fifteen acres, rattling around that big house by herself!"

Maggie cringed, stabbing at the salad. It wasn't *that* big a house, but Deb did have a point. It was huge for one person.

"She doesn't even have a dog!" Deb said as her own dog, Duchess, came wandering up. She was an older collie, very demure and posh but not above making puppy eyes and begging.

Maggie sighed as she petted Duchess's head. "I'm really fine with it," she insisted.

"You should come out with us for girls' night," Deb said firmly.

*Oh, hell no.* But before she could come up with an excuse, Cordy started coughing, her eyes bugging out.

"Cordy? Are you okay?" Deb asked quickly.

"What the hell *is* this?" the older woman said, her fork poking at her plate.

Deb turned, studying the food. "Maggie, didn't you make those?"

The entire table turned to look at her.

"Um, yes," she said. "They're chicken enchiladas."

"'Bout burned my mouth off!" Cordy made a big show of drinking most of her glass of water. "Good lord. You have to warn a woman!"

Maggie frowned. It barely had half a can of jalapeños in it and, frankly, enough dairy to douse most of the heat. She'd even drained the can before adding what she thought was a conservative amount. Normally she just dumped the whole thing in, liquid and all, enjoying what Kit called the "ring of fire" around her lips.

"I'm sorry," Maggie said. "Kit was fine with it that way, and Harrison never complained when he ate it, so it didn't even occur to me . . ."

"Well, teenage boys will eat anything, won't they?" Deb said indulgently, as if that explained everything. Maggie felt her frown deepen.

"So, Maggie . . ." Patience assessed her, tapping her chin with a long, manicured nail. "You're how old?"

Maggie had a tough time swallowing the bite of (unseasoned, mayo-heavy) potato salad on her fork. "Forty-eight."

"Really?" It was not a compliment. "Hmm. Are you looking to dive back in the dating pool, then? You could always go hang out with Deb and me. We know the best happy hours, and now that Harrison's moved out and she's letting me move in, I'm going to do everything I can to make sure my cousin has some *fun*."

"Um, no," Maggie said, in what she hoped was a self-deprecating way. "Dating really isn't my thing."

"It can seem hard," Patience assured her, "but don't worry. It's like riding a bike. You just have to get back on the horse."

Before she could respond to the mixed metaphor, Deb added, "You're not avoiding dating because of the divorce, are you? Or because you feel too old? Because that's ridiculous. Good grief, it's not like your life ends at fifty and you become some sexless robot. It's not like you're . . . you're *used up* or *broken* or whatever!"

Maggie sighed. *Tell me you're still pissed about being divorced without saying you're still pissed about being divorced.* "I'm not saying that. I'm just . . ."

"Well, it can make you feel a little broken at the time, I'm sure," Lisa said, and when Deb turned on her, she held her hands up defensively. "Just saying!"

"It's been five years since Trev walked out," Deb said on Maggie's behalf. "I've only been divorced once, and I'm *glad*. It was worth it. Totally the right decision! I should've divorced him sooner, if anything." Her eyes flashed for a moment. "I sure as hell am not *broken*!"

"Maybe it's different for different people," Klara said with kindness.

Deb ignored her. "Do you think there's something wrong with *you* just because he left?" Deb pressed, glaring at Maggie.

"Deb," Cordy interjected, her face both sympathetic and chastising. Patience leaned in, like she was watching *Real Housewives* or something. Klara looked placid—seemed like her default setting—and Lisa practically squirmed in discomfort.

Deb read the room, then grumbled. "I just think it's like giving up. You're *letting* him win."

Maggie took a few deep breaths through her nose. Deb's divorce had obviously hurt her deeply, and her vehemence was based on some personal issues.

That said, Maggie had also sworn to herself that she wasn't going to carry someone else's fucking baggage. Not anymore.

Maggie's divorce *had* broken her, no matter what Deb said. It wasn't an accident or some careless thing, like a mug nudged off a counter, a vase bumped by somebody's elbow. She was broken like a bottle on a bar edge, and it felt like she had rage pulsing through her every single day. Even after five years, she still had jagged edges that she'd only barely kept from Kit. Now that he was gone, it was like it had all welled to the surface, like a suit of armor made of razor blades.

Dating?

She was ready, maybe even eager, to cut someone.

"I am. Not. Dating," Maggie said, trying to keep her tone low despite her vehemence. "And I don't give a fuck what it looks like. To *anyone*."

They stared at her. Lisa's mouth dropped open, and Patience's eyes went wide.

Probably shouldn't have dropped an f-bomb at book club, but there it was.

She got up, heading to the kitchen to toss out her paper plate and plastic fork, and the rest followed suit. When she went back to the living room, Patience was hissing furiously at Deb. She fell silent, pasting on a wide smile as Maggie came near.

They talked around her, not surprising after her faux pas. This was why she hated going out to things, she realized. They were talking about quotidian details, people they knew, gossip she couldn't understand. Maggie felt awkward and bored, with a dollop of guilt at both.

With an eye toward escaping, she walked next to Deb, who was taking a break in her conversation with Patience. "Would you mind getting a selfie with me?"

"Really?" Her smile was delighted. "I wouldn't think you were the selfie type! Am I following you on Instagram?"

"Um, no," Maggie said. "This is just personal. For Kit?"

Deb's eyebrow raised, and she made a sort of tutting noise. "Oh, hon. He's off to college," she reprimanded. "I seriously doubt he's going to be thinking about what his mother's up to, don't you?"

Maggie gritted her teeth, counting to five before speaking. "He's a bit worried about me," she admitted. "I just want to show him that I have a life."

"Oh! Then sure," Deb said as Maggie got out her phone and wiped off the screen, flipping it so the camera was aimed at them.

Patience whooped. "I want in on this!"

Suddenly, the whole group squished in, and Maggie snapped a few shots. Her smile, she noticed, looked awkward, but it was better than nothing. Once she had the photo and everyone was chatting happily, she got ready to flee. "I should . . ."

"Lemon bars!" Deb trilled. "Made them myself. C'mon, have one!"

*Damn it! So close!*

Maggie sat down with the small paper plate and the dessert. She sat next to Klara, whose relative silence made her feel less awkward.

Of course, this was when Klara decided to start talking.

"So, Maggie," Klara said, leaning in, "what do you do for a living?"

"I'm an editor," Maggie said. "Mostly nonfiction. I work on business books and textbooks, things like that. You?"

"I work as a receptionist at the hospital," Klara answered.

They sat in silence for a moment as the others continued to chatter.

Then Klara picked up the conversational ball again. "What do you do for fun? If your son's worried about you not having friends."

"Oh, you know, the usual. I, ah, read, though not as much as I used to. Watch stuff." She paused, then decided *what the hell* and said, "I play video games, when I can."

"Do you and your son play?" Klara asked.

"When he was home, sometimes," Maggie said. "We could probably play online, but I don't want to embarrass him. The last thing he needs is his mother hanging around, you know?"

Klara frowned for a second, then nodded. "One of the ladies at church has a son . . . he's in community college, I think. And I think he has some kind of online game group—guild—with a bunch of other students? His mother said it sounded satanic, though. Blood something?"

"*Bloodborne*? *BloodRayne*?" Maggie asked. "*Blood Saga*?"

"That's the one, I think," Klara said. "Maybe you could join that?"

Maggie's ears perked up. She rarely joined guilds, though, because they were often too competitive. Or sexist. Or they would seem nice, until someone started spouting off white supremacist rhetoric, which had happened enough that she'd stopped looking.

"That sounds great, actually. Thanks for thinking of me," she finally said. She wondered if Kit would consider that socializing. Yes, it was online, but if all the members were local, surely that counted? Sophistry, maybe, but she'd take it.

"I'll pass your email along." Klara nodded, as if that settled things, then fell quiet again.

By this point, if Maggie was forced to be any more social, she'd probably be crushed under the weight of her own awkwardness. She got up, throwing out her paper plate, and then came back and cleared her throat. "I'm going to get going, thank you for having me," she said, all in a rush.

Deb made a little noise of protest. "So soon? Some of us were talking about going out to dinner!"

"All the single ladies," Patience half sang, with a grin.

"Not me," Klara countered, and Patience rolled her eyes.

"I'll go with," Cordy said, with a chuckle. "Show you girls a thing or two!"

Maggie could honestly say she'd rather perform an appendectomy on herself than go out on a girls' night. "I really can't," she said.

"Well, you're coming to my football party next weekend," Deb said. It wasn't a question.

"I'll see . . ."

"No! You're going, and I'm not taking no for an answer," Deb said, with an almost maniacally cheerful grin. "Kit doesn't want you to be lonely, right? I'll have Harrison talk to him and have him pester you if you don't!"

Maggie swallowed hard. "I'll see you there, then," she said begrudgingly. At least that gave her a week to find a good excuse to get out of it.

# CHAPTER 5

## THE MORE YOU KNOW

"As cool as it is to have breakfast with you," Aiden's old high school friend Riley said with a grin, "I get the feeling you're not here just to eat waffles. What's up?"

Aiden smiled despite feeling weary. Riley had been one of his closer friends, back when they were at Fool's Falls High. Riley, Aiden, and Aiden's best friend, Malcolm, had all been on the offensive line of the football team, which necessitated them spending a lot of time together. Back then, they'd gone on group dates and to keggers and big blowout bonfire parties in the woods down by the quarry. But where Malcolm had been his brother from another mother—the guy who'd shared his secret fascination with "those D&D books," the guy he'd turned to when college had gone horribly wrong, the guy he'd eventually opened a hospice business with—Riley was the golden-boy quarterback who had never left the Falls. He wasn't a gamer, he wasn't into geek culture, and if Aiden was honest, he was still basically the guy that Aiden remembered, only with alimony payments and some lower backaches. He'd gotten a job with a big local pump and well company straight out of high school when it became obvious that he was good but not good enough to get a football scholarship or move on to the NFL, and he had worked his way up to well drill operator. By all accounts he seemed happy to stay right where he was, here in the Falls. Since Aiden had moved back, the two of them had breakfast or lunch together at least twice a month. They were friends, or at least friendly-ish.

Malcolm, on the other hand, had moved to Seattle after graduation and was still running the hospice business he and Aiden had started. Aiden tried to text his best friend often, and they still played their online video games together, but ever since Malcolm had gotten married and had his kids, his free time had whittled away to nearly nothing.

Which was part of the reason why Aiden was sitting here, now, hanging out with Riley—hoping for some guidance.

It was Sunday, and he'd just gone to services at his mother's church. Now, they were at the Copper Kettle Diner, an institution in Fool's Falls. Almost exclusively decorated with antlers, the restaurant also featured really good food, including biscuits with elk sausage and gravy that were incredible. The after-church coffee klatch that his mother indulged in with women from her weekly Bible study was a similar institution, and Aiden had been taking his mother since the car had "broken down." She was in her element at a long table on the other side of the restaurant, talking and laughing and gossiping with the contingent of ladies of various ages. He usually had a coffee and read something or played a video game until she was ready to go home.

After he and Riley had put in their breakfast orders, he sighed. "I need to find a date."

Riley's eyes widened over the rim of his mug, which he then put down with a clatter. He visibly swallowed, then grinned broadly. "Hot damn! Finally!"

Aiden blinked. That was more enthusiastic than he had been anticipating.

"I have been *waiting* for you to get yourself out there," Riley continued. "You've been here, what, two years? Three?"

"Something like that." Aiden took a sip of his own coffee.

"In that whole time," Riley continued, "I haven't seen you out with anybody. Not *once.*"

Aiden frowned. "Um . . . my dad was dying? And . . . I was taking care of him?"

Riley looked abashed. "Fair. But he's been dead for a year, right? Besides taking care of your mom, what the heck have you been doing?"

"I do things!" Aiden protested. "I've been taking some community college classes. Stuff I'd wanted to try but never had time to. Took an English class and an art class, and I'm thinking of gardening next . . ." Granted, they weren't anything challenging—nothing that was leading to a degree—yet they helped him get out of his own head. The situation with his mother was getting him down, especially since he couldn't quite feel *settled* in Fool's Falls. He'd hoped that the college might help him find people to connect with, which had worked. Kind of.

"Did you meet anybody there?"

"Yeah. I set up my online gaming guild with a bunch of people I met in Contemporary Fiction."

Riley rolled his eyes at that. Aiden knew that as far as Riley was concerned, "online gaming" was right up there with "forty-year-old virgins" and "living in your mother's basement."

"No, I mean did you meet any *women,*" Riley emphasized. "Did you hook up with anyone?"

Aiden shook his head.

Riley's expression was one of patient irritation. "What you need is a dating profile," he said. "Couple of them! Man, if they'd had these back in our day, I would've gotten laid like carpet tile, you know?"

Aiden grimaced. "That isn't the . . ."

"I mean, I was making out pretty damned well," Riley continued with a laugh. "But now? Holy shit. Tinder! If you want to hook up, it's right there, like . . . like ordering a pizza!"

Even at fifty, Riley was striking. Much like Aiden, Riley still had a full head of hair, although his was dark brown, going gray at the temples. His pretty-boy looks had aged well, too, sort of Brad Pitt as a brunet. Since his divorce fifteen years ago, he'd cut a swath through the local women, and most of the women in the surrounding county. Possibly some nearby counties, as well. His expertise with all things dating was the reason Aiden was asking for his help, after all.

Still, Aiden didn't need quite this much eagerness.

"Riley . . . ," Aiden warned, and Riley rolled his eyes.

"Don't tell me: you want a *relationship*," Riley said, with a note of amusement. "You almost got married to someone you'd been with for years and years, so I get it. But I can help there too. I mean, *I* don't want to be in a relationship, but I've dated plenty of women who wanted more than I was interested in. I can think of at least five women off the top of my head who would love exclusivity . . ."

"*No*. I am *not* interested in a relationship!" The words popped out, more vehemently than he'd intended, and Aiden winced when Riley's eyes widened.

"No shit," Riley breathed. "You're *finally* going the casual-sex route?"

"Jesus, Riley." Aiden rubbed his hands over his face, suddenly uninterested in his biscuits and gravy.

"You are so west side," Riley teased with a chuckle. Ever since Aiden had moved away from Fool's Falls and Eastern Washington, Riley had been on him about turning into a "Seattle hipster" full of social justice, wokeness, and pretension. "There's no shame in my game, man. We're in our prime. I still get plenty of women, believe me."

Before Riley could regale him with any conquest stories, Aiden quickly jumped in. "I'm just looking for a date for Jason's wedding, okay? It's kind of important."

Riley actually recoiled. "Dude, *no*. If you're trying not to be in a relationship, then taking a woman to a wedding is the fucking third rail. You can't do that. That's, like, romantic and important and shit."

Aiden sighed, looking over at his mother, who was smirking at something one of the other women was saying. "If I just tell them up front, that'd probably work, though? That I'm not looking for a relationship, that I just need a date?"

Riley was still shaking his head before Aiden finished the sentence. "I have told women point blank that I wasn't interested in anything beyond sex, and I swear, a lot of 'em look at it as a *challenge*. Like I don't mean it, or I just haven't met the right woman—meaning *them*—yet. And it sucks, especially since they get this hurt look . . ." He shuddered. "That's why I don't stay all night. That way, they just kind of look surprised, and maybe a little pissed. You stay overnight, it's even worse."

Aiden stared, aghast. "That's kind of gross, isn't it?"

Riley shrugged. "I want sex, and I don't want to get remarried," he said. "I am perfectly honest up front. I'm not gonna live like a fucking monk just because women want something else and think they can get it out of me despite what I am *telling them point blank*."

Aiden squirmed.

"If a woman wanted to just have sex and didn't want a relationship, would you say shit about *her*? No. Because that's . . . what, slut-shaming." Riley looked triumphant. "That's a double standard!"

Aiden wasn't going to touch that one. Riley had always had a super-high sex drive, going through women like they were potato chips. Aiden wasn't judging (or was trying not to), but the thing was, it never seemed like Riley was really happy with all the sex. It was more like he had something to prove. It was kind of unsettling.

"Like I said, I just need a date for this. I won't even sleep with her." Aiden held up a hand, stopping Riley midprotest. "Don't start."

"Speaking of living like a monk," Riley said under his breath.

"Not the point, and shut up."

"So what's the big deal?" Riley tucked into his Denver omelet. "Why do you need a date for the wedding?"

"Long story short, if I get a date, Mom finally sits down and gets some of that medical and legal stuff handled." He glanced over at her again, then lowered his voice. "She is being *such* a pain in the ass about this, and she knows she's got me over a barrel. She doesn't think I'm going to go through with it."

"What does she care . . . oh." Riley's eyes widened as he figured it out. "Sheryl's gonna be there, isn't she? With Davy."

Aiden nodded, with a weary sigh.

"Shit. Well, yeah, you should totally bring someone," Riley agreed. "Somebody hot. Show them you don't give a damn that your little bro married the woman you were engaged to."

"Not the point," Aiden said with a groan. "I don't care who she is, I just need a live body at this point."

"Do you have any women friends?" Riley finally said, when he was finished chewing. "Somebody you can lay it all out to? Who won't have any expectations?"

"Not here in the Falls," Aiden admitted. "Hell, I don't have many friends, period."

"Um, hello?" Riley glared.

"Besides you," he amended. "Also, how many women friends do you have?"

Riley thought for a second. "Other than my daughter? I mean, I'm friendly-ish with Cassidy, but I guess that doesn't count."

Considering their divorce hadn't gone smoothly, even though Riley was a decent coparent, he wasn't shocked. "Don't suppose Cassidy would go with me to the wedding?"

Riley scowled. "Not cool, man. First, it's against bro code to take a guy's ex on a date, much less a wedding . . . especially a wedding including your own ex."

"You know I'm not looking for anything!"

"Second," Riley continued, "*I'm* going to Jason's wedding. We're friends, too, remember? And I was planning on hooking up with a bridesmaid or something. Weddings make girls horny. The last thing I need is my ex-wife there cockblocking me."

"Good looking out," Aiden said with a scowl. "Thanks for being absolutely *no* help."

Riley smirked. "I try."

"Well, if you can think of anybody, let me know, okay?"

"You know what? You should go to Deb LaFevre's football party on Saturday," Riley said. "Those parties are always fun. There'll be a lot of women there, too, I'm sure. You could probably find somebody there."

Aiden sighed. The last thing he wanted to do was go to a party. Still, this was important.

"If she won't mind me being there?"

"Are you kidding? From the looks she's been shooting over here, I think she'd fucking love it."

Aiden startled, glancing over at the table where his mother was. He saw a woman with brown hair looking intently at the two of them, then blushing and looking away, making a big show of talking to someone next to her.

"Are you sure she isn't looking at you?" Not that he cared, but he was honest: compared to Riley's dark good looks, Aiden looked like a goofy ginger lumberjack: stocky, bearded, his russet hair more unruly than it had been in years.

"Nah. She's the type who wants to settle down, and the women at the church know that's not me. She got divorced almost a year ago, so *you* should be careful, though."

"What? Why?"

"She wants to get remarried," Riley said. "And, from the looks of it, she's into you. But don't worry, you should still go to the party."

Aiden sighed. "I guess I'll show up."

"I'll give her your number," Riley said, almost gleefully.

At that point, his mother was looking tired, so he paid the bill, gave Riley a one-shouldered bro hug, and went to gather his mother and take her home. He also nodded politely to the assembled group, avoiding Deb's intent gaze.

When they were in the car, he asked, "Have fun?"

"They always overdo my eggs," she complained. She complained more since his father had died, Aiden noticed. "Oh. I have something for you."

He took a scrap of paper, an email scribbled on the back of it. "What's this?"

"Klara said some friend of hers wants to get involved with that crazy video game thing you do," she said. "Sounds like the lady's housebound or something. I don't know, I wasn't really listening."

"That's too bad."

"Must be older than me," his mother sniffed. "That's why I don't want to give up my car. That's when you know you're circling the drain."

Aiden winced. "Well, I'll invite her to the guild," he said, for lack of anything better to say.

Damn it, he needed that date—needed that leverage to get his mother to finally talk.

And then he needed to figure out a way to get his mother to accept a few facts without thinking of it as being one step away from dying.

# CHAPTER 6

## SQUEE VS. SQUICK

Maggie took a deep breath before signing in to *Blood Saga Online*. It wasn't a new game for her by any stretch. She'd started with *Blood Saga*, then *Blood Saga: New Dawn*, then kept buying them—*Hierarchy*, *Duskborne*, *Foul Moon*. When they'd introduced the online multiplayer version, she had hesitated a little, but despite some scathing reviews saying that it sucked, she was pretty happy with wandering around the large countryside. Yes, there was probably something ironic about her hiking through computer-animated wildernesses when she seemed to barely enjoy her own fifteen acres. That said, she'd never been bitten by mosquitos or ticks when she played *Saga*.

She sighed heavily. She *wanted* to love nature. Her ex-husband had loved it enough to convince her to buy this place. It was just . . . a lot to deal with. She hadn't realized that before she actually lived in a true rural area.

She went to the guild board. She'd gotten an email from the guy Klara had mentioned, her church friend's kid, the one going to community college. He'd sent her the invite to the Ship of Fools (a hat tip to Fool's Falls, which she appreciated) and said they were having a raiding party on Wednesday at eight. She signed in with the password he'd provided, bringing her character with her. She was an elf rogue, level twenty-seven, the lowest character she owned and a very awkward build.

That was a deliberate choice, since she'd already maxed out two other characters and had them at the ready. Basically, this was her "stealth" character—not in the game but in the guild. She was using it to see how the other players reacted and gauge if this was a group she wanted to stick with or not.

She waited through the intro screens, then found herself in a room with the party, a motley crew of rangers, warriors, wizards, and other rogues. Not a huge guild, she noticed. Nine people. She'd only played with Kit, and occasionally Harrison and a few of Kit's other friends, but she never wanted to be *that* parent—the one that horned in on her kid's social life. For all Kit's social anxiety, he was much more comfortable jumping into online social groups than she was. So here she was, entering this group, typing in the chat box with the name she'd chosen.

**BOGWITCH: Hi.**

She used the keyboard: no headphones, no mic, game music on but no player talk. For the most part, she didn't want to hear a bunch of kids swearing, and let's face it: when a big boss was barreling down on you like a howitzer shell, you were apt to swear. And she had chosen the name because she knew that women gamers were still catching shit, especially online. If they were going to think she was a bitch, she was going to embrace it.

The chat box exploded with text.

**OtterLeader: Hey. You're right on time. We're going to be doing a dungeon run at Castle tonight—not too hard, good way to break in. And we'll be dealing with Archduke Malekrin, who has some pretty good drops. Up for it?**
**BOGWITCH: Sure.**

DangerNoodle: Lev 27 WTF Otter don't need any more noobs

Maggie grinned at this. She'd been expecting this reaction.

BigDorkEnergy: Fucking babysitting
SneakyMeat: Quit ur bitchin—we babysit u don't we? :/
BigDorkEnergy: FUCK U SNEAKY
GandalfTheGay: Heathens. Hi, Boggy!
TheFerocity: Hi
Mouse5150: Hi Bogwitch. Everybody else, chill the fuck out or I'm cracking heads.
GandalfTheGay: Yes, Daddy
Cyrlaros21: Elves FTW

After a few more minutes of back-and-forth, and making sure they were equipped, they headed off to the castle. She hadn't done this particular run yet, strangely enough. She'd heard the boss was an absolute pain in the ass, and she figured the choice of tonight's run was deliberate. She was testing the guild to see if they were assholes; they were testing her to see if she could keep up. She couldn't really blame them.

They entered the castle, killing some low-level vampires and thralls and whatnot. Basic stuff, things she could handle easily. She did have to be more careful since her character was lower level. She couldn't just power through, counting on higher health and more experience points to carry her. Still, she'd logged countless hours on this thing, and she wasn't just a button masher. She'd learned how to actually battle, using her skills to avoid the bigger enemies until she was in a position to get in power shots.

More importantly, she was watching how the rest of the team fought together. She noticed that DangerNoodle, BigDorkEnergy, and TheFerocity were more impulsive, diving in and hammering away. They were warriors; that was to be expected. The rogues—SneakyMeat,

Mouse5150—hung back, either sneaking in and slashing or using ranged weapons like bows or wands, stuff that worked from a distance. And the mages—GandalfTheGay and Cyrlaros21—used spells to devastating effect.

Which brought up a point.

She was an anomaly in this world, to say the least. She was a rogue elf that was also a magic user. It wasn't impossible, but it was frowned on. And right now, she'd allowed a thrall to sneak up on her, taking out half of her health and starting to go critical. She snapped a quick spell that fortunately took the thrall out, but the damage was already done, and unless she went into a corner and hid, she needed something to fix her, fast.

BOGWITCH: Heal please

She felt like an utter ass, but it needed to be done. She couldn't heal herself—she hadn't progressed that far in healing with this character. But it pointed out the "flaw" in her setup.

They jumped on it, even as Otter healed her quickly.

BigDorkEnergy: Lol UR bad
DangerNoodle: Trash build
GandalfTheGay: Interesting choices.

Even Mouse, who had been somewhat sympathetic, chimed in.

Mouse5150: Maybe magic-using Rogue elf wasn't best idea?

Although she caught various levels of shit from the rest (except for Otter, who remained largely silent), she was at least gratified to see that they weren't complete dicks about it. She'd seen total flame wars break out when irate gamers felt like their teammates were fucking up. As a woman, it seemed to be ten times worse—she'd never been called "cunt" so many times in a five-minute period as she had the last time she'd tried to join a guild—so this was at least a step up.

They made it past lower-level bosses, finally arriving at the final boss. Most of the shit-talking had died down, thankfully, and the chat box had basically narrowed down to calls for healing or shouts for help, spells, and so on. They took a quick break.

> OtterLeader: All right, gear up. This guy is nasty. Fire magic, blood draw, blood poison, and if he hits you, good chance at death. I've got some re-gen, but Gandalf, want you to help.
> GandalfTheGay: On it
> OtterLeader: Cyr, need ranged ice attacks. Anybody got extra magic potions for him?

There was some quick trading and prep as people made sure their weapons and armor were charmed, that they were loaded up with whatever they needed. She switched from her now-battered armor to her fireproof Lev 100 armor that she'd gotten as a special drop from a limited-time mission a year ago. She also equipped her own ice attack, which was marginal—and then her close attack, a frozen blade of draining. It wasn't ideal. Some would argue she ought to use a shield and sword, or just be a mage. At least she wasn't still wearing heavy armor, like she used to. Kit had hounded her mercilessly until she'd accepted that elves needed to wear light armor, for a variety of reasons.

> OtterLeader: All right. Ready?
> DangerNoodle: Hell yah
> TheFerocity: Let's GOOOOOO
> BigDorkEnergy: Born ready

Maggie didn't bother to respond, just followed the others. Then she noticed a private note in the chat, from Otter.

**OtterLeader: If you start getting swamped, get by me, I'll keep you clear. Don't worry.**

She frowned, a little offended.

**BOGWITCH: I'll be fine.**
**OtterLeader: Just sayin**

Her frown evolved into a scowl, and she quickly typed as the boss did his monologue of *I will destroy your puny lives blah blah blah.*

**BOGWITCH: Because I'm a woman?**
**OtterLeader: Because you're level 27 and everybody else here is 50 or higher. I'm a level 100 healer. And this is your first time.**
**OtterLeader: No offense.**

After a moment's irritation, she relented. If she were leading a group, she'd probably feel protective of the noobs too. Well, unless they were acting like dumbasses. She probably wouldn't protect, say, BigDorkEnergy. She huffed out an irritated breath, then quickly typed:

**BOGWITCH: sorry**
**OtterLeader: No worries**

He seemed nice, this Otter guy. Good leader, good healer. She would've liked more women—any other woman—in the guild, but considering they were local and she hadn't met a lot of women who liked video games out here, maybe it was just specific to this crew. From what Deb had said, it sounded like they all knew each other. She was lucky they were open to taking her on, sight unseen. They seemed to have good stats, especially for a closed group.

Now the archduke had stopped blathering, and the real battle commenced. It was hard—maybe not *Dark Souls* hard, but pretty challenging. There were tons of "HEAL" calls going on in the chat, and "RE-GEN" came up a few times. She charged in, which made the chat explode.

**TheFerocity: Y would you do that**
**DangerNoodle: B R U H**
**BigDorkEnergy: FOH**

That is, until she started whaling on the archduke. She'd seen how it fought and knew its weak spots. She started stabbing at the back of its knees—a kind of Easter egg/shout-out to *LOTR*, maybe?—and the ice and drain did significant damage. Predictably, the group was shocked.

**Mouse5150: How are you doing that???**
**BigDorkEnergy: 2500 points? With two stabs? Ya right**
**DangerNoodle: B R U H**
**TheFerocity: She's hacking, fr**

She ignored them, continuing to kick the archduke's ass. With the help of the mages and the warriors, who were able to make sharper attacks with the archduke trying to fight off her combination of ice and draining, they took it out handily. She smiled.

**TheFerocity: U hacking?**
**BigDorkEnergy: obvs**
**DangerNoodle: Total hacks**

Now her grin turned sharp, and she typed furiously.

BOGWITCH: Don't hate the player
OtterLeader: Lol
GandalfTheGay: didn't think that would work, but you did it
DangerNoodle: Hack
BOGWITCH: enough hackusations. Unless you wanna go?
DangerNoodle: Nah—just sayin

Thankfully, Mouse—who appeared to be coleader—stepped in again.

Mouse5150: That was impressive. You're higher level than this usually, aren't you?

She took a deep breath. This was it. Time for the truth.

BOGWITCH: Got two level hundred characters. Just wanted to see how you guys would treat a noob before I committed.
OtterLeader: Lol
BigDorkEnergy: You fuckin smurf!
DangerNoodle: Lol Respect
TheFerocity: Totally gonna dominate the leader boards now
BigDorkEnergy: One of us! ONE OF US!

She shook her head, still grinning slightly. Until the next line.

DangerNoodle: Y named Bogwitch? R U ugly?
DangerNoodle: Or hot?

She scoffed. If she didn't stand up now, they'd start in. She knew it. It was prison-yard rules. Don't show fear. Don't show weakness. Establish dominance immediately.

BOGWITCH: Not interested.
DangerNoodle: Just asking
BOGWITCH: I'm old enough to be your mothers. Or grandmothers. And good enough to kick your ass.
BigDorkEnergy: Lol
GandalfTheGay: YAAAASSSS we stan a queen
TheFerocity: talk shit get hit
DangerNoodle: I'm not into GILF action gross
Mouse5150: And on that note . . . next week, we're tackling the citadel

They divided the loot, then did the whole "gg" good-game business and signed off. Except for Otter, who private chatted with her again, catching her before she logged off.

OtterLeader: GG
BOGWITCH: thx, same
OtterLeader: We play Thursdays, same time, mostly. Sometimes on weekends. Today was a one-off. People are welcome to team up for other stuff as well. I sent you the rules. You're good to join?
BOGWITCH: sure

She was never sure how to end these sorts of conversations. She wasn't clear on texts, either . . . always felt like she was either being rude by bailing or irritating by keeping someone tied up. It was close to eleven, though, and she imagined they'd have—school in the morning? Work? She didn't know.

OtterLeader: I think you'll be a good addition to the team. Looking forward to playing some more. If you have any questions or anything—I know you're a pro and all, but

**about the schedule or you want specific quests or whatever—just let me know.**

He was very polite. Maybe too polite?

**BOGWITCH: Again: old enough to be your mother. No funny stuff!!**

There. Just to really put paid to the idea of anybody hitting on her.

**OtterLeader: I would never. 🙂 See you tomorrow.**

She signed off, then looked at the chat. Well. That had gone better than planned. She had a life.

Sort of.

# CHAPTER 7

## THAT CAME OUT WRONG

Aiden glanced at his watch, and his mother finally called him on it.

"What, am I keeping you from some hot date?" She sounded a cross between annoyed and hopeful.

He winced. They were at Annabel's, one of the nicer restaurants in Fool's Falls. He had thought he'd take his mother out as a treat and as a sort-of apology for her car still not being fixed. It wasn't a terribly fancy place—there were no terribly fancy places in the Falls, honestly—but it was a sit-down restaurant that had a decent pasta plate and steaks, and his mother liked both those things. He'd deliberately taken her at five o'clock, when senior hour started. Now, it was two hours later, and she was lingering over her dessert. The waitress looked irritated, and Aiden promised himself he'd leave a good tip.

"I do actually have something to do," he admitted. "Not to rush you, or anything."

Her eyes widened, and she almost dropped her fork on her huckleberry cheesecake. "You really *do* have a date?"

"No!" He squirmed in the hard wooden chair. "Not a date. Just meeting up with some online friends."

She scoffed. "Fifty years old, still playing video games," she said, shaking her head.

"Lots of people do it now, Ma." He grinned. "That woman, the one whose email you gave me, just joined. I think she's your age."

"Pfft." She took another bite of cake. "Why would a woman, especially an older one, want to get involved in that foolishness? I don't get it."

"Tell that to TacticalGramma," he murmured. Of course, TacticalGramma was closer to his age than his mother's, but the point still stood: video games were no longer simply the province of pimply-faced teenage boys.

"What?"

"Nothing. Never mind." Despite the facts, he knew better than to get into a debate if he wanted to get out of here. He really was anxious to get back and get ready for tonight's quest. They were going to be taking on the citadel, and that would take a lot of focus and concerted effort, something they struggled with at the best of times. He'd met most of their team members relatively recently, at Fool's Falls Community College, so they tended to be on the younger side.

As his mother raked the edge of her fork through what remained of the cheesecake, he surreptitiously texted his friend Malcolm under the table.

AIDEN: Gonna be late to the guild meeting tonight. Are the guys behaving? How is Bogwitch doing?

MALCOLM: I'm not there, remember? Sophie's having her piano recital tonight.

Aiden winced. Sophie was Malcolm's twelve-year-old daughter, and Malcolm had mentioned this was coming. Even though Malcolm loved playing *Blood Saga*, between the demands of running the hospice business by himself (something that stabbed Aiden with guilt from time to time) and juggling his family's needs, he couldn't always play, even though the game was his best stress relief. Hell, the two of them had played earlier versions of *Blood Saga* when Malcolm and he had started the business.

AIDEN: Shit, sorry, forgot. Talk to you later.

He frowned at his phone before tucking it back in his pocket. That meant that the group was probably in the guildhall, unsupervised. Or at least, he *hoped* they were still in the guildhall. He noticed that BigDorkEnergy and TheFerocity tended to run off at the mouth *and* get themselves killed constantly without a little guidance. He could only imagine what they'd do left to their own devices.

He was also curious to see how Bogwitch held up, if she'd still play with the level-twenty-seven character or one of her level one hundreds. She was . . . unexpected. A power player, and a thoughtful one, even if her build was initially questionable. She could trash-talk with the best of them, but she wasn't a selfish player or a glory hound. She'd obviously been playing for some time and seemed to know the lore. He could see her being an asset in the guild if they didn't scare her off or simply annoy her into quitting.

Besides, he appreciated her sense of humor and feistiness and thought maybe she'd be a friend, sometime, down the line.

"Have you found a date to the wedding yet?" his mother said, interrupting his reverie.

"Um . . . no," he replied to stall for time. "But I'm working on it. I hung out with Riley Stone the other night—you remember him?"

"Your old quarterback?" She nodded. "Heard about him. Been divorced all this time, and acts like dating is his job. Nobody can pin him down. At least, that's what the church ladies say. You'd think that he was a blue-ribbon cow the way they carry on."

He snerked a laugh, finishing his decaf coffee. "Yeah, pretty much. Anyway, he said he might help me find someone." Okay, he'd more cautioned than offered help, but at least it showed effort.

"Does he even know any nice women?" his mother asked, her eyebrow arched with skepticism. "Because . . ."

"Oh, hi, Janine!"

Aiden looked up to see Deb there, smiling broadly at his mother.

His mother gave her a small smile. "Hi, Deb," his mother said, as warmly as he'd ever heard her. He remembered Deb from the after-church get-together at the diner, and remembered Riley's comments about her. *She wants to get remarried. She's into you.*

"We talked about you coming here for dinner on Thursdays," his mother said, and Aiden had a sneaking suspicion that there was a reason she'd lingered so long. "I didn't realize you ate so *late*."

"I like to treat myself from time to time," Deb said, sending Aiden a coy smile. "I didn't know the two of you were going to be here! How nice!"

"Did you want to join us?" his mother asked, and he panicked. He quickly cleared his throat.

"I actually just asked for the check," he said, and his mother scowled at him. "Sorry, Deb, I have a thing I have to do tonight, and I need to run Mom home first, so . . ."

Her face fell for a second, and then her bright smile came out in full force. "No problem! Maybe we can have dinner some other time?" She winked.

Was the wink to let him know she was joking? God, he hoped that was the case.

"Oh, but that reminds me. Riley said that you wanted to come to my football party?"

His mother's gaze shot to him, and she raised an eyebrow.

"If that's all right?" he asked. "I didn't mean to invite myself. I just thought . . ."

"No! I'd love to have you," Deb said. "You've been in town all this time, and you haven't really gotten out much. I mean, that was understandable, with your father and all . . . I was so sorry for your loss . . ."

His mother flinched slightly. After a year, the loss was still a tender spot. But she was also looking at him expectantly, her gaze flitting from him to Deb and then back, her intent clear.

Oh, God, this was uncomfortable.

"But it would be great for you to hang out with all of us," Deb continued. "It's not good to be alone all the time. Don't worry! We don't bite." Her smile was warm and welcoming and made him want to make a break for it.

"Of course he'll go," his mother answered before he could say anything, and he choked.

*And now my* mother *is setting me up?*

The waitress came up, interrupting them and handing him the check. He gave her his card, then turned back to where his mother was boring holes into him with her gaze as Deb grinned.

"Perfect! Want to give me your phone? I'll text you my address," she said.

Old school as it was, he'd planned on just jotting the address down on a napkin, or even asking Riley for it. Feeling uncomfortable, he nodded, unlocking his cell and handing it over. She happily texted herself, rather than simply putting in her contact info—which meant she had *his* number now too. "I'll get in touch with you tonight," she said. "It'll be fun!" Then the waitress came back with his card. He signed it as she ushered Deb to a small nearby table. Deb waved goodbye.

He got his coat and walked his mother to his truck. Seeing her carefully negotiate her way into the passenger seat, he felt a pang.

"Why don't you go out with Deb?" his mother pressed when he got into the driver's seat. "She's nice. Not much younger than you. Regular churchgoer . . ."

"I'll think about it," he said, rather than have some kind of long conversation that involved her picking apart his admittedly small romantic history.

"You'll 'think about it,'" she echoed, then made a grumbling sound. "I'm old, not stupid. You think I don't know you're just telling me what I want to hear?"

"No, I don't think you're stupid," he said, forcing himself to be patient and compassionate. He loved his mother, he really did, but he'd never gotten along with his parents. Not the way his brother, Davy, had. "And I'm going to her house Saturday. We'll just see how it goes."

"Hmph."

He dropped her off, then settled her in, making sure that all the doors were locked. She shooed him away "to play your games with your little friends," and while he felt a tiny bit offended at her characterization, he hurried back to the house he rented, grateful as always that he'd chosen to rent someplace else rather than try to live with his parents when he'd first moved back to the Falls. Even though he'd had to drive over there every day, he was glad to have a place where he could unwind, or break down if need be. If working in hospice had taught him anything, it was how invaluable having clear boundaries was, even more so when he was essentially "treating" family. He needed a separate, safe space to retreat. He needed time to himself, and he needed some peace.

Tonight, he fired up his Alienware and quickly navigated to *Blood Saga Online*, just a little late. He winced, hoping that the guys hadn't scared Bogwitch off or, worse, started the quest without him. That would be a chaotic disaster.

He opened their guildhall, the place where they started their adventures and were able to trade gear. To his shock, they were all there, and from what he could see, they were all chatting happily.

**OtterLeader: Sorry I'm late. Stuff came up.**
**BigDorkEnergy: Boggy hooked us UP**

GandalfTheGay: I have been trying to get this staff for fucking ever
TheFerocity: no fuckin way
TheFerocity: ur just givin away this shit?

Aiden frowned. What was happening here? It looked like the team had gotten a substantial amount of gear—*good* gear, at that. And most of it had come from Bogwitch?

BOGWITCH: I played a lot and got a lot of gear I couldn't use.
BOGWITCH: I am a quest treasure hoarder lol

Aiden grinned. If there was a way to this group's heart, it was offering . . .

His mouth dropped open.

OtterLeader: You've got 2 Crystal Swords of Savagery???
BOGWITCH: Sure. Want 1?

Aiden grinned.

OtterLeader: *grabbyhands*

Suddenly, there was one of the legendary quest items, right there in his inventory.

BigDorkEnergy: We are going to kick ASS in the Citadel!!! Fuck ya!!!

Aiden couldn't argue. He sent Bogwitch a quick private message.

OtterLeader: Really, thank you. You don't have to do all this. This is hundreds of thousands of coins worth of stuff.
BOGWITCH: *shrug* I have lots of coin and lots of stuff. I used to play a lot more than I have recently. With my son. It was kind of our thing.

He wondered what had happened to her son. Had he died? She certainly sounded sad, but he didn't know her well enough to want to pry and maybe cause more pain. It also sent a pang of jealousy through him. His own mother . . . he knew that she loved him, and that ultimately, she wanted what was best for him. The problem was, it was what *she* thought of as what was best for him, which wasn't necessarily what he wanted at all. She used to be more passive aggressive about it, nudging him, making "helpful suggestions"—until the blowup that happened after Sheryl. Now, she was far more direct.

And, if he was honest, far more disappointed.

OtterLeader: You're a good mother. I can tell.
BOGWITCH: I'm just lucky, he's a great kid. You ready to battle?

He got the feeling that she was uncomfortable with the praise. He could almost imagine the grumpy, crotchety expression—one that probably hid a gooey interior. She was the type to tear a strip off you for talking shit, but then give you a million-coin quest item and act like it was no big deal.

He immediately felt better.

OtterLeader: All right, gear up, then let's get going.

They went about getting their healing potions and their armor, then put away anything they could to free up carry space. Then they went on the mission.

It was, in a word, epic. The guys liked playing with the new gear and used it to good effect, cutting through enemies like a blowtorch through butter. The bosses were still a challenge, and the last boss, the Hierophant, was an absolute dickpunch. But he learned a few things.

When tempers flared (read: BigDorkEnergy), Bogwitch tended to get him to calm down . . . not by catering to him but with a quick, sharp retort and some applicable advice, even if it was "quit fucking around and notice the traps, dipshit" even as she tossed re-gen potions at him. Things that would've pissed off Dork if one of the other guys said it tended to go smoother when she did. Probably because he'd talked to them all offline, making sure they were nice to her.

"She's an old woman," he'd pointed out via private messages. "And she's got skills, so be nice, okay?"

Needless to say, between the fact that she'd essentially given them an early Christmas with all the gear and the fact that she was probably an octogenarian woman who swore like a trucker while killing bad guys like a Terminator, the guys had rallied and now looked at her as their own personal mascot.

After they'd trounced the Hierophant and gleefully split the loot, he sent one more private message to Bogwitch.

**OtterLeader: Thanks again for everything. And for tonight. You really kicked ass.**
**BOGWITCH: Ok. No worries.**
**OtterLeader: For real—it meant a lot.**

There was a pause, then a flurry of typing.

**BOGWITCH: You're not hitting on me, right? Because I will punt you into the sun.**

He let out another bark of laughter. He could *hear* the amusement in her tone.

**OtterLeader: You keep giving me legendary loot, I might consider proposing.**
**BOGWITCH: Right into the sun!**
**OtterLeader: Nighty-night, snookums**
**BOGWITCH: *raises fist* GET OFF MY LAWN!**

He shook his head, still chuckling, before signing off. It was kind of hysterical that she kept warning him off, telling him not to hit on her. Honestly, he had his own problems with dating *anyone* and tended not to hit on people, much less a grouchy elderly woman who he'd only "met" online. He wasn't like Riley, searching for someone to nail and bail, and this late in his life, he'd given up hope on having a relationship. But he'd begun to count her as a friend . . . and he was starting to realize he had precious few of those.

# CHAPTER 8

## GREAT BIG LIBRARY OF EVERYTHING

Kit video called Maggie on Friday night. He took after her: shaggy dark hair rather than his father's sandy blond, dark-brown eyes rather than hazel. It was yet one more thing that had alienated Trev, convinced that Kit had nothing in common with him, not even dominant genetics.

*Nope. Not going down that road.*

"How was this week?" she asked, forcing her voice to stay cheerful.

He shrugged. He had stubble, which continued to throw her, and he was wearing his favorite hooded sweatshirt, a black, thick fleece. She had to bite her tongue to prevent herself from asking if he'd washed it since he left the house. "This week was okay," he said. "Same shit, different day."

"Classes?"

"Fine."

"Is your roommate there?"

He smirked, shaking his head. "He's still rushing. I imagine he's getting paddled by chanting, masked individuals in a candlelit basement as we speak."

She chuckled. "You get the picture?"

"Of you with that duck-face lady with the peace sign?" He started laughing. "Yeah, I got it. You looked like you were being tortured."

He wasn't wrong, but she couldn't exactly admit that. "Doesn't matter. The point is, I *went*. So, what did you do?"

"I haven't gone yet."

She tutted. "No-hypocrisy card," she said, parroting his words back to him. "I got out there. Now you're on deck, pal."

He grumbled. "I am not taking a selfie," he muttered.

"No, you don't have to. I'm going to trust you," she said, even though her voice was stern.

"I don't know why it's such a big fucking deal," he said, and there was a definite edge to his voice. Because they were video chatting, she saw the shadow of pain that crossed his expression, one he might not have even realized until he saw himself on screen. He quickly schooled his features to a kind of implacable blank and shrugged again.

He'd learned to go featureless because of his father. She knew that.

Worse, she knew that he'd learned it from her.

She took a deep breath. "I joined a *Blood Saga* guild."

His eyebrow kicked up, and his forced calm turned into amusement. "No kidding? Been a minute since I played that. Are you playing with Mac or something? I didn't think she was that big a gamer. More into anime."

"Mac isn't into playing video games, especially online. Says that they're misogynistic cesspools, and generally speaking, I can't say I blame her. So this actually should count as making friends," she half bragged, even as she recognized the lameness of her boasting. When you were bragging that you had made friends with (presumably) a guy who promptly hit on you, then called you a grandma, then chanted *ONE OF US!* at you, you weren't winning any kind of extrovert awards. "They're based here in Fool's Falls. Theoretically, I could actually meet up with them face to face."

God, she hoped that was never truly an option.

"Sure," Kit said, with a genuine smile that warmed her. "Well, good on you."

"You still playing online with Harrison?"

He shrugged again. "Harrison's been busy, his job and stuff, and his girlfriend told him he was spending too much time playing video games, so . . ." He trailed off.

She winced. So not only was he alone in his new place, he was losing contact with his best friend, the closest person he had. He'd had a few other casual friends, but Harrison was like his brother. The physical distance was hard enough.

"Maybe you could join my guild?" she suggested. It'd be fun, hopefully for both of them, since they both enjoyed playing the game, and she knew the guild members, for all their shenanigans, were engaging and friendly. At the same time, it was perhaps a bit selfish. After all, she was supposed to be encouraging him to meet *new* people.

"What, have my mommy set up a playdate with people online?" His expression was both irritated and agonized. "Should I write 'LOSER' on my forehead in Sharpie, or save time and have it tattooed?"

She saw what he was saying, even as some irritation of her own struck her. "I just hate seeing you so alone," she snapped before she could stop herself, then sighed, taking a deep breath. "Sorry."

His expression softened. "I know," he said quietly. "But, Mom, you can't fix everything for me."

She nodded, knowing that logically. But she hated it.

"I just don't want you to devolve into some neckbeard incel who starts shit conversations with 'let me play devil's advocate here' and trolls people on Reddit," she tried to joke, forcing a grin.

He grinned back. It was small, but she'd take it. "Damn. And I was planning on gatekeeping comics and Marvel movies, and making girls prove their geek credentials."

She shook her head. "We both know I raised you better than that," she said. "Speaking of girls, though . . ."

"Ugh." He covered his face with his hands. "God, no. Please."

"I'm just saying, anybody interesting? See anybody in your classes or your dorm or anything?"

He put his hands down. "I don't know. I haven't really talked to anybody."

"But has there been anybody who caught your attention? Anybody who seems nice?"

He rolled his eyes. "Mom, I beg of you. Stop."

"Okay," she conceded, "that was invasive."

"You know, you don't need to have quite this level of interest in my personal life," he pointed out. "It's not healthy."

"Probably not," she admitted. "But besides loving you and, strangely enough, *liking* you as a person, I guess I just want to make sure that I didn't fuck you up irrevocably with my less than stellar parenting skills."

She winced. She was joking.

Kind of.

*But not really.*

She knew that he knew, too, when she saw him tilt his head, studying her in a way he had occasionally when he was in high school. When Trev had left and moved to Wyoming, he hadn't come back to see Kit and had barely called. He'd traded alimony for giving her ownership of the house, even though honestly that had been more of a burden than a gift. He'd paid child support, but there hadn't been a single birthday card or Christmas present. Kit had been hurt—but also somewhat relieved, since Trev had seemed incapable of hiding how disappointed he was with his only child and the wife who refused to let him be as harsh as he wanted to.

She'd done everything she could to make up the shortfall, but as amazing and wonderful a kid as Kit was, she still could see the cracks that the whole situation had left in him, the barely visible scars. It was why he tended to try parenting *her*, something she hated.

There was probably some psychological name for it. Maybe some German word with fifteen syllables. Basically, she'd tried her damnedest to make sure he was happy, healthy, and whole, without getting too creepily codependent about it.

She just wasn't sure if it had worked, especially when it looked like he was alone and doing nothing to change that condition. She knew enough to know that long-term isolation wasn't good.

*For him, anyway. For me, it's fine.*

"What about you?" he asked. "You meet anybody?"

"Eww," she replied reflexively, and he laughed.

"Just sayin'. You've been divorced for five years, and now you've got the place to yourself," he pointed out. "Time to cut loose."

"Ugh. You know I hate that," she said. "I went to Deb's book club, and there was a vibe of that—like a *Sex and the City* thing. Which, okay, they can do what they want, and I'm sure I sound judgy as hell. But they were pushing the whole 'single and ready to mingle' mindset. Sort of insistent that the best was yet to come, and that they were just as hot and beautiful and desirable as they were when they were young."

"I am not going to say my mom is . . . gack, I can't even hint at it," he said, shuddering and wrinkling his nose, "but . . . I guess they have a point? I mean, age ain't nothin' but a number, right?"

"First: if you were here, I'd smack you on the back of the head," she shot back. "Because no way are you quoting philosophical wisdom from R. fucking Kelly, especially considering he produced that song for a fifteen-year-old that he then *married*."

"Oh. Yuck." Kit grimaced. "Good point."

"Second: I have changed markedly since my twenties," she said. "I don't want to wear bandage dresses and club all night . . ."

Kit made gagging noises. "Ack! Brain bleach!"

She ignored his outburst. "I'm not saying that *other women* can't wear whatever the hell they want and feel however they want to feel. My *point* is, at this age, *I* don't want to get negged by some fifty-year-old douchebro who thinks I care about his opinion, just because he wants to sleep with me. I don't want to wear makeup or shave my legs or buy matched underwear . . ."

"I regret everything," Kit groaned. "You're right. You're old. You don't need to date, and I never want to have this conversation ever again."

She grinned at his pain. "Although, you know, the guild is all guys, except for me. I could probably have my pick."

*"Mom!"* He looked shocked. "Hook up with somebody you meet online? Are you *trying* to get on a true-crime podcast?"

"I'm just saying, they're friends with Deb—or somebody in her church, or something," she teased. "So they're not *complete* strangers . . ."

Kit paused, studying her. "You're just messing with me, right?" he asked suspiciously.

"Of course I am," she said, bursting out in laughter. "Fuck's sake, there's a guy named BigDorkEnergy. He's pretty much what you'd expect."

Kit finally relaxed, chuckling in response. "Are they all tools?" he asked. "I've been playing a lot of *Vicious Squad 4*, just joining online groups. And yeah, there's a lot of dickheads out there."

She shrugged. "They're actually pretty decent," she admitted. "In skill level and manners."

"Did you bribe them?"

"Shamelessly," she said. "Totally worth it. Between that, my stats, and my smack-talking, they have accepted me as one of their own. Leader's really good too. Keeps things calm, schedules our games, helps out where he can. He's a healer, if you can believe it. He even offered to protect me when I played with my level twenty-seven. Chivalrous."

Kit's eyes narrowed, even as he smirked. "Sounds like you *like* him." Now his eyes popped wide. "You wouldn't date *him*, would you?"

She snickered. "These kids are all in community college. I think they're probably your age, eighteen or nineteen. Maybe in their twenties.

That's not dating. That's grooming." She mimicked a vomiting sound, and was gratified to hear Kit's laugh.

"Nobody wants that," he admitted. Then he looked at the clock. "Guess I'd better go. Toby's gonna be back soon, I think."

Toby. The roommate.

"You're going to go back to the book club?" he pressed. "I just don't want to come home for Christmas break and find you wearing a tinfoil hat, speaking in tongues, because you haven't interacted with a human in real life in months."

"Yeah, well, I don't want to hear that you've been wearing the same clothes all semester, wearing Febreze as cologne," she pointed out, "and that you've been communicating solely in grunts or simplified pantomime, okay? Get out there and say hi to someone."

He rolled his eyes.

"Just one person."

"What are you gonna do?"

"Hey, I went to book club! I'm ahead of the game!"

His look was askance. "So if I do one token thing, we're square?"

Dammit. "And . . . I'm going to Deb's house again," she said slowly. "She's having some football thing Saturday. For the Washington State game." After the debacle of her showing at the book club, she was frankly surprised that Deb had followed up on her invite, much less that she'd been insistent. Perhaps she should be nicer to the woman and more charitable about these social outings.

"The Cougars. Boo, hiss," he said with a grin/wince. They were his college's nemesis. "But you hate football."

"Well, I can say hi to her dog," she said. "I didn't get a chance to at the book club. So that's something."

"All right. I will"—he frowned—"check out the anime club on campus."

"Pics or it didn't happen," she said.

"BEGONE, THOT!" he yelled.

Any other mom—or at least, any other mom who knew that "thot" essentially meant "whore"—would be horrified. She just laughed, knowing that he was quoting a YouTuber and that . . . well, she'd laughed, too, when she saw the gamer playing and yelling at the character on screen.

"We are so weird," she said. "Be careful, have fun. Make good choices."

"Oh, shut up," he said, shaking his head, then smiled. "Love you, Mom."

"Love you, too, kiddo."

They signed off, and she sighed. She hadn't wanted to go to Deb's thing. She'd just sort of ignored it when they'd talked about it at the book club. And then she'd ignored the mentions in the group text (and she hated the fact that she was *on* a group text with the rest of the book club) and replied tepidly to Deb's personal nudge. But she knew that she could take another picture, and maybe . . . okay, just maybe she could guilt Kit into trying harder. He knew how much she hated social stuff. After all, he came by his antisocial tendencies honestly.

This might boost him into trying, she thought, ignoring the tiny, squirming thought that she was being emotionally manipulative. Ultimately, Kit's well-being was what mattered. She'd do a lot to justify that.

# CHAPTER 9

## YES, YES I AM

That Saturday, Aiden gritted his teeth and drove from the Falls all the way to Spokane Valley, about two and a half hours. He hated going to Spokane. He especially hated when he had to go see his little brother, Davy. Not that he hated Davy, particularly—he wasn't very close with his brother, but there was no animosity, despite what people believed. Davy was, in a lot of ways, what his parents had always wanted: he was successful, he was married, he had kids. He'd stayed in Eastern Washington, rather than fucking off west side to hang out with "those hippies and losers."

He sighed, pulling up in front of the white two-story where Davy and his family lived. Not the time to focus on bitterness. Although right now, he was bitter. Not because of the past, but because Davy refused to answer his repeated attempts at contact.

Now, this was happening.

Girding himself, he strode up to the front door, ringing the doorbell. It was nine in the morning . . . early, but he knew that the kids usually got up early. Or at least they used to.

The door flung open, and he saw a pretty little girl with large hazel eyes, light-brown hair in a ponytail, and a generous sprinkling of freckles across the bridge of her nose. She wore a pink T-shirt that said

"Daddy's Got a Shotgun" and a pair of jeans with flowers embroidered on them. He blinked momentarily.

"Hi," he finally said. "Which twin are you?"

"Patricia," she said. "Hi, Uncle Aiden." And she gave him a hug, which he returned.

"Patricia, I told you not to open the . . . oh."

He glanced up. Sheryl, Davy's wife and his own ex-fiancée, was standing in the hallway, glaring at him.

He released Patricia. "Hi, Sheryl," he said gruffly, then saw the shyer twin standing by her mother in a purple outfit very similar to her sister's, with a T-shirt that said "Girls Rule, Boys Drool." "Hi, Elizabeth Anne," he added. Then he sent her a wave, and she shyly waved back with a grin.

"What are you doing here?" Sheryl said, her voice crisp as a new dollar bill.

He sighed. He'd hoped that five years would've thawed her out a little, but apparently no dice. "I'm here to see Davy, actually."

She clenched her jaw. "He's—"

"Hey, hon?" Aiden heard his brother's voice just before he stepped into the kitchen, at the end of the hall. "Where's Bug's backpack? He needs . . ." Then, over her head, he caught sight of Aiden. "Whoa! Aiden. What are you doing here?"

Despite the fact that it was the exact same phrase that Sheryl had used, Davy's voice was warmer, if puzzled. He strode forward, giving Aiden a one-shouldered hug. Aiden saw Sheryl take Patricia's hand, tugging her away.

It hurt.

"Well, you weren't returning my texts or calls," Aiden said, trying to keep his voice even. "And we really need to talk."

Davy rubbed his hand over the back of his neck. "Yeah, sorry. I've been hellishly busy . . ."

"Got time now?" Aiden pressed. Because if you didn't corner Davy, he'd wriggle out. The guy was so allergic to commitment and confrontation, he acted like a straightforward conversation would send him into anaphylactic shock. "I drove almost three hours, dude. I wouldn't have if it wasn't important."

Davy glanced over his shoulder at his wife, who arched an eyebrow imperiously. She took Elizabeth Anne's hand.

"Honey, we talked about not calling him Bug anymore, he's too old for that," she said firmly. "I'm taking the girls out to breakfast. You still need to drop *David* back at his mother's for his sleepover. And then we're going to my parents' this afternoon, remember? The Cougars game is going to be on, and they'll want to eat early."

"Okay, sure," Davy said, turning to give her a kiss on the cheek. With another glare at Aiden, she hurried the girls out the door to their minivan.

"So, she's still pissed," Aiden said, under his breath.

"Yeah, well, what did you expect? It's only been a decade," Davy responded. Then he called up the stairs, "Bug! Buddy! C'mon, you know your mom hates it when I drop you off late."

Aiden grinned as Davy's twelve-year-old son, a.k.a. Bug, walked down. "I had to make sure I had all my Magic cards," he explained. Then his face lit up. "Uncle Aiden!"

Aiden gave Bug a big, crushing hug, gratified by the kid's laugh. Bug took more after his mother than his father—the deeper tan, the jet-black hair, the dark-brown eyes. His grin was like distilled sunshine.

"Still playing Magic, huh?" Aiden ruffled the top of his head, making a mental note to send the kid another pack.

"Yeah, but we keep it quiet," Davy said, looking a little embarrassed.

"Sheryl doesn't like it," Bug muttered, rolling his eyes.

"Hey," Davy added. "Be nice to your stepmother."

Bug's sigh was long-suffering.

"We're taking him back to his mother's early," Davy said.

"My best friend, Tom, is having a birthday-party sleepover," he said. "We're gonna play Magic all night!"

"Or at least until they fall asleep," Davy said, with obvious fondness. "You have your backpack?"

"Yeah."

"Got everything?" Davy prompted. "Toothbrush? Birthday present?"

"Yup."

"Pajamas?"

Bug froze, and Davy sighed.

"Go get your pajamas, Bug."

Bug bolted back up the stairs.

Davy looked at Aiden. "Ah, the joys of fatherhood," he joked, then winced. "Sorry."

"Don't be. I mean, sometimes I wonder what it would've been like to be a parent," Aiden admitted. "Then again, sometimes I see shit like that kid who climbed a column right in the middle of an airport, or see those screamers running around in a restaurant, and I think—I could barely handle a houseplant, you know?"

Davy laughed as Bug returned. "Okay!" the boy said, out of breath.

"All right. Mount up." He looked at Aiden. "Why don't you talk to me on the way?"

Aiden grimaced. This was not something he wanted to talk about in front of a kid. "We'll talk on the way back," he said pointedly.

Davy winced. Then the three of them climbed into Davy's big, shiny truck. There were perks to owning and running three of the most successful car dealerships in the Eastern Washington area, apparently.

Aiden asked Bug a bunch of questions about school and his friends, and Bug chattered away. Before long they were in front of Bug's mother's house. Maria was out on the lawn, watering some flowers with a hose. "Bug!" she called, then wrapped her arms around him. Between the two of them, Aiden could definitely see the resemblance, the Latinx genes popping to the fore. Then she glanced over. "Aiden? I haven't seen you in ages!"

Aiden accepted her exuberant hug. "Hey, Maria," he said. "How're you doing?"

She winked. "All right," she said. "How are you? I was so sorry to hear about your father."

He sighed. Her relationship with his parents had been . . . tense would probably be underselling it, but it was close enough. "Thanks," he said.

"And you're still in the Falls?" she asked. "Wow. I don't know how you do it."

He shifted his weight from foot to foot, uncomfortable. "It is what it is."

She looked at Davy. "So, you're good for next weekend, right?"

"Aren't I always?" Davy answered, then gave her a quick hug, before hugging his son. "Be good, behave, and I'll see you next weekend."

"Bye, Dad!" Bug said cheerfully, then scampered off with his mother.

Aiden climbed back into the truck. Now that Bug was taken care of and he had Davy in an enclosed space, it was time to get down to brass tacks. "Mom's health is failing," he said, almost before Davy closed his door.

"What?" Davy's hand stilled on the ignition key. "The fuck, Aiden? Why didn't you tell me! What does she have?"

Aiden sighed. "It's not like that," he explained. "It's not like she has . . . just one thing. It's not like cancer."

*It's not like Dad.*

"Jesus, you scared me," Davy said with a scowl, starting the car. "Dude, she's just getting old. It happens to everybody."

"I know that," Aiden said, with more bite than he had intended. He took a deep breath to calm himself down. "I worked in hospice, remember? And I was a nurse for the elderly for a few years before that. I've been in nursing homes. I know the drill."

"Mom's only, what, seventy-six?" Davy said with a shrug. "And she's healthy. Ish."

"She's been falling. A lot," Aiden emphasized. "She almost gave herself a concussion on the tile in the bathroom. Gave herself a black eye when she fell and hit the kitchen table. And the car . . ."

"Oh, right," Davy said, with a snap. "That reminds me. She's been bugging me, so I thought I'd give her a new car for Christmas. I mean, her old car is a piece of junk, always breaking down."

"It's not breaking down!" Aiden growled. "I told her that because I was afraid she was going to take out a fucking school bus full of kids!"

Davy sent him a quick, startled side-eye. "Seriously?"

"That's why I've been texting," Aiden said. "That's why I've been calling. She's having issues, and we need to deal with them. We can't wait until the last minute. Remember what a mess it was with Dad?"

Davy rubbed the back of his neck with one hand. "All right."

"I need you to come to the Falls," Aiden said. "She'll listen to you. She likes you better, anyway."

"Aiden, that's not fair."

Aiden shrugged. "I'm not trying to be passive aggressive with that, or anything. It's certainly not your fault. I'm just stating facts. She will listen to you. And we need to get her to understand that decisions need to be made. All right?"

Davy sighed heavily. "I have a bunch of stuff I need to deal with at the dealerships," he grumbled. "And I'm opening the new one in Coeur d'Alene. Dammit, I don't have time for this."

"Well, it's got to be soon. She's getting worse. And you know how she is," Aiden added. "She doesn't listen, she's stubborn as hell, and she thinks I'm full of shit."

"All right. Tell you what . . . I'll come back after Jason's wedding," Davy finally relented. "Does that work?"

"That's *two months away*!" Aiden yelped. "What the hell?"

"Best I can do." Davy could be stubborn, too, and he saw that this was as much leeway as he was going to get. "You can hold down the fort until then, right?"

Aiden took a deep breath. "Fine."

"Speaking of. You're not going to the wedding, are you?"

"Mom is insisting that I do," Aiden said, rolling his eyes. "What? You think I shouldn't? Because if you could tell *her* that, it'd be great."

"Shit." Davy winced. "Why does she want you there?"

"She thinks seeing me there, with a date, might smooth things out with all the gossip." Aiden shook his head. "All these years. You'd think they'd be over it."

"It's because they don't know the details," Davy said, and to his credit, he sounded genuinely sorry.

"Do you honestly think that would help?" Aiden said, stunned.

"God, no!" Davy snickered, and in that moment, Aiden wanted to throttle him. "No," Davy continued, more seriously. "Although—hmm. You know, you bringing a date might be a good idea. Let some people think you've moved on, that Sheryl's cool with it, that everybody's happy, and put the whole thing behind us. Hell, hire some woman if you have to."

"This isn't a Julia Roberts movie," Aiden said, with a small smile.

"Not with that attitude," Davy replied, grinning back. "So there isn't anyone you're even remotely interested in?"

Aiden hated when Davy, or anyone, said shit like that. Like it was his fault. Like there was something wrong with him. He sighed.

"Well, there is a woman who just joined our guild," he finally said, setting the trap.

"Really? That could be perfect!" Davy seemed genuinely happy. "She'd have something in common with you. Have you met her? What's she like?"

"She's a badass. Has two level-hundred characters, fully kitted out."

"Like I even know what that means," Davy said. "What's she *like*?"

"Funny," he said, thinking of Bogwitch. He really did like her—what he'd seen, anyway—and was glad she'd joined the guild. "Snarky. She doesn't take shit, but she isn't mean if you don't deserve it. Also super generous."

"She sounds great. So why don't you ask her out?"

Aiden finally burst out laughing. "Because I think she's like eighty. Old enough to be Mom."

"Oh, fuck off," Davy said, and Aiden laughed some more. "Hey. Wanna go grab some breakfast? There is a diner I know that is amazing."

Aiden's eyes narrowed. "Is it a Sheryl special?" Sheryl had gotten onto a health kick lately, which as a nurse he agreed with—to a point.

"Not a scrap of kale in sight," Davy said. "And some of the best bacon I've ever had, I swear. And pancakes the size of manhole covers."

"You had me at bacon," Aiden said. "Let's go."

At least he had a time frame, he thought as they drove off. He just had to manage his mother past Jason's wedding. And get a date. And then his brother would come home, and the three of them would hash it all out.

Then . . . maybe, just maybe, he could move away from Fool's Falls. For good.

# CHAPTER 10

## HILARITY ENSUES

Maggie showed up to Deb's "First Home Game Party" just a few minutes late. All right, half an hour late. She'd considered wearing her T-shirt that said "Sorry I'm Late, I Didn't Want to Be Here," but she felt it was too on the nose. She knew that there would be a good deal of other people there, and though the thought made her skin itch, she was determined. She hoped that Harrison was there so she could maybe nudge him to reach out to Kit, and also to back up that she had indeed left the house and been social.

That said, after seeing the book club's style, she had a feeling there would also be eligible bachelors there, and frankly, she didn't need that shit. So while she was showered and in clean clothes, she wore no makeup—which was pretty standard—and had her hair pulled back in a low ponytail that basically made her face look like a large moon. She also wore a bulky sweater that wasn't ugly enough to be ironic or a conversation piece but was ugly enough to seem accidental and which should persuade people to avoid her. Her jeans and mostly clean UGGs completed the ensemble.

"You made it!" Deb said, giving her an awkward hug. Deb, on the other hand, was dressed to kill, in a Cougars V-neck shirt made of a thin material. Maggie realized that her pea-green sweater was going to get really hot, really fast, considering Deb had cranked up the heat.

"Thank you for inviting me," Maggie said, handing her a tray of homemade cookies.

"Oh, aren't you sweet," she said. "Your cookies are always so good! Harrison always loved them."

At this point, Deb's cousin Patience walked over, taking the plate from Maggie. "If I ate carbs, I would be all over these," she said, with a friendly smile, even if she looked askance at Maggie's outfit. "I'll put them in the kitchen. You can put your coat in my bedroom. Game's already started, beer's in the kitchen, and we've got the dining room table for the food."

Maggie nodded, heading down the hallway and opening the door to Harrison's room, which was now Patience's room, if what she'd heard at book club was true. Harrison must've taken down the things that she remembered when he moved out—posters of various video games and memes, things that he and Kit had found hilarious. Now, there was a crafting area on his desk, with Deb's sewing machine set up and a pile of fat squares fanned out for color. There was also an open set of luggage on the floor with what looked like women's clothes that had been pawed through, like it belonged to someone who didn't unpack and was just living out of a suitcase. The bed was piled high with winter coats.

The coats reminded Maggie of Nana Birdie's parties, and she felt a pang. It had been years since she'd thought of that.

As she put her coat near the foot of the bed, at the bottom of the pile, she heard a little chuff. Looking over, she saw Deb's dog, Duchess, sitting like royalty in a plush dog bed against the wall by the closet.

"Hello, puppers," Maggie crooned, automatically going to the floor. Duchess lifted her head, allowing Maggie to give her skritches behind her ear and then slow strokes down her lustrous thick coat. She nudged Maggie to keep petting her, and Maggie finally laughed.

"Let me put in an hour," she whispered, glancing at her phone to mark the time, "and then I'll come back and pet you more. Okay?"

Duchess let out a long exhalation, then seemed to roll her eyes before putting her head back down on the bed and promptly falling asleep.

Maggie shook her head. Grinning, she took a picture of Duchess before shutting off the light and closing the door behind her.

The party was in full swing and surprisingly crowded. She didn't really recognize anybody and felt that cloying awkwardness that always happened in those situations. Forcing herself not to fidget, she washed her hands in the kitchen, then went to the dining room. She wasn't particularly hungry, but having food was a party-survival technique—giving her something to do, and if necessary, giving her a reason not to talk to anyone by stuffing her mouth. It was like standing in a doorway when playing the video game *Diablo*, a technique that allowed you to take on your foes one at a time. She looked at the archway between the dining room and the living room.

It seemed defensible. She hovered nearby, hugging the wall.

There was another man at the dining room table, talking to a woman. She squinted. "Mr. Roeper?" she asked tentatively.

He turned, then grinned at her as the woman wandered away to say hello to someone else walking in. "Mrs. Le. Kit's mom."

She bit her lip against correcting the "Mrs." She'd told him she preferred "Ms." so many times, but it wasn't worth it. "Yes. How are you?"

"Good, good," he said, holding a plate full of finger foods—mini quiches, pigs in a blanket, cheese cubes. And several of her cookies, she noticed with a tiny bit of pride. "Still teaching the boys and girls, you know how it goes. And how is my star pupil? I miss him."

She smiled. *You and me both, mister.* "He's . . . adjusting," she said carefully.

"Is he pursuing computer science?"

"He's looking at game design, yes," she said.

"I'd like to think that my classes helped with that," he said with pride.

"Your computer classes were some of his favorites." She gave him that. Of course, Kit had practically *taught* the last semester he'd had with Mr. Roeper, at that point, before taking a computer science class at the community college in nearby Turnball his senior year. "He's definitely feeling the challenge."

"Well, that's great," the man said. Then the conversation petered off, as they so often did.

She was conversationally challenged, was the problem. She popped a tiny quiche in her mouth. It was good for a frozen brand, she thought. She might have to pick up a few.

"Oh! I see Jerry," Mr. Roeper said, then nodded at Maggie. "It's been great to see you."

"You too," she said around some spinach, then swallowed and watched the couple walk away.

She often found herself in that position. Nana Birdie had often bemoaned her complete lack of grace, her inability to manage conversations. "When I was your age," Nana had said breezily, "I could make sure a party never lacked for topics of conversation, I made sure everyone felt at home. I could single-handedly have a dinner party for twelve or a backyard cookout for a hundred! What is so difficult about just talking to our guests?"

Maggie had grumbled. "I didn't grow up in the South, Nana."

"No, of course you didn't," Nana had sniffed. "I blame your mother."

Maggie winced. Then again, Nana had blamed her mother for everything, including her parents' deaths, even though that had been because of an icy road and a drunk truck driver. Maggie shouldn't have been surprised that Nana blamed Maggie's very existence, problematic as it was, on her mother, period.

She took a deep breath. If she was going to survive—she glanced at her phone—another forty-five minutes here, then she needed to stay out of dark mental rabbit holes. She could already feel the creeping signs of anxiety. No need to chuck a dollop of depression to the mix.

She reluctantly gravitated back to where Deb was, in the kitchen, having an animated conversation with a number of people, none of whom Maggie knew except for Patience. She hovered at the edges of the group.

"Riley!" Deb said, smiling at a man about their age with dark hair, then looking past him. "Where's Aiden?"

"I know where I rate around here," he said, with a laugh. "He'll be here, don't worry. Had to take care of something for his mom, I think."

The crowd of women let out a collective *awwwww*, and Deb's expression was rapt. "He's *so* sweet."

The guy—Riley—chuckled.

Patience's smile was less enamored, more predatorial. "And *hot*, right?" she pointed out. Deb flushed, but laughed along and didn't deny it. "You sure he's going to come? Haven't you been trying to find an opening with him for months?"

"I think I was too subtle," Deb mused. "He's shy."

Now Riley snorted.

"What? You don't think he is?" Patience pressed. "Is Deb just not his type?"

"I have no idea what the guy's type is," Riley said. "It's not something we talk about."

Now it was another woman's turn to scoff. "Like men need a type," she teased, with a bitter edge. "Men just need an opportunity."

Maggie sighed. It felt like a high school party—not that she'd really gone to many of those either. But the few that she'd attended had people congregating around the kitchen, red Solo cups of booze and mixers. She'd usually had a cup full of soda. People gossiped, and teased, and eyed each other with interest. Flirtation, gossip, bitching.

It was like watching middle-aged versions of high school comedies. Was this what adulting was like? At fucking *fifty*?

Then again . . . what was she expecting? She so rarely went out—she didn't know what anything was *supposed* to be like. Besides, she was still staying in, playing video games, much as she had when she was younger. Maybe she shouldn't throw stones.

She wanted to go home so very, very badly. Anxiety itched over her skin like frantic ants.

"He's *shy*," Deb repeated. "But don't worry. He just needs a nudge! Spend some time with us, you know? See how much fun it is to have friends to hang out with. I mean, he was gone for*ever*, and then when he came back, it was to take care of his father, who was *dying*. If I'd known, I would've made sure that he was getting out more. Even if you're caretaking—especially if you're caretaking!—you really need to make time to decompress and hang out with others."

"You didn't know?" Patience asked. "Aren't you friends with his mother in church group? And he's been back, what, a couple of years now?"

Deb's expression flattened. "Well, I was busy too."

"You mean you were married," Patience murmured under her breath.

The group seemed to freeze. Maggie stared at Patience, who simply smiled as if she hadn't said anything. Maggie got the feeling that Patience was a drama magnet. She'd known several in her time.

Nana Birdie came to mind, unbidden, and she shoved the thought aside *again*.

Riley seemed to see someone across the room, giving an up-nod and walking away before Maggie had the chance to also escape without being obvious. Deb's mouth drew into a tight line before she spoke again, unfortunately turning to Maggie. "It's important for people to get out," she said. "I mean, look at you now! You've been burying yourself in taking care of Kit since you got divorced, and you never came to any of my parties. No more puttering around, all alone! God, you convinced yourself that video gaming was somehow *having a life*. I'm sorry I didn't reach out sooner! If I'd known, I would have."

*Grrrrrrr.*

And the worst part? Deb genuinely thought she was helping.

"Don't you worry, we're going to make sure you have lots of fun. You won't even miss Kit, and you'll start *living* your life, not just pretending." Deb shot a glare at Patience, who was trying and failing to hide a smile. "It helps to have someone show you that they care and drag you out of your rut. That's what being a good friend *is*."

"Her kid's eighteen," Patience pointed out. "Why didn't you push her before?"

"I was too wrapped up in Barry, okay? I admit it," Deb said. "Marriage takes up a lot of time! But now, I see where I went wrong . . ."

"Other than Barry?"

"*Meaning* that I'm going to help my friends more," Deb said resolutely, talking over Patience's disparaging comments.

"I'll just bet you want to help Aiden," Patience purred.

"Maybe I'll . . . I'll help Maggie start dating!" Deb beamed. "That's a great idea. Maybe we can double-date!"

Oh *hell* no.

Maggie felt her throat go dry. "I'm . . . going to go . . . somewhere else," she muttered, then beat a hasty retreat as Deb continued to snipe at Patience.

She was *not* going to make it a full hour in this nightmare. She glanced at her phone. She'd barely made twenty minutes.

*Too bad.* She was too old and too tired to hang at a middle-aged kegger. She didn't even *like* football, and after years of nodding like a bobblehead when Trev bored her senseless about sports stats, she would be damned if she was going to keep pretending.

She'd done her time.

She pushed through the small crowd to the spare bedroom to grab her coat and give Duchess a good long skritch goodbye. But as she did, she paused, motionless.

There was a big guy already there, kneeling on the floor. Duchess was giving him her belly, completely shameless, her tongue lolling out in doggy ecstasy. The man was chuckling. He looked huge. He had big shoulders and was built solid: some extra pounds, padding around his middle, like an athlete who'd gone to seed. He had red hair . . . well, *reddish* hair. Not flame red, not copper, not blond, not quite brown. She wasn't sure what she'd call it. A neatly trimmed beard, lighter, with more gray.

He looked at her over his shoulder. He had gray eyes, currently looking at her curiously. She thought she saw a little bit of a blush, high on his cheeks, above his whiskers. He gave her a little up-nod.

She up-nodded back. Then she grabbed her coat and fled. *Fuck this social shit,* she thought.

Then realized, abruptly, three things.

One: she hadn't gotten proof or a picture of the party.

Two: she felt bad for that Aiden guy they were talking about. She could tell Deb had plans for him. Then again, if it was a choice between Deb digging into her life or trying to snare this guy—well, Maggie was going to throw him right under the bus.

And three: she wanted to play some video games. *Immediately.*

# CHAPTER 11

## TOO GOOD FOR THIS SINFUL EARTH

Aiden watched the woman go, scurrying away after snatching up a blue fleece jacket from the mountainous pile of coats. She'd looked unsettled, he couldn't help but notice, and surprised to see him there. She'd also waved goodbye to the dog, which made him grin. He was a pet person and got the feeling she was too.

She also wasn't a party person, if she was bailing this early. He couldn't help but envy her the exit.

*Suck it up. You just need to ask somebody on a date. To a wedding.*

He straightened after giving the dog one last long scratch behind her ear, leaving her lolling in canine delight. He had a mission. He'd come to this party to ask a woman out. Riley was right. It wasn't brain surgery, and it wasn't going to kill him. For that matter, simply being social shouldn't be that big a deal. When he'd been with Sheryl, she'd dragged him to restaurants and birthday parties for her friends, concerts and comedy clubs. He hadn't always enjoyed it (okay, he had *rarely* enjoyed it), but he'd also spent time with Malcolm and his family, and he'd gone on outings with people from the hospice organization, so it wasn't like he was a complete recluse.

With renewed resolve, he grabbed the tray of cupcakes he'd purchased at Tasty Great, and headed for the kitchen. Everybody knew that the kitchen was the epicenter of any party.

As he'd expected, Deb was there, talking to some women. She saw him, and blushed, even while smiling broadly. "Aiden! Welcome! So glad you could make it." She reached for him, surprising him with a hug. He carefully held the cupcakes to the side.

"Thanks for having me," he said. "I brought dessert."

"Perfect!" She handed them off to a pretty blonde who stood beside her, brushing her long hair over her shoulder and studying him intently. "Patience? Can you put these out on the table? Maybe next to the cookies?"

"So this is Aiden," Patience said. She looked him over like she was going to be tested on his appearance later. He tried not to squirm self-consciously.

Deb made a low, impatient noise. "Sorry. This is Patience, my cousin. She's younger than I am, so you probably don't remember her."

"I would've remembered *you*," Patience said. Flirted? He felt fairly certain she was flirting.

"The cupcakes, Patience?" Deb pressed.

Rolling her eyes, Patience complied. "I'm gonna be right back," she promised.

Deb sighed, then lowered her voice. "She had a bad breakup, just moved back from Las Vegas. I'm letting her stay with me, since Harrison moved out. That's my son," she clarified. "He just graduated from the high school."

"Congrats," he said as she grabbed a glass out of a cabinet and got him water from the fridge door. He thanked her absently and took a sip, grateful that it gave him something to do with his hands.

"Aiden!"

Aiden looked up to see Riley walking over from the living room, where the bulk of partygoers were congregated around the TV, watching the game. "Hey, man," Aiden said, giving Riley a half bro hug. "We winning?"

"Nah," Riley said, with a laugh. "But hey, we're trying."

"Know how that feels," Aiden muttered.

"Soooooo . . . ," Riley said to the group at large. "Who here is interested in dating this guy? I mean, he's a total catch, right?"

Aiden goggled. "The *hell*, dude?"

Riley shot him a don't-worry-about-it look. "I am being your wingman," he said, with no chill whatsoever.

"Were you planning on opening an auction or something?" Aiden hissed.

Deb laughed. "You're like me," she said to Riley, with an approving grin. "Proactive."

"He does need a date, though," Riley continued.

"Throat punching you," Aiden growled under his breath, which only made his friend laugh.

"Who needs a date?" Patience said, rushing back, her face the picture of curiosity.

"Aiden," Deb said, looking very intent, her face both friendly and encouraging. "Which I can completely agree with."

Now Aiden was taken aback. "You can?"

"Your mom has said to our church group, many times, that you're just too alone," Deb said, with a nod.

"I was busy," Aiden felt compelled to point out.

"Oh, I know," Deb said, and now he felt really, really uncomfortable. "Taking care of your father! And helping your mom . . . I get the feeling she probably doesn't thank you much for it, I know how independent she is . . ."

*That is for damned sure,* he thought.

". . . but still, you need to take time for *you*. And I'll bet finding the right person would make her feel happier too. She's worried that you're shutting yourself off, just burying yourself in your computer and away from people."

"I connect with people," he protested. "Just . . . online."

For a second, it seemed like everybody in the small circle looked at each other with a note of pity, a sort of group *bless your heart*. He forced himself not to bristle.

"Well, yes, that's nice, to have friends that you have things in common with," Deb reassured him. "But it's not the same as flesh-and-blood *people*. The connection's just not the same."

Aiden gritted his teeth.

*You need a date. You don't have to see them again after Jason's wedding. If you go off, you are going to ruin it.*

"I suppose you're right," he finally said, when he was sure he could say it without sounding strangled. "And I'm here, aren't I?"

Deb beamed. "Exactly! Hopefully, we'll be seeing a lot more of you."

He looked around. "Maybe I should see how we're doing," he said, nodding at the TV. "Been a while since I watched football."

Not that he had any interest in this particular game. He'd largely stopped watching football on a college level when he'd moved to the west side. Still, he needed a chance to regroup and see what his prospects were. He got the feeling asking anyone his mother knew to the wedding might be an issue, especially if she'd been lobbying for someone to take him off her hands, for God's sake. He was fifty years old, and his mother was trying to set him up like getting married was a playdate?

"But what about the wedding?" Riley said, stopping him before he could take a step.

*Goddamn it, Riley.*

"What wedding?" Patience asked, and Deb frowned.

"It's no big deal," Aiden said, at the same time Riley added, "Jason's wedding."

"Oh! Jason, your cousin, right?" Deb asked. Patience was still staring, although the conversation seemed to be boring her.

"Right."

"And Sheryl's gonna be there," Riley said. "So of course Aiden needs to be there with a date."

They all went silent: Aiden in frustrated irritation, the rest in quiet shock as a result of Riley's revelation. The group in the living room cheered at something happening in the football game, oblivious to the social faux pas that had detonated in the kitchen.

"Of course," Deb finally said. "If your brother's going to be there . . ."

"Oh my *God*, you're that guy?" Patience yelped. "The one whose brother married his fiancée? Like, immediately after they broke up?"

*Kill me now.*

Aiden tried to get ahold of the conversation. "That was years ago," he said, although no matter how many times he pointed this out, no one seemed to get it. "And trust me, we're all past it."

Well, Sheryl wasn't, but he wasn't about to admit that.

"If you're past it, why haven't you dated, then?" Patience probed. "And why do you need a date now?"

"*Patience*!" Deb snapped.

"What? I'm just asking what everybody's thinking!"

Aiden was really, really starting to dislike this woman.

"Like I said, I've been busy the past two years. And I just haven't met anyone I felt like I could connect with. I don't want to be with anyone just to be with someone, you know?"

Deb stared at him, hearts in her eyes. "That is the most romantic thing I've ever heard," she cooed. "Especially from a man."

"Hmm." Patience, on the other hand, had one dark eyebrow quirked, and she was studying him with suspicion. "I don't think I've *ever* heard that from a man."

He shrugged, unsure what to say.

"At least," Patience continued with a flirtatious grin, "not one that wasn't trying to sleep with me, anyway."

Aiden winced. "Trust me, I would never."

They all fell silent for a second, and he realized that might've sounded really bad. To his surprise, Deb actually burst out laughing, and Patience flushed an unattractive color, glaring at him.

"I mean . . ." He cleared his throat. "Honestly, I was too wrapped up in other things—work, then taking care of my dying father—to be focused on anybody else. Sheryl marrying Davy, who loves her to pieces and can devote time to her, is really the best thing for everybody."

He'd practiced that, used it in various family occasions. It was the truth.

Just . . . perhaps not all of it.

"Oh, you poor thing," Deb said. "Putting everybody else first, no time for yourself. But doesn't it get lonely?"

"You could be his date, Patience," Riley pointed out, although he was giving the woman a subtle once-over himself. She smirked back coyly. "Nothing says 'I'm over it' like walking in with a beautiful new partner, am I right?"

Deb frowned. Patience, on the other hand, sent him a flirtatious wink.

"Maybe I'll be available," Patience said, with a careless shrug, even as her eyes sparkled. "If you want me to make her jealous, I'm happy to help!"

"For God's sake, Patience, could you not stir up shit for one night?" Deb snapped, then startled, as if she'd suddenly heard the words she hadn't intended to say. "I mean . . ."

"No, that's fine," Aiden said quickly. "I have time. The wedding's months away. And it isn't a big deal. Oh, hey!" He made a big show of pointing to the dining room table, laden with food. "You have mini quiches. And, um, chocolate chip cookies. They look amazing. Did you make them yourself?"

“Nah,” Patience answered for Deb. “Those are . . . what’s her name?”

“A friend of mine,” Deb said. “Mother of Harrison’s best friend.”

“I’ll have to try some.” He used that as the excuse to jump. He should have known that any conversation involving people from Fool’s Falls would bring up his past with Sheryl. It had seemed like the scandal of the century, or at least, his mother had claimed so. Apparently, it was still something to talk about.

Maybe he should rethink finding a date on Craigslist at this point.

His phone buzzed in his pocket, and he pulled it out, retreating into the bedroom with the dog again for a little privacy and to get his head together.

To his surprise, it was Bogwitch.

**BOGWITCH: Hey. You up for a dungeon run?**

He found himself grinning. It wasn’t one of their designated guild play nights, but there had been times when a few of them did impromptu missions. She kept typing.

**BOGWITCH: Sorry to reach you this way, but nobody else is in the guild hall, and I don’t have anybody else’s contact info.**

He thought about it. He could stay and tough it out at this party, but now, he wasn’t sure that this was the right approach. He’d have to hang out with Deb, who seemed intent on pushing him into some social makeover, and deal with Patience, who seemed like a gossip at best and who was now eager to dig into his past. Riley would probably find some woman he hadn’t slept with yet—if there were any left in Fool’s Falls—and probably bail early, leaving Aiden to halfheartedly watch the Cougars game and talk with people he didn’t know very well.

He took a deep breath, then typed his response.

**Aiden: Why? Just felt like playing a game?**

There was a pause, the dots appearing and disappearing. Finally, she sent:

**BOGWITCH: I feel like killing shit.**

He smiled at the screen. After that little group weigh-in on his past love life, he knew exactly what she was talking about.

**Aiden: Respect. Give me like 30 minutes? I'm not at my computer.**
**BOGWITCH: Okay. See you in the guild hall.**

He shut his phone off, then took a deep breath and prepared himself to do something he was really, really bad at.

Namely: lie, to get the hell out of this party.

# CHAPTER 12

## THE SNARK KNIGHT

Maggie waited patiently in the guildhall. She could've played one of her other games, she supposed. She still had a few kicking around. But ever since she'd gotten home from what would go down in history as the Debacle at Deb's, she realized that she was angry. She'd initially tried settling down and watching a movie, but scrolling through the different options on all the streaming channels just increased her rage. And doing something sweet, like *Stardew Valley* or *Animal Crossing* or something?

She'd probably set everything on fire.

No, like she told Otter . . . she wanted to kill things. The tougher and bloodier, the better.

In the meantime, she treated herself to a quick meal of chicken fingers, fresh out of the air fryer. She'd been hyperfocused on work and hadn't eaten lunch, which probably hadn't helped her attitude at Deb's party . . . something she should've thought about. So now she felt even angrier—at herself, at the situation.

Self-care was hard. Rage wrangling sucked.

She needed some escape.

She heard the announcement bell that someone else had entered the guildhall.

OtterLeader: Hey Boggy.

She smiled. Gandalf's nickname had started to catch on, she'd noticed, just in the three times or so she'd played with the guild.

BOGWITCH: Hey Otter.
BOGWITCH: I don't suppose you checked to see if anyone else was interested in joining?
OtterLeader: I did send out a few texts. Everybody else is busy, from the sounds of it.
BOGWITCH: So just us?
OtterLeader: Fraid so.

She couldn't help but feel a pang of disappointment. Just two people would really limit the kind of boss they could tackle, the kind of mission they could pursue. Which was frustrating.

OtterLeader: Still up for a dungeon run?
BOGWITCH: What's the toughest opponent you think we could handle? Just the two of us.
OtterLeader: Huh. Never really thought about it.
OtterLeader: Actually, we're probably one of the best pairs in the guild.
OtterLeader: Because I am a badass healer, and you are just a badass. Total tank.

She grinned fiercely. That felt good to hear.

BOGWITCH: Damned right.
OtterLeader: You ever take on the FireMiser?

She blinked in surprise, shoving some hair out of her eyes. The *what*?

BOGWITCH: That is NOT what he's named.
BOGWITCH: Oh my God. All I can think of is that weird, angry Claymation dude.
OtterLeader: lol no it's not his real name
OtterLeader: He's this fire demon, up in this hidden cave at the upper North-East quadrant of the dessert map.
OtterLeader: *desert

She felt a little curl of curiosity starting to twist and break up her foul mood.

BOGWITCH: How are the drops? How tough is the boss?
OtterLeader: Don't know. Never run it. Guys think it's a waste of time, it's kind of apocryphal. Nobody I know has actually done the mission. It's kind of an urban legend.
BOGWITCH: So why's he called FireMiser?
OtterLeader: Don't know. I imagine he looks like it? Don't know what his real name is, either. Just saw it on some of the boards and in the wiki.

She quickly called up the *Blood Saga* wiki, typing in FireMiser in the search bar. Sure enough:

"The FireMiser is rumored to be in the northeast quadrant of Tryal desert biome. Few enter—none leave to tell the tale. Easter egg. Developer's notes."

BOGWITCH: Do you even know where to look?
OtterLeader: Kinda?

Maggie grimaced. On the one hand, it did not fulfill the "kill shit" adrenaline-elimination purpose she'd initially wanted. On the other hand . . . she was curious. Kit had said she was viciously tenacious when she decided to figure something out. "It's a good thing you're not into true-crime podcasts like I am," he'd said, shaking his head, "or you'd be like that dude from *Always Sunny*, looking wild eyed in front of a murder board with, like, pins and strings and newspaper clippings all over it."

**BOGWITCH: What the hell. Let's try it.**

They geared up and then ported over to the desert biome, heading for the far corner of the map. Since they hadn't been there before, it meant traveling by foot rather than using a spell and teleporting. Which meant a lot of boring travel. Which meant they had time to talk—or rather, text.

**OtterLeader: Bad day?**
**BOGWITCH: Why do u ask?**
**OtterLeader: You said you wanted to kill things. I just figured.**

She took a deep breath, then tried using Kit's favorite method of deflecting.

**BOGWITCH: Bold of you to assume I don't want to kill things as a default.**
**OtterLeader: lol**
**OtterLeader: Well, do you?**
**BOGWITCH: It's not my factory setting. But more often than not, probably.**
**BOGWITCH: I'm guessing you're all sunshine and light.**
**OtterLeader: I have my bad days, sure, but I try not to let them get me down.**

OtterLeader: Too many people have it really bad. I look like a punk ass bitch in comparison.
BOGWITCH: You saying I'm a punk ass bitch?
OtterLeader: I would never. :)

She laughed.

BOGWITCH: Fuckin' A right.
OtterLeader: lol

She bit her lip. She didn't owe him anything—no explanation. But something about the fact that he'd asked, that he was concerned, kind of tugged at her. She finally sighed, then typed.

BOGWITCH: Bad day. I hate people-ing.
OtterLeader: Hard same.
OtterLeader: Social stuff sucks ass.

She let out an actual laugh. He was usually so much more . . . professional wasn't quite the right term, but he struck her as the type that shepherded the rest of the knuckleheads in the guild, like a teen tour guide amid his ragged, unruly band. Mouse was good at cracking skulls, but he didn't have Otter's implacability. Otter tended to be calm, soothing.

Maybe she was responding to that.

BOGWITCH: I have reached the age when I give absolutely zero fucks about what anyone else thinks. Mostly.
BOGWITCH: Ever see that meme, from anime, where one school kid is chasing another school kid? And they're labeled "fuck around" and "find out", and they're being

**followed by a reporter who's talking to a camera and he says "as you can see, the gap is narrowing . . ."**
**OtterLeader: LOLOLOL**
**OtterLeader: You're pretty cool for an elderly person**
**BOGWITCH: Picture me flipping you off.**
**BOGWITCH: And then letting Mr. Fire Miser or whatever eat you.**
**OtterLeader: which would leave you healer-less, and then where would you be?**
**BOGWITCH: Worth it. I am just that petty.**

They kept bantering like that as they got to the corner, a Mordor-like environment with some nasty steam spouts and what seemed to be mini volcanoes. They searched fruitlessly for about an hour. Ordinarily, she'd be getting more fixated—and more frustrated. Now, she was wondering if maybe they'd missed it because they were too busy chatting. Not so much about themselves—she liked the anonymity, and frankly, she'd had enough of small talk for one day—but talking about . . . concepts? Life? Just silly observations, things they liked and hated, things that made sense and didn't make sense.

**BOGWITCH: So that's why I think it's impossible to go back in time and kill your grandfather.**
**BOGWITCH: Which is why I think the movie TENET is kind of ridiculous.**
**OtterLeader: That's sort of wild. I have never thought of time travel that way.**

She had never actually told anybody her time-travel theory. Well, other than Kit, who had heard her as she refined it over the years, to the point where he covered his ears if she so much as breathed the term "time travel." Otter, on the other hand, not only "listened," he proved that he was paying attention *and* that he understood the concepts by asking her some very good questions.

OtterLeader: I have mixed feelings about Christohper Nolan. I appreciate his obvious influences from Andrew Niccol, like Gattaca . . .
BOGWITCH: YOU watched Gattaca? Isn't that, what, vintage for you?
OtterLeader: lol I'm not that young

She wondered what that meant. Maybe he was all of twenty-one or something. *Kids these days.* She shook her head, even though he couldn't see it, feeling indulgent.

BOGWITCH: Kiddo, you probably tell people your age still using halves and quarters.

It looked like he was about to type, but she quickly saw something behind a crevice they'd walked past easily twenty times.

BOGWITCH: Oh my God do you see that??
BOGWITCH: The purple stones.

Whatever he'd been about to type, he didn't seem to complete, because she saw his response.

OtterLeader: Holy shit is that a door??
BOGWITCH: Let's gooo

They entered tentatively. And then spent the next five (yes, *five*) hours exploring a small cavern that opened into a bigger cavern. That brought on one of the toughest, weirdest bosses she'd ever fought in *Blood Saga*.

One that looked, funnily enough, like the damned Claymation villain.

After getting killed three times, they finally decided to return to the guildhall and then try to convince the rest of the team to work with them to take down the boss. Hopefully they would be able to find it again. As it was, it was now two in the morning, and Maggie was starting to feel exhaustion descend on her like a storm.

BOGWITCH: 2 am I gotta sleep
OtterLeader: I'm sorry
BOGWITCH: Why?
BOGWITCH: I make my own decisions. If I wanted to sleep earlier, I would've told you. Don't be ridiculous.
OtterLeader: lol
OtterLeader: Okay. I like hanging out with you.

That took her by surprise. The thing was, she'd never had any intentions of staying up quite this late. But she'd had a great time, and her need to "kill shit" had been replaced with a warm, drowsy, happy feeling. She couldn't quite remember the last time she'd felt that way, actually.

Huh.

OtterLeader: Besides, I imagine at your age you need less sleep anyway, right?
BOGWITCH: Don't make me regret my decision
OtterLeader: LOL good night, Boggy
BOGWITCH: 'Night, Otter.

She signed off, then looked at her computer for a long second. She felt tired, yes, but she felt *better.* Better than she had in weeks. Better than she had since Kit left. Longer than that, if she was honest with herself: since the year leading up to Kit leaving—figuring out the money for his tuition, trying to organize all the things that would help him get there. Hell, even dealing with Kit's temperamental roller coaster of emotions as he tried to figure out where he wanted to go and what he wanted to do. She'd been wrung out like a sponge.

She enjoyed fighting with the guild. But this, this one-on-one with Otter, had been the most connected she'd felt to someone else in a long time.

She was still for a moment as her tired brain processed that.

*You felt close and comfy "hanging out" with a guy who is, tops, twenty-one.*

That . . . might not be a good thing.

# CHAPTER 13
## BEING GOOD SUCKS

Aiden gritted his teeth so hard, he was surprised his molars hadn't turned to powder. He was at his mother's. He'd managed to pretend that her whole engine had blown up and he needed a slew of replacement parts (and had even gotten Davy's buy-in to bolster the lie). Meanwhile, Davy said that he'd get her a new car, but it was going to take time to get the right one. Since she liked Davy better, she took the explanation with a degree of pride and grinned smugly at Aiden. It didn't bother him as much as it used to that he wasn't her favorite. Although it did still bother him. Especially on days like this.

She'd called him at six in the morning, telling him there had been a loud noise, a crash. In a panic, he'd tossed on sweats and driven over like a demon, hoping that there wasn't any black ice—it had gotten cold. Still, he lived only ten minutes away, on the other side of their small town.

When he arrived, she was drinking coffee . . . and there was a small, angry, barking little dog.

"Are you all right?" he asked.

At which point she got up, still dressed in pajamas and a thick flannel robe, and shuffled her way to the living room.

His father had been many things, but a carpenter he wasn't. Still, he'd surprised Aiden's mother with a "built-in bookshelf" one year, on their thirtieth anniversary, and they'd put every book in the house on it, including a now-ancient set of children's encyclopedias. Year after year, with every visit, Aiden had noticed that the weight of the books had caused the shelf to continuously sag, like a slow, tired smile. Now, all the books were strewn across the floor, and the shelf itself was wrecked.

He took a deep breath.

"Scared the hell out of me," his mother said, going back to the kitchen and turning on the small TV there. It was her habit: get up, get a cup of coffee, then watch the news or a rerun of *Murder, She Wrote*. "And Prince Albert here was terrified. Spent about half an hour barking."

Aiden looked at the dog with narrowed eyes, and the dog glared at him right back. Or at least, it seemed to, from underneath a thick fringe of beige hair. It was a Pomeranian or something, from what he could tell. He liked animals and generally loved dogs, but he preferred bigger dogs. Also, he couldn't imagine why his mother, who wasn't particularly a pet person, would be responsible for one. "When did you get a dog?"

"I'm watching him for Gladys," she said instead.

He kept his face completely impassive as he crouched down and tried to befriend the dog, who growled at him with suspicion. The last thing she needed was a dog to take care of, but he knew better than to say so, or to even show his uncertainty. He chose his battles.

After having a cup of coffee of his own, he gathered up the books, piling them on the coffee table and along the wall in the living room. The thing was, he'd inherited his father's unhandiness. He was decent on a computer, and he felt like he had a real skill when it came to taking care of someone sick. But wood, nails, plaster? Not his wheelhouse. At all.

"You know, maybe Riley knows somebody," he started, only to have her instantly up in arms.

"No! I don't want to spend money on this!" she said, and as cranky as she sounded, he could see the genuine panic in her expression, and he relented.

"Mom, if I try to fix this, I'm just afraid it's going to be a nightmare," he said. "I can pay for it."

She huffed. "You should be saving your money," she said. "You're not even working. Not even *looking* for work, for God's sake, Aiden. You can't just throw your money around."

He pinched the bridge of his nose. "I can't fix this, and neither can Davy." *Even if he ever made it out here.* He forced himself to smile encouragingly. "So . . . here's what we're going to do. We're either going to hire someone to make you a built-in—"

"No!"

Startled, he saw that she was teary eyed.

It occurred to him that this shelf, one of the things his father had actually built for her on their anniversary, wasn't something she'd want replaced by Random Handyman. He nodded.

"I'll see what I can do," Aiden finally agreed, even as he felt a falling sense of doom.

A few days later, after much discussion with talkative guys at Fool's Falls Hardware, he had a vague idea of what he needed to do. To add insult to injury, the dog was slowly won over, and was currently trying to get his attention. He gave the puffball some skritches that had him wriggling until Aiden thought his butt would wiggle right off. "I need to do this, buddy," he said firmly, but the dog was intent on getting in the way. "Mom, can't we shut him in the bedroom or the spare room until I'm done with this?"

"He'll pee," she said, shaking her head. "He gets nervous when he's left alone. He already peed on my bedspread when I took a shower."

Aiden sighed, making a mental note to change out her bedding. He couldn't leave the dog in the yard, either, since she had no fence. Well, he'd just have to make do.

So, clenching his jaw and trying to find a stud, he found himself ignoring the yipping antics of the dog, the high volume of his mother's television (which was spouting something that he knew, had he been paying attention, would've pumped his blood pressure up by a dangerous amount), and fielding questions from his mother as he tried to work.

"Did you find a date?" his mother asked, apropos of nothing, as the news complained about immigration. Prince Albert let out a little sharp bark, like punctuation. He was cute, if somewhat demanding. At least his mother wasn't tasked with taking care of, say, a Great Pyrenees.

"Not yet." The stud finder lit up, and he marked it off with a pencil. Then he went to find the other stud.

"You aren't trying hard enough," she said. "You can't just sit in your house, playing video games. You're not a kid, for God's sake! You should go out, date. Get married."

His eyes widened, and he was surprised enough to stop looking at the wall, turning to her. "*Married*? That's a little excessive, isn't it?"

She sighed, shaking her head. "Never married, never dating in college, never dating since Sheryl. At *fifty*." She looked both mournful and frustrated. "People talk."

He turned back to the wall, trying to draw a connecting line between the two *x* spots he'd marked. Then he took out his measuring tape, hoping that he'd gotten the right-size piece. "So let them talk?" he suggested.

A quick glance showed her scowl had deepened. "It's a small town, Aiden," she said. "And I have to *live* here."

*You know, you really don't.*

But that was *not* the conversation he was going to have with her now.

The thing was, she loved Fool's Falls. Her church was here. Her friends were here. She'd scattered his father's ashes in the Bureau of Land

Management forest that he'd loved—which Aiden wasn't quite sure was legal, but up here, folks looked the other way.

"I went to Deb's party." Aiden said, trying for deflection. She was nice, Deb. Not his type, but . . . nice.

His stomach knotted uneasily. She was perhaps too nice.

His mother turned down the TV, and he suppressed a groan. "So you're dating?" she asked eagerly.

"What? No!"

The dog started dancing between his feet, which would be cute in any other circumstance, but not when he was trying to deal with heavy boards and a drill, especially as someone not very handy.

"Stop that, Prince Albert." He held up the first board replacement for the shelf. He wasn't sure if he was doing this right. He needed to put up the side pieces first. He got the braces screwed in, glad that he seemed to be hitting something solid. "You know, Mom, the shelf might've fallen because the books you had on it were too heavy. Do you really need these old encyclopedias?"

"Don't change the subject. Is there something wrong with Deb?"

"No. She seems like a kind person. Really . . . outgoing." He huffed out a breath. "I'm serious about the encyclopedias, Mom. You might want to think about weeding out some of this stuff."

"I like all those books."

"When was the last time you read any of them?"

Two bright spots of color flared on her cheeks. "Dammit, Aiden! What are you doing with your life? It's like you're fifteen again!"

He couldn't help it. He'd tried so hard to be patient, to keep cheerful, to help her, but something just snapped.

"Mom, I am currently *retired*. I sold my half of the company, remember? To Malcolm!" He didn't mean to, but his voice sharpened, turned loud. "I came *back here* to take care of Dad! And now I'm trying to take care of *you*!"

It was the absolute worst thing he could've said.

"TAKE CARE OF ME?" she shouted back. "I'm not some . . . some child! How dare you!"

At that moment, he would've given his entire savings—and they were substantial—to take the words back. Even more than that if he could somehow port to his house, playing *Blood Saga*.

As his mother started shouting vitriol, he focused on the shelf, tuning out the worst of the insults.

*Looks like I'm texting Boggy again.*

It was funny. One senior citizen was driving him up a wall, while another was quickly becoming his best friend. Of course, his official best friend would probably always be Malcolm, but Aiden was honest with himself. Malcolm was married, he had kids, and he was running the business by himself at this point. He was on another track. While Malcolm tried to stick with the *Blood Saga* missions, he was slowly stepping away from his guild responsibilities and playing less and less. Aiden missed his friend, but he certainly didn't blame him.

That said, Aiden couldn't see himself having a heartfelt discussion with TheFerocity or even Gandalf. They were too young, too . . . frivolous. They lacked life experience.

Boggy, on the other hand, was someone he enjoyed talking to, as well as playing with. She was an octogenarian who cursed like a sailor, fought like a shield-maiden, and had both no filter and no tolerance for bullshit. Which she'd proved many times. At this point, whether there was a group mission or not, he found himself either doing dungeon runs or just exploring with her every night. Once, they'd just hung out in the guildhall for over two hours, typing back and forth.

He kind of wished his mother was better friends with her, so maybe Boggy could talk some sense into her. Although he could only imagine what kind of conversations they'd have.

"Are you listening to me?" his mother demanded.

Braces in, he picked up the solid plank of oak that he'd chosen. Moment of truth. Time to put it up. "Let me get the shelf up, Mom," he said firmly.

"Sometimes, I think that you just do things to hurt me," she snapped as he placed the thick piece of wood up, then took a step back. It looked . . . okay? Like a shelf? He supposed that was the best he could hope for.

That is, until there was a creak, and a snap.

"Shit!" he said as he saw the long, heavy board start to fall—right toward the little puffball of a dog.

Everything was instinct from that point on. He moved forward, scooting the mop-like creature out of the way with his ankle before he got hurt—just before the heavy board slammed into his own foot.

"GODDAMN MOTHERFUCKER!" he shouted as pain erupted, shooting up his leg from his instep.

"Oh! Oh!" His mother was at his side in a second as he shoved the board away. "Are you all right? What happened?"

He stared at her for a second. "It . . . the board . . . really?" he asked, his voice strangled. "What happened? *Really*?"

"I mean, why did the board fall?"

"I have no fucking idea," he snarled. "I don't know how to build stuff."

His mother waved her hands like frightened birds. "Give me your keys, I'll drive you—"

*"No, you won't,"* he growled. "Just . . . call for an ambulance. I think I broke my foot."

# CHAPTER 14

## TREACHEROUS CHECKPOINT

Maggie sat in her office, trying her damnedest to stay focused. She'd taken to exchanging texts and GIFs with Otter during the day, stuff that had nothing to do with *Blood Saga*. She wasn't sure if he was texting her during class or what, but she was starting to smile every time her phone chimed with a message notification. Which was strange, she had to admit. For the past few weeks, she'd grown from just enjoying the guild to playing with Otter every day to texting and messaging him and hanging out with him in the guildhall. She spent more time with him online than she did with Mac, and she texted him more than she did Rosita.

She tried not to think about it too much. Her connection with Otter was weirdly intense. It was just . . . he seemed to *get* her. He was mature, and sort of artlessly wise. And relaxed. She desperately needed relaxation in her life. He was a good friend.

*A young friend.*

She frowned at herself. She hadn't actually come out and asked him how old he was. She tried not to think about it, because it frankly *didn't* matter. It was platonic.

She wasn't quite sure why she was so insistent, mentally, about that point. Probably because of his nondisclosed age.

The other guys in the guild weren't aware of how much time they spent together, although they'd noticed a closer camaraderie. BigDorkEnergy, as usual, had been the first to pipe up.

BigDorkEnergy: R U 2 fuckin or what
OtterLeader: not funny
BigDorkEnergy: GILF man lol
OtterLeader: Seriously. Knock it off.

Maggie got the feeling that Otter, who generally had the patience of a saint, was probably offended by the suggestion, or was perhaps embarrassed by their friendship. It made her sad, a little, but it was also understandable.

Before BDE could get Otter too riled up—or, worse, kicking people out because of things that any shit-talking guild would say—she decided to simply address things head on, as was her wont.

BOGWITCH: Y'all youngsters couldn't handle me.
BOGWITCH: I've got a toy drawer full of fun and a lifetime of being disappointed by men. Why the hell would I settle for you amateurs now?
GandalfTheGay: uh TMI
TheFerocity: OH GROSS
BigDorkEnergy: NOBODY WANTS TO HEAR THAT
BOGWITCH: lol
BOGWITCH: FAAFO, dipshit
SneakyMeat: Hey, no judgment. Get some!
BOGWITCH: Sometimes you have to provide your own fun
BOGWITCH: are we killing shit tonight or what?

Otter then messaged her privately.

**OtterLeader: You okay?**
**BOGWITCH: What, because of them asking if we're fucking?**
**BOGWITCH: It's fine. Srsly. No prob.**
**OtterLeader: I can make an official rule. These assholes need to quit it.**
**BOGWITCH: They're kids. It's not a big deal.**

It occurred to her—he was a kid, too, and he'd never treated her with anything other than respect. It was . . . nice, she realized, absently.

**OtterLeader: After the mission, want to hang out? We could live text a movie again.**

She felt herself blush—which was ridiculous. But she still said yes.

Everyone in the guild seemed to have plans for Halloween, despite it being on a Monday. Now, it was Tuesday, All Saints' Day. She'd already done the bulk of her editing, waiting for a few clients to turn in projects or turn around revisions. She did some administrative stuff—invoicing, social media scheduling, making sure bills were paid. Even got some pho broth out to thaw. She usually made a big batch of broth with oxtail, and then fixed a big bowl of noodles with Thai basil, jalapeños, and the usual accoutrements.

She really was a foodie, even if she hadn't had a chance to indulge in it in years. When Trev had suggested they move out to the Falls, it hadn't even occurred to her that they would be moving to a small town that only had fast food, an "upscale" restaurant that was basically an Applebee's Plus with an emphasis on pasta, a sports bar that served nachos and burgers, and a Mexican-food restaurant that she couldn't really recommend.

Logically, she knew she'd been spoiled for choice in California. Actually living here, where she couldn't even order Domino's, had shown her just how spoiled she'd been. Now, she'd had to learn to make a lot of things she'd easily ordered, back in the day.

Not that it would've changed her choices. When she'd gotten married, she'd known that Trev would never cheat on her, and while he'd been demanding, he'd also loved her, in his way.

Until she'd had Kit.

She shook her head, erasing the thoughts like clearing an Etch A Sketch.

One of her favorite cuisines, hands down, was Vietnamese. Even though she'd never had pho as a child, she'd fallen in love with it, as well as banh mi and cha gio, when she'd gone to college. Maybe it was silly or strange to try to use food to connect to a culture she'd never been raised with, since that part of her background had died with her mother—Nana Birdie had made sure of that. Her grandparents had tried to pretend that her mother wasn't Vietnamese, that she was somehow just some brunette Yankee who had stolen away their son from college.

Maybe that was why Maggie had always loved Vietnamese food, semipretending that it was more authentic to her than her grandmother's shrimp and grits or banana pudding. It was definitely the reason she'd changed her last name to her mother's maiden name on her divorce. She was tired of her name being tied to people who had tried so hard to mold her into what they wanted her to be.

Her stomach grumbled a little, and her heart ached. Dinner was hours away. She might just indulge herself, and have the pho for lunch.

She needed a distraction. She'd joined the guild only to show Kit that she could interact with people. So far, her IRL interactions had crashed and burned spectacularly. Deb kept inviting her to things—*"Girls' night!" "Mimosa brunch!" "Casino weekend!"*—that were really not her cup of tea. So far, she'd managed to dodge Deb's good intentions and stayed polite, but she was running out of options. At this point, she was afraid Deb might simply come over and kidnap her. Maggie might need a moat. Possibly a minefield. Good spiked barriers made good neighbors.

The problem was, the guild was becoming her focus—and Otter himself was becoming close to a fixation. Maybe Kit was right, and her antisocial tendencies were damaging her. She'd never have thought that she'd be soaking in some twenty-year-old's attention like sand sucking up water.

She sighed. It had been a while since she'd talked to Rosita. Rosita had moved away sophomore year of high school, but the two of them had managed to stay in touch all these years. Not religiously or anything, but usually about once every two months or so. They caught each other up on their marriages (including Maggie's divorce woes), their kids, their lives. She was due a call. She texted Rosita, only to have her text back: WORK IS CRAZY. CALL YOU TONIGHT?

That pruned off that avenue. She sighed, then went on Twitter, DMing her friend Mac.

Maggie Le Editor: Hey, you there?

Macross Sagittarius: As it happens. What's up?

Macross Sagittarius: Surprised you're not on Blood Saga. Seems like that's your go-to hang out lately.

Maggie Le Editor: Yeah. It's been fun. I like my guild.

Maggie Le Editor: Too much, maybe? I was thinking of taking a break from it for a while.

Macross Sagittarius: Okay, spit it out.

Maggie Le Editor: ??

Macross Sagittarius: You only DM me in the middle of the day—your day, not mine—to either scream about problem clients, tell me about worries about Kit, or let me know something about Pedro Pascal.

Maggie Le Editor: I could be just whiny and feeling blue. Or have something amazing to tell you.

Macross Sagittarius: No, you tend to save that stuff till nighttime, when you know I'm having insomnia and because you don't interrupt your workday.

Macross Sagittarius: What's the deal, sweetie? Tell Auntie Mac. Some spoiled client driving you up a wall?

Maggie briefly considered making something up, just so she wouldn't be called out like this. That said, Mac never pulled her punches. It was one of the reasons they got along so well.

Maggie Le Editor: No.

Macross Sagittarius: Is Kit all right?

Maggie Le Editor: Still having some trouble connecting. He sent me a selfie from some anime club, and his roomie apparently turned down the fraternity life, but they seem to be having some trouble in the dorms. He just sounds so lonely.

Maggie Le Editor: It's why I joined BSO in the first place. To show him how to get out of his comfort zone.

Macross Sagittarius: So why would you walk away from it, then? If it's to set an example for Kit?

It took Maggie a long time to actually type. Then she gritted her teeth, typed quickly, and hit send before she could stop herself.

Maggie Le Editor: I've kind of been talking with the guild leader. Like, a lot.

Maggie Le Editor: Like, maybe every night.

Maggie Le Editor: And we text even when we're not online. During the day.

Maggie Le Editor: Pretty much every day.

There was a long—and in Maggie's worried opinion, possibly judgmental—pause on Mac's end.

Macross Sagittarius: Are you two like dating or something?

Maggie Le Editor: GOD, no! He's like, 20 or something, I think? Maybe 21.

Maggie Le Editor: And you know I don't date. That's not something that interests me.

Macross Sagittarius: What interests me is, if I'd asked that about anyone else, you would've said "I don't date" as the FIRST thing. This time it was second.

Macross Sagittarius: Hmm.

Maggie Le Editor: Hmm? What hmm? No! This is not hmm worthy!

Macross Sagittarius: Well, it's good you're not dating. Because ick. There's age differences, and then there's age differences with someone who's practically a minor.

Maggie felt nauseated.

Macross Sagittarius: Is he hot?

Maggie Le Editor: I have no idea. I've never seen him IRL.

Maggie Le Editor: I'm not horny for him, FFS. I just really like him. He's my best friend, other than you and Rosita.

Macross Sagittarius: Oh! That's so cute.

Maggie Le Editor: I will end you.

Macross Sagittarius: It's even cuter you think you can.

Macross Sagittarius: Sweetie, if you're just worried because you've got a platonic friendship with a guy who's a lot younger than you, you're fine. It's literally no big deal.

Maggie nodded, feeling the knot in her chest slowly release.

Macross Sagittarius: I wouldn't meet him in IRL though.

Macross Sagittarius: And maybe watch your innuendos? 😉

Maggie Le Editor: Well, there goes half my sense of humor.

She closed Twitter, then sighed. Mac was right. She just had to be careful, and honest with herself. She genuinely cared about Otter, and would do anything to make sure they stayed friends. She needed to make sure she didn't make anything . . . *weird.*

So the kid was nice. Emphasis on *kid.* She just needed to keep it together. Focus on the game, rather than the players. Maybe reframe the relat—*friendship*, she quickly corrected herself. Keep their interactions in game, rather than live texting and stuff. That was the slippery slope toward . . . well, she wasn't sure what it was toward, but it couldn't be anywhere good.

Which, of course, was when her phone pinged. She didn't even have to glance at it to know it was Otter.

Otter: Hey Boggy. You around?

Maggie: Yup.

Otter: I have a big favor. Can you run the mission on Thursday?

The guys will listen to you. Mouse has a thing he can't get out of, and he's stepping down as co-lead anyway.

Maggie smiled, pleased that he trusted her with this. From what she could tell, *Blood Saga* was one of the biggest things in Otter's life.

*Knock it off, you twit.* She frowned at herself, or tried to.

Maggie: Sure thing. You okay? Just busy? Got a date or something?

She winced after she hit send. *Got a date?* What the hell?

Mac would be so disappointed in her right now. Rightfully so.

Maggie: You should date. Get out there, sow some oats. Enjoy yourself.

She winced again. Did that read as cringe-tastic to him as it did to her?

*Stop making this worse!*

His response was slow.

Otter: Actually, no. Not really big on dating.

Otter: And especially not right now. Minor fracture in my foot . . . long story.

Otter: Just getting around is a PITA and I'm hobbling around getting food, generally gorked by the meds. Not fun. :( They make me too sleepy.

Otter: If I feel better, I'll play, but I don't think I'm up for leading a big mission. Gandalf can handle healing, but he's not quite as high leveled, so the rest will probably be grumpy about it. Just tell them I told them to knock it off.

Maggie: You're adorable. Like I can't handle the crew if they start bitching.

Maggie: Back up tho. You BROKE YOUR FOOT?

Maggie: What happened?

Otter: was at my Mom's fixing a bookshelf, dog got in my way, dropped a big board on myself. Could've been worse. But yeah, this sucks.

It occurred to Maggie that he was going to community college. They wouldn't have dorms. She frowned, typing.

Maggie: I don't mean to pry, and you don't have to tell me, but do you live with your Mom? Are you there now? Is she able to help take care of you?

Another long pause.

Otter: It's kind of complicated. But don't worry. I can manage.

She took a deep breath. It was the kind of breath you took before jumping off a super-high dive . . . or walked into the woods in the middle of the night in a camping trip . . . or ate something doused in the dubiously named Super Nuclear Face Melter Hot Sauce. It was scary, sort of thrilling, with an undercurrent of "I know this is a poor decision, and yet here we are."

Maggie: Want me to bring you lunch?

She stared at the words she'd sent. She should take them back. She should block his number. She should uninstall *Blood Saga* and then possibly move across the country.

Not that he'd even care, right? She prayed that he didn't care. Hell, maybe he'd think it was weird that he was friends with her, or be repulsed that an old . . .

Otter: I would love some lunch, actually. I was kinda low on groceries, and I just ate tuna out of the can. Which is a clear sign of desperation, amirite?

She couldn't help but laugh. She wondered if he added mustard, or if he even had any mustard to add. If he was down to naked tuna out of the can, he was truly scraping the bottom of the barrel. She also felt a grudging sense of solidarity. The guy needed lunch.

He needed her.

Otter: But you don't have to. I mean, if it's trouble. I can take care of myself.

She blinked. *Dammit.* Too late now.

What had she done?

Maggie: I'm bringing soup. Just text me your address.

This was foolish. So intensely, ridiculously foolish. But with any luck, she'd see him—and more importantly, he'd see *her*, in her feral, frumpy, middle-aged glory—and then he'd probably drop their conversations himself. Her heart actually hurt at the thought, and she immediately regretted volunteering. Still, from that standpoint, it was probably a *smart* move, if she thought about it. She was getting a little squirrelly about Otter. The fact that she was volunteering to take him lunch, to check up on him after being hurt, was definitely foolish.

*This is probably going to be a disaster.*

With a sigh, she got up and started to get pho ready to travel.

# CHAPTER 15

## SUSTAINED MISUNDERSTANDING

It took about forty-five minutes for Maggie to get the pho stuff together and packed, and then to make her way down from the Upper Falls, where she lived, to "downtown"—such as it was—where Otter apparently lived. She pulled into the driveway of the house. It had white siding and a sort of rock-patterned set of panels on the front, and while the colors looked tired, it was nonetheless nicer than she had expected. The lawn was strewn with some fallen leaves. She frowned. It looked bigger than she'd thought, too—maybe a two-bedroom, or even three.

Kinda big for a kid to rent on his own.

Little pings of alarm started dancing along her spine.

She'd been so intent on helping out a kid in trouble, or at least so she'd perceived, it had never really occurred to her she was going to a man's house. One she didn't know, not really . . . online didn't count: Kit was right. She glanced around. At least he had nearby neighbors. She lived on fifteen acres, and her nearest neighbor was nearly a mile away.

She'd probably be fine. Right?

She grimaced, lugging her reusable shopping bag full of pho broth and accoutrements.

Now that she thought about it, she probably *should* have discussed more personal details with Otter. She knew his stance on, say, *Star Wars* versus *Star Trek* (and the fact that above all he was a *Doctor Who* fan, which she felt spoke well of him). She knew that his favorite flavor of ice cream was butter pecan, even though it was a "grandma" flavor. She knew that he loved graphic novels like *Sandman* and *Bone* and *The Dreamer*, even though they weren't the typical superhero comics that his friends were into.

But she didn't know why he lived alone.

And she didn't know why his mother wasn't helping him out, despite him having a foot fracture.

Her steps slowed as she headed to the front door.

*I also don't know if he has, say, a large basement . . . with, say, manacles.*

Suddenly, she had another twinge of pure self-preservation. She knew he was the son of Deb's friend. Probably like Kit . . . although, considering how geeky Harrison and Kit were, why weren't *they* friends with Otter?

It had never occurred to her to ask. Maybe he was a little older than twenty, she realized. Yes, he'd just started community college, but maybe he had been doing something else beforehand? Like . . . a gap year? Or he might've been working. Kids around here did that, like Harrison himself.

Maybe he'd gone to another high school?

She bit her lip, then frowned as she saw a note on the door.

*IN SHOWER. JUST LET YOURSELF IN.—OTTER*

She felt . . . conflicted. A little nervous.

*Okay. Naked guy somewhere in the house. No big deal.*

Oh, who was she kidding? If she was any more stressed, she'd implode.

Setting her shoulders and gritting her teeth, she grabbed the doorknob and opened the door.

It was nice. Nicer than she'd expected, honestly. The door opened up to a set of stairs that led to the upper story. Looking off to her left, she could see the living room and the kitchen beyond. She expected to find the usual plank-and-milk-crate decor that was typical of college students, mismatched furniture that was cast off from older relatives, maybe some posters on the wall. But Otter had a nice couch, a decent TV. The dining room table was a smallish circle, with just two chairs.

She meant to close the door gingerly, but the bag of soup stuff swung, slamming it shut.

She could hear the shower upstairs running, and then heard a loud, deep voice.

"Boggy? That you?"

A *lot* deeper than she'd realized. Of course, he was in the bathroom, so . . . maybe an echo? And Harrison's voice had turned into a frickin' Barry White bass when he hit freshman year, even as Kit's had stayed more in a low tenor range.

"Boggy?" Otter sounded a little more concerned when she didn't answer.

"Yup," she croaked, then cleared her throat. No. She knew this guy. And if he tried anything funny . . . well. She'd do . . . something. "It's me."

"Sorry! I'll be out in a minute, swear," he called out. The shower sounded louder, so she imagined he had opened the door and was now dripping and yelling. The image made her smile, not for any pervy reasons, but because it seemed so *Otter*. Polite, thoughtful. A bit harmless.

"It just occurred to me I hadn't showered since I got my air boot, and you were nice enough to make lunch, and I didn't want to, you know . . ."

"Stink?" she called, then started chuckling when she heard him laugh.

"Yeah. So . . . things take a little longer with the whole foot thing. But I will be down in a minute!"

"Take your time," she responded, then added, "Mind if I use a pot? I can microwave this, but it's not as good."

"Sure. Make yourself at home," he called. Then she heard the door close, and she headed to the kitchen. Again, it was cleaner and nicer than she'd thought it would be, even though it was pretty much a typical, built-in-the-seventies-style kitchen. Nicer appliances. She wondered if he rented.

She riffled around through cabinets and drawers until she found where he kept the pots and pans. Grabbing a lidded pot, she got out the broth and dumped it in. She then grabbed a big bowl and put the rice noodles in. It would take half an hour's soaking, she realized.

Maybe she should've just gotten him a damned sandwich?

She realized that she might be really, really foolish here.

She pulled out her phone, then took a deep breath. Something wasn't quite right, and she wasn't sure what, but after all these years, she knew better than to ignore it. She quickly typed a message to Rosita.

Maggie: Hey, I know we're talking tonight. Six o'clock.

Maggie: On the off chance you don't hear from me—I went to this address.

Maggie: I'll let you know if I'm going to be late, though.

She sent the address, then put the phone back in her pocket. Still, she should've expected it when Rosita instantly texted her back.

Rosita: Can't talk, in a meeting, but . . . are you on a date?

Rosita: Because if you are—you're damned right you're calling me!

Rosita: Wait, why are you at his house? Whose house is this?

Maggie: Long story. Am at house of kid I told you about a while ago. Otter?

Rosita: One of your video game friends?

Maggie: I'm sure it's fine? It just occurred to me that Dexter was a kid once, and I wanted to cover my bases.

There was a pause, then a quick ping.

Rosita: Get the fuck out of there RIGHT NOW.

Maggie: No, srsly, I am just being weird. I will be fine, I will call tonight.

Maggie: I promise. Just chill out.

Before she could read Rosita's next text, she heard Otter's voice. "I am *so* sorry," he called. "Everything takes twice as long as I think it's gonna at this point. And the boot's supposed to help, and be better than crutches, but it's like . . . *urgh*."

She couldn't help it. He sounded like he did when he texted (other than the deep-voice part)—gently self-deprecating, mild mannered even when irritated.

"It's fine," she called back, not looking around the kitchen wall. "Just getting the soup ready."

She felt her chest squeeze a little. She turned the burner on.

She'd thought the biggest worry she might, *might*, have was that she was somehow feeling inappropriately toward the closest thing to a "local friend" she had. Now, she had a whole different set of concerns.

She swallowed. This was *Otter*, she told herself.

He was limping this way, she could tell. She could hear a sort of shuffling drag-thump down the hallway, then a staggered step down the stairs.

Her breathing went a little shallow. She glanced out the kitchen window. It looked like he had a big garage . . .

Wait.

The house had a carport beside it. So that would be a workshop?

Her throat went dry.

*Oh, God, I am terrifying myself.*

"I just wanted to thank you." She heard him just before she saw him. "I hope it wasn't too long a . . ."

Then he saw her and stopped, staring at her in disbelief.

She, on the other hand, felt her eyes widen and her eyebrows hit her hairline.

This was no kid.

He was about six foot one, easily, and built like a linebacker. Auburn hair, glinted through with gray. He had a beard that defined his jaw.

"I'm . . . you're . . . ," he spluttered, in that deep, rumbling voice, looking completely at a loss. "You can't be . . . *Boggy*?"

She, on the other hand, suddenly had enough adrenaline in her system to wrestle a bear. Without thinking, she yanked open the nearby drawer, grabbing the cast-iron skillet she'd seen when pot hunting.

"Who the *fuck* are you?" she demanded, brandishing the pan with both hands.

He blinked.

Then he laughed.

"Yup," he said, a deep, satisfied sound. "You're Boggy, all right."

# CHAPTER 16

## BEWARE THE QUIET ONES

Aiden stared at the tiny woman who was currently standing, wild eyed and wild haired, brandishing his cast-iron skillet. She was staring at him with a combination of fear and pure, unadulterated fury. She was wearing an oversize sweater that hung past her hips, and a pair of jeans that disappeared into a blocky pair of sheepskin boots. She looked biracial, if he had to guess—some kind of Asian?

From where he stood, he could see the pulse thumping in her throat, just along the column of her neck. She was going to stroke out if she didn't calm down.

"It's okay," he said, holding up his hands gingerly, trying for soothing. "It's just me. Otter."

"You're . . . Otter?" Her voice was sharp, and the pan didn't move an inch, despite being heavy. Her phone buzzed in her pocket, but she ignored it.

"My real name's Aiden, if that helps?" He put his air-booted foot out. "I really did break my foot. And I sent you the text, asking for your help, and you volunteered to bring me lunch. Which was really nice, by the way."

Her dark eyes narrowed with suspicion, or at least, one of them did. The other was behind a long, frizzled lock of dark hair, shot through with strands of silver. She blew at it, still frowning fiercely, and he chuckled.

"We've been talking for weeks—well, texting," he corrected. "Remember? We live texted that old movie—"

"Classic movie," she interjected. The pan went down a fraction of an inch.

He grinned. "*Classic* movie, the black-and-white one. Where the old ladies murder people." He laughed. "I thought maybe you were giving me a message."

"*Arsenic and Old Lace.* And how are you this age—whatever age that is—and you don't know Cary Grant?" she asked, shaking her head.

Her phone rang again. She glanced down for a minute, looking torn.

"Wait a minute," he said as something clicked in his mind. "Didn't I see you at Deb's football party?"

Now she blinked slowly, and he could almost see the cogs whirling in her head. Her eyes were even darker than they'd first seemed, he noticed, with really long eyelashes. Presumably natural, since it didn't look like she had any makeup on.

"You were petting Duchess?" she asked tentatively.

"You were grabbing your jacket."

"Oh my God." She put the skillet down, then wiped her palms on her jeans. The phone stopped, then rang again. "Hold on."

She grabbed it and answered, her dark gaze never leaving his.

"Rosita, it's fine."

*"Get the fuck out of there!"* Whoever Boggy was talking to, she was loud. "I don't care if he's a tween, or a priest, or a fucking *sex god*, you get the fuck out of that house!"

"It really is fine."

"You sent me a safety check out of nowhere, saying you're at his house in the middle of the day and feeling nervous? Hello, red flags! You need to—"

"Rosy! It's all right!" Her cheeks were now flaming red, he noticed, and she turned away. "False alarm. He's a friend of my friend . . . it turns out I've met him before, I just didn't know he was him. If you know what I mean." She paused. "And . . . erm, he's not a kid. Apparently."

He grinned. "You thought I was a kid?" he mouthed.

She covered the mouthpiece. "I thought you were twenty, all right? Or twenty-one. Young."

*I'm old enough to be your mother!*

It was kind of hilarious.

"You want to send her a picture of me? My address?" he asked softly, not wanting to interrupt.

She looked over at him, surprised.

*"Is that him?"* the woman yelled. *"Put him on the phone!"*

"Oh my *God*, I am not putting him on the phone," Boggy said, sounding mortified. "It's fine, I promise. I will call you tonight."

"*You're goddamned right you are*," the woman said. *"I went out on a pee break to make sure you weren't being murdered. YOU ARE TELLING ME EVERYTHING."*

"I'll, erm, send you a pic," Boggy said. "Love you, talk tonight."

*"GRRRR!"*

Boggy cut off the call, then held up her cell. "Um . . ."

He smiled as she took a picture. "Is there anything else I can do?" he asked gently. "I should've thought it through. Going to any stranger's house is going to be, y'know, kind of fraught. Especially for women. But you were *Boggy*, and I figured if anybody could handle herself, it would be you. Of course, you're not exactly the way I, uh, envisioned you. So if there's something else I can do to help you feel safe . . ."

"No, that's fine," she said. "And to be honest, I already sent my friend your address and told her where I was, before you walked in." She said this with her chin up, completely unapologetic.

"Good," he said, and meant it. "I mean, bad that you had to, that it's the world we live in. But safety first."

She looked at him, and her expression softened a fraction before she cleared her throat, looking grumpy again. "Why didn't you tell me?"

"Tell you what?"

"That you're old!"

He stared. Then he burst out laughing. Jesus, this woman. His chest warmed. Even in person, she cracked him up with her bluntness and energy.

"Not . . . oh, shut up. You know what I meant," she grumbled.

"Actually, that never occurred to me either," he said.

"How old *are* you?" she asked carefully.

"Fifty this May."

"Holy shit," she said. "You're older than I am!"

"If it's any comfort," he said, "all this time, I've thought you were in your eighties."

She spluttered. *"What?"*

"Well, you kept saying you were old enough to be my mother," he countered. "My mother's the one who gave me your contact info. So . . ."

"Oh my God," she muttered, rubbing her hands over her face. "Rosita and Mac are going to have a field day when they find this out."

He wasn't sure who any of those people were, but at least she didn't seem scared or angry at this point. He liked that the tension seemed to leave her body. He'd take embarrassment over fear any day, and with luck, he'd be able to get her past even that. "The soup smells good."

"It's pho. Have you had it before?"

"It's been a long time," he admitted. "There used to be a place in Issaquah that had some decent stuff. Miss that place."

"You lived on the west side?" she said.

He grinned. "Even worked in Seattle for a while."

They studied each other. Then she made a wave with her arm.

"Do you need to sit?"

"Nah, this is fine." He took a deep inhale.

"Well, the noodles need time to soak, and I'm going to get a plate to put out the toppings. Do you have a cutting board?"

He nodded. She made dainty piles of herbs—mint, a sort of dark purple-green basil, sliced jalapeños, wedges of lime. She arranged them on a plate, her movements deft, with purpose.

"I don't suppose you have sriracha?" she asked.

"In the fridge," he said, then watched as she opened it, whistling a low note.

"You weren't kidding about being out of food. Do you just . . . not eat, normally?"

He laughed. "I go out a lot, I'll admit. And I buy groceries every couple of days, or I have ramen."

"I tend to stock up, and I never go out," she said. Each word came out grudgingly, like she still blamed him for not being some pimply-faced teenager. "So I cook a lot. Or I have a lot of bread and butter. Or I, ah, forget to eat."

He frowned. "That's not healthy."

"Hey, I like carbs," she said.

"No, I mean skipping meals isn't healthy," he said, then took a deep breath. "Sorry. I'm a nurse—used to be a nurse. Health is kind of a thing for me."

"Says the man who has no food in his house," she pointed out, and he grinned.

"You wouldn't be Boggy if you didn't call me on my shit, I guess."

She tilted her head. "Maggie," she said, with a tiny quirk of a smile. "My name's Maggie. Maggie Le."

"Huh." He held out his hand. "Hi. Officially, I mean."

She looked at his hand, then rolled her eyes. Then she washed her hands, muttering something about jalapeños, before giving him a quick handshake.

He couldn't help smiling at her. Her palm was small and soft and warm, engulfed by his. She was, in a word, cute, like a disgruntled baby duck—and the fact that she'd hate the word made her even cuter.

He would face a firing squad before saying that out loud. He got the feeling her retribution would be swift and decidedly not cute.

"Weirdo," she teased.

"Polite," he countered.

"Yeah, well, I gave up being polite in person years ago," she said with a graceful shrug. "As my behavior in the guild will probably attest." Suddenly, her eyes widened. "Oh, shit. The guild."

He felt a cold chill of prescience. "Please tell me you're not thinking of quitting the guild," he said quickly.

She looked guiltily off to the side, then dove into her bag, pulling out a piece of beef and popping it into his freezer.

"Because . . . okay, I'm just going to say it. I consider you a friend of mine," he said, feeling squirmy and vulnerable, but still determined. "I don't want to lose you, and the guild would definitely be pissed if they realized I was responsible for driving you away."

She stirred the broth, sighing, then pouring a spoonful of fish sauce and what looked like grainy brown sugar into it. "It's just weird, isn't it?"

"Why? Because we're basically . . . Wait, how old are you?"

"A lady doesn't tell," she said, then laughed at herself. "And I'm no fucking lady, so forty-eight."

"We're practically the same age, then," he said.

"Yeah, I figured that out myself." She scowled.

He suddenly felt a ball of ice in the pit of his stomach. "So, you thought I was twenty or something . . . and . . . you're weirded out because I'm not?"

Was she attracted to the barely legal, or something? He felt his stomach rebel. Then his mind threw forward another thought.

*Why are you wondering who she's attracted to?*

That was a weird place to go, mentally, wasn't it? Especially for him. He leaned against the wall, stunned.

"What? *NO.*" She bellowed it. "I . . . I don't know. It was more like I saw you as this kid who was nice and polite, even when he was surrounded with rowdy dickheads about his age. I came because you needed help. All this time, you were fun to talk to, and I like playing in the guild."

"So why would you *stop*?" he repeated. "I don't understand."

She looked mulish for a long second, then she crossed her arms in front of her, the folds of her voluminous sweater shifting.

"I am not dating you." Her words were sharp.

He blinked. "Okay. Didn't ask, but that's good to know . . . ?"

"If you were twenty, I could tell you that," she said slowly, "and just sort of laugh it off. Guy that age, and me nearly fifty? It'd be like disciplining a misbehaving puppy."

He chuckled at that image.

"Not that you'd be interested. That was part of the comfort, I guess? Then we could just be friends. But you're . . ." She waved her hands at him, as if to say, *Well, look at you*. "You're . . . you're *tall*, and all *rugged*, and you're my age!"

Now he felt mildly unnerved.

So . . . was she attracted to *him*? What she knew of him?

Ordinarily, with anyone else, this would be the moment that he felt a bite of panic and guilt. Because he rarely felt attracted to anyone, for whatever reason. He didn't know why, and while he'd made peace with it, around other people it could be a cause of great discomfort. The last thing he wanted was to hurt this woman, who was quickly becoming one of the best friends he'd ever had.

Although . . . doing a quick gut check, he realized that he didn't feel *unattracted*. He was actually . . .

Curious?

Maybe something else?

He blinked slowly, like she'd actually hit him with the skillet she'd been brandishing.

"And I *don't date*," she said, with so much vehemence, so much venom. "I don't see people, I don't hook up. I don't even socialize with the possibility of romance. *Never*."

"Damn." He grinned, shaking his head. "There goes my promposal."

She stared at him. Then, slowly, she started laughing, and he joined in.

"What if I promise not to date you, not to fall in love with you . . . maybe to not even make any sort of physical contact?"

"Well, we blew it with the handshake thing," she said wryly. "But yeah, no physical contact sounds good. You ready for lunch? I just have to get the steak sliced, then we'll get everything set up."

He took a deep breath. "Sounds good."

This was weird. In a lot of ways, it was perfect. But something felt different.

He'd need to think about it. For now, he was just having soup with his new friend . . . and seeing what happened.

# CHAPTER 17

## PLUCKY COMIC RELIEF

Aiden tried not to slurp the remaining broth and noodles, but it was impossible. "Oh my God," he said, catching his breath, feeling like a pig but also very, very happy. "That was *so good*."

She sent him a little smile, or rather the suggestion of a smile, her eyes crinkling at the corners, the pinched edges of her lips tilting up. Then she nodded, getting up and clearing the table, which made him feel guilty.

"Shush," she said dismissively. "You probably are supposed to be resting that foot anyway, right?"

He shrugged, then nodded. "It's just a hairline fracture anyway," he said.

"Does it hurt?"

"Well, yeah."

"Then *shush* and rest it." She rolled her eyes, carrying their bowls to the kitchen. He could hear her loading the dishwasher. "I put the leftovers in a container in the fridge, okay? Noodles separate. Trust me, you never want to dump the noodles in with the broth. They act like a sponge, and then you've got weird pho gummy worms, because all the broth's gone. It's gross."

He sighed. Now that she mentioned it, his foot *was* throbbing. He probably ought to take some painkillers and maybe nap. But he was having a great time talking to Boggy—*Maggie*—and in some weird way, he was afraid that when she walked out the door, she'd bug out completely.

He saw the potential. If she decided it wasn't worth the trouble, or it was some sort of threat to her sense of well-being, she'd vanish like Keyser Söze. She'd drop out of the guild, delete her character files, block his phone number . . . *change* her phone number, probably. Vanish like a puff of smoke.

Which, of course, she had every right to do, and he'd never want her to feel threatened or even uncomfortable. But frankly, this had been the nicest lunch he'd had in years, above and beyond the fact that the pho was freaking *tasty*. It was like his conversations with her, when it was just the two of them exploring *BSO*, or when they live texted movies.

It was just . . . *nice*.

It had been a long time since he'd had pure, uncomplicated *nice* in his life. So long, in fact, that he hadn't realized just how much it soothed him.

"Want to hang out awhile?" he asked when she came back out, looking around awkwardly. "I mean, I don't want to keep you if you're busy. But . . . I don't know. We could watch a movie or something."

She frowned, her weight shifting, her hands fidgeting, hiding themselves in the overlong sleeves of her sweater. The neckline was large, showing off her delicate collarbones, the long, graceful line of her neck. Her skin was a tawny amber, not tanned but not pale either. Her hair was long, a tangled, uncontrolled mess of waves, and she started to tuck some behind her ear before frowning, obviously becoming aware of her actions.

*Why do I* notice *her so much?*

"I should go," she said, firmly, almost as if to herself more than to him. "I shouldn't stay."

He sighed. "Okay. Thanks again for lunch. It was above and beyond, and I really appreciate it."

She rolled her eyes. "Sure, fine. Really. I was going to make it for myself—it wasn't any big deal."

"Do you have a bunch of work to do?" he asked, then paused. "Actually, what do you even do for a living? We talked about everything but ourselves, and it's starting to occur to me that we really ought to know a little more about each other in real life. So there aren't any more nasty surprises." He chuckled at that.

Another small, reluctant grin. "Bad time to mention I'm a cyborg?"

"And here I am, a cyborg hunter from the distant future, sent back to protect Earth from the rise of the machines," he said, and her grin widened. "Awkward."

"Shh. Just bow to your robotic overlords, it'll be fine."

He barked out a laugh.

"I like you," he said, without thinking.

She froze.

"You remind me of my best friend, Malcolm," he quickly added, trying to rectify his error before she got defensive or thorny. "You just make me feel comfortable. You're nice."

"You take that back."

Strangely, he couldn't tell if she was just being a smart-ass or if she was really pissed. There was an edge to her words. "Okay. You're . . . a terrible person?"

He could see her relax fractionally. "You suck at smack talk," she pointed out. "I've noticed that in *BSO*, actually. You should take lessons from Dork. Although, good God, I never thought I'd be saying *that* in any context whatsoever."

"So you're staying on? With the guild?" he nudged, as gently as possible.

She tilted her head, staring at him, long enough that he squirmed in his seat. His foot was starting to hurt more.

"Does it really mean that much to you?" Her question sounded baffled, with a touch of suspicion.

"Yeah. It does."

"Don't worry. I'm not planning on going anywhere. I like the guild too." She shrugged.

He felt like he was on thin ice, but he pressed just a little further. "And . . . we can keep texting? Because your friendship means a lot too."

She crossed her arms, her dark eyes boring into him. "I mean, okay. But we're not going to, like, hang out in person, are we? This is a special circumstance."

"Okay." He felt relief that she wasn't just fleeing, especially considering he felt like that was a real possibility. But that disappointment was still there too. "Just curious, no judgment, but what do you have against in-real-life interactions, anyway?"

She huffed out a breath, leaning against his wall. "I have some social anxiety issues. Nothing clinical. Just . . . I'm not good with other people."

"Me neither."

"No, really. At book club—I just didn't know what to say to anyone, I didn't care what anyone else was talking about. Then, I was at Deb's party, and they were all talking, and there was this one woman who just seemed to love causing drama and needling people. I couldn't get out of there fast enough."

It sounded like she was talking about Patience. He nodded. "I get being uncomfortable." Then he had a thought. "She wasn't mean to *you*, was she?"

He didn't know why, but the thought suddenly incensed him. He hated it when the guys in the guild gave Boggy shit, so he imagined it was an extension of that . . . even though he now knew she wasn't some fragile eighty-year-old. And let's face it, even when he thought she was eighty, she was far from fragile.

"No, but I don't have the time or the bandwidth to put up with privileged women who need to pick on other people just because they're bored or want to feel better." Maggie's eyes blazed. "And if she's stupid enough to try it with *me*, she gets what's coming to her."

"Start shit, get hit," he replied, thinking of DangerNoodle's frequent quote.

"Yeah, well, I imagine that's frowned upon at casual suburban get-togethers." Maggie looked frustrated, and there was a hint of a blush on her cheeks. "Kit's continually telling me to chill out. And Deb is the mother of Kit's best friend, so . . . yeah. I don't want word to get back to him that I went full feral at a football party."

"Kit is . . . ?"

"My son." Now she smiled, a little wider, more natural. Just a little rueful. "He went to college this year. U Dub."

"Miss him?"

"A ton." She took a deep breath. "I tried harder, when he was here. To fit in, I mean. To not be quite so . . ." She gestured down at herself. "*Me*. He had enough shit going on."

Aiden desperately wanted to ask what kind of shit she was referring to, but knew enough about her to know now wasn't the time.

"I've just found it's best not to interact a whole lot," she muttered. "In person."

"Not to pry, but . . . what do you do for a living, then?" he asked. "Because that's got to be challenging."

She let out a short laugh. "I work from home. Freelance editor." He must've seemed skeptical because she laughed again. "Don't worry, I present well in writing when I want to. I even use smiley faces and exclamation points when necessary."

His eyebrows went up. "I can't even imagine that from you."

She rolled her eyes, then shifted to a hyperfriendly expression. "Hi! This is Maggie Le from Le Editorial. Here are the critique notes for your textbook. They may seem comprehensive, but I do hope you find them helpful. Thank you for your business!" Then she shot him a wide smile.

He cracked up. "You sound like a sociopath!"

"Yes, well, I have a different voice when I don't get paid, but otherwise, you're not wrong." Her grin was tiny but evil. Adorably evil, if that was a thing.

*When was the last time I thought of someone as adorable?* First cute, now adorable? Other than, say, someone in a movie or TV show, or animated characters and whatnot, he couldn't remember the last time he'd considered anyone either of those things.

"What do you do, then?" she asked. "I just figured you went to community college, maybe had a day job too. Are you studying for anything in particular?"

"I'm not trying to get a degree or credential, or anything like that." He leaned back. "Once Dad died, I knew my mom needed help, but she didn't need, you know, constant care. Not like Dad. But I didn't want to go back to the west side until things were settled, and I had all this free time. So I tried a bunch of different things."

"Like what? Basket weaving?"

He grinned. "If they'd offered it, I might've. I considered pottery, but I don't like the feel of clay, and I can't draw for shit."

She grinned back.

"Besides, I met Gandalf and Dork in English class, and wound up starting the guild with Malcolm—Mouse, you know—and that's been a nice distraction too."

They were quiet together for a moment, a comfortable sort of quiet, just surveying each other with amused affection. Despite the pain in his foot, he couldn't remember the last time he'd felt this content.

She glanced at her phone. "I really ought to go," she said, and this time, she sounded more regretful than wary. "I should get a little more work in, and if I don't call Rosita by six, she's going to probably get in the car with all five of her brothers and go hunting for your ass."

He chuckled. "They look out for you, huh? That sounds nice."

"They've got my back." She smiled. "Sometime, I'll tell you about them. Maybe."

She started to put on her jacket. Out of habit, he got up, then winced and almost immediately sat down.

"Shit." Maggie rushed to his side and, to his shock, felt his head. Then her eyes widened. "Sorry. Habit. I wanted to see if you had a fever. But I guess that's not the point? Your foot hurting?"

Unable to speak, he nodded.

"You take anything?"

"I'm probably due for painkillers."

She sighed. "Okay. There's enough soup for you for tonight. You set for, like, coffee and breakfast?"

He cleared his throat. "Um, yeah. I don't really eat breakfast anyway, but I have some English muffins." Somewhere. Probably.

"You're a nurse, you know the drill. Have some food with your pill tonight and tomorrow morning." She looked determined. "Then, how about I stop by, and we'll grab groceries? Special circumstances, and all."

He felt unaccountably lighter at the thought, especially after her whole "no more IRL interactions!" bluster, but he forced himself not to smile too much, lest he scare her off.

"Thank you," he said, hoping he could somehow get across how grateful he was. Then he frowned. "Um . . . I'm sorry, I hate to add this, but I usually grab groceries for my mother as well. She doesn't live that far. Would it be . . ."

"You want to drop off groceries for her too? No problem." She sounded so "don't be silly," he felt relief hit him in a wave.

"God, you're a lifesaver," he groaned. "I was not looking forward to asking anyone else for help. Not because, y'know, toxic masculinity or anything. Just . . . couldn't think of anybody I'd be comfortable asking."

"Believe me, I get it. You get points for recognizing toxic masculinity, by the way," she tacked on, with a tiny, surprised smile. "Especially at our age. You okay to get to bed?"

"I would squash you like a bug if I fell on you," he pointed out. "But I appreciate it. Don't worry. I'll take a pill and take a nap."

"All right. I'll be here at eleven tomorrow. That work?"

"Perfect." He felt like hugging her, but they'd already agreed: no physical contact. Instead, he gave her an up-nod. "You're surprisingly personable for a hermit."

"Yeah, well, you're surprisingly old, period," she said with a shrug. "Besides, I've got your back now."

She gave him an up-nod in return, as well as an adorkable little wave. She tugged on the heavy coat she'd slung over a kitchen chair. Then she grabbed her reusable grocery bag, crossed the living room, and left, closing the door behind her.

He hobbled up the stairs, slowly. He really should've taken the pill earlier. Or maybe even crashed on the couch downstairs so he didn't have to maneuver this. But it had all been worth it. He couldn't remember the last time he'd felt like this. Someone having his back.

He had not expected it to come in the form of a tiny woman with no filter and lots of attitude.

Somehow, it made it even better.

# CHAPTER 18

## TOO BLEAK, STOPPED CARING

A few hours later, Maggie was still processing her IRL interaction with Otter.

Or rather, Aiden.

The considerably older, very-different-than-she'd-pictured Otter/Aiden.

She'd barely managed to keep focus enough to go through some brief edits, and she got half as much done because her brain kept flitting back to the strange turn of events that afternoon.

No wonder he had seemed so mature. The man was her age, not some barely legal . . .

She frowned at herself. "Really?" she said to herself aloud, irritated. "You're going to fixate on that now?"

It wasn't like he'd deliberately catfished her. If anything, it had been a series of comedic misunderstandings and a lack of information. At any point in their texts and messaging, it could have come out. But they simply *hadn't* talked about it. They both knew they were in the same town and they had some common acquaintances, but they'd never brought it up. If anything, it reminded her of days in college, when she'd hung out with her few core friends and they'd talked about everything under the sun: whether ghosts were real, how to right social wrongs, whether you could swim in bubble tea, whether marriage was a social construct or not.

The one thing they didn't do was small talk.

In true introvert fashion, she and Aiden had focused more on deep dives into esoteric topics than the mundane realities of "Hey, how old are you?" Frankly, it was part of what she had *liked* about him. She liked that, for a few hours at least, she wasn't Maggie, frazzled, divorced, empty-nest-facing editor. She was Bogwitch, a badass bitch who wielded a mean blade and liked black-and-white movies. And she had enjoyed the too-pure-for-real-life Otter, who kept his rowdy cohorts in line, was a force-of-nature healer, and liked animation in any form. Also, the fact that he was a college kid meant she didn't have to worry about any potential romantic expectations, period. He was not a viable candidate, he wouldn't hit on her, and she sure as hell would not hit on him.

But that seemed to fly out the window now, although she wasn't sure *why*. She'd been single for years, and had no desire or intention to date.

*Not that I want to now!*

But . . . there was something there, and she had to admit, it had her rattled.

That night, at six on the dot, Rosita called her. "Tell me everything," she said without preamble.

Maggie sighed. She didn't talk to Rosita all the time. Her job, her family, her extended family's restaurant, her aging parents—all this stuff kept Rosita busy, so they tended to send each other little texts, memes, and GIFs periodically. When they did talk, it was usually a big download of words, catching each other up. There was never awkwardness: it was always like they'd spoken to each other the day before. So she wasn't surprised by her best friend's eagerness, even if she was dreading it.

"There's not really much to tell," Maggie hedged. "It's actually kind of silly. Total fluke. One-in-a-million shot."

"How is it a fluke that you wound up in a hot guy's kitchen, afraid he was going to kill you?"

Maggie let out a sound that was half frustrated sigh, half growl. "It wasn't . . . it was a safety check, Rosita!"

"What were you doing at his house?" Rosita countered. "Sidebar: I notice you're not protesting his hotness."

"Like I said, he's a friend from a video game group I joined. I texted you that I was playing with a guild, and he's the leader," she said. "I thought he was just this dorky local college kid who'd fractured a bone in his foot. He seemed like he was having a tough time, and I thought I'd bring him some soup. Then once I got there, I just kept hearing Kit saying 'This is how you wind up on a true-crime podcast' in my head, and I freaked myself out. Then I found out that just because Aiden's going to community college does not mean he recently graduated from high school, which was a stupid assumption on my part."

Rosita snickered.

"And he found out I wasn't an octogenarian grandma," Maggie added. "So I wasn't the only one who was guilty of misassumptions."

"So . . . you laughed it off, and left?"

"I mean, I heated up his soup," Maggie said. "Guy is on medication and wearing an air boot. He was kind of out of it."

"And then you left?"

"I had lunch with him . . . what?" she snapped when Rosita burst out laughing. "I was going to make lunch for myself anyway, and it was pho, which you know I love, and—"

"You gave him some of your pho?" Rosita interrupted. "Damn. You must like this boy. Man, I mean." More laughter.

"Goddamn it," Maggie muttered. "Listen, I would've done this for one of Kit's friends. As far as I knew, he *was* Kit's age. Why would I bail on him just because he's my age?"

"He's your age, huh?" Rosita pounced. "Hmmm. That's interesting."

"No, it's not." Maggie scowled. "You stop that."

"I'm not saying you have to marry the guy, for God's sake," Rosita said.

"What are you saying, then?"

"I'm saying he's the first guy you haven't chased off with either your looks, attitude, or your baton since Trev left," Rosita pointed out. "Don't think you're fooling me, chica. You started to let things go when Trev moved you out to the fucking wilds, and ever since he left, you're leaning in, trying to pull a whole Sasquatch thing. I haven't heard you so much as mention a male of the species. No dating apps. No setups. Certainly no hookups, because you'd have told me."

"If you hadn't married Oscar," Maggie said, "you would probably be in the same boat."

"The hell I would. I need sex, sweetie."

"I'm having plenty of orgasms. Men just aren't involved."

A pause. "Women, then? Or nonbinary?"

"Pure silicone," Maggie said, with a short laugh and the comfort that came only with being friends with someone for over thirty years. "Gotta say, I'm better than anybody I've ever been with. I'm never breaking up with battery powered."

"Oh, hon." Rosita sounded pitying. "You just weren't with many people. You slept with that guy from high school, and let's face it. Sex in high school is pretty wretched. Nobody knows what they're doing. Then you dated that asshole in college . . ."

"He wasn't as bad, skills-wise," Maggie clarified. "Probably because of all the practice he had with other women at the same time he was sleeping with me."

"And then you married Trev." Rosita sighed. "Three people. Any scientist is going to tell you: that's a small data set."

Maggie stepped outside. The sun had set, and it was pitch dark, the clear, cold skies showing the first sprinkling of stars. She pulled her sweat jacket closer around herself. "I have no interest in pursuing the research," she said. "I've come up with a better alternative through technology. They've been automated out of a job."

She knew from Rosita's huff of breath that she was frustrated. "You know I don't want to hound you," she said. "I haven't brought up anything in the past five years. I know you were totally focused on getting Kit to school. I know you've been working your ass off to keep that house, even though *I* voted for you to sell that fucking thing and move back to California . . ."

"You know why I couldn't," she said. "It'll take a while to sell this house. Besides, I didn't want to rip Kit from his friends and his school when he'd already lost Trev. He was dealing with a lot of shit, and he had Harrison and his other friends. He needed the stability."

"Again, I know," Rosita said, far more gently. "But Kit's in college now. You can focus on you."

That sounded terrifying. "I can. I am," she said, hoping she sounded more convincing to her friend than she did to her own ears.

"And you seem to like this guy."

"Otter?" She made a *pffft* sound. "He's . . . a friend. Video game friend."

"I know you. You don't make friends easily, anywhere on the gender spectrum," Rosita noted. "So what's special about this one?"

"I wouldn't say special . . ." When Rosita made an inarticulate sound of disbelief, she relented. "He's a nice guy. Total cinnamon roll. Kinda old fashioned. You know the dude-bro culture online. He keeps them from being intolerably dickish."

"What's he do for a living?"

"He's not working right now."

"Aha. Gotcha." Rosita's quick dismissal was sharp. "So, living in his mom's basement? Looking for someone else to pay his bills?"

"God, no," Maggie said immediately, remembering their conversation that afternoon. "He had a hospice business on the west side, with his best friend—who is also in the guild, by the way—but he sold it to move back here. He grew up in Fool's Falls. He needed to take care of his father, who had cancer, and then his father died, and he's been taking care of his mother, who's getting older and starting to need help and care. So he's dealing with that."

Rosita let out a low whistle. "That's not easy."

Maggie immediately remembered that Rosita's parents were getting older. "How are your—"

"Nope. I will talk to you about Mama and Papa in a sec, but we're not finished with this yet," Rosita said, and Maggie heard the smile in her voice. "You immediately defended this guy. If you didn't like him, you wouldn't care if I thought he was a useless dickbag. Therefore, I have to assume you not only care about the guy, you *really* like him."

"Bold assumption."

"Are you going to see him again?"

Maggie winced. She'd been asking herself the same question. Mac had specifically counseled her not to see him in the first place—and boy, she'd screwed that up. "It's probably better if I don't see him more in real life," she said carefully. "I mean, after I help him with his whole foot thing. I figure I can still game with him and the rest of the guild, but it's not like we're going to, you know, socialize or anything."

"What do you mean, help him with his foot thing?"

"He needs help getting groceries," she said. "And his mother needs groceries, too, so we'll grab some for her and deliver them."

"Okay."

"And he'll probably have a doctor's appointment or two, I'm sure. And he doesn't want his mother driving."

"Sounds reasonable."

Maggie pouted. "Why does it feel like you're mocking me?"

"I'm not, I swear." Rosita's amused tone did not reassure her. "So, he's going to just be sitting there in his house, huh? And you're going to deliver some groceries, and play chauffeur, and that's it?"

"Yes. That's it."

"He *is* cute, though, don't you think? I mean, objectively?" Rosita pried. "Kind of auburn hair, built like a linebacker. Total bear material."

Maggie sighed. "Can straight women date bears? Is that a thing? Are we appropriating the term from gay culture?"

"For the love of . . . Do you think the man's cute or ugly? Quick, don't think about it!"

"He's not ugly," Maggie finally relented. "That said, he's not exactly *pretty* either. He's . . . rugged?"

"Is he ever," Rosita purred.

"Listen, that's not the point here. He's *nice*." Maggie paused for emphasis. "And yeah, we get along. Talking to him's like talking to you. He doesn't talk my ear off with stuff I'm not interested in, never noticing that I'm not interested. He doesn't try to impress me with stuff. He doesn't just wait for a pause in my conversation so he can jump in with his own shit. He asks questions and actually listens. He's funny and smart."

"Sounds like you've given this a lot of thought."

"I value him," Maggie said, realizing as she said it that the words were true. "And I'm not going to fuck this up by romanticizing it. That is the *last* thing I need. So it doesn't matter if I think he's attractive or not. I am not letting myself be attracted to him or anyone."

"All right, I'll stop pushing," Rosita said. "I still think this is hilarious, though. He thought you were eighty, you thought he was eighteen. You were like this cross between *You've Got Mail* and *Harold and Maude*."

"Again: we're not romantic."

"Hey, you can't control my ships," Rosita teased. Then Maggie heard a crash and the raised voices of tweens in an obvious argument. Rosita rattled off to someone in quick, sharp, loud Spanish. "Dammit, I am going to have to break it up. Those kids are going to drive me right up the wall. Let's talk this weekend, okay? Love you."

"Absolutely, and love you too," Maggie said, before hanging up. She meant every word . . . she wasn't just protesting to protest. She did like Aiden. She hadn't had good luck with sex, and had even worse luck with relationships—well, outside of her sweet relationship in high school. As clichéd as some people might've found it, her marriage had really done a number on her, and the last thing she wanted was a man in her life to take care of, to humor, to shrink herself to accommodate. Otter—*Aiden*—was a friend, and barely that. She wasn't going to somehow romanticize what they had or add pressure she didn't want to something that didn't exist.

She sighed, hugging her jacket to herself a little tighter. The air smelled like rain, even though she couldn't make out any clouds. It felt like a storm coming.

*Damned metaphors,* she thought, and scowled at the sky.

# CHAPTER 19

## IT'S JUST A FLESH WOUND

Aiden's foot still hurt when Maggie picked him up the next morning. It wasn't that bad—he'd probably gotten injured worse in football, back in the day. Of course, "back in the day" was over thirty years ago, and while nursing was physically demanding, he'd been riding a desk for years. Now his older body was grumping at him nightly.

The air boot made him feel like he was walking on his tiptoes, and it made him walk funny because his right foot was suddenly higher than his left. There was also no way he could drive, so he was thankful that Maggie was helping him.

This would also give him more of an opportunity to get a sense of her and how she was reacting to their strange first meeting. After she'd left, it was almost like she had been a result of the meds . . . some weird, hazy figment of his imagination.

The sensation had been amplified that morning, when she'd texted him that she would pick him up at eleven if he still needed to go grocery shopping. He hoped she didn't feel obligated and wasn't helping because she felt pressured, but the more he thought about it, the more he realized that this was one woman who would probably never feel obligated nor pressured. If she didn't want to do something, she'd tell him to fuck off and find another way. Advise him to live off the remainders of his condiments or something. He grinned at the thought.

She might not be eighty years old, but she was still Boggy.

He was waiting near his driveway when she pulled up in a forest-green Forester that looked like it had some years on it but could still tackle the feet of snow and sheets of ice that hit Fool's Falls in the winter. He hobbled over to the passenger side, grunting as he maneuvered his way inside. "Thanks for this," he said.

She shrugged, looking embarrassed. She was still wild haired if not wild eyed, wearing the same thick coat he'd seen the day before. She shot him a sideways look. "Tasty Great all right?"

"Sure." There was a little combination organic market and specialty food / antique shop in town, but only the bougiest of Falls citizens went there. He'd considered it, but had balked at the prices they charged for even the simplest things. And much as he liked it, he couldn't really justify stuff like Kerrygold butter.

"You got a list?"

"I'll, um, figure it out."

She arched an eyebrow at him quickly, before looking over her shoulder and backing out of the driveway. "How about your mom? What does she usually need?"

Now embarrassment zinged through him. "Um . . . actually, she's okay. And I don't need a lot. We'll be in and out quickly, I promise."

Another quick, sharp glance. "Please tell me you're not starving your mom because you feel awkward about asking for favors. Don't be weird."

"First, I can't help it, I am weird," he said, with a lopsided grin. "But second . . . she, um, got help from the ladies at her church."

One woman specifically, in fact.

When his mother hadn't shown up for church, and the news had finally filtered through the various women friends, Deb had taken it upon herself to get his mom loaded up with groceries "to help," something his mother had quickly pointed out to him when he'd called to check in on her that morning and asked what she'd need from the store. She'd insisted that he thank Deb, which he'd felt was warranted, so he'd called.

Unfortunately, it had caused a domino effect.

Deb had then immediately volunteered to help *him* out, as well, pointing out all the ways he'd need care. Maybe he was being paranoid, but there had been a *tone* to it, something more than just being neighborly. Then it had gotten downright suspicious. Maybe Riley's admonishments had gotten into his head—he didn't know. But he had said no, quickly and vehemently, and he hoped that would be the end of it. The last thing he wanted was to be *surprised* by a "helpful visit." He shuddered at the thought.

Maggie must've caught it. "You okay?"

"Yeah. Just . . ." He thought about telling her, then decided against it. "Yeah."

She drove silently for a minute. Tasty Great wasn't that far from his house—nothing in the town itself was that far from anything else in the town, that was what small-town living was all about—and then she sort of grunted. "Okay, spill."

"Spill what?"

"What happened since yesterday that's making you squirrelly about grocery shopping?"

"The woman who helped my mom . . . actually, you know her," he realized as he said it aloud. "Deb?"

"What about her?"

"She texted me and said she wanted to help me out while my foot recovered." He squirmed in his chair.

"Did she already buy you groceries or something?" Maggie sounded puzzled. "Do you not need to go? I mean, you could've told me before I drove here, but it's not that big a deal."

"No! No," he said quickly. "It's just . . . I told her I already had help."

She was quiet for a long second.

"She said she'd not only grocery shop for me," he said, feeling his cheeks heat, "but she'd cook for me, and clean my house, and help me get around. Make sure I was, uh, well taken care of."

He felt kind of like a dick for putting it that way. Deb was probably only being kind. That said, his Spidey senses were on full alert around her, and while he would not and could not be rude to her, he didn't want to be put in a position where he had to tell her he really wasn't interested in her.

"Don't tell me," Maggie joked. "She volunteered to help you bathe too."

He winced. She *had* mentioned in passing that it was "tough to shower" when you broke your foot, and that they were "both adults, it wasn't a big deal."

"Shut the front door!" Maggie breathed as she pulled into the parking lot of the supermarket, her tone one of shocked glee. "She *did*!"

He rubbed his hands over his face. "Sorta, yeah. And I threw you under the bus by insisting I already had help. I'll pay you if you want. But please don't make me have to be mean to this nice lady because she wants something I am not interested in giving to her."

Maggie was still smirking. "I'll protect you, you big soft teddy bear," she teased.

He grinned back. Strangely, this felt right. It felt like hanging out with the guild—just easy, just comfortable. Just friends. Only it was in the real world.

*Weird.*

She parked the car, and the two of them strode slowly toward the door. She grabbed a cart. "Okay, Mr. No List," she said, matter-of-factly. "What are we grabbing, then?"

"You're right, I should've made a list," he admitted. "I'm so used to just driving over to a restaurant or drive-throughs, I barely have any staples."

"And I don't know how long you're going to want to be on your foot cooking either," she pointed out. "Actually, do you even cook?"

He shrugged. "This and that," he said. "Nothing gourmet or anything. I used to cook more, back in the day."

"You've got a microwave," she mused. "Frozen stuff?" He must've made a face, because she laughed. "Yeah, I don't like that shit either. Don't even like frozen pizza, honestly."

He pushed the cart, leaning on it like a walker as they ambled through the produce aisle. "Foolish Pie's pizza is pretty good," he noted.

"I don't go into town itself that often, and usually not at dinnertime," she said. "And I live too far up the Falls for them to deliver. How about salads?"

"Kinda cold for salads," he noted, "but yeah, that's pretty simple."

She grabbed salad makings, studying the prebagged stuff for freshness, then grabbing some add-ons: cranberries, candied pecans. "You okay with feta? Or chèvre?" she asked, not looking at him.

His stomach grumbled. He'd only had a cup of coffee that morning, which was probably a mistake. "Yes to both."

"We'll grab some when we get toward the deli," she mused. "And we'll grab a rotisserie chicken. Then you can have a simple salad with chicken, cranberries, pecans, and feta. What kind of dressing do you like?"

"With that? Maybe a light vinaigrette?" he suggested, his mouth watering. "Damn. That sounds really good."

"I should make it more, myself," she agreed, "but it's edging into winter, and I'm not as much of a fan of salad outside of summer. Now, I'm all about soup."

"I like soup too," he said.

"Grilled cheese and tomato soup, maybe?"

They went back and forth like that, wandering the aisles, getting food. He was by necessity going to have more at-home meals than he'd had in the past two years, he realized . . . and he was looking forward to it.

"Do you eat like this? All the time?" he found himself asking.

She shrugged. "I cooked more when Kit was home," she answered. "I liked making more experimental stuff. Indian food. Vietnamese food, of course. Mexican food. His father didn't really like ethnic food, so once he left, I went a little wild."

It was the first time she'd made any mention of her son's father, despite talking fondly at length about Kit himself during their lunch the previous day. It piqued his interest, but he got the feeling now wasn't the time to ask. He really, really hoped there would be more opportunities to delve deeper, if he just bided his time.

They eventually got him enough food for a week, and she promised that she'd help him after that, but insisted that "next time, buster, you'd better have a list." They'd bantered back and forth easily. Hell, he'd had more fun grocery shopping with her than he'd had at the football party, or even having breakfast with Riley, by a long shot.

They drove back to his place, and she helped him put all his groceries away. By which he meant she snarked "Oh, sit down before you fall down" and then moved like a whirlwind, putting away stuff with a ferocious efficiency that was startling. She was done in minutes, it seemed, and he stared in awe.

"I put away your food, dude," she said, rolling her eyes. "I didn't perform trachea surgery."

He shook his head. "I'm just . . ."

But before he could finish, there was a knock on his door. He frowned.

"Expecting anyone?" Maggie asked.

He felt a ball of ice in the pit of his stomach. "Oh, please God, no," he whispered.

She grinned. "You just sit there," she instructed, then went to the door and opened it. From his place at the dining room table, Aiden watched in horror as Deb emerged on the other side of the door.

"Maggie?" she said, eyes comically wide. "What are *you* doing here?"

"Helping Aiden." Maggie sounded matter of fact, like it was something she did all the time. "We just went grocery shopping."

"Oh. I . . . um, brought a lasagna?"

"That's really nice, thanks," Aiden called, and Maggie threw a look over her shoulder that pretty much said *shut up if you want to live*, but he would hate being rude.

"I'll take it and put it in the fridge," Maggie said, relieving her of the burden.

"Is there anything else I can do?" Deb asked. "Because I've got plenty of time. I know how much you hate being around people, Maggie, and you're working so hard. I'm happy to stay, help Aiden with whatever he might need . . ."

"No, no, I'm fine," he tried to reassure her.

"C'mon, men never admit they need help," Deb insisted, her super-cheerful, super-efficient, just-this-side-of-pushy demeanor returning full force. She turned back to Maggie. "Don't worry, I've got it from here, Maggie. Maybe we can catch up some other time . . . ?"

"Actually," Maggie said, overpowering Deb's runaway-train monologue, "we were just about to watch a movie and hang out before dinner."

Deb's words screeched to a halt, and her mouth fell open a little. She looked at Aiden.

"You two are . . ."

"Just gonna talk about guild stuff," Maggie said firmly. "That's how we know each other: video games. He's a good friend, so if he needs me, I'm on it. Don't worry. He's okay."

Deb looked stunned, like none of what she was witnessing computed.

"Uh . . . okay. Well, if you need me, Aiden, you know how to reach me," she finished, her tone weak. She nodded at Maggie. "Good seeing you," she added.

"Great seeing you too," Maggie said, then shut the door behind her. She shook her head. "Awkward. But hey, over with."

He looked at her. "*Am* I keeping you from work?" he asked. He hated the thought.

She arched an eyebrow at him. "If you were, I'd say: I have to work, I'll take you shopping later."

He chuckled. Then he looked at her hopefully. "*Do* you have to go do work later?"

She stared back at him. "Oh my God. You're like six feet and you're built like a tank, and you have the audacity to try puppy dog eyes at me?"

He added a comically exaggerated lower lip.

She cracked up. "Lucky for you I'm waiting on some client stuff and I got up early to do billing," she grumbled, but laughter still hinted around her eyes and lips. "Besides, I ought to probably watch something with you, just in case Deb is waiting around the corner for me to leave or something."

"Movie?" he pleaded, then sighed. "We could even watch something old in black and white."

She shot him an indulgent smile. "You know I like cartoons and anime too. How about something animated?"

He grinned broadly. "*Now* we're talking."

# CHAPTER 20

## MUNDANE MADE AWESOME

She'd been at Aiden's all damned day, and now well into night. And she really *ought* to go. But she . . . well, didn't.

It was ten o'clock, and they'd just knocked out a bunch of *Jujutsu Kaisen* episodes while eating Deb's lasagna, which was quite good. She supposed she ought to feel sorrier about cockblocking the woman (or whatever the female equivalent of cockblocking was—clam slamming? cunt shunting?—she'd have to ask Mac) but frankly, she hated it when people got invasive. Sure, Aiden needed help, but he was also a grown-ass man. If he didn't want to accept *Deb's* help, she couldn't just politely and passive-aggressively nudge her way into his life and his living room because she thought it was best. The fact that Deb was also apparently interested in Aiden, romantically speaking, made it a big no-go for Maggie. Like she'd taught Kit: consent was crucial. That was across the board, and it applied to men as well as women.

He hit pause, stretching, and she couldn't help but be a teeny bit drawn to the way his broad chest looked. He had some cushioning. Her ex-husband, Trev, had been whipcord thin, like he was carved out of wood, like a young Clint Eastwood. Aiden was, as Rosita had noted, more like a bear. Or possibly a sofa. He was squishy, and with his russet beard and wild hair, he was furry as well.

He also smelled good, although she couldn't pin down any of the scents. A little woodsy? And clean. And . . . warm? Also, he gave off heat like a furnace, which, for someone who was usually cold enough to burrito herself in blankets at any opportunity, felt like a bonus. Between his heat and his overall sofa-esque comfy vibe, she wondered absently what it'd be like to snuggle up against him.

*Wait. What the HELL?* Her subconscious reared back, and she cleared her throat.

"Aren't you glad I thought about ice cream?" she found herself saying.

He grinned, shaking his head. "Lasagna *and* ice cream. I should've broken my foot ages ago," he said, and she snickered. "Although I am gonna be paying for this when I recover. But what the hell. Speaking of"—he gestured to the TV—"wanna watch another episode?"

She bit her lip. "I shouldn't," she said slowly. "I don't like driving late, and it's almost ten o'clock." Which was nuts. She was *never* outside her house this late at night if she could help it. "But I really like binging stuff. And I like Gojo—I can see him being played by Ryan Reynolds, you know? And the kid who only speaks in sushi ingredients." She put on a fake serious expression, mimicking the character's somber tones. "'*Bonito flakes. Salmon. Salmon.*'"

Aiden laughed. "I'm all about Panda, myself," he replied, "although his backstory's surprisingly sad. Still, he's the best." He frowned. "Wait. If you don't like driving late—are you going to be okay? Driving, I mean?"

"Sure. Just because I don't like it doesn't mean it's not safe," she said, mentally adding *as long as I drive slowly*. "And it's full dark. Moose and deer tend to wander more at dusk, anyway."

He looked thoughtful. "You know . . ."

She felt her muscles tense. She liked Aiden, which continually surprised her. Probably because they'd gotten to know each other for a while before meeting face to face. Also because they were just good at being friends: they had compatible personalities.

What he asked next would probably determine whether or not they stayed friends, frankly.

"You could—and let me say, this is with absolutely no pressure and no weird, creepy, horndog vibes," he temporized, "stay here. In, like, my spare bedroom. And again, no pressure. I just don't want you on the road and, like, crashing or freaked out or anything. That's why I *have* a spare room, in case a friend needs it."

She felt her shoulders slowly retreat from where they'd pinched themselves, somewhere around her ears. "That's sweet," she said, with a relaxed smile.

Then, because her subconscious was an asshole, it pointed out:

*Well, he's not sexually or romantically interested in you at all. And why would he be? You look like a troll that lives under a bridge, and you're slightly more domesticated than a coyote.*

She found herself frowning at herself. The thing was, she didn't *care* about how she looked, and she would be damned if she acted like she had under Nana and Trev's influence. Nana had constantly insisted that she bob her hair and that she wear—swear to God—a pastel-pink twinset. Trev had been less specific, but it seemed like no matter what she wore, he wasn't happy with it, the bar a consistently moving target that she couldn't ever meet.

*Never again.*

"I'll be fine," she reassured him.

He nodded. Then he looked . . .. embarrassed?

"I know that you got conscripted into hanging out with me because of the whole Deb thing," he said, with a heavy sigh. "But I really had fun hanging out with you today."

She sent him a small smile. "It didn't suck," she teased. "And it's not like I didn't have options. I chose to stay here. Chill out."

"Was I mean?" he asked, his expression hangdog. "To Deb?"

"No," she said firmly. "If anything, I get the feeling you're too nice for your own good."

"You may not be the first person to notice that," he grumbled.

"Well, knock it off." She paused, then smirked. "I am obviously not burdened with an abundance of niceness at this point."

He grinned warmly at her, and she felt her chest heat in response. "You're honest. That's awesome . . . I admire that."

She shrugged offhandedly, feeling her cheeks start to burn with embarrassment. "I just don't think that you should get pushed into doing anything you don't want to do. Period. Life's too short, you know?"

"I heard a lot of regrets, when I was working hospice," he said, his gray eyes looking thoughtful. "There were regrets about what they'd done, and what they hadn't done. A lot of them said they wish that they'd taken more risks. And even more said that they wished they'd lived the way they had wanted, instead of letting other people tell them what they *should* do, and living that way."

"*Yes,*" she said. "I feel that on a cellular level. I don't regret the choices I've made because I got my son out of it, but if I didn't have Kit . . ." The mere thought had her teeth on edge, and she balled her hands into fists.

He seemed to take in her posture, the set of her jaw, and nodded along with her. "I'm lucky," he said, and to her surprise, his rumbly tone actually helped calm her down. "I've lived in a way that I felt was true. It might be kind of small, and I might not have been the son my parents expected—my truck-driving father was *not* expecting a nurse, let me tell you—or the partner the people I've dated thought I should be, especially since I never got married or had kids. But I was always true to *me*."

The words struck her. "I see that about you," she said, not even monitoring her words. "You've got that quiet strength about you. I don't know a lot of people like you."

Then she immediately felt embarrassed. Seriously—what, and she couldn't stress this enough, *the hell*? Was she going to start writing sonnets to the guy now?

She bounced to her feet. "I gotta go," she said. "You all right from here? Need any meds? I loaded up the dishwasher, and the rest of the lasagna's covered in foil in the fridge."

He grinned, then got up slowly, balancing on his air boot. "Nah, I'm good. Probably won't need anything more than ibuprofen, and then I'll go read and then sleep, I guess."

"Good." She sent him a stern look, but still, she felt her resolve soften. "If, for some reason, you find yourself in a lot of pain, or you need . . . I don't know, food, or whatever . . . you can text me."

He smiled back. "Careful, Boggy," he teased. "People will say we're in love."

It was like a splash of cold water in her face. "Emergencies only," she said, wagging a finger at him. "Not ringing a bell like I'm your fucking butler. And I'm not scrubbing your back. Not that kind of party, pal."

He chuckled. "I would never," he said, which was quickly becoming one of her favorite quips from him. "Drive safe, and text me when you get home, okay? Just ease my anxieties and overprotectiveness?"

She humphed. Then she nodded sharply. They stood there in front of each other. She got the feeling that they should . . . do something. Hug? Shake hands? Wave in a weird way?

He leaned in, and in a panic, she did this weird bro hug that was, in a word, humiliating. Especially since he was taller than she was, and she almost brought him toppling down on her.

"You okay?" he said.

"Shut up." She straightened her clothes and pulled her jacket back on. "Get some sleep."

With that, she shut the door behind her. The cold night air was like a slap. She got into her car, her teeth almost chattering by the time she got the heater going. Slowly, she made her way up the winding mountain roads that led her back to her house. She really did hate driving in the dark.

*Maybe I should've slept at his house.*

But that would've been weird. Not that she didn't trust him. But the fact that she *did* trust him . . . was perhaps not a great thing. Historically, her judgment when it came to people in general, and men in particular, was horrible.

*Thank God he doesn't seem interested,* she tried to console herself. Because the last thing she needed was someone interested in her romantically, for more reasons than she could list on a piece of paper. But . . .

God, if she caught feelings, she would have to kick her own ass. This was *not* going to happen.

# CHAPTER 21

## GIVING THE SWORD TO A NOOB

It was now Saturday, and Aiden was absolutely miserable.

He'd actually been doing pretty well since Wednesday night, when Boggy (*Maggie*, he reminded himself) had helped him with food shopping and they'd binged *Jujutsu Kaisen*. Since then, she'd stopped by to check on him Thursday. The guild had done their weekly dungeon run, and she had smack-talked and brutally sliced her way through like the seasoned tank she was, earning accolades from the rest of the crew. It was actually even funnier seeing her brutality and picturing her tiny IRL self, or hearing her vicious insults in her relatively sweet alto.

Then, on Friday, they'd talked via cell while watching another movie, this time his choice—*Buckaroo Banzai across the Eighth Dimension*. It turned out she'd seen it before, and loved it, which made it that much funnier. She could actually *quote* it, and he laughed hard enough to tear up.

Sheryl had never watched his "nerdy" stuff, had not understood his sense of humor. She was sweet, and supportive, and would've probably taken a bullet for him when they were together . . . right up to the point when they *weren't* together, and then she'd been tempted to shoot him herself. And in college, Jordan had been charming and vivacious, ushering him to parties and helping him fit in, loving him to distraction . . .

but there had been pitfalls, too, and heavy expectations. In retrospect, as much as he'd loved them, he'd found himself being what the people he was in relationships with wanted him to be.

*Not that two relationships is a lot of history to compare.*

"Aiden!" Deb's voice rang out. "C'mon! The game's starting!"

He grimaced. Now it was Saturday afternoon, around three o'clock . . . and he'd been ambushed by Deb yet again, this time with a cadre of friends in tow. At his mother's insistence, apparently.

"Your mother figured you must be bored, all by yourself, stuck in the house," Deb had said when she showed up, armed with seven-layer dip and chips and an extremely bright smile. "I know it's got to be pretty lonely. So I thought, if you couldn't go out with your friends, why not bring your friends to you?"

"But . . ."

"I called Riley, he's right behind me," she pointed out, and true enough, Riley's truck was parking on the street right in front of Aiden's house. "And you know my cousin Patience."

"Yes, but . . ."

"I also invited my friend Lisa and her husband, and Klara," she said. "And a few other people from our church, and from the old football team. They love watching the Cougars play, and I figured you haven't seen them since my party . . . and you weren't able to stay long, because your stomach was bothering you. So now you can. It'll be like a mini reunion!"

He blinked. "Um . . ."

There was a reason he hadn't connected with his ex-teammates, other than Riley. Not that he disliked them, per se. He just didn't have a lot in common with them. When they were teens, they'd had football. Now they had . . . nothing, really. Other than living in Fool's Falls.

The party was a done deal, apparently. More cars showed up, and within an hour, the house was packed with thirty people. Which, though well intentioned, still felt *rude as hell.*

That said, he couldn't bring himself to be a dick and kick them all out, especially when Deb just kept being solicitous, making sure he had a drink or food or whatever.

He gritted his teeth. *Who does this?*

The thing was—he'd lived in the Falls long enough to remember this sort of thing happening. Hell, his mother herself had performed a similar intervention when her friend's husband died. The woman had withdrawn, refusing to socialize, to her own detriment. His mother had then taken a posse of her church ladies, and they'd descended on the woman's house like a tornado of cleaning, casseroles, and kindness. He knew, in his heart, that Deb was trying to do the same. She really did mean to be kind. The fact that she was attracted to him—he assumed?—was secondary.

That said, it was part of why he had a hard time living in Fool's Falls. He was actually lucky he hadn't gotten the "be more social, be a part of the community" treatment before. The clock had been ticking. Now, his luck had run out.

He sat in his armchair, watching Riley smile and charm the ladies, watching Patience wander through like a butterfly, grinning and gossiping and flirting as she flitted about. The game was starting, and the couch was crowded with his old classmates, all older (and several, like himself, a bit larger), all watching the game and yelling and hooting with encouragement, armchair quarterbacking, or booing and howling in despair.

Between the conversations, the TV, and the cheer squad, it was a wall of sound that made his head ache and his chest hunch in on itself.

It seemed like his cell phone was in his hand before he even consciously thought about it, and he started texting Maggie automatically.

Aiden: Kill me now.

BOGWITCH: What's going on? Your foot?

Aiden: Deb's here. In my house.

BOGWITCH: LOL

BOGWITCH: So kick her out.

Of course that would be Maggie's first response. He grinned.

Aiden: She brought a bunch of people. My "friends" from h.s. Said she didn't want me to be lonely.

BOGWITCH: Are you lonely?

He was about to type, then found himself pausing. He would've thought the answer was obvious: *no*. And he certainly wasn't lonely enough to find this spontaneous football party fun, that was for damned sure. But . . .

Maybe?

Aiden: Not that lonely. *screams silently in introvert*

BOGWITCH: Then kick 'em all out.

Aiden: Not that easy. She's taking care of my Mom's groceries. A lot of these people are part of Mom's church. And I run into these people at the store and stuff. Small town living: can't afford to be a dick.

BOGWITCH: Pfft. People. Who needs them?

Once again, Aiden was sure that Maggie had more reasons as to why she was so virulently antisocial . . . or at least, why she clung to the front. Because nobody who was supposedly such a curmudgeon would watch bad movies with a guild buddy or help out an injured friend. Or even *have* any buddies or friends. Still, she was prickly enough that he knew not to poke at the facade.

BOGWITCH: How long is this thing supposed to go on?

Aiden: Till the game's over? I'll tell them to go if they don't get the hint. But it's just loud. And I kinda stopped watching when I stopped playing—I mean, I want the Cougars to win, and all, but I don't really care *that* much.

BOGWITCH: So you're watching a program you're not interested in, with people you don't know anymore *and* whom you didn't invite, and you can't hide somewhere?

Well, when she put it that way . . .

Aiden: I guess?

BOGWITCH: Dude.

Aiden: I know! I know.

Aiden: But not all of us are rude AF, darlin'. Or at least, not all of us pull it off as beautifully as you do.

BOGWITCH: I may be rude, but I'm not putting up with a bunch of bullshit from well-intentioned people who are running roughshod over my life, am I? 😉

He winced. Dammit. She had him there.

Aiden: Touche.

Aiden: Tell me your night's going better.

BOGWITCH: Actually, no. My internet's fucking up, and I can't figure out what's wrong. I can't type and edit on my damned phone, and I don't want to use it as a hotspot because my booster's not working as well either. ARGH.

Aiden straightened in his chair.

Aiden: Maybe I can help? I was essentially the I.T. guy at our hospice. I know things.

BOGWITCH: I don't know. Every time some customer service tries to talk me through computer stuff, I usually want to throat punch someone.

Aiden snickered.

Aiden: You, wanting to throat punch someone? SHOCK. I AM SHOCKED.

BOGWITCH: Quiet, you! *Doofenschmirtz gif*

Then an idea of such brilliance, such beautiful *elegance*, hit him like a lightning bolt. He could practically hear the choir of angels emphasizing it.

Aiden: Come get me, and I'll fix it for you. In person, no charge.

Aiden: Least I could do for the groceries and stuff anyway.

BOGWITCH: What about your insta-party?

Aiden: I'll tell them it was an emergency, you need my help.

BOGWITCH: So you're throwing me under the bus?

Aiden: Yes. RESCUE ME DAMMIT

BOGWITCH: lol

BOGWITCH: You really need to learn how to stand up for yourself, my dude

BOGWITCH: Still . . . you really think you can fix it?

Aiden: I'm a good 80% sure.

There was a long pause. Then, to his eternal gratitude, another text.

BOGWITCH: Deal. I'll be there soon

There was another roar as the Cougars scored, and he cheered along. Just not for the game.

Twenty-five minutes later, Deb was, needless to say, surprised when Maggie showed up. "Oh! Hi, Maggie!"

Maggie gave her a small smile. Then she looked at Aiden, giving him a small up-nod.

He got to his feet, wincing just a tiny bit at his foot. Deb flew to his side. "Do you need something?"

"I have to go," he said, with a sheepish smile.

Deb's face fell. "Go?"

"I promised Maggie I'd help her with her internet."

"You're actually *leaving*?" Deb's shock was evident, as was her undercurrent of irritation.

Riley walked up, obviously sensing trouble. "What's going on?"

"I gotta go," Aiden repeated stubbornly. His foot was throbbing a little. He looked over at Maggie, who was standing in his open front door like the party was some kind of black hole. "Maggie? Give me a sec, let me take a little more ibuprofen."

He hobbled to the kitchen with Riley at his side, leaving Deb in the living room. "Who's the woman who showed up, and why are you just leaving?"

"That's Maggie—the woman I was telling you about." He took the ibuprofen bottle out, shook a few into his palm, and then got a glass of water.

"You did *not* tell me about a woman," Riley protested.

"Bogwitch?" he reminded him. "From my online gaming thing?"

"Right. The *gaming* thing." Riley frowned, then muttered, "Well. Bogwitch, huh? The name's kinda on the nose, isn't it?"

*"Hey."* Aiden leveled a sharp look at him.

Riley held up his hands defensively. "No! No. I mean, that coat probably isn't helping any. And . . . sorry, but she's got kind of a Cousin Itt thing going on with the hair, doesn't she?"

Aiden growled.

"But I bet with some makeup and maybe some clothes that . . ." Riley stopped, chuckling and shaking his head. "Okay, I'm lying. You can't even tell what her body looks like. She's swimming in that shit. How's a guy supposed to know what he's dealing with when a woman wears that?"

"I know, right?" a new voice chimed in.

Aiden and Riley spun to find Maggie standing in the kitchen doorway, obviously hearing them.

"For Christ's sake, what was I thinking?" she added, with an amused smile. "It's like I'm doing it on *purpose* or something."

Riley actually flushed. Aiden didn't think he'd ever seen his friend embarrassed before.

"Sorry! I, uh . . ."

She waved a hand dismissively, the smile still in place. "No worries, I literally don't care. Aiden, you good?"

Aiden smirked back, feeling his chest warm as he suppressed a laugh. "Yup."

"Then let's go. That connection's not going to fix itself."

"But why do you have to do it *now*?" Deb had returned, this time flanked by Patience, who must've sensed drama and naturally gravitated to it. *Like demons to misery.*

"Because she doesn't have internet," he explained.

Deb rolled her eyes, then looked at Maggie. "I'm sure you can manage without internet for a weekend," she said, then added with some reluctance, "Maybe you could hang out here. I mean, I told you I'd help you get out more. Although I know football's not your thing." She sounded sympathetic.

Almost.

"Maggie needs to send out things for clients. She needs to download new projects and get ready for the week. She works from home, *Deb*," Aiden said, a little sharper than he intended. But he didn't like the way Deb was pushing. It was one thing to foist her friendliness on him. It was another entirely to dismiss Maggie's actual problems in the name of "being a good neighbor," which apparently only applied to Aiden. "This is important."

Deb's mouth dropped a little, and Riley and Patience were both looking at him—and Maggie—with open speculation. To his surprise, Maggie was looking at him, similarly stunned.

"Huh." Maggie blinked, then shook her head. "Yes. Thanks. I really do need this problem fixed."

"And I told you I'd fix it," Aiden reassured her. "So let's get going."

Without another word, Maggie turned and almost sprinted out. He started to follow her more slowly—damned foot—but Deb put a hand on his forearm, stopping him.

"I know you're just trying to be nice to her," Deb said in a low voice. "Trust me, I get it. I've been trying to help her too. It's easy to feel sorry for her. But . . . I mean, you have a whole house full of people. You can't just walk out. They're here for *you*."

He had what his mother called a long fuse. It took a lot to piss him off.

He'd reached the end of his fuse.

"Did I invite them, Deb?"

"That was the surprise, Aiden." Deb half laughed. "We're just trying to—"

*"Did I invite them, Deb?"*

She blinked. Then, dammit, her lip started quivering, and her eyes brimmed with tears.

"I was just trying to help, though," she said. "I swear. I didn't mean to upset you."

He felt like an ogre. "I know you were," he said, his voice more exhausted than anything. "And I do appreciate the thoughtfulness and the intent behind it. But first *ask me* before you think about doing anything like this again."

She bit her quivering lip, nodding.

"Second," he tacked on, "Maggie's my friend."

He thought back to the words Maggie had used, when she'd thought he was some kid with a broken foot who needed some soup.

"I have her back. Always. So I'm going to go. Just lock up when everybody's gone, okay?"

"You're going to be gone that long?" Deb's voice sounded stunned.

He honestly had no idea how long it would take to fix Maggie's problem. But no matter how long it took, he wasn't coming back to this.

"Yes, I am."

Then he walked away.

Maggie was waiting for him, car door open. "Look at you go," she said. "Pretty soon I'll teach you how to tell people to fuck off like a Bogwitch!"

"Shuddup," he muttered, but he felt himself smile, and his chest warmed when she smiled back. "Let's get out of here."

# CHAPTER 22
## YOU CAN'T FIGHT FATE

Maggie gnawed on her lower lip as she watched Aiden in her home office. The house wasn't palatial, but she did have her own little spare room in addition to Kit's old room. Her office was her kingdom, her refuge. She wasn't used to seeing anybody in it. Especially not a big ginger cinnamon roll of a man, who was currently humming under his breath as he clicked through her computer.

She was glad that he had stood up to Deb. Not that she had anything against Deb, per se. They just didn't have anything in common. Deb was an extrovert. When they'd scheduled playdates, or worked together on things like the school fair or whatever, she tended to listen to what Deb had going on but didn't share much about her own life—largely because she didn't know what to say about Trev, especially as things went downhill. She'd genuinely felt bad when Deb and Barry had gotten divorced a year ago and had sent over a chicken pot pie and a baked rigatoni casserole for her and Harrison. But they hadn't hung out just the two of them, ever, and Maggie was fine with that.

After shutting down Deb not once but *twice*, Maggie got the feeling even the cheerful Deb might shank her in a dark alley. Still, Maggie hated seeing anybody get rolled over, and Aiden was definitely letting

Deb run roughshod. Which shouldn't be her problem . . . but here she was, allowing him to futz with her internet.

She could fix it herself. Eventually. With a lot of crying and cursing. She might not have been a programmer or anything, but her life was largely lived online. Which was why this whole thing was so frustrating. She'd tried everything.

She wondered if Aiden was bullshitting his knowledge of things. She really hoped not.

He frowned. "Where's your router?"

"My router?" She frowned. She pointed to a high bookshelf. "It's over there."

He hobbled over, staring at it. Then he started chuckling gently.

"Sweetie," he said, surprising her with the endearment. "It's off."

"That's it? My router's off?" It was too high for her to see—supposedly the best place in the house for it, but still. "Goddamn it! I should've looked at that first! I *know* better!"

He nodded. They tried messing around with that for a while; then he rubbed his bearded jaw. "You have a power outage recently?"

"Here in the Upper Falls, we have outages all the time," she said. "Short ones, though, unless it's, like, a windstorm or snow knocking down a tree onto the line or whatever. We've had a lot more recently because they installed a new line too low."

"What, are vehicles hitting it or something?" Aiden looked horrified.

She giggled. "Actually . . . apparently, they're being hit by turkeys. Who are then electrocuted . . . and also, somehow, knock out the power."

"Turkeys." He started laughing, shaking his head. "Well, you had it plugged directly into the outlet. You should have a surge protector."

She tried to get on her tiptoes, then swore. "Kit," she said. "He needed another one before he left, and I forgot we cannibalized my office. I meant to get a new one, but I sort of spaced out."

"They've got that supercenter, couple towns over," he said. "Maybe an hour drive. I can go with you if you want to go now."

She glanced at her phone. It was about four thirty, and the Walmart was an hour away, easily. "I'll grab it tomorrow," she said instead. "Too late now. I'll just have to make do."

He nodded. Then he looked around. "I like your office."

She felt her cheeks heat. Which was silly, but there it was. "Thanks."

She watched as his gaze moved over her bookshelves, taking in her Funko dolls, her LEGO hobbit hole, various reference books, and novels that she loved.

"Love that you have graphic novels too," he said. "I read *Sandman* over and over as a teen."

"Somehow, I have trouble picturing you as a goth kid."

He rolled his eyes. "Yeah. That would've gone over. If the football team didn't rib me endlessly, my parents would've lost their minds. Especially if I dyed my hair black." He chuckled.

She grinned back. She wondered, absently, what he looked like in high school. What he *was* like.

"I suppose you were a goth kid?" he asked.

She shook her head. "No. My Nana Birdie would've been appalled and kicked me out, no question." She did not chuckle, because she wasn't kidding. She'd always subtly—or not so subtly—felt like she lived on borrowed time in Nana's house. "I was your typical honors student. Editor in chief of the school paper. Stuff like that."

"Huh." Now his curious gaze was trained on her. "Got any pictures?"

"None I'm willing to share," she said, shooting him an *are-you-nuts* look. "C'mon. I figure you're going to be here for a bit, so I should get started on dinner. Nothing I cook seems to be quick."

"You're taking awfully good care of me," he said, slowly shuffling after her and heading toward her kitchen. She settled him down at the table. Her living room, dining room, and kitchen were open plan, so it was easy to prep dinner and talk to him at the same time. "Seriously. I owe you, for grocery shopping, and saving me from Deb—*twice*. I feel like you deserve a kidney or my firstborn child or something."

She frowned, pulling out the ingredients for cottage pie. It was hearty, perfect for fall. She used to make it all the time when Kit was home, because he was a growing teen with a black hole of an appetite and they could cruise on the leftovers for longer than a day. She put ground beef, vegetables, and potatoes on the counter, and started to go to work.

"You don't have any kids, do you?" she asked. "I seem to remember you saying something like that."

He'd made a passing remark about not being married or having kids, actually. Yet she remembered it clearly.

He made a face. "No," he said. "I like kids, and I hope I would've been a good dad if I had any. But I would've wanted a solid marriage first. And at this point—God, this might sound like shit, but the thought of kids is exhausting."

"You are not lying," she said. "Kit is my heart, but there's a reason we were one and done."

Pain, sharp and unexpected, slapped at her.

"You okay?"

She looked up, startled. "What?"

"You just . . . I'm sorry," Aiden said, and his deep rumble was impossibly gentle. "I didn't mean to upset you."

"No. No, it's fine."

Aiden shifted in the chair, studying her intently. "Was it your ex? Didn't want children?"

She threw carrots, onions, and celery in the food processor, buying time by pulsing it before letting it whirl the large chunks to bits. Then she put it all in the large pan to brown in some ghee. "He didn't want the child he had," she said. "He probably didn't want children at all. Kit was an unexpected accident . . . although I guess if it's expected, it's not an accident." She laughed, but it was a dry, dusty sound. "And this is why I'm a paid editor, am I right?"

Aiden didn't take the bait. "That sounds incredibly hard. Did . . ." He paused. "Did Kit know how his father felt?"

"Yes." Fury burned, quick and familiar. "I thought I could compensate. I acted as a buffer for a while, but it never quite worked. Honestly, I probably shouldn't have hung on for as long as I did, but . . ." She shrugged.

"You didn't just tell him to fuck off, Bogwitch-style, I guess?" Aiden said, with a small, teasing smile, but his eyes were compassionate. Possibly just a tiny bit pitying.

"Eventually. Just took a while to get there. Too long." She added some garlic and stirred, probably a little too vigorously, like the vegetables had somehow wronged her. "But he's gone. Out of the state. Last I checked, he was in Wyoming."

Aiden's face darkened like a storm cloud. "He hasn't even been in touch? With Kit, I mean?"

"No." She added tomato paste, letting it brown with the mirepoix she'd created. "It's probably better that way, honestly. They didn't have a lot to talk about when they were under the same roof. But yeah, sometimes, I could strangle him with my bare hands. It's probably safer for him, and better for my life outside of a prison, that he stays at least a state or two away from me."

"I . . ." Aiden looked like he was gearing up. "Sorry, but . . . how did you marry this guy in the first place? How'd you meet?"

"He was from the town I grew up in," she said. "I lived in a smaller city, outside of Napa, California. His family was friends with my grandparents, who raised me."

"Nana Birdie?"

She smiled. "You *are* a good listener. You remembered that I had assignments coming up when you told Deb why me having internet was important, and you remembered my grandmother's name. That's impressive. Not a lot of people pay attention when other people are talking."

"Thanks," he said easily. "Although with a name like Nana Birdie, it wasn't as hard. I was definitely curious."

"She was from Tennessee," she said. "Big Memphis family. She moved to California to be with my grandfather, who moved there after World War II. He was in charge of a farm there . . . was from a family of farmers. They made a decent living."

"What about your parents?"

"Died. Car accident." She saw the sympathy on his expressive face, and she shook her head. "I was two. I have no memory of them."

"Still hard."

She nodded, acknowledging it. The tomato paste had browned nicely, and the whole thing smelled good. She added red wine and beef broth, as well as peas, then set the whole thing to simmer as she peeled potatoes.

"So your grandparents knew your ex's family?"

"It was sort of like the Falls, now that I think about it," she said. "They went to the same church, and they were just tight. After my grandfather died, they basically absorbed my grandmother and me. We went over there for holidays and birthdays and things, all the time. I'd see Trev when he was in town. He didn't like hanging out, because his parents kept bugging him about not getting married and not settling down nearby. He was four years older than me, so I didn't really get to know him until after I dropped out of college." She bit her lip. "Anyway, my grandmother decided to move to Tennessee to be with family, younger cousins and her sister, I think. I didn't feel like I'd fit in there, so I stayed behind. I told Trev I wanted to move out of state, and he did, too, so we moved to Washington. It took a while for us to get settled—he got a bunch of different jobs, and we tried a bunch of cities, but he hated the west side. So we finally found property in Fool's Falls, and he got a job, and we moved Kit . . ."

*Shut up. Shut up. Why are you telling him all this?*

It was like she'd been alone for so long, she was willing to unload all of her shit at once, on any ears that were even halfway friendly.

No. That wasn't it. It was the fact that it was *Aiden*. She felt like she could trust him. So she did.

"Anyway, I hope you're okay with cottage pie," she said, cutting the potatoes and putting them in a pot of water to boil. "I'm making a full batch, so you'll be able to bring home half if you like it. It'll be one less meal for you to pull together."

"I dropped out of college too," he said. "Well, that's not entirely true. I dropped out of Washington State, and moved to the west side and changed majors and graduated from Bellevue College. I was pre-med, but I decided to go into nursing." He looked rueful. "The decision didn't go over too well with my family, needless to say."

"Nursing is tough," she protested.

"Yes, it is," he said. "But apparently it isn't all that manly. And they . . ." He cleared his throat. "Me being manly was kind of a big deal."

She made a *pbblt* noise in rebuttal. "Fuck manly," she said. "I haven't met a single self-proclaimed 'manly man' that wasn't an asshole, I swear to God."

He burst out in surprised laughter. "Well, that's a first."

"Trev bought into that bullshit," she added, since the rage was still simmering, much like the cottage pie filling. "He was the stereotype. Fixed cars, drank beer. Got his six-point buck every season. Fished. Watched football with the guys down at the Trick Shot. He certainly didn't understand having a sensitive son who seemed the opposite of all that."

"Not into sports or cars, or hunting?"

"Decided to become vegetarian for a year when he was eleven," she said, with a small, sad smile at the memory. "Part of it was because he was really freaked out by hunting, but I also think part of it was to piss off his dad, who couldn't give a shit about video games or anime."

"Sounds like Kit takes after you."

"Couldn't be more like me if I designed him in a lab," she agreed with a nod.

Aiden smiled. "I'd like to meet him, then."

She startled. It had never occurred to her to introduce Kit to any of her friends. Probably because she hadn't *had* any friends.

"I'm doing all the talking," she said, suddenly flustered. "What about you? Surely you've made some disastrous romantic decisions in your past. I'm gun shy because I made the most massive of all unforced errors with my previous marriage. What happened to you?"

He blinked slowly. Then he turned red.

"I . . ."

"Oh, God," she said. "I am being a total Deb right now, aren't I? Pushy as hell?" She was aghast. "Never mind. Don't answer that. I don't want to make you uncomfortable."

"No, that's all right," he said, even though his tone was tentative. "I just . . . I don't really talk about it much? To anyone?"

"That's okay . . ."

He took a deep breath, looking like he was going to jump off a high dive. Then he blurted it out.

"I have trouble with sex."

# CHAPTER 23

## YOUR NORMAL IS OUR TABOO

Aiden hadn't meant to say that. At all.

Maybe it was the normally prickly Maggie just dropping all these truth bombs on him. Being brave. Or maybe it was the fact that he felt so unbelievably *comfortable* around her. He hadn't even admitted this to Malcolm, and Malcolm was his best friend for life.

Maggie's eyes widening slightly was her only outward show of surprise. "Okay."

"Not like . . . I have problems *doing* it," he clarified, although he was pretty sure he was just making things worse. He felt flushed, and swallowed hard. "But that attraction? Doesn't happen that often." He let out a little jagged laugh. "Like, *really* not often."

"So . . . ," she drawled slowly, as if she was processing it. "You're . . . what, ace?"

This was not the reaction he was expecting. "I'm what now?"

"Asexual," she said easily. She drained the potatoes, then took a big masher out, squashing them. If he hadn't broken his stupid foot, he'd help, because she had to practically get on her tiptoes to get leverage on the spuds. "Familiar with the term?"

"Not really. Never came up in hospice, anyway." Or anywhere in conversation with Malcolm, and certainly not at Fool's Falls. Even back when he was in high school and college, he hadn't really been cognizant of LGBT stuff, not like kids were today. He didn't think there were any gay kids in his high school. He frowned. There probably were, actually—they were just closeted. In Fool's Falls, he couldn't blame them.

"Asexual, as far as I understand it," she said, her face going pink across the bridge of her nose and the apples of her cheeks, "is when you don't feel physical sexual desire for people the way allosexual people do. But keep in mind, I know just enough to be dangerous. I'm no expert."

"You know more than I do," he said. "What's allosexual?"

"Kind of the opposite of ace—asexual," she corrected. "Ace is also called 'graysexual.' Lots of people call allosexual 'normal' sexuality, but that's a crock of shit."

He frowned, rolling the term around in his mind. *Asexual.* "That's not entirely true. I mean, what I said," he quickly added. "I have liked sex in the past—a lot. Under the right circumstances, anyway."

Why was he being this honest? He ran his fingers through his hair, no doubt turning it into a ginger-colored haystack.

She nodded encouragingly, adding butter and cheese to the potatoes. "You don't have to prove anything to me. Trust me, I'm not judging."

He knew that. He was just being defensive. "It just doesn't happen very often. I'm apparently insanely picky."

He felt like his stomach was knotting, but the words were tumbling out like snow in an avalanche. He didn't think he could stop them if he tried.

"I thought it was, um, low sex drive," he said. "Please, for the love of God, stop me if this is too much, by the way."

"No, it's fine. I mean, unless *you're* uncomfortable."

"I never talk about this," he muttered. "But you just seem to *get* it. You're a good listener too."

She smiled—not her little grumpy smile. A genuine one.

"Anyway, I definitely felt desire in my relationships," he said. "In the beginning of the relationships, anyway. But I've only had two relationships in my whole life."

He waited for the curious look. The bafflement. Surprise. Ghoulish curiosity. Instead, she looked very unbothered.

It was nice.

"I started to become a workaholic just to have an answer when people asked why I didn't have a girlfriend, or why I didn't get married," he admitted. "I just wasn't attracted to many people. *Any* people. I didn't want to *find* anybody. My life was fine as it was. And the idea of, like, Tinder? Or hooking up off an app?" He winced. "Yeah, *no*."

She mixed a little half-and-half into the potatoes, then some salt and pepper. Whatever was going on with the beef and stuff she was cooking smelled like pure heaven, and his mouth watered in appreciation.

"Two relationships," she repeated, again with no judgment. "When were they?"

"It's a little complicated," he replied. "The first was in high school . . . that is, it *started* in high school. Sheryl. An absolute, utter sweetheart. We were friends first, then it seemed natural when we got together. We were crazy about each other. I thought we'd get married, honestly."

"High school sweethearts," Maggie mused. "So what happened?"

"We broke up when I went to college," he said. "She wanted to go to college out of state, or at least on the west side . . . anywhere but Spokane. She wanted to get away from home. Her parents were growing their car dealership, and they wanted her to go to school in Spokane because they were going to move there and really expand. Her family was kind of rich, I guess. *Is* kind of rich?"

Maggie took turns paying attention to the casserole she was constructing, putting the filling in the large square dish, then spreading the mashed potatoes over it. She carved the top with a fork, then threw the whole thing in the oven. Having her walk over and sit next to him at the table was comforting and daunting at the same time.

"You said that was when it started," Maggie said. "I assume you two got together later? What happened in the meantime?"

"I was heartbroken when we broke up, but I couldn't afford to go out of state to college. My parents weren't even sure they wanted me to go to Spokane. Anyway, I was single for most of freshman year. Then I had a relationship in college. Jordan."

This was the tough part. The part he didn't talk about. Malcolm knew about it, because he'd been there to pick up the pieces, the disastrous fallout.

Could he talk about this? His heart started beating, hard and fast, and he swallowed against the lump in his throat.

"I wasn't really expecting Jordan either," he said.

"How'd you meet?"

He took a deep breath. Then another. He felt his heart hammering in his chest like he was going to have a panic attack.

"He was my roommate."

"Ah."

He studied her, looking for any scrap of disappointment, or disgust.

Instead, she looked . . . well, more like his computer, when the wheel went around as it worked on something. Then she nodded. "So you're . . . bi? Pan? Sorry. If this is uncomfortable, let me know. You don't have to label, obviously."

He felt his body release tension like a wave. "You're taking this well," he rasped.

"What's to take? It's not my business. And so what?" She shrugged. "I didn't always live in the Falls, Aiden. I went to Berkeley, I lived in Napa, and we moved around the west side for a while when we first moved to Washington. My best friend from middle school, although married to a guy, is bi. Granted, I don't think her parents know, and sometimes she feels like she doesn't represent it well since she's married to a guy and has several kids, but I tell her that's total bullshit. It's not like you have to get verified like Twitter, for fuck's sake."

He found himself heartened by her stubborn and profane vehemence. It made it that much easier to keep telling his story.

"Anyway. Jordan was amazing. Handsome, charming . . . everything I wasn't."

"Hey," she said, lightly tapping his forearm until he looked back at her stern expression. "Don't insult my friend."

He grinned, surprised. "Well, I was awkward and lonely and felt completely out of my depth. Most of my high school friends hadn't gone on to college, or they'd just gone to Falls Community or gotten certified. Hell, most of them had jobs. I'd never met anybody like Jordan. He seemed to know *everybody*. He went to parties and dragged me along. He took me to clubs. And by the end of freshman year, he hit on me." He shook his head. "I don't think I'd ever been so turned on in my life. It was mind blowing."

"Big change from Sheryl, I imagine." There was a hint of a question in her tone, but again, no judgment.

"I loved Sheryl, and I loved being with her . . . that way," he said. "Being with Jordan was different, but also sort of the same? It was ridiculously hot, and he knew so much more than I did—I mean, Sheryl and I were virgins, and Jordan really wasn't. I fell totally, uncontrollably, passionately in love with him." He felt his lips curve in a bittersweet smile.

"Uh-oh. What happened?"

"One problem," he admitted. "Jordan was in the closet at home. And I didn't mind staying there, myself, especially then. My parents—my *father* would have lost his damned mind if I came home as a freshman and said I was gay, which I figured I must be at that point. I didn't want to deal with that. We were having fun, and as far as either of our parents were concerned, we were just really good friends and roomies."

"Parents, right?" She grinned, shaking her head. "I'm sure there are things about Kit's life that I am oblivious about that will seem totally obvious in retrospect."

"By the time I was a junior, I was so in love, I didn't care if other people knew about us. We'd been together over two years. I *wanted* other people to know about us, and I couldn't understand how he could keep up the pretense of us just being roommates. I started pushing him."

She was hanging on every word. His throat got scratchy.

"It . . . went bad. Especially when his parents came to visit. We'd had a fight. Then they mentioned how he might want to bring his girlfriend around." Aiden still felt that stab of betrayal. "I thought he'd been lying to them. Turns out, he'd also been lying to *me*."

Maggie gasped. "He was *cheating* on you? With a woman?"

"Someone his parents liked, in fact," he said. "She wasn't even his beard. As far as she knew, she was actually his girlfriend back home. It was a mess."

"That *asshole*," Maggie hissed, looking like she was ready to hop in her car and beat his ass. Weirdly, that helped.

"Obviously we broke up. I couldn't handle bumping into him on campus. I couldn't handle *anything*. So I dropped out," Aiden said. "My best friend, Malcolm—you know, Mouse, from the guild? Well, I wound up telling him everything, sure that he was going to shun me but not even caring. But he didn't. He told me to come out to the west side. He was going to U Dub, and I crashed with him in his apartment. My parents were *pissed*, and they didn't even know about my whole thing with Jordan. They just thought I was a quitter. And when I said I didn't want to be a doctor, I wanted to be a nurse? They didn't talk to me for a few years."

She shook her head. "I am so sorry."

He shrugged. "It's okay. I mean, it wasn't at the time, but . . ."

"No. I get it. Unsupportive family is the absolute worst." Again, she looked ready to go vigilante.

He smiled. "Anyway. I got my nursing degree, and I was working at some care facilities, focusing on elder care and hospice. And you won't believe it, but I ran into Sheryl again."

"Sheryl from high school?"

"The same," he said. "She was just as sweet and just as kind, and we wound up having dinner. A couple of times." He sighed. "I told her about having a bad breakup—not all the details, obviously, because Jordan was still in the closet and I wouldn't do that to him."

"I should hope not," Maggie murmured. "I mean, the guy's a dick, but that wouldn't have made it better."

"Anyway, I told her that I had a broken heart. And she wanted to make it better. So we got to know each other, hung out a lot. Next thing I knew, we were dating. I was still attracted to her, and I knew how rare that was. To my shock, I found myself falling in love with her. Again." He frowned, still puzzled. "So . . . yeah, bi? I guess? Although . . ."

"You want a drink?" she asked. "I mean, I don't have much, but . . . um . . ."

"Nah." Actually, he kind of *did* want a drink, but it wouldn't help. He was spewing out his life story like a broken sprinkler head. "The thing is, I wasn't interested in anybody else. Sheryl and Jordan, that was it. People kept saying I should get out there and date, and I'd *try*, even try to hook up. But I just couldn't get there."

She looked sympathetic without being pitying, and he could've hugged her for it. "What happened with Sheryl?"

"That's a whole long story, and one that will probably require more liquor than my pain meds will allow at this point," he said, already feeling too vulnerable. He'd shared more with Maggie in the past hour than he had with anyone in the past few decades. "Long story short: We got back together. Almost got married. Then we broke up."

"I figured."

"In the interest of full disclosure," he added, "she's now married to my younger brother."

Maggie's mouth formed a perfect O of surprise. *"No. Shit."*

"Swear to God."

"It's like a K-drama," she marveled. "Or a telenovela."

"Glad my life can provide some entertainment."

Now she stared at him speculatively. "Both times, the relationship aspect sort of blindsided you?"

He thought about it. Since he'd told so few people, no one had really *asked*. "Now that you mention it, yes."

"You were friends first?"

"Yes . . . ?"

"You know," she said slowly, "it sounds like you're demi, maybe."

It was his turn to stare, puzzled. Ace, demi . . . there was a whole world out there he didn't understand. "I . . . don't know what that is?"

She reddened. "Again, *I am no expert*," she cautioned. "But from what I understand, demisexual people don't feel sexual attraction until they form, like, an emotional attachment. They're never going to be love at first sight, and they're not going to have one-night stands. Where allosexual people might be drawn to people sexually and then build a relationship after that spark, you'd be kind of the opposite."

He stared at her.

She rolled her eyes. "No sexy fun times until you feel close to someone. And even then, not everybody you get close to. Just some people."

He felt gobsmacked. "That's a thing?"

"Yes, it is."

"Huh. Demi," he said, testing the word out.

He felt a strange lightness in his chest. He was going to go home and google the shit out of this stuff—asexual, allosexual, demisexual. The idea that there might be an explanation for something he'd always felt like a freak about was eye opening. The thought that he wasn't *alone* in it was more comforting than he'd ever realized.

The timer on the oven dinged. "All right. Grub's on," she said, like she hadn't just changed his life with one conversation. She got up, taking the casserole out and putting it on the stove top, putting the oven mitts away. "We'll give it a few minutes, because it's currently hotter than . . . ack!"

He'd gotten up and stumbled over to her and hugged her on instinct. "Thank you," he said quietly.

She reared back, staring at him with her mouth slightly open. "For what?"

"For listening to me. For not judging me," he said. "For teaching me about this stuff. You have no idea how much you help."

She grumbled . . . and for a second, leaned against his chest. "S'okay."

They stood there for a long moment, her head tucked under his chin, his arms wrapped around her. Her arms tentatively sneaked up to embrace his chest, and he could've sworn she sighed. Her hair was soft, and she smelled nice. Like coconut, a bit, and some kind of spice. Between that and the delicious smells of the kitchen, he took a deep breath, snuggling against her.

It felt like home. Or at least, the way he'd always imagined home ought to feel like.

Some part of him felt like he could've stood there forever, but she nudged him. "Let me get some bowls," she said, her voice scratchy. "Go sit down."

He did as instructed. "How do you know about all this stuff, anyway?"

She looked grumpy for a second, then huffed out a breath. "I read a lot of romance," she muttered. "All kinds."

"You?" He stared at her. "*You* read romance? Really?"

She crossed her arms. "You have something against romance?"

"Absolutely not," he said. He couldn't help it. He laughed, just out of a joyous sense of relief. "It's just so *hopeful* of you. That's awesome.

Like you're less of a grumpy butt than you pretend." He was delighted with the image of cranky, cantankerous Boggy tucked in with a love story.

It showed she was more of a marshmallow than she let on.

"Shut up," she growled, but there was a little smile at the quirked corners of her lips. "I'll show you fucking grumpy."

He shook his head. She was a very good friend, and he was lucky to have found her.

As she put the dishes in front of them at the table, he looked at her. "And . . . they talk about stuff like this? In romance novels?"

"The ones I read do," she said, with a firm nod. "You'd be amazed. Anyway, *dinner* . . ."

# CHAPTER 24
## OBLIVIOUS TO LOVE

Maggie had her woodstove going and the TV on for background noise. She'd been puttering around her house aimlessly for most of the afternoon. She'd tried to get some work done but had trouble focusing. She'd thought about cleaning, but she'd find herself in a room, unsure of why she'd decided to come in and what she ought to be doing next. It was like brain fog. She wondered if it was menopause, which made her want to growl. Like the hot flashes and irritability weren't bad enough, there needed to be confusion too? *Thanks, body!*

But she knew that her current state had less to do with hormonal chemistry, and more to do with Aiden. More than she wanted to credit, if she was honest.

She'd taken him to the doctor that morning, and he'd finally gotten the all clear to lose the air boot. His hairline fracture had healed, and he was now under his own steam. He'd been so happy, his smile broad and genial and so *him* that she'd found herself staring. She couldn't remember the last time she'd felt like that, and she found herself drawn to it, like a lizard sunbathing on a hot rock.

She'd dropped him off at his house, and he'd thanked her profusely, which she'd brushed off with embarrassment before fleeing back to her own home. It occurred to her that since Aiden's injury, she'd spent time with him almost every day. Sometimes to help him get groceries, and sometimes to cook. She'd found herself loading up his freezer, showing him easy meals to make and having him help, although never straining his foot. Afterward, they'd watch something, or eat something together, or sometimes just drink coffee and bullshit together. She'd even brought her laptop to his house, and they'd played *Blood Saga* together, laughing and smack-talking in real life and real time, without any of the rest of the guild being aware.

It felt . . . nice.

It had been a long time since she'd felt that close to someone. When Trev had suggested they move to Fool's Falls, she'd agreed, hoping that it would patch the gaping cracks in their marriage, even though she wasn't sure Trev even *wanted* that. But it was like trying to repair a suspension bridge with Flex Seal . . . despite the miraculous promises, it was never going to work. With five years' distance in her rearview mirror, she was astounded at how scared she'd been about failing in the marriage, how determined she'd been that she could somehow, some way, make Trev and Kit have an improved relationship, that she could be the kind of wife that could raise her son *and* make her husband happy.

Fool's Falls was a good community—or at least, she had to assume it was, since Deb and Harrison and even Kit seemed to do well there—but she'd never felt like she fit in. It was so weird how something so Hallmark could make her feel so isolated. She knew being in a bad marriage hadn't helped matters, and the divorce had made her isolate, an injured animal licking her wounds in her den. Since then, she'd found herself lost, and cranky with exhaustion, and simply drifting.

Aiden was the closest thing to a true friend that she'd made in a decade.

She didn't know what to do with that. Her stomach twisted with awkwardness. Should she text him, see if he wanted to maybe play some *Blood Saga*? Of course, she'd just seen him that morning. And he'd just gotten his cast off. Surely, he'd want to see someone else, do something else?

*Gah.* This was why she didn't make IRL friends. It was easier when she had a *task*, an *assignment*. When she was useful. Just asking for his attention felt wrong and twisted her already knotty anxiety into a braid.

*Fuck it. Just eat something, watch something, go to bed.* She probably wouldn't get much sleep (read: any sleep), but at least she had a game plan.

Before she could turn to her kitchen, she saw the flash of headlights through her kitchen windows, and her stomach dropped.

*Who the hell is coming to my house on a Friday night?*

She felt her heart pound with adrenaline. As irritated as she'd been with Deb's observation, she had made a good point: it was hard to be a woman alone in this house, on this property. When Trev had first moved out, she'd cried herself to sleep, not because she missed him—they were too far gone for that—but because she'd been *scared*. The place had seemed too wild, too big, too frightening for her to handle on her own. It was only her stubborn love for her son, her determination to protect him and not to fuck up his life, that had provided the fuel in her engine to continue.

Only now Kit was gone—and despite her big attitude, she knew, practically, that she was a five-foot-tall biracial Asian woman in the middle of fucking nowhere. Maybe Deb was right: she ought to have gotten a dog.

Gritting her teeth, she went to the hall closet, grabbing an aluminum bat. Whoever was there came up to the door, knocking. She peered through the peephole. Then she opened the door, slowly. "*Aiden*?"

He grinned. His light-auburn hair was tamed a bit, suggesting he'd had a shower since seeing her that morning. He was bearing a pizza box and a bag. "Hey there," he said, before taking in her holding her bat. "Bad time?"

"No, no. I just . . . I didn't know who you were."

Now his cheeks pinkened a little. "Shit. I should've thought of that," he said, sounding sheepish. "I would've called, but I wanted to surprise you. I know you said that pizza doesn't deliver out here, so I figured I'd bring you some. We'll probably need to heat it up, though. And I got some ice cream too."

She felt relief pour through her like cool water. She leaned the bat against the wall and took the pizza and the bag of ice cream. "You didn't have to do this."

"Yeah, well, you didn't have to babysit me and help me out with my foot, but you were awesome, and I wanted to say thank you."

"You don't have to say thank you either," she said, that embarrassment squirming through her insides as she tucked the ice cream in the freezer and checked the pizza, trying to figure out how best to heat it back up. She preheated the oven, getting out a large cookie sheet and placing the whole thing on it.

"I wanted to."

She glanced over to find him smiling at her, a warm, almost amused smile. "It was no problem at all."

He glanced around. "Did you have plans for tonight, or anything? Damn. I thought . . . I probably should've thought this through more, I guess."

She barked out a laugh. "Dude, what plans would I possibly have? I am the least social person you know."

"Other than me," he said, chuckling in response. "I love that about you, actually."

She blinked. He looked startled.

"I mean . . . you're an introvert, like me. I don't feel exhausted with you."

"That's a ringing endorsement," she said.

"I'm sorry! I mean . . ."

"No, I wasn't being facetious," she quickly added. "Trust me, I get it. Most people drain me like an old cell phone battery. You don't exhaust me either. I feel better after I hang out with you."

She frowned. She hadn't meant to say that. She hadn't realized she actually *thought* that, come to it. But it was true.

She cleared her throat, busying herself with the pizza. "You're sharing this with me, right?"

"If that's okay?"

She rolled her eyes, feeling bristly and vulnerable. "Sure, sure. Maybe pick something to watch on Netflix, huh?"

He fiddled with her remote, and she felt her heart beating funny again. It was similar to fear, but she wasn't sure why. Maybe it was residual adrenaline.

Yeah. She'd go with that.

They settled on her couch. He'd decided to choose *Arcane*, and she found herself swept up in the story and the gorgeous art style. Just like they always did, they chattered back and forth as they demolished the pizza, making comments about the show and the characters. When she'd gotten them both bowls of ice cream, they'd debated the pros and cons of different flavors, letting the series roll from one episode to another.

She wasn't sure when she fell asleep. Between the heat from the fireplace and the heat from Aiden at her side, she found her eyes going low lidded, felt herself yawning. Now, she snuggled a little against the hard pillow under her cheek. Bleary, she looked up.

Aiden was looking down at her, his smile gentle, his gray eyes bright. He was stroking her hair, petting her as soothingly as he'd petted Duchess.

Which was when she realized her head was in his lap.

She sat up so fast she got a head rush. "I'm sorry!"

"For what?" He grinned. "For falling asleep through *Arcane*? Because I'll probably make you watch those episodes, not gonna lie. You need to see them to get the full story line."

"That I . . . that my head was . . ." A blush heated her cheeks, and she felt like a complete idiot. "That I used you as a pillow," she eventually landed on. Which sounded not-great but was better than *sorry I had my cheek really close to your dick there.*

The blush intensified. She could feel it heating her cheeks like the woodstove.

He chuckled, squirming. "You must be tired," he said sheepishly. "And I guess I should probably go. But I had a good time tonight."

"I did too. I wasn't sure if I'd get to see you again." Goddamn it. She wasn't fully awake. Why else would she admit something like that?

"Why wouldn't you see me again?"

She covered her face with her hands, feeling like an idiot. "No reason. I am an antisocial hedgehog. I don't leave the house if I don't have to. That's all."

He tugged her hands from her face—which showed her how close *his* face was to hers. He was staring at her like a very sweet interrogator. "Did you think we weren't going to hang out anymore because I didn't need your help?"

She groaned. "Maybe?"

Now he frowned . . . and to her shock, tugged her forward into a hug.

"You are one of my best friends," he said, squeezing her. She could hear his deep voice resonating through his chest, which then rumbled against *her* chest. Her sweater was no defense against that kind of sexy rumbling, she immediately noted.

*Oh, God.* What was happening here?

"So of course I'm going to see you again," he continued, obviously completely unaware that her pulse was now dancing the rumba in her throat and she was feeling rushes of heat that had nothing to do with hot flashes. "If you're okay with it, I mean. I'm not going to, like, force you to see me."

"I like seeing you," she admitted in a quiet voice.

He pulled back. "Same."

They stared at each other for a long second. She swallowed hard.

It had been a long time since she'd wanted to kiss someone, and suddenly, there were all those *feelings*. And she was frozen, unsure of what to do, her heart beating like a power hammer in her chest.

He stroked her cheek. She leaned into the touch, still staring.

*Just go for it.* She started to lean forward, her body tense as a coiled spring, when he spoke.

"Um . . . would you go to a wedding with me?"

She blinked, yanked out of the moment by his uncomfortable tone. "Sorry?"

"Wedding." He sighed, leaning back. "My cousin is having a wedding, and I need a date. It's in Coeur d'Alene, at this fancy hotel. Any chance you could come with me?"

She recoiled. She'd thought . . .

*Oh, God.*

"Um . . ."

"Please don't feel pressured," he said quickly. "It's not a big deal, I'm not . . . I'm just . . . my ex Sheryl is going to be there, with my brother obviously, and . . . it's a favor. I hate to ask . . ."

Now she felt like she'd been slapped.

*I hate to ask?*

She'd been about to *kiss* him. But he'd come out to her as demi—maybe, anyway, but somewhere on the ace spectrum probably—and he'd made it clear that he rarely felt attraction, and she'd almost . . . oh, God, what the *hell* had she been thinking?

She got to her feet in a rush, humiliation and pain flooding through her at what she was feeling, at how close she'd been to making a truly horrible mistake . . . with a guy she now realized she really liked.

"Maggie? You okay?" He got to his feet, cursing a little. "Sorry. My foot's still a little tender . . ."

"I can't," she said. "I'm sorry."

"I didn't mean to upset you," he said, and to his credit, he sounded concerned.

"No, no, it's fine," she hurried out. "I just . . . can't."

He nodded. "I'm sorry I asked. I know you don't like crowds, and family gatherings are a lot of pressure. I don't blame you. You've helped me so much, I don't want to make you feel uncomfortable . . ."

Now guilt was added to the weird emotional cocktail she was wrestling with. "No, no, that's . . ."

"I'm going to go," he said. He looked like he was going to hug her goodbye—they were getting pretty good at those—but instead, he dropped his arms, giving her a weird, awkward nod. "Talk to you tomorrow?" His voice sounded hopeful. And a little sad.

She didn't trust her own voice, so she just nodded, before closing the door behind him and locking it.

# CHAPTER 25
## PRAGMATIC ADAPTATION

Aiden felt terrible.

He hadn't meant to pressure Maggie. Especially after everything she'd done for him. The fact that she somehow thought the only reason he was friends with her was because she *did* things for him—helped him cook, drove him to appointments, kept him company—was disheartening. And then what had he done?

*I asked her for a fucking favor.*

After *literally* just telling her that he liked her without her needing to do anything.

He knew that she was introverted. They'd talked about it at length. They'd laughed about how they'd almost met at Deb's football party, even as his heart hurt at the idea that she'd barely been able to keep it together for twenty minutes. And he'd remembered her text, saying she wanted to "kill shit." While it had been prime Bogwitch, now that he knew the woman behind the screen name, he also saw that her grumpiness and lashing out were an extreme coping mechanism. She was trying to protect herself.

*You are such a dickhead.*

He grimaced. All day, he'd waited for Maggie to text him after he'd sent her another quick apology. She hadn't. Now, he was out at the Trick

Shot on a Saturday night, something he very rarely did. And an even more rare occurrence: he was drinking. Now that he was off pain meds, he just wanted to numb himself. He'd called Riley, asking him for a ride and explaining that he might get a little trashed.

As expected, Riley was all about being wingman and designated driver. "Because *goddamn*, you need to loosen up" had been his response.

So here he was. At a bar. Trying desperately to loosen up.

"Wedding's coming up," Riley said next to him. "Did you finally get a date?"

Aiden drank some more, emptying his pilsner glass and gesturing to the bartender to get him another. "No."

"I'm telling you: ask Patience," Riley said. "Sheryl's eyes will bug out, and it would serve her right."

"I'm not trying to get revenge on Sheryl," Aiden said, his irritation bleeding out. "I'm just trying to prevent gossip and bullshit. I don't know Patience very well, but from what I've seen? Nothing about her screams 'There's a woman who knows how to *defuse* a situation.'"

Riley laughed. "All right, you've got a point there." He munched some of the cheese fries he'd ordered from the bar. "How about Deb, then?"

"You're the one that warned me off of Deb, remember? Because she wants to get married?"

"True," Riley said. "But you're kind of running out of time for Tinder. Hell, even for hiring someone on Craigslist . . ."

"I am *not* doing that," Aiden snapped, then sighed over another sip of beer.

"Look at it this way," Riley said matter-of-factly. "You want a date. Deb won't stir up shit, she's good in a crowd, and your mom likes her. Hell, your mom would be over the moon. Wouldn't it be good to get her off your back? You're going to be stressed out enough with Davy and Sheryl there."

Aiden took a deep breath. *He has a point.*

"Lucky for you, she just walked in." Riley smirked, nodding his head at the door.

"What?" Aiden swung his head around. Sure enough—Deb and her cousin had just walked in, surveying the place. He hadn't talked to Deb since the disastrous "surprise" party at his house. He felt his stomach turn into a ball of ice. *"Fuck."* He quickly turned back to the bar.

Riley looked surprised. "Do you hate her or something?"

"What? No!" Aiden grimaced. "I don't even really know her. She's Davy's age, maybe a little younger, and it's not like we ever hung out since I moved back, other than seeing her with my mom's church group, and going to her party."

"And her throwing *you* a party," Riley teased.

"*I don't know her*," Aiden repeated.

"Yeah, well, now's your chance," Riley said, his tone surprisingly serious. "Because it is going to *suck* if you're at Jason's wedding alone. You know people are going to talk. They're going to say that you still haven't gotten over Sheryl. Hell, they might say worse."

"Worse like what?"

"I dunno. Like you're gay, or something." Riley shrugged, then narrowed his eyes. "You're not, are you?"

"No." Aiden took a deep breath. "Not exactly. I'm not particularly straight either."

And he waited for that bomb to detonate.

Riley's eyes widened as the gears in his head whirred. "So . . . you're . . ."

"I don't know what my particular label is, but yeah. I'm interested in guys as well as girls—when I'm interested. Which isn't often."

Another moment of quiet. Apparently, when he decided to come out, he came *all the way out*. But ever since he figured out that what he was—whatever he was—was something that other people were too . . . it had been hard to walk back. He didn't want to. It was like he'd known for years that there was something wrong with him—and now he knew there *wasn't*, that this was a *valid thing*.

It was still blowing his mind.

"Okay, first things first." Riley looked grim. "You're not into *me*, are you?"

Aiden couldn't help it. He laughed. Hard.

"Not with a gun to my head," he said honestly, and Riley looked both relieved and insulted.

"All right. Shit." Riley frowned. "Should you maybe be asking a guy, then?"

"It's complicated."

"How the fuck have you not been dating left and right?" Riley then asked, completely serious.

*Bisexual misunderstanding for the win.* Aiden shook his head. He'd read about the stereotypes, the erasure. He wasn't about to have that conversation with Riley. "That's part of the complication. I'm not *interested* in people." Aiden squirmed uncomfortably. It's not like anyone was listening in to their conversation at the bar—there was some kind of sports commentary show on the multitude of screens, and it was busy enough that there was a wall of conversation. Fortunately, Deb and Patience had not made their way over, and since he hadn't spoken to Deb since the disastrous surprise party, he hoped she'd continue to avoid him. He wasn't ashamed, per se. He just didn't want it to be public. Especially since the small town's commentary would make the sports show look like amateur hour. He didn't need all of Fool's Falls weighing in and armchair quarterbacking what he was, why he was, and how it might have happened.

Riley looked like his brain was still wrestling with the information he'd just been presented with. "You're . . . okay, I still don't get it."

"You don't need to," Aiden said. "You're taking it better than I'd expected, though."

Now Riley looked affronted. "You're still my bro. I mean, I'm an asshole, but I'm not *that* much of an asshole."

Aiden actually felt heartened at that. "Trust me, if I brought a guy to the wedding—which, I don't even know any guys, either, certainly none that I'm interested in—then my mom would lose it, and the deal I have with her would be off. The idea is to cause *less* talk, not *more*."

"That, I get." Riley nodded. "Then I have to say, again: Deb's your best bet."

Aiden wanted to howl with frustration. *Not Deb!* Just the thought of her on the verge of crying because he had chastised her made him feel sick.

"Just be up front with her. Maybe don't tell her the not-straight bit," Riley added, "but say you just need a date for one thing, just as friends, nothing more."

"And you think she'll be okay with that?" Aiden said doubtfully. "Without being upset or having any other expectations?"

"Hell no," Riley said, with a shrug. "But that's not the point. You want to settle this deal with your mom? Then suck it up."

Shit. Riley did have a point.

He sighed. "All right. I'm going in."

"Good man." Riley raised a nacho in his honor. "Good luck."

Aiden gritted his teeth, finished his second beer, then walked over to where Deb and Patience were sitting. Patience was flirting with some guy, who then asked her to dance on the tiny dance floor. Aiden nodded at the empty seat. "Mind if I sit here?"

Deb looked away, shrugging.

"How are you?" he asked. He hated small talk, but he needed to ease into this conversation.

She shrugged again, then finally looked at him. "I'm so sorry," she blurted out. "About the surprise party at your house, I mean."

"It's no problem," he assured her, hoping she didn't get weepy again. "You meant well, and I'm sorry if I sounded ungracious. I don't do well around people."

"Except Maggie."

He blinked. "Sorry?"

Deb's expression shifted, and for a flash of a second, he saw resentment. "Are you two an item? You seem really close."

"She's just a good friend. Nothing romantic at all." His chest pinched, and he rubbed at it absently.

"Is she going with you to your cousin's wedding?"

Aiden winced. "No."

"Your mom did say you were looking for a date, and so did Riley, a while ago. *I* could go with you," Deb said, her blue eyes large and sincere. "If you want."

There it was. His chance. He'd get a date, talk would be quelled, his mother would be appeased, and they'd finally get her to deal with her shit. He didn't even have to ask. She was presenting it on a silver platter.

But the look in Deb's eyes . . .

"Are you attracted to me?" he asked.

Now there was dead silence for a long moment before a high-pitched, nervous giggle. "Let's not get ahead of ourselves," she teased. "I mean, you're cute and all. Of course I wouldn't mind spending some time with you, but I don't *know* you."

He almost felt better for a split second until she added:

"But we could get to know each other," she said, with a sweet smile. "Better, I mean. Isn't that what dating's for?"

He let out a long, slow exhalation. "I don't want to lead you on, Deb," he said. "The thing is, I'm not interested in dating. Not anyone." He waited a beat. "Trust me. It is literally me, not you, in this case."

She looked crestfallen. "You're not interested in even *trying* . . ."

He winced. "I'm . . . I'm sorry," he said, swallowing against the lump in his throat. "I just . . . I'm not attracted. To people. In general."

It wasn't like his blurted admission to Maggie, which had been received like an egg dropped in about ten feet of cotton batting on a safety net. It wasn't even his fumbling confession to Riley, which was more like a juggled near-drop on a hard kitchen floor. This was like an egg being thrown at a sidewalk from ten stories up. Or possibly shot from a bazooka.

Still, he wasn't prepared for the response.

"You don't want to date me, that's fine," she said, her voice low and cutting. "But you didn't have to *lie*."

"I'm sorry?"

"You're in love with Maggie!" Deb snapped. "It's obvious."

"What? I'm not!" he protested. "I haven't even known her that long. Just a few months!"

More to the point, that wasn't how his attractions worked. All two of them, admittedly. They usually blindsided him. He was in love before he knew . . .

Before he . . .

*Oh, shit.*

"Aiden?"

He realized that Deb had asked him something, or told him something, and he'd been momentarily struck deaf by his realization.

He was attracted, *really* attracted. To Maggie. Maggie the prickly. Maggie, who would probably smack him upside the head and yell *SNAP OUT OF IT* if she had an inkling of how he felt. Even though there had been that moment on her couch . . .

Had there been a moment? He had no idea. It happened so infrequently, and it wasn't something he tuned in to at this point.

"Aiden!"

He blinked. Deb was scowling at him.

"I'm so sorry," he said. "I appreciate the offer, and I'm sorry I was blunt, and . . . I'm just sorry. But I can't do this."

He got up, feeling terrible, even though he was glad he hadn't gone through with it.

He had feelings for Maggie.

He was *attracted* to Maggie.

It was the last thing he needed, and he had absolutely no idea what to do with any of it.

# CHAPTER 26

## ARMOR-PIERCING QUESTION

Maggie had managed to keep herself occupied for four whole days since the Incident. She hadn't texted Aiden since his apology, and he hadn't texted her again. While she felt a pang at this—she missed the easy camaraderie, just the sheer comfort of texting with him during the day—she also knew that if she texted him, it'd be awkward.

He'd apologized for asking her. She hadn't responded until Sunday, and all she'd been able to cobble together was "I'm sorry too" without being perfectly clear *what* she was being sorry about, possibly because she was still confused about that herself. If he hadn't noticed that she'd almost planted one on him, she didn't want to tip him off to it and make things worse. If he *had* noticed, maybe they could . . . pretend she hadn't? And go back to normal?

Forget seeing him in person, though. "Normal" was going to have to be guild stuff, playing online. And hopefully texting. God, his texts had brightened her day more than she'd realized.

*You're still crushing.*

She gritted her teeth. How the fuck could she have a *crush* at nearly fifty?

Not that she was going to judge other people who had crushes . . . they could have them at 108, for all she cared. But after Trev left, she was so angry, she thought her fury had basically burned away any residual feelings of that nature. The first year, the thought of being with anyone had made her almost bug eyed with wrath.

By the next year, she'd settled into a semiroutine with Kit, and the insidious stuff she'd ignored in the name of making the marriage work had sprouted from the wreckage, and she'd been too busy second-guessing how she might be fucking up Kit's life to think about a relationship. Trev had been adamant: Her approach to parenting would ruin their child. Her approach to *everything* would ruin his life. The idea of opening herself up to any sort of criticism, from *anyone*, was abhorrent . . .

So no crushes. No interaction.

When Kit had gotten to his junior year of high school, she'd stopped being quite so scared. She'd settled into their life, a nice, quiet, insulated little bunker of solitude. It wasn't that she was angry at men, or afraid of them, anymore. It was that she quite firmly didn't want the hassle. Her life had finally gotten uncomplicated. She didn't need to add one more thing.

Then Aiden had showed up, with his geeky-healer charm, and his gentle sense of humor, and his absolute lack of pressure or expectation.

Trev had criticized her mercilessly by the end: how she'd looked, what she ate, what she liked or didn't like.

Aiden thought she was amazing *for simply heating up soup*.

Her phone rang, and she jolted, her heart pounding. Was he calling her? She'd hoped that they'd gradually move back to their old patterns, the gaming, the texts. Why would he want to talk to her?

Then she saw the display: KIT.

She sniffed, got herself together, then answered. "Hey there. I was going to call you, but didn't want to cramp your style. Or be that old person who calls." She paused. "Come to think of it, why are *you* calling?"

"Just checking on you," he said. "Hadn't heard from you in a while, and I thought . . . Do you have any big news, maybe?" His tone was leading.

She blinked, her mind scrolling through what he was talking about. Had she missed something? It wasn't her birthday—that wasn't until next month. It wasn't *his* birthday either. She thought of the shows they both liked, the games. "Um . . . I don't think so?" she finally admitted.

He waited a beat. "Seriously? You're not going to tell me?"

"What are you talking about?" She knew she sounded a little peeved, but she just wasn't in the right headspace for guessing games.

"You're *dating*."

She spluttered. "I'm *WHAT*?"

"Wait, so you're not dating?" Now Kit sounded confused. "But Harrison said you were."

"Harrison? Why does he think that?" She felt bewildered, and vulnerable. Her irritation meter, which had already started creeping up, was starting to bury the needle in the red. "What did he say? What did he tell you?"

"Whoa, hey! Calm down," Kit said, and she shut up. It wasn't his fault, after all. "Harrison just said that his mom said you're dating some guy she knows. That you guys have been seeing each other for a while."

She goggled, her mouth moving like a fish flopping on the bottom of a boat. No sounds came out other than strangled protesting noises.

"So I take it you *aren't* dating some guy Ms. Deb knows?" Kit's tone turned dry.

"No!"

Kit sighed. "Why does she think you are? She said that he'd probably asked you to some wedding or something."

*Oh, for fuck's sake.* That had happened *in her house,* not in some public arena. Did Deb have her living room bugged at this point? With the speed of gossip transmission in Fool's Falls, and the ferocity with which it was pursued, it was like Nextdoor meets TMZ. She'd probably find Patience hiding in her hedges with a telephoto lens next.

"Mom?"

"It's fine."

"Really?" Kit now sounded amused. "Because you're doing your Linda-Hamilton-in–*Terminator 2* voice."

"I'm just annoyed," she replied. "It's a nothingburger. Aiden's just a friend."

Another pause. "Aiden?" Kit asked, sounding amused. "Who's Aiden?"

"He's the healer, the leader of our guild. It's *no big deal*," she tacked on with a tone she hoped shut him down.

"And he knows Ms. Deb?"

"His mom goes to her church, or something. One of the ladies at book club hooked us up." She froze. "*Connected* us, I mean."

"Is he the healer guy you were talking about? The one who volunteered to protect you when you first joined the guild?" Now Kit sounded scandalized and a bit sick. "Didn't you say that he was like eighteen or something?"

"Funny story, that," she said, rubbing her temple. "It turns out he's a little older than me, actually."

He let out a startled laugh. "How'd you find out?"

"I, um . . . went to his house."

"Jesus, this is a roller coaster," Kit said, sounding bewildered. "Moving past the inherent dangers involved in going to a stranger's house . . . Why did you go to his house? You don't even like to go to the grocery store. And you need to do that to *survive*."

"He'd broken his foot, and he needed a hand, and I brought him some soup, and that's how we met. IRL, I mean."

"And Ms. Deb thinks you're dating because . . . you brought him some soup? Why? And what was the wedding thing about?"

"She may've gotten the wrong idea because we've been hanging out a lot," she admitted, debating how much to tell him. But she'd tried so hard not to lie to him if she didn't have to. "And there may have been an incident at his house where she went full hyper-helpful hamster and threw a surprise party for him. In his house. Without his consent."

Kit sighed. "That does sound like Ms. Deb."

"So I gave him an out, and helped him escape. He came up to the house and fixed our router, sort of, so that was a thing. Also, we watch movies together, and stuff." She bit her lip. "He's actually really nice. You'd like him."

"Are you dating this guy or not?" Kit asked. "Because it honestly sounds like you're dating him, and I am confused as hell right now."

"I'm . . . we're . . . friends." She huffed out a breath. "It's complicated!"

They were both quiet for a second. "Mom, it's all right if you date," he said softly. "You know that, right? I don't want you to be all alone. If you like this guy, I don't want you to avoid a relationship because you think I'm going to hate it, or something weird. I *want* you to get out there, and have fun, and . . . I don't know. Find somebody who's nice."

She swallowed hard, her throat suddenly feeling scratchy, her eyes prickling with tears. "It's not about you."

"Is it about Dad?" Kit asked. "Because I have to assume that they're not all like him."

"No." She gritted her teeth. "Not exactly. I mean, he influenced me up to this point, but this has some weird specificity that I literally cannot and will not talk about. Anyway, long story short, Aiden and I aren't dating. He asked me to a wedding, and I said no, and that's it."

"Wait—he asked you to a thing . . ."

"*To a wedding,*" she emphasized.

He ignored her. ". . . and you said no? Why? Do you not like him?"

"I like him a lot." The admission leaped out of her mouth, and she felt horrified.

"So why aren't you going to the wedding with him?"

"Because it's not like that between us!"

"His choice? Or yours?"

She was quiet.

Kit sighed. "So he's an asshole?"

*"No!"* The vehemence of her words startled even her. "No. Not even a little bit. He's a sweetheart, and I mean that. He just . . . doesn't feel . . ." She let it trail off.

Kit sighed. "I'm sorry, Mom. I wish I could make this better."

Her laugh came out tear laced, and she cursed herself silently. Clearing her throat, she reminded him, "I'm the parent here, not you. And don't worry about it, okay? The shocking thing here, really, is that I made a friend. I'm ahead of the game for a change."

"You're still going to hang out with him?"

"Maybe. Eventually. I just need a little time to . . . process."

There was a commotion, a jumble of people's voices and laughter on Kit's end of the line. "I need to go, but call me if you need me, okay?"

She wanted to ask if they were friends of his—how *his* life was—but she didn't want to keep him, and she didn't want him worrying about her further. "I'll be fine, okay? Talk to you next week." With that, she hung up.

She felt like she could explode from emotions, like Mentos stuffed into a Diet Coke bottle. She was angry at Deb's presumption. Embarrassed at needing to explain herself. Upset that she'd inadvertently made Kit sad and concerned. Most of all, she felt that weird, empty, achy feeling in her chest at the thought that she'd somehow fallen heavily in *like* with Aiden and that there was really no pathway that worked there, not without pressuring him or hurting him or losing his friendship.

She wanted to scream. She wanted to play video games until her mind shut off. But video games made her think of Aiden, and there was no way she was texting him to play when *he* was what she needed to forget right now.

She swallowed hard. Then she turned on the TV, and called out the big guns.

She played *Encanto.*

And she wept her damned eyes out until she felt a little better.

# CHAPTER 27
## CRAPSACCHARINE WORLD

"Thank you all for coming to our rehearsal dinner," Jason said to the group of family in the hotel's restaurant. Jason was beaming, as was his lovely bride-to-be. Their respective parents were also beaming. People were eating the food, drinking copious amounts of booze, enjoying themselves, and toasting in preparation for the joyous occasion to come the next day.

*It'd be great if this wasn't such a clusterfuck.*

Aiden drank a glass of water, recognizing that it was, technically, only a clusterfuck for *him*.

"What did you do?" his mother had snapped when he had picked her up to go to Idaho that morning. "I thought you were asking Deb! I told her you should!"

"I changed my mind," he admitted. "It's not fair, Mom. She wants to be my girlfriend, and I am just not interested in her that way. At all. It's a dick move."

"Watch your mouth," she'd sniped. Then she hadn't talked to him for the rest of the ride. It should've been a relief, but it wasn't. It was more like sitting in the same room as a time bomb. He was waiting for the explosion.

Now, in the cordoned-off dining room of the restaurant, sitting at one of the four-tops sprinkled around the room, he felt the tension rising. He doubted his mother would make a scene in front of the rest of the family, simply because it would humiliate *her* and add even more gossip and questions. But he knew she was probably ready to chew nails at this point, and he wasn't sure how much longer she could hold herself back.

To make matters worse, she'd insisted that they sit at the same table with Davy and Sheryl, the four of them uncomfortably close. He had Davy and his mother on either side of him, which meant Sheryl was sitting across from him, deliberately avoiding making eye contact. She ate the chicken with grim determination.

"I thought you were bringing a date to the wedding?" Davy said, with all the grace of a Sherman tank.

Aiden squirmed slightly, taking in his mother's venomous look. Sheryl shot a matching one a beat later, finally looking at him.

"He didn't ask anyone," his mother said in a low voice, each word sharp as a scalpel. "If you can believe *that*."

"Oh, I can," Sheryl muttered, slicing off another piece of chicken. The chicken piccata was nice and tender, and there really was no reason for her to use quite so much force.

"And I *know* someone who was interested," his mother added, glaring at him.

Davy looked startled. "What happened?"

"Long story," Aiden said. "And it would've just been as friends anyway. I'm not interested in her that way."

"Nice, churchgoing girl," his mother all but spat under her breath. "Would've loved to get remarried, has a grown boy. A decent, community-centered woman!"

"Not your *type*, I take it?" Sheryl's voice was almost imperceptible.

He tried not to glower.

"Now, hon," Davy said, with a note of warning in his voice. She looked away again, so Davy turned his attention back to Aiden. "Well, it can't be helped now. But if we just all stay calm—and be *civil*"—this seemed directed at his wife—"we should be able to get through this without any big deal."

"People are going to talk!" his mother hissed.

Aiden couldn't help a disgruntled sigh. "They talk anyway. I don't give a fuck."

Now, all three of them stared at him.

"What has gotten into you?" his mother said. "You've never cussed like this! You're like a sailor!"

Surprisingly, he felt a smirk affix itself to his face.

*No, like a Bogwitch.*

He knew better than to say that aloud, though.

"I'm going to the restroom," his mother said—almost snarled—and then got up.

He saw it first . . . the sudden unease, the way she instinctively grabbed for the table and the back of the chair. The way she swayed. He was on his feet and helping her in an instant.

"Mom?"

"I'm fine," she said, stubbornly, closing her eyes and taking a few breaths. "I'm fine!"

When her eyes opened again, he studied her. "You got dizzy again," he said, not asking.

"The wine," she argued . . . but there was just an edge of uncertainty, of defensive posturing. "And I need to go to the bathroom."

Aiden looked at Sheryl, who had also gotten to her feet. When their gazes met, she nodded, shooting Davy a quick look before helping their mother. "I need to go too."

"Don't baby me, Sheryl," his mother growled in a low voice, but she still took Sheryl's arm as they made their way toward the bathrooms. Aiden and Davy watched them as they headed down the hallway.

"She's gotten worse," Davy said, and his voice was a mixture of surprise and dismay.

"I've been fucking telling you!" Now it was Aiden's turn to growl.

"Well, how was I supposed to know? She sounded fine when I talked with her!"

"And how long ago was that?" Aiden asked, before rubbing his temples. "Listen, we've got to get her to think ahead, okay? She's managing, but that's with me grabbing her groceries, cleaning her house, driving her around. Even with all that—she's still falling, Davy."

Davy grimaced. "What does her doctor say?"

"She's not letting me talk to her doctor," Aiden said. "I don't have medical authority. Besides, you know what the facilities are like in the Falls. If she needs to see a specialist, it's a two-hour drive to Spokane, easy. Having her in the car for four hours round trip, every week?"

Davy fell silent, looking troubled.

"She won't talk with me, Davy," Aiden said, quietly, urgently. "We're gonna hit a point where I can't take care of her on my own. I don't mean hospice, although that'll be a thing at some point, I imagine. I mean just day-to-day care."

"But you're doing fine now," Davy protested. "I don't see why—"

"No, *you don't see*," Aiden said. "She doesn't like me. She hasn't liked me in years."

Davy spluttered. "I thought it was better, since—"

"It isn't." Aiden kept going, implacable. "Dad barely came around before he died. In fact, I think that's part of why Mom's still so pissed. She relies on me, and hates it. Dad didn't get me to change who I am before he left, and she feels like it's on her. Leaving her in my care is not doing her any favors, Davy. And it's only going to get worse."

"What do you want me to do about it?" Davy shot back, eyes sparking.

"*Help me.* Talk to her. Get her to think about the legal stuff, the medical stuff." He swallowed. This was going to be the hard part. "And . . . we're going to need to think of long-term care."

Davy paled. "But she loves the Falls, dude."

"You think I don't know that?" Aiden felt like his chest was going to implode from the weight. "I don't want to make those kinds of decisions. But—the doctors. The drive. The in-home care. The Falls is not equipped for what she's gonna need, probably sooner than we realize. I've seen it happen, too many times."

Davy was subdued, silent. He looked like a guy who'd been cornered in an alley, trying desperately to think of how to escape.

Eventually, Sheryl and his mother came back to the table. His mother sat down with a sigh, then looked her sons over. "All right, what's going on?"

"Mom," Davy said quietly. "Aiden was telling me—"

"I'm going to stop you right there." For as frail as she looked, their mother sounded like a drill sergeant. "If this is about all that lawyer stuff and medical stuff, and how I apparently can't take care of myself—"

"Mom," Aiden tried to interrupt, but it was too late. Here was the explosion. He glanced around, but fortunately, most of the other guests were already pretty wasted, and few were paying any attention to the drama that was quietly unfolding at their table.

To his surprise, his mother unleashed a wide smile. "But here's the thing. You told me I don't have to talk to you about any of this stuff. You said you'd *drop* it. So we're not going to talk about it."

"What?" Aiden gaped. "When did I say *that*?"

"When you said you'd have a date." She looked smug.

He narrowed his eyes, trying to remember their "agreement." "Mom, just because I don't have a date doesn't mean it's not important. We have to talk about this!"

"Nuh-uh." His mother looked triumphant, crossing her arms as a waiter put little bowls of ice cream in front of all four of them. "We had a *deal.* No date, no discussion. I get to drive again. And if you bring up any of that 'long-term care' crap, I will boot you out of my house!"

He felt a chill run down his spine, exchanging a worried look with Davy. "But . . . *I don't live with you.*"

There was a split second of surprise.

No. Not surprise. *Confusion.*

"Well, you're there often enough," his mother carped, but her tone was more hesitant. "That's what I meant."

Aiden felt like his shoulders were made of granite. He wanted to howl. Part of him felt like throwing up his hands and saying, *Fine! Do what the hell you want!* Just walk away and leave her to her own stubbornness. She'd hated so many aspects of him, for so long. The nursing. The "gay thing." The potential scandal. Never getting married, never having kids. What the hell did he need her judgments for? Why keep helping her when she made his life so miserable?

But then he'd think about the times she'd stayed up with him when he had a fever, or when she sat with him at the ER when he'd broken his clavicle playing football. The way she'd read stories to him when he was a kid, including doing the silly voices. The games she'd shown up to. The way she and his father had scrimped and saved to make sure he and Davy went off to college, even though they never had, because they wanted better for their kids.

It was complicated, and it hurt. But he couldn't walk away.

"I'm going up to my room," his mother said, once they'd finished their dessert, with Davy doing all the talking . . . too-cheerful, totally surface chatter about something that had happened at one of the dealerships. Aiden assumed it was supposed to be funny. He couldn't focus enough to tell. "Davy? Sheryl? Why don't you walk me. It's on this floor."

Aiden went to give her a hug, and she grudgingly let him. Appearances, he knew, and that hurt his chest just a little bit more.

He waved to some people, hugged Jason and Hailey, and retreated to his own room.

He thought briefly about drinking, but decided against it—just because tomorrow was going to be almost unbearable as it was, and it would only be compounded if he was hungover. The last thing he needed was to have people reading into his alcohol consumption as well. He didn't know how they were going to interpret the little scene his family had going on tonight, but he could imagine the family grapevine was already hard at work.

He wanted desperately to talk to someone. He even considered talking to Malcolm—but it was Friday, the sixteenth of December. He knew Malcolm was picking up last-minute presents for the kids and doing holiday stuff. He didn't want to bother him.

*You know who you* could *call . . .*

He closed his eyes. He hadn't talked to Maggie since she'd turned him down. It wasn't that they weren't in contact—they still texted, even if it was more stilted. They still went on raids with the guild. But they hadn't met in person. He didn't want to make her feel awkward or defensive, and was afraid he'd managed to do both.

He missed her. Man, did he miss her.

*I can call a friend, can't I?*

But he didn't want to *use* her. She wasn't his soother. She deserved more than just being his woobie when he was down.

But it was more than just needing her as an emotional grounding rod. He liked talking to her. He'd hoped that she felt the same.

Did she feel the same?

Maybe . . . maybe he could just talk to her. No emotional demands. Just . . . be friends.

He sighed. Then he picked up his phone.

She answered almost immediately. "Aiden?"

"Hey there," he said—but his damned voice rasped, and he cleared his throat. "Just . . . it'd been a while. Thought maybe I could call, if that's okay?"

"Of course it's okay," she said, but she still sounded off.

"I'm sorry. I could . . ."

*Could what? Give her space? Not call her?*

Why did this have to be so hard?

"It's fine, Otter," she said, and he couldn't help himself—he smiled at her no-nonsense tone and the guild nickname. "We're friends, you can call. I *like* talking to you. Stop being weird."

He chuckled. "Got it."

After that, he was able to spend twenty blessed minutes talking with her about nothing in particular. She told him that Kit seemed to be doing well. Her friend Mac had a new boyfriend, and her latest editing client had changed his manuscript five times. He'd commiserated, laughed, and felt his muscles relax even as his chest warmed.

God, he liked this woman.

"Now, your turn," she said. "You at the wedding? Because you sounded tense."

"No." He sighed. "Rehearsal dinner."

There was a pause, like she was weighing his words, then a sigh. "Right, spit it out," she said, with some of the sharp fire he was used to. "What's going on?"

"Nothing," he quickly replied.

"I didn't just fall down on the last drop of rain, y'know." He could almost imagine her stern frown.

"What does that even mean?"

"I don't know. Something Nana Birdie always said. Now, *spill*."

He huffed impatiently at himself. "I am having a kind of shitty night," he admitted. "But it's not a big deal, okay? I don't want you to think I just call when I'm in trouble. I like talking to you. I don't want you to feel obligated."

"Oh, shut up," she said, and he barked out a laugh. "I told you already: I've got your back. That doesn't change. Now, talk."

# CHAPTER 28

## EVEN EVIL HAS STANDARDS

Maggie was nervous. Which was ridiculous. She hadn't even wanted to answer the phone, but at the same time, she missed hearing from him. She knew that the wedding was this week—he'd missed that night's dungeon run—and she had been curious. Had he wound up asking Deb? Maybe someone else?

That bugged her a little, although she didn't want to think of *why* it bothered her.

But now he was calling, and he was upset, even if he didn't want to show it. He said he was having a shitty night. The fact that he was nervous about talking to her, afraid of using her, made her hard little heart melt like a sugar cube in coffee. Which was the last thing she needed if she was trying to get past this crush, admittedly.

What could she say? The guy was her kryptonite.

She settled into her bed, where she'd been tucked in with a book, a large mug of tea on her nightstand.

"Did something happen at the dinner?" she pressed.

He let out a huff of breath. "Nothing I wasn't expecting," he said, and he sounded so sad, so bitter . . . so *un-Aiden-like,* she was upset on his behalf. "My mother gave me hell about not having a date, even though technically it meant her winning our bet—but that's a different story. She insisted we sit with Davy and Sheryl, which was a nightmare. Nothing overt, just the usual little stabs and snarking."

"Davy snarks at you?" she said, incensed. His little brother had hooked up with his ex. Surely he wasn't the offending party here?

"No. Sheryl." Aiden sighed. "It's been ten years. I swear, I keep waiting for her to get over it. It's actually kind of hurtful to my brother, if you think about it."

"Wait, why is *Sheryl* pissed?" she asked. "Did you dump her? Because I don't understand this at all."

"It is a little complicated," he said.

When he was quiet for a beat, she gritted her teeth, blowing out a breath. Then she said, "You really don't have to tell me, Aiden. It's all right. I'm just trying to understand. Because it doesn't sound like you did anything wrong."

"No, it's okay. I don't know that I've given anybody the gritty details, except Malcolm, now that I think of it."

She took a sip of tea.

"So, remember, I broke up with Jordan junior year of college? I was working for a few years after that. I didn't date anybody, because I was heartbroken, and I was trying to figure out what I wanted, and I thought there was something wrong with me. Sheryl had gone to school in Chicago, but she'd had kind of a bad experience too. I think she wanted to have this rebellious period, and I guess she did go a little wild, but ultimately she didn't like what was happening. I heard her parents needed to bail her out of something—I think a trashed apartment or something, and some debt she'd run up—but by the time I saw her, that was all in the past. She graduated, had gotten a job in HR in Seattle. After Malcolm and I had started the hospice . . . I was like twenty-eight or something when we connected again. I ran into her at a grocery store, of all damned things."

Maggie felt like she was on the edge of her seat.

"It was nice. She was still kind, and fun, and supportive. She didn't know why I'd left Spokane and went to the west side, but she was supportive of me being a nurse, and thought the hospice was a great business to get into. We started seeing each other regularly. She felt like home, in a good way. And I was still attracted to her, and she was still attracted to me and single at the time we bumped into each other, so it just kind of happened. Organically."

Maggie felt her stomach twist. Why was she begrudging him? This was his life. She was just listening to him tell this story. But there was a Spidey sense tingling too. She didn't trust this woman.

"Anyway, after we'd been together a few years, I started noticing some things that had changed. She'd always prided herself on being different from her parents, who were pretty conservative. Now, she was starting to say she saw their point. She complained about living in Seattle. She wanted to get married, and have kids. Settle down in Spokane."

Maggie's jaw clenched hard. She would *not* interrupt. No matter how badly she wanted to.

"I started to realize that I wasn't really feeling as connected. I should have broken up with her immediately . . ."

"Hindsight is twenty-twenty," Maggie blurted out. "It's not your fault. People grow apart. I can't imagine that many people reconnecting with their high school sweethearts and still being the same people, much less maintaining a relationship."

He sounded startled. "I . . . guess that's true," he murmured. "The thing is, my family was pressuring us to get married. *Her* family was pressuring us to get married and move back to the east side. I wound up asking her to marry me, but I kept putting off setting a date. That should've been a sign, right there."

Maggie made a sympathetic noise.

"Sheryl started talking about me either opening a branch of our hospice company in Spokane, or taking over her parents' car dealerships. I put my foot down on that one. I had absolutely no interest in selling cars."

She could all but picture him shuddering. "Yeah, I don't see you as a car salesman," she said, with a little teasing in her voice.

He chuckled, but it was brittle. "I didn't want to move to Spokane either. It felt like we were fighting more than anything, and I guess the writing was on the wall, but I . . . well, I so rarely felt like this for people. I didn't know what to do, and if I screwed up with her . . . although by that time I didn't even want to have sex anymore anyway." He paused. "Thanks for the demisexual and asexual information, by the way. It really cleared some things up. About me, I mean."

"Glad I could help," Maggie said, swallowing against a knot in her throat.

"Wish I'd known it then," he added ruefully. "So we were arguing one day, because I'd been working a lot of overtime or staying up late so I didn't have to, you know, go to bed with her. She asked what was wrong with me. She asked if I'd ever even dated anyone else, and how we'd lost our virginity to each other, but she'd slept with other people in Chicago and had boyfriends and stuff, and she hinted that something might be wrong with me and maybe I should see a doctor . . ." He cleared his throat. "It really sucked."

"Jesus." *That bitch.*

"I brought up my relationship in college, in Spokane. She actually doubled down and said it was impossible, because my family didn't know, or they'd have told her. So I spit out that I had been dating a man in college, and he was in the closet, so nobody knew, least of all my parents."

Maggie let out a low whistle. "Bet that went over like a lead balloon."

"She lost her shit. Kicked me out that day. I had to move in with Malcolm and his wife until I could get a new place to live."

Now Maggie didn't hold back. "That *bitch*!"

"No, she wasn't," he said. The sheer *virtue* this guy had. "She was angry, sure. But it was my fault too. I knew we weren't working, but I didn't do the hard thing and just break up. I just kept thinking things would work out somehow."

"I bet you put in a ton of effort," Maggie countered. "Because I *know* you. You probably did all kinds of shit you didn't like to try to make it work. And again: Why is she pissed *now*? She kicked you out!"

He let out a long exhalation. "Because I should've been honest," he said. "I should've been up front with her, right from the start."

Maggie blinked. "Why?"

Now there was a long pause. "What do you mean, why?" Aiden asked, sounding genuinely baffled. "Because . . . I should've disclosed it."

"Again: Why?" Maggie felt anger bubble in her bloodstream. "I don't hand over a résumé of my past partners when I start seeing someone. Did she tell you all about her boyfriends from college? Provide you with a list of past lovers?"

He was still quiet.

"Wait. 'Disclose.' *That's* why she's still angry? Because you didn't *disclose* you were bi, or whatever?" Maggie was almost shaking with fury by this point. "You come out when you're ready, when you feel safe with it. Obviously you didn't feel safe."

"She thought we were going to get married," Aiden said, but his voice was softer.

"Did you, though?"

"I thought we were supposed to."

"There's a difference."

He seemed to mull that over. "She said she felt cheated. Like she wasted all that time with me. Like I'd lied to her, tricked her. She is convinced that I'm gay. I think she's hurt, thinking that I never loved her."

"Did you?"

"I did," Aiden said, and Maggie could hear it, the truth of it, resonating through his voice like a tuning fork. "I really, truly did. But we both changed, and we both wanted the other person to be different than we turned out. She wanted me to be more like the husband she'd envisioned, more conservative, close to her family, living in Spokane. I wanted her to be someone who understood me and accepted me for who I was. Neither of us was happy. But yeah. I really did love her. At heart, she's a good person."

Maggie felt her heart break for him. "I'm so sorry, Aiden." Then she frowned. "How the hell did she marry Davy?"

"Davy came out to the west side to help me move out of our apartment, actually," he said. "She was a little younger than me . . . same age as Davy. Turns out Davy had always had a thing for her. She moved back to the east side shortly after I moved out, back to Spokane, where he was working in the sales department of this manufacturing company. He comforted her, listened to her. They got closer."

"You must've been hurt."

"I was," he said. "Again, I did love her. But I felt guilty, too, for not telling her. And I wanted her to be happy. Davy seems to make her happy . . . happier than I ever did, anyway. The fact that he already had his son and was eager to have more kids was a big plus for her, as well."

"Shit. And now you're stuck at this wedding with the two of them." Speaking of guilt: she should've gone. She could've kept her crush locked down, her feelings buried. This wasn't about attraction. This was about helping a friend.

"Yeah. Hopefully I can sit somewhere else at dinner. Or maybe I'll fake stomach cramps and just disappear until I have to drive Ma home the next morning."

His mother . . . her memory jogged. "You said that your mother was winning a bet with you. What's that about?"

"Oh. We had a deal," he said. "If I brought a date to the wedding, she would finally agree to talk to Davy and me about some stuff that we really need to discuss. Like her not driving. And finally filling out some legal paperwork: durable power of attorney, life directives, stuff like that. Stuff she doesn't want to deal with, but really, really needs to."

"Are you kidding?"

"No. Too many people think it's macabre and put it off, but it's—"

"No, I mean you had a deal with your mother? *That's* why you needed a date to the wedding?" Maggie said, aghast.

"Well, yeah."

*For fuck's sake.* "Give me the name of your hotel, where the wedding is."

"What?" Aiden sounded startled. "Why?"

"Because you're going to have a date," Maggie said in her best Linda Hamilton impression. "No arguments. I'll meet you there."

# CHAPTER 29
## BEAUTIFUL ALL ALONG

Aiden was wearing a suit he hadn't worn since he lived on the west side, a black suit with a snow-white shirt and pale-blue tie. He looked like a funeral director, but a classy one. According to Malcolm, who had forced him to buy it, it was his "power" suit.

If he had ever needed a boost of confidence, it was now.

The wedding wasn't for another hour, but people were getting together already. He was at the bar, debating whether he should drink or not. So far, he'd settled on a very light gin and tonic. He generally didn't drink his troubles away—he didn't often indulge in liquid courage, and he didn't like feeling out of control.

*Maggie's coming.* Or at least he hoped so, looking at his watch. She said she'd try, anyway.

Maybe she wouldn't make it.

He'd put up a token resistance when she'd volunteered, but as she'd pointed out, resistance was futile. He hoped that she was driving okay from Fool's Falls. He wasn't sure what she'd turn up looking like . . . hell, for all he knew, she'd wear her usual jeans and baggy sweater, her hair a wild nimbus around her head.

He wouldn't care.

*I just want to see her.* Because things were *better* when Maggie was around.

"Why the hell didn't you just take Deb?" Riley asked by his side. He'd shown up that morning, not having been invited to the rehearsal dinner. He was the one who had suggested the bar in the first place once he'd realized that Aiden was stag.

"She's got feelings for me."

"Sounds like a 'her' problem, not a 'you' problem," Riley said with a shrug. "I guess that's why you couldn't go with that Bogwitch, either, huh? She's hot for you too?"

The thought made Aiden's neck flush. Not with embarrassment, exactly. With interest.

Would Maggie be interested in him? She was so guarded, so deliberately grumpy. And he wasn't sure about her past, other than her really bad divorce.

"Did you friend zone her too?" Riley continued, oblivious to Aiden's pensiveness. "Because . . . shit. People are talking; your mom was right on that front. They've only ever seen you with Sheryl—you know, as in dating or whatever—and she's married to *your brother*. And you haven't been with anyone since, and nobody knows what the hell went wrong. So they're talking up a storm. It's like a Reddit board out there."

"Yeah, well," Aiden said, which he knew was a poor comeback, but he wasn't sure what else to say.

Riley was trying: he'd give him that. He frowned, assessing the increasing crowd of wedding-goers who were filling the bar and flooding into the lobby beyond. "You could pick up somebody," Riley said, even though his tone was dubious. "One of the bridesmaids is single, and a bunch of Hailey's cousins and friends. Well, maybe not a bunch. At least four, though. And one or two of them are seriously cute."

"I've got it covered," Aiden said, glancing at the dressy watch he rarely wore. It had been his father's.

Riley made an impatient noise, almost splashing him with his own whiskey sour as he gesticulated vehemently. "Do you? You need to find somebody hot and give people something *else* to talk about. Otherwise . . ."

"Did it ever occur to you that I don't give a shit?"

Riley stared, and Aiden realized he'd made the statement out loud, drenched in exhausted irritation.

"Still think you should get laid, though," Riley muttered, scoping the crowd like a lion in the savanna.

Aiden sighed, considering a second gin and tonic. It was going to be, as Maggie would say, a long fucking day.

He was facing the bar, still contemplating a refill, when he saw Riley's expression out of the corner of his eye. Riley had been leaning against the bar, but now stood up straight, like he'd been goosed, and his eyes widened with surprise. No—disbelief.

God, he hoped Sheryl wasn't behind him. He started to gesture for the bartender. If it was Sheryl, he was going to need at least a double.

He felt the delicate hand on his shoulder, tapping him, and he turned, feeling warmth and comfort and relief. She was here, she'd gotten there safely, and he'd . . .

Then he got a look at her, and his brain went completely offline.

It was the closest thing he could compare it to. Initially, he didn't know who he was looking at. Rather than her usual tangle of hair, she had an absolute riot of dark curls tumbling down her shoulders. In place of her baggy clothes, she wore a very simple, formfitting black dress. Even some long dangling silver earrings and a silver cuff bracelet. She had sheer black stockings and black heels. Her dark walnut eyes were lined in black and dramatically done up, and her lips pouted full and dusky. She studied him intently.

He didn't know how long he stared at her. He could feel his mouth going dry and his heart beating harder in his chest than it had since he'd run practice in high school football. He felt hot, then cold, then hot again.

*Maggie.*

Riley, on the other hand, was grinning like an idiot. "Hi, sweetheart," he said, in his worst, cheese-tastic, utterly Joey Tribbiani impression. "Here for the wedding?"

She turned to Riley briefly, and her sneer could've frozen Puget Sound. Then she pointedly ignored him, turning back.

"Aiden," she murmured, and she looked embarrassed. And annoyed that she was embarrassed. "Told you I'd make it. Sorry I'm a little later than I wanted."

"Maggie," he breathed, the word hesitant—like he could still be wrong.

She bit her lip, then crossed her arms, a tiny black clutch in her hand. "You look good," she said. "I mean, the suit. Looks good." She glowered. "I'm shutting up now."

"Maggie?" Riley said, goggling. "Wait—Maggie, from your game thing? From Deb's house? The one you left with at your football party?"

She ignored him.

"You really didn't have to come all this way," Aiden said, even though every cell in his body seemed to shout *Thank God she's here, everything is now awesome.* "I could've handled it."

"Nobody's saying you couldn't," Maggie said. "But that doesn't mean you *have* to. This is about what *you* need, okay?"

"But you always help me."

"Aht! None of that," she said, looking into his eyes like she could pin him with her deep-brown gaze alone. Hell, maybe she could. "You seem to think that just listening to you is some herculean feat. Like bringing you some soup and grabbing some groceries is indentured servitude. You helped me figure out what was wrong with my router, and watched a bunch of movies with me, and you're a good friend. That's what friends *do*, Aiden. So let me be a friend, okay?"

He swallowed hard.

No one had cared about him, supported him, like this.

He'd been won over by Jordan, swept along in a tidal wave of enthusiasm, but he'd also felt shut out as Jordan kept his worlds from colliding—and he'd ultimately felt betrayed. As much as they'd had shared interests, ultimately they only had one real thing in common: they'd *both* loved Jordan, above everything else.

While Sheryl had been caring and supportive, she could also be judgmental and critical. He'd gone along to get along. He never cared about things that seemed so critical to Sheryl, like how their apartment looked or what neighborhood they lived in or what they drove. They had butted heads politically from time to time, until they'd agreed to disagree and avoid hot topics like the proverbial third rail.

Maggie challenged him. She poked at him, teased him, joked with him. But she was also one of the few people on earth he felt like he could tell all his secrets to—and the one person he'd ever met that he felt accepted him completely, just as he was, and would fight to make sure he could exist happily that way.

"I'm glad you're here, Boggy," he admitted, hoping her guild name would help him keep a lid on his runaway emotions. His voice still came out as a rough croak.

She smiled. "I am, too, Otter."

"You're *Bogwitch*?" Riley interjected, still unable to move past that particular tidbit of information. "But . . . but . . ."

She arched an imperious, perfectly manicured eyebrow at him. "What?"

"You look amazing!" he said, and it was almost an accusation.

She looked down at herself, then shrugged. "Yeah."

Now Riley really looked stunned, and a little impatient. "This is because you're into Aiden, isn't it?" he deduced. "You decided you'd do that movie thing, where you got a new dress and you'd find someone to give you a makeover? Cinderella, am I right?"

She huffed out a breath, popping a hip and crossing her arms. Despite being shorter than Riley, she looked like an Amazon looking at an ant, considering crushing him under her impressively high heel. "Here's the difference between you and me," she said. "I *always* knew I could look like this."

Riley tilted his head, like a confused Labrador.

"This outfit's over five years old. I didn't go to anyone. The makeup, the jewelry, the hair—I did all that shit myself. No makeovers involved. It's not perfect or anything, but the bottom line is," Maggie finished, "just because I don't put in this kind of work every day doesn't mean I *can't*, for fuck's sake."

Her confidence—her regal dismissal in the face of Riley's disbelief—was glorious.

"But if you could look like that," Riley asked plaintively, "why the hell *wouldn't* you? Why would you . . . ?"

"Why would I look like a hag by choice, you mean?" she finished, amusement warring with a light of anger in her eyes.

Riley nodded.

"If you can't handle me in sweatpants, you don't deserve me in stilettos," she said, each word ringing with finality.

She then pointedly turned her back on Riley, who choked on his inadequate words—Aiden wasn't sure if Riley was pissed or defensive or, worse, trying to protest his innocence. She moved to flank Aiden and slipped her hand in the crook of his arm.

"Shall we find seats?"

Aiden smiled, covering her small hand with his. Her smile back was warm, melting away the frost from her interaction with Riley.

"Let's," Aiden said, and escorted her to the ballroom, arm in arm.

# CHAPTER 30
## I REJECT YOUR REALITY

*So far, so good.*

They'd made it through the ceremony, which really was beautiful. Jason looked so happy he could explode, and Hailey, in her tiered, lace-and-bead-bedecked dress "experience," looked like something out of the proverbial fairy tale. He'd taken Maggie back to the (now crowded) bar as the wedding party had pictures taken and servers broke down the wedding-chair setup and moved in the dance floor, as well as putting finishing touches on the tables where the nearly two hundred guests would be eating dinner.

"Quick question," Maggie had said on tiptoe, her mouth hovering close to his ear because with the chattering crowd, it was difficult to hear yourself think. "Do we need a cover story?"

"What do you mean?" he said back. He felt her shiver, and knew that his beard was probably tickling her neck. "Sorry. I put in beard oil and everything . . ."

"No worries," she rasped. She cleared her throat. "What I mean is, I've just shown up as your date. Did you want me to say I'm your friend? Or did you want me to be your girlfriend—fake relationship?"

He blinked, pulling back enough to study her face and see if she was joking. She looked serious as a tax attorney. He couldn't help himself; he laughed anyway.

"Do you really think you can make that kind of a stretch?" he asked, close to her ear. "I didn't think you were that kind of an actress."

She smirked back, even as he noticed a faint flush creeping along her neck and jawline. With the noise and the crowd, she was snuggled up to his side, and he automatically put his arm around her waist, fitting her to him. It was amazingly comfortable. And a little arousing . . . which compounded when he thought about *her*, how she knew what he was like, and now they were here together. It was like butterflies on meth in his stomach, and he wasn't quite sure what to do with it.

*I am definitely going to examine that more closely. Soon.*

She grinned, shifting her weight from one heel-clad foot to another, in a surprisingly mesmerizing motion. "I pretended to be happily married for years," she said, with an impish grin. "I can pretend to be in love with you for a night."

He grinned—until the import of what she had started with hit him like a slap. "Years?"

She winced. "Sorry. Ignore me," she murmured. "I'm just saying, for one night? For you? I could be Meryl fucking Streep."

He knew that her ex had been an asshole, but that long? He would definitely ask her more about that later. "I guess we can just say we're friends, and you didn't think you could make it, but then something happened where you could?"

"Sure, I can do that."

Someone shoved his way to the bar, and Aiden pulled Maggie more protectively against him. "Sorry," he repeated.

She was looking up at him, her eyes huge somehow, her breathing shallow. Her smile was bright. "S'okay," she assured him.

"I figure we can get through dinner, maybe a few dances, and then we can bolt," he said, close to her jawline. He wrapped his other arm around her, because . . . well, it seemed fitting? Especially given the sardine-packing job the bar was currently. If it hadn't been fifteen degrees Fahrenheit out, they might've gone outside and gotten more of a breather.

"I'm at your disposal," she murmured back in his ear. Now it was his turn to shiver. "You can take as much time as you need."

He grimaced. "Were you planning on staying, or driving back tonight?" He knew she didn't like driving in the dark, and with the cold and the ice, he wasn't sure he was comfortable with her driving back nervous.

"I didn't really think this through—a little bit impulsive," she admitted. "I can get a room, though."

"Um . . . actually," he admitted, "the hotel's booked up. The wedding's pretty big."

She looked at him indulgently, and for a split second, he thought about offering *his* room. The king deluxe room, with the fireplace and claw-foot tub.

And just the one king bed.

"You realize there's a Best Western not fifteen minutes away from here?" she pointed out with a grin.

"Um . . . oh. Right." He felt like a dork. "That makes sense."

She shook her head as Jason's father yelled, "Grub's on! Go find your tables!"

Which led to the second hurdle: dinner. The tables were set for six, stylish rectangles with black-and-silver tablecloths and centerpieces of silver candles and black-and-white chess pieces and bits of quartz and other pretty stones. At their table, he was with his mother again, as well as Davy and Sheryl. Riley rounded out the number. He greeted Aiden with a wink and a bro hug.

"I switched seat numbers," he said in a low voice. "Which put your cousin Robert at a table full of hot girls. But I got your back, bro. *You're welcome*."

Aiden shook his head.

"Who's this?" Davy asked, surveying Maggie with surprise.

"My date was able to show up after all," he began, only to have his mother step in.

"You said you didn't have a date!" Her tone was accusatory.

He shook his head. "I asked Maggie, but she thought she wouldn't be able to make it," he said, his voice tight. He knew his mother recognized Maggie from one time, when Maggie had helped him walk the Pomeranian his mother had been dog-sitting, and they'd dropped off lunch from Annabel's. He shrugged, trailing off, hoping that would be enough. "But it worked out. This is Maggie Le."

He watched as Maggie *transformed*. He was used to her scowl, her sharp smile, her eyes twinkling with amusement. Now, she still had the twinkle, but it was like she'd turned into some slightly shy, polite, *personable* creature.

It was kind of fascinating, and a little creepy, if he was honest.

"It's nice to meet you," she said to the table, with just the right amount of enthusiasm and a smile that would've turned Scrooge into a softie, no ghosts required. "Aiden's told me so much about you."

"Funny," Sheryl said, arching an eyebrow. "He's never mentioned *you*."

*Fuck.*

To her credit, Maggie never missed a beat. "You must be Sheryl," she said. "Which would make you Davy? And it's nice to see you again, Mrs. Bishop."

His mother pursed her lips, nodding in acknowledgment. Davy just looked startled.

"And that guy down there is obviously Riley," Aiden finished.

"We've met," she said, with a wry smile. Riley grinned unrepentantly.

They sat down, and the servers swooped in with appetizers. Grilled-cheese "bites" served with a cup of tomato soup, and flatbread with figs and feta and some kind of balsamic drizzle. Hailey's family had pulled out all the stops for this wedding, it looked like.

"So you weren't able to make it to the rehearsal dinner," his mother said. "What happened to get you here now?"

Aiden's stomach tightened. Nothing like diving right into it.

"I thought I'd have to work," Maggie said. "But I finished and drove down this morning. The roads were better than I expected, and there wasn't much traffic, so I was in luck. I'm just glad I could make it in time."

His mother's eyes narrowed. "I'm surprised he even asked you."

He suppressed a groan. *Jeez, Mom, really?* "I wanted Maggie here. The whole time."

Now the whole table was staring at him—Maggie included.

He cringed at himself.

Maggie shrugged. "We're good friends," she said, acting as if he'd wisely kept his mouth shut. *Which he should have.* "He's my best friend in Fool's Falls, really."

His mother still looked sour—like her candidate, Deb, had somehow gotten knocked out of the running by this usurper. Davy looked puzzled. Riley looked highly entertained. And Sheryl . . . well, Aiden couldn't get a bead on what was going on with her. Her expression was impassive—which, from experience, made him nervous.

"Friends," Davy echoed, turning over the word like it was a Rubik's Cube he couldn't figure out. "How'd you guys meet?"

"We're in an online video game guild," Maggie said, shooting a quick, warm smile at Aiden. Then she dipped the little triangle of grilled cheese in the tomato soup, and her eyelids fluttered for a second. "That's good! Oops, sorry."

He watched as her tongue darted out to catch a stray drop of soup. It slicked her full lower lip, just for a split second.

He found his own mouth going dry. Yeah, he'd definitely need to explore this more, sooner rather than later.

It was *really* weird sitting with Sheryl and Maggie. All it needed was for Jordan to walk in the door, honestly, and he'd hit the hat trick of relationship weirdness.

*Not that you're in a relationship with Maggie.*

But . . . maybe? If she didn't beat the crap out of him, metaphorically speaking, for even asking? He didn't know how it would work, or if she'd be open to it. But for the first time in ages, he really wanted to try and see where it went.

He ate his own appetizers as Maggie and Davy chitchatted about her job and, naturally, her car. He also supplied some embarrassing stories from their childhood, which Maggie giggled at with an almost supernatural charm. She tossed her curls over her shoulder. She ate daintily.

She didn't say "fuck" once.

It was eerie.

As Davy and Riley swapped some stories about people they knew, catching up, and Sheryl and his mother talked about the kids (who were staying with Sheryl's parents, while Bug stayed with his mom), Maggie leaned closer to him.

"Hey. Doing okay?" she said, in a low voice.

"You're not being *you*," he noticed.

"Of course I'm not," she whispered. "Are you kidding? You're trying to make a good impression, or at least blend in. So I'm finally using those manners and socializing skills Nana Birdie kept trying to drill into my skull."

He snickered, shaking his head. "I don't care about any of that. I like who you are."

Her cheeks went pink. "I . . . like who you are too."

Oh, yeah. They were *definitely* talking soon.

He nodded in response. They were already halfway through their risotto and beef tenderloin medallions. "Just need to get through this, eat some cake, listen to some toasts," he whispered to her, close enough to her to smell her perfume, "and maybe two dances? Then we're home free."

She smiled, nodding. "Been a while since I danced," she murmured. "Then I guess I'll find a place to crash for the night."

He'd been facing her—she was sitting on one end of the table, and he sat to her left, while his mother sat to her right. Davy was at the other end, with Sheryl between him and Aiden, and Riley sitting next to his mother. He took her hand under the table, giving it a squeeze.

"Maybe we can talk a little, hang out? Before you hit the Best Western," he added.

She nodded, and he turned back to see the rest of the table staring at them. He realized they had perhaps gotten a little close, physically. He felt his face flush, even as his body was tightening in response.

"I'm going to hit the restroom," he said quickly, then got up. He felt a little concerned about leaving Maggie alone, but she'd been exemplary, more than able to handle anything. She played the perfect combination: just friends, with a suggestion of more. She'd shocked Riley and made an instant friend with Davy, and even his mother seemed to be thawing out, asking Maggie about her cottage pie recipe and talking about Kit's time at Fool's Falls High. Only Sheryl still seemed aloof, which was probably the best he could hope for at this point.

He went about his business, and bumped into Riley on his way back to the table. "Dude!" Riley enthused. "I can*not* believe that your Maggie looks like that. Hell, I didn't even know she had legs!"

Aiden sighed. He liked Riley, he did. But he was quickly getting tired of the whole "dude-bro, let's nail some chicks" attitude that had been progressing from old school to offensive, no matter what his rationales were. "Be nice."

Riley's eyes popped wide. "Are you dating her?"

"I want to. But *don't say anything*," he warned. "I haven't even talked to Maggie about it yet. But I really like her, and I want to give us a shot if she's open to it."

Riley hooted, and Aiden hissed at him, causing him to quiet down. They were close enough to the table that several heads turned to look at him. He felt heat creep up his neck, and for a moment, he wanted to kill Riley. Riley looked immediately apologetic, at least.

"Looks like we missed the cake cutting," he said, quickly taking his seat.

Aiden sat next to Maggie. Their dinner plates had already been cleared away, and they each had cake on small plates. He took a bite. It was good. He went to say as much to Maggie, only to see that she'd eaten only a bit and was systematically cutting the rest into a paste with the edge of her fork.

"You've only known each other for a few months?" Sheryl said to Maggie. There was a *tone* to the question.

He felt his tension ratchet up. He didn't know what Sheryl's problem was, other than the usual, but he wasn't about to let her take potshots at Maggie.

"Yes." Maggie took a sip of water. "Longer online than in real life."

"She took care of me when I broke my foot," he added. "She's been great. She's one of my best friends."

Davy smiled. His mother shrugged.

Sheryl didn't change expression. She took a sip of water, mirroring Maggie's action. Then she leaned over, enunciating clearly and firmly.

"Then he told you he's gay?"

# CHAPTER 31

## HEART BEAT-DOWN

Maggie's jaw dropped as she stared at Sheryl's expression—a facade of boredom, with a sharp bitterness peeking through the cracks. "Excuse me?"

"Didn't you know?" Sheryl's voice was low and unemotional, like she was talking about the Seahawks game or her favorite taco recipe. The fury in her eyes belied her calm tone. "He's *gay*."

Aiden's face went ashen. His mother looked like she'd swallowed a live octopus, her mouth working, her eyes bulging. Davy face-palmed. Riley, on the other hand, went very, very still.

Maggie's back stiffened. She glanced at Aiden, checking his response.

Anger etched his expression. "Dammit, Sheryl," he said, his voice so low it barely carried to the other side of the table.

"Sheryl, this isn't the time . . ." Davy said, but it was too late. She was on a roll.

"And it wasn't just experimentation," Sheryl spat out. "I wouldn't have cared about that. Hell, *I* experimented in college! But no. He was in love with the guy. They had a full-on *relationship*."

"Hold the phone. *You* experimented?" Riley asked. "Like, with another girl? Or . . ."

"For *years*," Sheryl finished, ignoring Riley. Which, understandable. But still.

Davy spun on Aiden. "Wait. I knew about . . . your, um, interests." Like sleeping with men was a hobby. "But who the hell were you dating for years?"

Riley stared hopefully at Sheryl. "*More* than one girl? Maybe?"

"Oh my God," Aiden's mother groaned, covering her face. Maggie felt like she was witnessing a hundred-car collision.

Aiden glowered at Sheryl. "Why are you doing this? Why can't you move past it, and just . . . just let me live my life?"

"Like this is your life." Sheryl sneered. "Isn't it obvious? I don't want to watch you lead some other poor woman on."

Davy looked shell shocked. His mother looked agonized. Riley just looked uncomfortable—and was still staring at Sheryl curiously.

Maggie had been on her best fucking behavior, and after five years of being a hermit who forced herself to be polite only for Kit's sake, that was really saying something. Tonight, she'd been a goddamned *delight*. Still, Sheryl had been grating on her nerves all evening. Maggie had managed to talk about cars and baseball with Davy. She'd even gotten the somewhat dour Mrs. Bishop to warm up. But Sheryl was acting personally affronted, which still made *no* damned sense. Now, this? With Aiden's face looking like a storm cloud . . . this gentle teddy bear of a man, upset and furious?

Yeah, the time for good behavior was *over*. As Ms. Sheryl was about to fucking find out.

"Quick question," Maggie interjected, before Aiden could say anything. "Was Aiden still sleeping with that guy, from college, when you found out? Are you implying he cheated on you?"

Sheryl crossed her arms. "I don't know, do I?" she taunted. "I mean, if I didn't know about that, what else didn't I know? How could I trust him?"

"That is *such* bullshit, and you know it," Aiden growled. "I never cheated on you! And just because I was with a guy in college doesn't mean I didn't love you."

Sheryl's eyes blazed. "You . . . you tricked me!"

Maggie held up a hand, and thankfully, they quieted down. "Few points of clarification," she said, her voice cold and flat as a frozen lake. "First. You *are* aware that bisexuality is a thing, right?" She pitched her voice deliberately, strongly suggesting that Sheryl was too ignorant to know this basic a concept.

At this point, Aiden's mother popped her face out from behind her hands, hissing a fast, panicked "*Shush*."

"Oh, come on." Sheryl rolled her eyes. "Sure, whatever. If you believe that one."

Maggie's temper ratcheted up another notch. "Second point: did you hand over a list of everybody you'd been involved with when you got into your relationship with Aiden . . . including your experiments?"

"What are you talking about?" Sheryl hissed. "I might've experimented, but I wasn't in a *relationship* with any woman!"

"Not what I asked," Maggie growled. "Did you tell him about every man you dated or slept with? Go into exhaustive detail about your previous sexual history?"

"No. Because I was in relationships with *men*!"

Like that explained it. Like that justified it.

Even Trev would've known that this was the moment that even a six-foot MMA fighter should be afraid, because she'd truly left all fucks behind her. It was salt-the-earth mode now. Adrenaline pumped through her veins like rocket fuel. Maggie's voice went liquid-nitrogen cold. "Point three—and *this* is the important one—"

Riley, Sheryl, Davy, Aiden, and Aiden's mother all stared at her, uncertain, expectant because of her emphasis.

"You didn't know." Maggie bit out every word. "You probably thought I had no idea. In fact, you probably *wanted* me not to know."

"What are you talking about?" Sheryl asked, her expression impatient.

Maggie's voice went low and vicious. "*You didn't know* if I knew about Aiden's sexuality. You decided, on your own, to share something you had absolutely *no* right to disclose without his consent. To someone he presumably cares about. Am I right?"

His mother looked confused, as did Riley. Davy looked embarrassed, and kept shooting looks at his wife. Aiden stared at her with a small, stunned smile.

Sheryl looked *smug.*

"You should be thanking me. I'm doing you a favor," she responded. "I would've appreciated the courtesy when I was dating Aiden."

That was it. It was like the click of a mercury switch. All the protectiveness and sadness and sheer rage Maggie had felt building hit a critical point, and there was no turning back.

Maggie reached her hands up, calmly, and took the studs of her dangling silver hoops out of her ears. "Hold these," she said, handing them to Aiden blindly, feeling his big hand reach over hers.

"Why?" Aiden sounded baffled.

"Because the gap just closed."

Maggie moved quickly when she wanted to. Sure, she could've gone around the table to reach Sheryl . . . but really, it wasn't *that* big a table, and going over it would be quicker. If Sheryl was going to be a smug, hurtful bitch, she was going to *learn today* why it was a bad idea to mess with one of Maggie's best friends.

But in a split second, Aiden's big arm snaked around her waist, catching her before she could complete her catapult. She saw the exact moment when Sheryl realized she was about to get messed the fuck up, too, and felt a furious kind of frustration at being stopped.

"Whoa!" Aiden said, tugging her back. Maggie got the sense that other tables were now riveted to the action that was happening there. She didn't care. "It's okay! It's okay."

"It is *not* okay," Maggie growled, her eyes never leaving Sheryl's. Sheryl had gone Elmer's-glue white, and her mouth flopped open like a trout's. "This woman has been bitching since I sat down, making snide remarks, and I took it. But it's been over a decade, and now she's acting like *you* did her wrong, just because you had a relationship she didn't like, years before you got back together with her!"

"He *lied*!" Sheryl wailed.

"He didn't tell you," Maggie shot back. "Seeing the way you're acting, I don't blame him. If anything, maybe you should've disclosed just how queerphobic you were!"

Sheryl's mouth opened and shut, but no words came out. "I'm not phobic," she said. "You can't turn this back on—"

"You are *absolutely* phobic," Maggie snarled. "You've been punishing Aiden for years, over something that's just a part of who he is. He's one of the best people I know. He's committed, and loving, and wonderful, and you're *still* bent. Even after marrying his *brother*? And letting his whole family gossip about what kind of a bastard he is? How the *fuck* do you feel you've got the moral high ground?" A thought struck her, and she glanced at Sheryl's husband. "Jesus, are you even considering how Davy feels, seeing you get all jealous and bitchy about your ex? About not moving on from that relationship, *and* trying to sabotage any new relationship Aiden might have? Punishing him because *you* loved him? *What is wrong with you?*"

Sheryl looked like she was ready to cry.

Maggie bared her teeth. *Good!*

"C'mon, they're playing music, let's dance," Aiden said to her gently. "Davy, can you make sure Mom gets back to her room?"

Davy nodded, his lips pulled into a taut line. His face was displaying a range of emotions in a whirled mess. He was glaring at Maggie, but also at Sheryl, which Sheryl seemed surprised about. Aiden's mother looked angry but also upset, her eyes darting around the room, obviously intent on damage control.

Aiden tugged her out to the dance floor. It was a slowish song, one of her favorites—the sad but strangely romantic "All This Love" by J. P. Cooper. Aiden kept his arms around her, his broad palms resting on her waist. It probably read as romantic, although she suspected it was actually insurance so she didn't go back to the table and beat the shit out of Sheryl.

Which—okay, wise move on his part.

"Easy, easy," he breathed in her ear, his beard tickling the outer shell, the heat of his breath brushing against her jawline. "It's okay."

"It is *not* okay," she protested in a hiss, her breath still ragged, her heart barely calming down. "It is *far from fucking okay*. That bitch outed you."

"I know." He held Maggie tighter.

"Let me go," Maggie muttered. "I just wanna talk."

*With my fists.*

"Yeah, right, killer," he said. "Maybe you calm down a little before you pursue some conversation."

Maggie probably shouldn't have gone that far, all things considered. It was good that Aiden had stopped her from straight-up beating Sheryl. But still—the whole thing was *so* toxic. They'd wanted Aiden at this goddamned wedding with a date. They should've been more careful what they wished for.

She struggled a little, then sighed, forcing herself to take deep breaths. "You're taking this awfully well," she finally noted, a song later, after her pulse settled.

"Nobody's stood up for me the way you do," he said.

She stroked his face. It just felt natural. She wanted to just wrap him in a weighted blanket and . . . protect him from all the small-minded, hurtful people in his life. She wanted to hug him tight and never let him go.

It made her heart hurt and her head ache with confusion, but she was going to lean into it.

"Your mom knew, didn't she?" she said instead. "About Jordan. That's what she was afraid people would talk about. That's why she wanted you to have a date."

He nodded, and she felt him exhale. "My parents were so pissed when we broke up, demanding answers, and I was angry and hurt, and I told them it was because I'd been with a man. Then they didn't talk to me for a few years, until my dad got sick and wanted to reconnect."

Oh, God. Maggie's heart broke for him, and she hugged him, stroking his broad back.

"Davy knew bits and pieces, too—probably because Sheryl said I was gay, and he thought it was true and that I'd been just using her, especially since I didn't date anyone afterward. It turns out he'd always had a thing for Sheryl, and he'd recently been divorced, and when they got together, I felt like . . . I owed it to her. At least she was happy."

Maggie couldn't help it. She let out a strangled noise.

"I know," he said. "I mean . . . now, I know. I didn't have to feel so guilty. I didn't need to become the villain in this narrative. It's just been a hard habit to break, y'know?"

Maggie wrinkled her nose. Aiden had contributed, sure—all communications problems took two to tango. But Sheryl was far from the blameless victim that she tried to portray herself as.

"I hate that you went through all that," Maggie said. "I'm just so sorry. And I'm sorry she acted this way now, here. You deserve so much better."

To her surprise, Aiden was smiling at her, his gray eyes glowing with happiness. "It's fine. No, really," he reassured her, when she went to protest. "Nobody has *ever* gone to bat for me like you have. Anybody else would've blamed me, until they heard more of my side of the story. Maybe even then. But you just . . . well, had my back. Just like you promised."

She shrugged, feeling a little weird. "You're one of my best friends," she pointed out.

"More than that. I have never, ever felt as supported and cared for as you make me feel." He leaned down, kissing her forehead. "Thank you, Maggie."

She felt it, like a combination of heat and chills, dancing over her skin. She involuntarily clenched tighter.

He must've seen it. His eyes were suddenly glowing for a different reason. She swallowed hard against the sudden lump in her throat.

"Maggie," he rasped, leaning forward slowly. "Can I kiss you?"

She knew she should say no. That she really, *really* ought to say no.

But she couldn't.

So she heard herself say "yes," and closed her eyes.

# CHAPTER 32
## MOMENT OF AWESOME

She felt his breath before she felt his lips, warm and inviting, smelling like chocolate and coffee buttercream from the slice of wedding cake they'd eaten before all hell broke loose at the table and she'd come close to committing assault. He tugged her closer to him, even though that was barely possible. His hands were so big and strong and yet comforting as he pulled her tight.

When his mouth covered hers, she felt unmoored as the soft brush of his mustache and beard tickled against her lips.

She sighed and leaned in.

Heat and energy rang through her, tingling through her nerve endings and lighting her up like a scoreboard. She made an involuntary soft sound of surprised pleasure, and kissed back, hard. Gentle be damned. She had wanted this too much and for too long, whether she was conscious of it or not, and now that he'd opened the door, she was running right through that mother. She licked at the seam of his lips, and he opened with a stunned small groan that she felt more than heard over the overloud pop music the DJ was playing.

He was too tall, that was the problem. Even with her heels, which she was managing to wear more easily than she'd thought (it was like riding a bike, apparently), he towered over her, and she was in serious danger of climbing him like a jungle gym.

He pulled away, suddenly, his breathing harsh and ragged. His gray eyes were wide and alight with hunger, and she was *there for it.*

"Maybe we should have that talk now," he croaked. "Probably somewhere without spectators?"

She blinked. Then she looked around to see people staring, some whispering, all with varying expressions of curiosity or shock. The blush that ran over her covered every square inch, it felt like. Even her knees and elbows. At the same time, another, louder part of her wanted to say: *So fucking what? I kissed Aiden Bishop, and it was* glorious. *Ten out of ten, would do again. And will, as soon as he gets his mouth back down here.*

But he was right. Privacy was good . . . and her body was signaling, not so subtly, that more privacy would be best for what it had in mind.

*Knock it off,* she chastised herself. Aiden liked kissing, it seemed—he was physically affectionate. That said, she didn't know *that* much about being demi, but she knew that he might be good with some things and not others. Just because she was turned on like a lighthouse didn't mean that he matched her intensity, and that was *fine.* She wasn't going to put him in a position he was uncomfortable with, not ever.

*And why is that, do you suppose?*

She ignored the voice in her head, instead walking with him to the table and grabbing her purse. His mother had already left, as had Davy and Sheryl, probably off to their respective hotel rooms. A quick scan showed Riley dancing with a pretty woman in a pale-peach dress—bridesmaid, she registered. She picked up her purse and then looked at Aiden with a nod.

He had an arm around her, gently guiding her to the stairs. He was on the upstairs floor. She noticed his hand was shaking slightly as he pulled out his key card and opened the door, then held it open and gestured her inside.

She vaguely took in the room. It was cute, with hardwood floors, and a chair and desk, and what looked like a big bathtub in the bathroom beyond. But what dominated the room—and her attention—was the giant king-size bed with a dark craftsman headboard.

*Perfect to hang on to.*

She startled. What was she thinking? It had been a while since she'd had sex, and honestly, even then it had been pretty vanilla and infrequent.

Maybe it was deprivation?

She turned to find Aiden staring at her, a small, happy, eager smile on his face, his eyes shining.

*Nope. It's definitely the guy.*

The fact that it was Aiden, who had always been consistently kind and understanding to her, who had always listened and supported her . . . that seemed to dial the intensity up to eleven.

She shivered, and it had nothing to do with her having left her coat at the coat check the hotel had set up for the wedding. He was looking at her like she was the most sumptuous dessert he'd ever seen and he hadn't indulged his sweet tooth in too long.

"Is this weird?" she asked, putting her purse down, feeling nervous.

He wrinkled his nose a little, and even *that* was adorable. She was losing her mind.

"Because I'm demi, you mean?"

"Maybe?" She hadn't quite meant that. Well, perhaps she had meant that, now that she thought it through. "I don't want you to be uncomfortable. Ever. And I'll be honest, I really don't know what the boundaries are, and I don't have any expectations, and I know we probably ought to talk . . ."

He stroked her arms softly, his gray eyes shining, and he shook his head. "It's not uncomfortable," he murmured. "Trust me."

She swallowed hard. She could feel her pulse like a bass drum in her throat, almost a tangible bump. She swayed a little closer to him.

"What did you want to talk about?" she murmured, smoothing her hands along his chest, moving them around until she was hugging him. It wasn't like their usual hug-hellos—which she hadn't realized had become "usual" until that moment.

"I like you." He huffed out a laugh, tucking her head under his chin and squeezing her a little. "God, that sounds so high school, doesn't it? I mean, I'm interested in you."

She felt her cheeks heat, and she squirmed. "Really?"

"In a relationship-type way."

Man, the way his voice reverberated through that barrel chest was amazing. Even better when she got to lay her cheek against his sternum, feeling all that bass rumble through her. "Mmm."

"You have an opinion about that?" he teased gently . . . but she could sense an underlying tension. Which, given his romantic history, was completely reasonable. Actually, even without his romantic history, putting yourself out there with someone you were interested in was terrifying.

She was grateful he'd gone first.

"I'm interested in you too," she admitted, then rubbed her face against him, like she could snuggle into his chest and smother all the embarrassment out of herself. "But I didn't want to pressure you. Also, honestly, I didn't quite know what to do about it."

"I have a few ideas," he volunteered dryly, and she laughed into his dress shirt. Then abruptly remembered she was wearing makeup and yanked herself away, checking for residue. "You okay?"

"Forgot I looked like a grown-up for a minute there," she admitted, and he laughed.

"I think you look beautiful," he said, with a little half smile. "Then again—I always thought you were beautiful."

She rolled her eyes. "Yeah, right."

He stroked her cheek before cupping her chin in his large palm. "It's more than looks. You aren't like anybody I've ever met. You're snarky and snarly and sweet and generous. You're helpful and kind and act like a honey badger to anyone who tries to point it out. You aren't as mean as you think, but you're not to be messed with either. You're brave and smart and loyal and funny. You are amazing."

God, why were her eyes starting to prickle with tears? She cleared her throat, taking a quick swipe at them with the back of a hand. "You're amazing," she pointed out. "You're consistently compassionate in situations that would have me shrieking like a banshee. You're patient, and empathetic, and helpful. You care about people, at a time when I swear I'd have left every last fuck behind."

He snickered. Then he pressed slow kisses against her jawline, his hands moving up to weave into the waves that brushed her shoulders. She sighed softly, submitting to his ministrations.

"You're also, um, hot," she whispered.

She gasped when he brushed his beard down her neck, before pressing open-mouthed kisses along her exposed clavicle. She closed her eyes, then let out a little huff.

"Super hot," she muttered, almost to herself. "Are we . . . should we . . ."

"Just spit it out, Boggy," he teased, and it was just what she needed.

"Are we going to have sex?" She laughed, shaking her head at herself. "I haven't had sex with someone else in five years. I haven't *dated* anyone in over twenty. I don't know how to do any of this." She wondered if she looked as lost as she felt.

He let out a breath, tugging her to sit down on the bed and sitting next to her. "First, I'm in no rush," he said, and she chuckled again, a little nervously, wondering if that should've been *her* line. "Second, I haven't dated in over ten years, and I haven't had sex in that same amount of time."

"So we're the blind leading the blind here," she summarized.

"*So*, we don't have to do anything," he countered. "That said, we don't have to follow any kind of rules either. I know I'm attracted to you. Really attracted," he added, his eyes heated. "But there's no pressure."

She swallowed. "We could make out," she ventured. "See how it goes?"

"That sounds good." He grinned in response. Then he leaned down, and covered her mouth with his.

It had been ages since she'd really been kissed. As her marriage had gone on, and gone south, kissing had become something that fell by the wayside . . . a perfunctory peck here and there, something that accompanied a greeting or goodbye. She couldn't believe how turned on just pressing her lips to his got her. She felt like she was getting the spins, but in a good way, feeling overwhelmed and yet dreamily floating in the sensations. She moaned softly as he tugged her tightly to him, tilting his head and feasting on her lips like she was the best dessert he'd ever had. His tongue tangled with hers lazily, and she almost forgot how to breathe.

After some period of time (time had lost meaning by that point), she tugged away to take in a shaky breath, absently realizing that they'd gone from vertically sitting side by side to lying down on the hotel bed and taking turns rolling over each other, hands groping, kissing whatever they could reach. It wasn't quite frantic, but it was close.

It was *amazing*.

She felt her body vibrating like a crystal wineglass that had been rubbed just the right way, all but keening with the sensations zipping through her. "Oh my God," she said as he pressed hot kisses against her throat and held her waist. "I could fucking *devour* you. Are you okay with this?"

His laugh was wrecked and light and tinged with shock, the good kind. She hoped, anyway. "I am so turned on, I would *let* you," he responded. "You snuck up on me, then you fucking blindsided me."

"F-bomb, huh?" She nipped at his earlobe, gratified by his deep growl. "I'm rubbing off on you."

"If only."

She froze, realizing she was on top of him . . . and kind of straddling him. She could feel his hard length pressed against her, and she shivered, pressing back and spreading her legs just a *tiny* bit more.

He slotted right into place, and they both groaned.

"Sex would probably be a bad idea, huh?" she said, half joking . . . half really, truly *not*.

He sounded breathless. "Whatever's clever," he murmured. "It's your call."

She hesitated, then clumsily dismounted, trying to get her bearings. This was madness, wasn't it? It was . . . too soon. Sure, they'd been friends for months, and technically they'd had "friends dates" of sorts, having meals, watching movies. But shouldn't they have a date-date, if they were going to have sex?

Actually, *did* they need to?

"Just putting it out there," he said, and those gray eyes of his glowed with warmth and sincerity. "I'm serious. I want to see what we could be together, as a couple, romantically. I care about you."

She swallowed hard.

She was excited. She was nervous.

She might be making a horrible mistake.

But she trusted him. She cared about him too.

"All right," she said, her voice filled with determination. "Let's maybe . . . get comfortable. And see what happens?"

# CHAPTER 33

## LOVE EPIPHANY

He couldn't help it. He chuckled at her determined expression. "Relax. You're making it sound like we're storming Omaha Beach."

She rolled her eyes and wrinkled her nose at him, even as she was grinning, and amazingly enough, he went even harder. Because it was so *Maggie*. Aiden hadn't been this turned on in longer than he could remember.

That wasn't to say that he hadn't been turned on in the past ten years. He'd jerked off plenty of times, of course. Being demi didn't mean he wasn't interested in coming, apparently. When he was stressed, a fantasy and a Fleshlight tended to help him shut down his brain. But he hadn't actually had sex with another person in a decade . . . and let's face it, he was a different person at fifty than he had been at twenty, or thirty. Or even forty.

Thankfully, the adrenaline rush of finally getting the obstacles out of the way, of admitting he genuinely cared about and *wanted* Maggie, as well the glorious sight of witnessing her defend him like some kind of gleaming Arthurian knight, was doing a lot to push him past any sort of performance anxiety he might have otherwise felt.

"C'mere," he said, pulling her against him and kissing her soundly. They'd get clothes off in a minute. He'd forgotten how awesome kissing could be, honestly. It wasn't the sort of thing you did by yourself, and in weird ways, it could be more intimate than sex. It was so easy to overlook that until you'd gone without.

But soon enough, he could feel his body tightening, growing impatient. His hands were roaming over her back, pulling her taut against him. Then, with a growl of impatience, she nudged him down onto the bed and straddled him again, picking up where she had left off.

This was a *great* escalation. He laughed against her lips, feeling incredible. He wove his fingers into her hair, ruining whatever hairstyle she had and genuinely not caring. She half purred, half growled in return, moving her hips and cradling his increasing hardness. His heart was beating a mile a fucking minute, and he felt like his nerve endings were on fire, and he just wanted to devour her. He tore his mouth away from hers, trailing hot open-mouthed kisses on her jawline, her throat, nipping at her ear and luxuriating in her sharp, sexy gasp as she rolled herself against him, involuntarily and uncontrollably.

"Aiden," she murmured, shivering.

He rolled her under him, and she squeaked, then grinned at him, looking at him through her lashes. "What are you going to do to me?" she said, nudging his erection, her skirt hiking up over her hips, her legs wrapping around his, drawing him closer.

"What do you want me to do to you?" he teased back. "Because I could kiss you for days."

"Just kiss?" she asked breathlessly.

He nudged back, his body notching to hers. "Or more," he teased, even though on some level, he was completely serious. "I'd be happy to do whatever you want. *Whatever* you want," he repeated, staring at her with emphasis.

He saw the heat of a blush creep over her face, and she bit the corner of her lip, and it was so fucking sexy he couldn't stand it.

"Maybe lose some clothes?" she suggested. "Hot as you looked in your suit, I wouldn't mind seeing you out of it. And it *would* be more comfortable."

"True." He quickly rolled off her, his hands clumsy on his buttons. He growled at them, like each piece of plastic was personally trying to cockblock him, and Maggie let out a peal of laughter.

"Oh my God, let me do that before you pop them off." She stood in front of him, her hands moving nimbly as she undid the front, then pushed his shirt off his shoulders. Her heated gaze took in his torso, her hand smoothing over his arms as she pulled his shirt off and tossed it aside.

He reached for her. "Need some help with your dress?"

"It is a bitch to zip," she admitted, turning her back on him. He tugged the offending zipper down, revealing her light-olive skin, flawless and smooth. He teased its surface with his fingertips as he opened the dress and slid it down her arms, then pulled her closer, nuzzling his nose against her spine. She let out a low moan. He tugged her onto the bed between his legs as she dropped the dress, letting it pool on the floor. She was in a black bra and panties and a garter with thigh-high stockings, and he kinda wanted to come just looking at it.

He might not feel attraction often, but when he did . . . well, in his case, he *really fucking did.*

He pressed hot kisses between her shoulder blades, against the side of her neck, until she was writhing against him. She spun around, and he scooted farther backward on the bed as she advanced on him like a lioness stalking prey. She smoothed her hands up his thighs; then her fingertips rested on his fly. She raised her eyebrows, questioning.

He nodded wordlessly, then stretched out. She unzipped his pants and stripped him out of them, tossing them the way of his shirt. There he was, tenting his boxer briefs, while she looked on.

But something had changed. She was rubbing her arms, crossing them in front of her, and now she looked unsure.

"What's wrong?" he said. "We don't have to do anything you don't want."

"Not that," she said, and there was a rueful sound in her voice. "Maybe . . . maybe we shut the lights off?"

"What? Why?" he spluttered. "No way. You look sexy as hell, and I want to see you when you . . ."

She blinked. So did he.

"Oh," she said, a little dazed, then a tiny grin spread into a full-blown smile. "So you're planning on making me . . ."

"Hell yes," he said. "If you're good with it, I absolutely want to 'make you.'" He paused. "We're talking about orgasms, right?"

She threw back her head and laughed. *"Oh my God, Aiden."*

He laughed too. He couldn't remember the last time he'd had this much sheer *fun* having sex. He'd had good sex, hot and overwhelming sex, content and gentle sex. It had been a while, but that didn't discount it. But this was just joyful.

This was what it was, to be with Maggie.

She tackled him, and he let her. She then peppered his face with kisses. Of course, now all they had between them was his thin layer of boxer briefs and her silky panties . . . a fact they both seemed to clue into immediately, as they froze.

"Um. It's suddenly occurring to me," she said, her voice dragging reluctantly, "but do you have a condom?"

He winced. "No. I don't suppose you do?"

She shook her head. "I told you: haven't had sex in five years, and this wasn't even on my radar."

"We don't have to," he said, even as his dick screamed at him. "That is . . . we don't need to do things that require condoms for you to get off."

She smirked. "Or we could call down to the front desk . . . ?"

"I think I'd rather die," Aiden admitted. "With my luck, it'd get charged to the bride and groom somehow, and next thing you know, I'm on a group text with the entire family asking who I hooked up with."

She framed his face with her hands, stretched out on top of him like a blanket. A molten-hot, shivery-sweet, sexy-as-hell blanket. Her smile was like sunshine. "How do these things keep happening to you?" she asked, with fake seriousness.

"I have no idea." He stroked a few wayward waves out of the way, studying her face. "What do you like? What can I do for you?"

She kissed his chest as she hummed in thought. "What are my options?" she asked casually, before running her teeth around his nipple and making him groan.

When his brain got back online, he cleared his throat. "Well, I have fingers . . ."

"Sounds promising."

"And a mouth." To demonstrate, he kissed her hard.

"Mmmmm." The noise felt rich with approval against his lips.

"Also . . . well, it's sort of juvenile, but . . ." He lifted his pelvis, nudging at her entrance and making them both moan. "There's always the old-fashioned grind."

"Oh, God," she said, rubbing against him and arching her back a little. "Yeah. That. Let's do that."

He started to chuckle, but it cut off like a record scratch as she rolled her hips. "You are really good at that," he said, in a broken voice, as his body ramped up and his breathing went raspy.

She didn't acknowledge it with words, just kept rubbing against him. Her nipples were sharp points in the cups of her bra, and her breathing was just as jagged. Her pupils were blown, her skin flushed. She was the sexiest thing he'd ever seen in his life.

She leaned down and kissed him ferociously, and he met her stroke for stroke, his tongue tangling with hers as their bodies rubbed against each other. They were moving, faster and faster, the bed creaking with their exertions.

And suddenly, she let out a rippling cry, her body convulsing on top of him, her thighs clenching his hips so hard he thought they'd leave bruises. Her eyes flew open in surprise, even as she shuddered.

It was *so fucking hot.* His body was reacting before he was aware of it. She squeaked again, throwing herself off him as his body was wracked and he temporarily went whiteout *blind* as the orgasm tore through him, soaking through his briefs.

They lay, side by side, breathing unevenly. Gasping, messy, his arms at his sides, hers crossed over her stomach.

Then she started laughing, soft at first, but gaining in momentum. He turned to look at her, wrung out but happy, taking in her delighted expression. He started laughing, too, until they were both collapsed against each other, her giggling, him chuckling.

"So that happened," he said, peeling off his underwear before it could get uncomfortable. He turned to see her taking in his nakedness, eyes widened. "You keep looking at me like that, I'm gonna call down to the front desk."

If possible, her eyes went even wider. *"Really?"*

"Well . . . I wouldn't be able to use anything right away," he admitted, and she laughed again. "Hey. I'm fifty, not twenty."

"Still," she said, with a mischievous smile. "You'd actually brave the front desk and any possible gossip?"

To prove his point, he went over to the phone, hitting the number. "Front desk, how can I help?"

He took a deep breath, then quickly muttered, "Would it be possible to have a few condoms sent up to room 212?"

There was only the slightest pause before the man answered, "Of course, sir. We'll have them delivered as soon as possible."

"And you can bill them to the room?"

"Don't worry. No charge." Aiden could swear there was a smile in the guy's voice. He hung up.

Aiden turned to see Maggie covering her face with a pillow. "I can't believe you did that!" she said, her voice muffled.

He pulled on a robe. "If you can't believe that," he teased, pulling the pillow from her and kissing her soundly, "just wait till you see what I *do* with them."

# CHAPTER 34

## I HAVE NO SON!

It had been an incredible night . . . more incredible than he could've dreamed. They hadn't used the condoms after all, unfortunately, since room service hadn't come for almost an hour. After a smirking delivery, they'd cleaned up, teasing and talking in robes. Then they'd snuggled naked under the covers, whispering and laughing until they fell into a dazed sleep.

The next morning was chaotic. He'd forgotten to set their alarm, which meant a mad rush.

He'd forgotten how intimate, sweet, and downright *hot* it could be, being with someone he was actually attracted to. Not just the sex, nonpenetrative as it was, but sleeping wrapped around someone you genuinely cared about. This was all so different. He was different. He wasn't a young high school or college student, intrigued and confused and awkward. He wasn't a heartbroken adult, either, looking at getting married and going on the traditional "grown-up" path. He was in the enviable position of being old enough to not feel pressured, not worry about fulfilling anybody's expectations. Even better, he'd been with Maggie, who had her own insecurities, sure, but she'd had no qualms about him, and there had been no pressure. They'd just been *together*, and that had been glorious.

Unfortunately, now he was paying the price for his fantastic night.

After kissing Maggie goodbye, he'd collected his mother from her room, and from that point on, she had been giving him the quintessential cold shoulder. She looked exhausted, but more than that, furious.

He brought her slowly back to the car, carrying the luggage. She was silent. Now, they were nearly to Fool's Falls, and she was *still* silent. It had been over two hours. She'd never been that quiet with him in her life unless she was sleeping.

"I'm guessing you're angry," he said, deciding to simply lance the conversational boil.

"Don't talk to me."

"What happened was *not* my fault," he pointed out. "You told me I needed to bring a date to the wedding—"

"I *meant* Deb!"

"Do you honestly think that Sheryl would've treated Deb differently?" he asked. "This is Sheryl's fault. Maggie and I were being—"

"*Maggie*," his mother said, her voice dripping with venom. "That woman! Causing a scene!"

"Maggie caused a scene?" he echoed. "Did you not remember Sheryl saying that I'm gay—incorrectly, I might add, not that she seems to understand that? Or dragging up all that stuff from the past? How is any of that Maggie's fault?"

"Sheryl shouldn't have said anything either," his mother conceded, after a long pause. "But that *Maggie* was just throwing gasoline on a fire. And it's not like Sheryl was lying, was it?"

"For fuck's . . ." He gripped the steering wheel, forcing himself to count to ten. "My point is, Sheryl's the one with the problem. I could've brought the most Instagram-perfect woman on the face of the earth, and Sheryl would've *still* given me shit and tried to ruin it!"

"You didn't cuss half this much before you met *Maggie*." He glanced over to see his mother crossing her arms, scowling so hard it had to hurt her face. "Deb wouldn't have caused this kind of trouble.

Sheryl would've *understood* her. They're . . . you know, the same kind of woman!"

Now his eyes narrowed. "Mom," he asked carefully. "Is this because Maggie's Asian?"

"What! No!" Her voice was shrill. Defensive. "I'm not *racist*!"

"Good." His voice, in comparison, was cold and laced with doubt.

"But Deb goes to church, like Sheryl does. Deb has the same, you know, *values* as Sheryl. Deb knew Sheryl in school, was just a year behind, you know! They would have been *friendly*!"

"That would've made Sheryl even angrier. She'd wonder why I could be with Deb, and not make it work with her. She'd definitely have spilled the beans on my past anyway . . . which, incidentally, I'm realizing I'm sick of hiding."

"Don't," his mother breathed. "Don't you *dare*."

"Don't what, Mom?" he said. "Don't tell people I'm bi? Don't let anyone know I was in a relationship with a man in college? For God's sake, Mom, I'm fifty years old and I'm still in the closet!"

"Deb is never going to date you if she finds out!" She sounded reedy, a bit desperate. "Don't you understand? *No* one will! She'll tell everyone. The church group, her book club . . . oh, God, she knows *everyone* . . ."

"I *don't fucking want to date Deb*!" he roared. "I want to be with Maggie!"

The car was quiet for a second, except for the low hum of the radio, playing some old country songs . . . Patsy Cline, maybe. It sounded hollow and twangy and sad.

"You're supposedly *gay*," his mother finally said. "You said Maggie was a friend of yours, doing you a favor. She knows that you were with a man, and somehow . . . she's *fine* with this? And now I'm supposed to believe that you're 'dating' this woman?"

"We didn't start officially until last night," he admitted. *At least, I hope that's where we're going.* "She was going to just help me, true. But we both realized we can have something more."

"I don't understand this." His mother crossed her arms. "I don't like her."

"You," he said, through gritted teeth, "don't need to. *I* like her."

Another long silence.

"This isn't up for discussion," he added. "My relationship with Maggie isn't something I need to justify or debate."

"Relationship," she scoffed.

He huffed out a long sigh. "The wedding's over, Ma. And I'm sorry that it didn't go the way you wanted, but let's face it: it was *never* going to go the way you wanted. If I'm in the same room with Sheryl, it's going to be a nuclear train wreck. She hates me, and she's always going to hate me."

"Whose fault is that?" his mother yelled.

"*Hers!*" Aiden snapped back. "Because being bi is not a fucking *crime*!"

"Watch your mouth!" He wasn't sure what she was more pissed at—the f-bomb or the term "bi." "You broke Sheryl's heart. I was so grateful that she finally found happiness with Davy after what you did."

"I didn't do . . . !"

Aiden gritted his teeth. This was futile. And maddening. And heartbreaking. He could keep going, but what was the point?

The worst part was, Maggie was right. He'd bought into Sheryl and his mother's argument for years, like it had been his fault for "disappointing" Sheryl . . . *by being who he was*. By finally telling her the truth.

"It's over," he reiterated.

Her anger was a tangible thing, emanating from her like microwaves. He sighed.

"Are you going to Davy's for Christmas?" He, himself, wasn't welcome, but he knew his mother would like to see her grandchildren.

She made a little noise that he took as assent.

"I'll have him pick you up," he said slowly, his brain working out logistics. "When he brings you back . . . the three of us will discuss the legal stuff: power of attorney, advanced directives. And we'll talk about your driving."

"I'm not going to discuss a goddamned thing with you."

He shot a shocked glance at her . . . although really, how surprised should he have been? "We had a deal," he reminded her. "I bring a date to the wedding, and you agree to talk about this stuff. I held up my end of the bargain."

"You didn't bring a date. You dragged a woman you barely know and caused a scandal. I don't owe you anything!" She let out a long, frustrated exhalation. "If you had just kept your mouth shut and settled down with Deb, this would be different. I'd give up *driving*, even! Do whatever goddamned paperwork you wanted. But you just *couldn't do that*!"

*"Settled down?"* He looked over at her, appalled. "You have got to be kidding. You can't . . . you think this is something I'd bargain with? That I'd just keep lying about who I am, and, what, *marry* someone I don't love, so you'll do the right thing? Are you insane?"

"You just have to keep acting so . . ." She trailed off, as if she was too angry to find the word. "I am finished. Discussion is over."

"Mom . . . ," Aiden growled in warning. "You gave me your word!"

"I don't care!"

He should have known. He should have *known*.

She'd never had any intention of addressing his concerns—the driving, the legal paperwork. None of it. This was just one more way to manipulate him, one more way to get what she wanted. Now that it had blown up in her face, she was going to punish him for it.

"I know you're pissed at me," he said, gritting his teeth, "and I'm . . . sorry. But this is *important.*"

"I don't care," she repeated. "In fact, I don't want to talk to you. I don't want to *see* you. You want to be this . . . whatever the hell you are? Want to boss me around? Then you don't have to be in this family!"

The words hit him like an axe. "What?"

"You heard me."

In previous years, this would have crushed him. He'd be emotionally devastated. He'd twist himself in knots, try to find some way to patch the breach.

Not today.

"Even Dad was okay with my past," he said. "By the end. He told me he was." It might've been the closest they'd ever been.

"He was dying," she said coldly. "He made his choices. And he was on all those medications. Who knows what he was thinking?"

"Jesus, Mom."

They'd gotten to her house. He helped her get out, or at least tried to, until she waved him off. He brought her luggage into the house.

"I mean it," she said, her eyes snapping like a log fire. "I don't want to hear from you until you're ready to . . . to snap out of whatever the hell's gotten into you. I'm certainly not going to give up my driving because *you* think it's necessary, and I'm not going to be the brunt of gossip of Fool's Falls because you're . . . you're . . ." She spluttered, gesturing at him. "Whatever *this* is."

Aiden swallowed hard. "Fine."

He turned, getting back into his car. He felt . . . he wasn't sure how he was feeling. Strange. Angry, without question, but it was different. It wasn't laced with the same hopeless desperation that he often felt, dealing with his family.

He didn't want to go back to his empty house. Instead, he found himself driving to the Upper Falls, to Maggie's. Her car was in the driveway, thankfully. He knocked on the door.

She opened it, looking like the usual Maggie: no makeup, her hair a tangled, wavy, wild mess. She was wearing the green sweatshirt he'd loaned her that morning, despite the fact that she'd obviously showered, and a pair of oatmeal-colored sweatpants, her feet in thick heather-gray wool socks. Her eyes widened as she took him in.

"Aiden?" She sounded surprised, and he noticed her cheeks went pink before she studied his face. "You all right? What's going on?"

He swallowed. "I'm sorry. I should've called. Just . . ." He took a deep breath. "I wanted to see you."

"C'mon in," she said, then opened her arms. He walked into them and held her tight. "It's okay," she soothed.

It wasn't okay . . . not really.

But here, in Maggie's arms?

It was better, and that was a pretty damned good thing.

# CHAPTER 35

## TRUE LOVE IS A KINK

Maggie looked at Aiden's face. He was still wearing the clothes he'd hastily thrown on that morning, which suggested he hadn't stopped at home. At least she'd changed . . . well, mostly. She was still wearing the sweatshirt he'd loaned her, the one that she'd thrown over her dress when she'd shame-walked out of the hotel and fled to her car.

Thankfully, she hadn't run into his family or Riley. After the brouhaha from the previous night, she'd calmed down, but she did not want to think what she'd be capable of if they tried to give her shit for being with Aiden. Worse, if they'd tried to give *Aiden* shit for being with *her*.

"What happened?" she pressed, leading him to the couch and nudging him to sit down before sitting next to him.

He let out a bitter chuckle, running his hands through his hair, making it stick up almost comically. "Guess I'm disowned," he said. "Had it out with my mom on the car ride home."

Maggie felt a stab of guilt, and let out a long breath, looking away. "I'm sorry. That's probably my fault."

"It wasn't," he said staunchly, nudging her chin so she was facing him. "I mean, yeah, she's blaming you, and me. But it's *not our fault*. I'm tired of feeling like the bad guy for just being myself."

"Yeah?" She searched his face for any trace of remorse. Instead, she found anger, and . . .

Was that relief?

"You really are okay?" she double-checked.

He nodded, stroking her cheek. Which was *awesome*. The pads of his fingers were rough and broad and warm, and she was there for it, smiling before she realized what she was doing. He smiled in return. She got the feeling there would be emotional fallout for him, but for now, she wasn't going to prod. She'd just . . . be there for him.

That felt amazing.

"You're not the bad guy," she emphasized, hugging him tight for a long minute. "You didn't do anything wrong. I'm glad that you're finally getting that. Don't fall into beating yourself up again, got it? Or I'm going to go full Bogwitch and kick your ass. And theirs. It'll be a bloodbath."

He nuzzled his nose along her throat, making her pulse jump like water on a ripping-hot skillet. "You," he murmured, adding some kisses and stroking her arms, "are one of my favorite people on earth. You know that?"

"You've got some pretty nice qualities yourself," she said. Or tried to say. Her breathing was awfully uneven for this. Every gasp she took in brought a delicious whiff of luxury-hotel shampoo and soap and that yummy smell that was just Aiden. Comfort, now shot through with a scent of pure *heat* that was making her body throb.

"Mmm." He breathed against her skin, heat trailing wherever his mouth went.

Her body was going bananas. It occurred to her that after dry humping him like a teenager last night, she'd been more than happy to cuddle up with him and conk out, rather than stay up and have some kind of wild sex marathon. Partially because, after the long drive and the emotional upheaval with the family drama, with one of the most powerful orgasms she'd had in her life on top of it, she was pretty fucking wiped out. But there was also the realization that, despite really enjoying said orgasm, she was running pretty damned impulsively with this. They had been friends for months, true, and she genuinely cared about him—more than she had realized she would at this point. Still, jumping into sex on the heels of all that adrenaline was, quite possibly, a foolish move.

Of course, now they'd had a surprisingly good night's sleep. He'd had a rough morning with family from the sounds of it, but he was here, and he seemed . . . happy?

She loved when he was happy.

She loved him.

He sucked a little harder on her neck, making her eyes roll back in her head.

*Okay, not going to think about that right now.* Because she didn't have the bandwidth to get a grip on what was happening to her emotionally *and* what was happening to her physically.

"You . . . don't happen to . . . have those . . . hotel condoms?" she said, around choppy, rasping inhalations.

His responding deep, rumbly laughter did *things* to her, dammit. Like she was being painted with fire.

"I might've stuffed one in my pocket before I came in here," he admitted. "Y'know. Be prepared."

"Boy Scout?" she said, with a giggle that was wildly disproportionate. It was like she was so filled with effervescent *need*, it was going to bubble out somehow.

"You know it."

"Awesome," she said absently, doing some kissing of her own before tugging at his shirt. "Semper fi, and all that."

His laughs got louder. "That's the marines."

"Oh, fuck it," she said, then wriggled out of his grasp, turning and grabbing his hand. "C'mon. It's no hotel bed, and it's the middle of the damned day, but this is *happening*."

"Take me, you wild woman," he joked, but still moved pretty damned quickly, following her and then scooping her up as they got to the end of the hall. She yelped, then joined his laughter when he dropped her on her unmade bed.

She watched in wonder as he tugged his shirt off, then pulled off his pants, losing the boxer briefs as well. In the late-morning sunlight creeping through her gauzy undershades, she could see every detail of his body. He was solid, chunky, with broad shoulders. His pale chest was firm and substantial, covered in auburn hair that led down to . . .

She gulped audibly.

"That didn't seem as intimidating in underwear," she admitted.

He let out a surprised chuckle. "You know," he said, stretching out on her bed and looking at her with bright gray eyes, "I've never had as much fun with anybody as I have with you."

That warmed her up.

"Your turn, by the way," he said, nodding at her body with encouragement.

She reached for the hem of her sweatshirt—*his* sweatshirt, technically—when it suddenly occurred to her that she wasn't going to have sexy matching black undies and garter-suspended stockings to help her seem alluring. She'd scrubbed off all makeup. Sure, they had wrapped around each other naked the previous night, but she'd dived into bed like a cormorant while he was in the bathroom, and he'd climbed under the covers and shut off the light soon after.

She felt a teeny bit less sexy than she had a second ago.

"Hey," he said, reaching for her. "What's up?"

"Was wondering if I could draw the blackout curtains?"

He raised an eyebrow, leaning on his elbow. "Thought we were past this?" He reached for her, and when she hesitated, he made grabby hands, which made her giggle. Slowly, she stretched out next to him.

He engulfed her, kissing the giggles from her lips like a butterfly sipping from a flower, tickling her with his beard . . . which of course made her giggle more, as she wrapped her arms around his neck.

"I think you're sexy, and gorgeous, and amazing," he murmured, nibbling at her throat. "If you're going to be self-conscious, I can't stop you. But you have to know . . . I don't feel this way about just anybody. Not to, y'know, make it weird or anything."

She felt her body unwind and start to relax. "Sorry," she said, biting her lip. "I gained some weight after having Kit, and . . . well, things stretch and sag and, um, readjust."

"I used to have a different body too. A football body," he said, wiggling his eyebrows. "Are you disappointed that I look like this now?"

She stroked her hands over him, feeling a shiver go through her, matching the small shudder he gave beneath her palms. "Not even a little."

"Again," he reassured her, "you don't have to do—"

"Oh, shush." She knew, or should've known, that Aiden wasn't like Trev. He wasn't going to point out that she'd gained some weight, or warn that not wearing a bra around the house would make her sag more, or recoil from stretch marks. The way Aiden was touching her now was almost reverent.

Taking a deep breath, she shucked off the sweatshirt, and wiggled out of her leggings and undies and socks. Then she looked at him, almost defiantly.

His smile was tender and encouraging, and his gaze was fucking *hot.* He stroked his hands over her, in broad daylight, caressing her and taking note of every time she trembled or let out an inadvertent moan. Before long, she felt feverish and shivery and so turned on her toes curled.

She wasn't going to say it was like riding a bike, although that would be a funny analogy. It had been a long time since she'd had full penetrative sex with anyone, and considering how enthusiastically she'd responded to him the last time they'd been together, even if they hadn't "gone all the way," she was amazed at how easily they seemed to just *click*. He tasted like cinnamon Altoids and smelled like a rainy morning and gave off heat like a furnace, and she wanted to just rub herself all over him, like a cat in catnip. So she did. She wanted to bathe in the moment, and at the same time, let it rush over her in a shock.

They got close, then closer, then closer still. By the time he was inside her, she could no longer hold on to a thought for more than a second, her body moving on pure instinct, her heart so impossibly full that she thought her chest would burst.

"You all right?" he asked breathlessly, pausing when she froze.

"More than," she said, then kissed him as he started moving again, grateful for his thoughtfulness even as she felt like she was melting. They moved together, like dancing, until she wrapped her legs around his waist and clutched him tight and shook with her release. He lost tempo, burying himself in her with uneven thrusts until he shuddered and collapsed, propping himself on his arms so he didn't squash her as his forehead rested against hers. Their harsh, jagged breaths mingled as they looked at each other face to face.

Then she smiled, and he smiled, pressing a soft kiss to her lips.

"Hi," he said.

She snickered. "Hi." Then nuzzled his nose with hers.

He rolled off her, getting up and going to the bathroom, presumably taking care of the condom. She smiled when he came back, all but bouncing her off the bed when he jumped onto it, causing her to dissolve in laughter and grab him to stay on the bed.

"Wanna watch a movie?" he asked, grinning like a kid.

She laughed even more, then ran her fingers through his hair. "Yeah. But I get to pick."

"Then, I was thinking . . . maybe I could make you lunch." His gray eyes were so gorgeous, and his smile made her feel like she'd swallowed the sun.

"Mmmm." She kissed him. Because she *could.* And it felt amazing.

"And then," he said, cuddling her to his chest, "maybe . . . if you're up for it . . ."

"We could do that again?" She buried her face in the juncture of his neck and shoulders as he chuckled. "Absolutely yes."

# CHAPTER 36

## AND I MUST SCREAM

Aiden woke the next morning feeling disoriented. It was dark, but the clock—a digital crimson readout he didn't recognize—said it was eight, and even in December the sun ought to be up. He didn't have blackout curtains at the house he rented. Usually, it didn't even matter, because he'd be up by seven or so naturally.

So why was he up late, and where the . . .

He took a deep breath, and inhaled Maggie's coconut-tinged scent. He rolled closer to her, encountering a lump in the center of the bed. It was a comfortable mattress, but old . . . and that lump had been formed by years of two people sharing but not cuddling. It was the demilitarized zone of marriage. He didn't fit in the divot the previous occupant had left, he realized. Just like he realized that Maggie did not wander from her side either. Rather, she was cocooned in a perfect Maggie-shaped indentation. He could hear her breath whooshing softly. Otherwise she was perfectly still.

*Maybe we can buy a new bed.* He grinned, thinking about breaking it in. And cuddling with her afterward.

He stretched out. Even if they hadn't said so explicitly, he was starting a relationship with Maggie, and that was mind blowing. He was still upset about everything that had happened with his mother, and with

Davy and Sheryl at the wedding, but at long last it seemed *over*. Even if they all hated him, he'd tried his best, and he didn't have to prove himself or try to assuage their feelings anymore. He was himself, completely.

He didn't have Maggie to thank for that, per se. But her unflagging support, her grumpy, nearly violent brand of friendship, had meant the world, and he appreciated it. And now, this . . . whatever fledgling thing was happening between them . . .

That meant a lot too. That meant everything.

He got up, got cleaned up a bit. Maggie was still sleeping like a rock. She'd been so good about cooking for him, about *doing* things for him, when he was hurt. He was happy to help. And it wasn't quid pro quo, balancing the favor scales. He wanted to help, to do things that would make her life easier and make her feel better.

He wanted to do that for a good long time, if at all possible.

He went out, down the hallway from the bedroom, as quietly as possible. Sunlight poured in through the windows. The house was clean, if a little disheveled. There was a blanket and pillow on the couch where they'd watched the black-and-white version of *The Scarlet Pimpernel* and where they'd made out before taking it back to the bedroom. There was a plushy sea turtle on the love seat, and mismatched throw rugs that still managed to make the place look homey. He took the time to look at the photos on the walls. They were mostly of Kit, her son, he had to assume. A gap-toothed elementary school photo . . . a kid with a buzz cut, holding up a fish proudly . . . him towering over her in a cap and gown, tasseled cords hanging loosely over his shoulders. She was wearing the black dress, he noticed. Her special-occasion dress.

It made him smile.

Her kitchen was a little messy, so he took the time to do dishes, especially when he discovered (with some horror) that she didn't have a dishwasher. Then he checked out what she'd stocked her pantry with and decided to make pancakes. He liked cooking when it wasn't just him, and he was looking forward to learning more challenging recipes since it seemed like Maggie was a foodie at heart. Fortunately, he'd memorized his grandmother's pancake recipe because it was one of his favorites. He was picky about pancakes.

He hoped Maggie liked them too.

He puttered around, cooking, until he had a tall stack on a plate in the oven, the heat of the oven's light keeping them warm. It was now nearly nine, and he wondered if he should wake her. He had no idea what her schedule was like. Fortunately, he heard her making noises and saw the ribbon of light under the bedroom door.

"Hope you like pancakes," he called out, with a grin.

"Let me shower really quickly first," she called back, muffled through the door. "Then I'll be right out. There's maple syrup in the fridge. And some Nutella."

"Got it." He cleared off the dining room table, set plates and cutlery, then got the syrup and spread.

He was apparently so engrossed in it that he hadn't noticed the crunch of wheels on the gravel driveway. He only registered the thump of heavy footsteps on the deck, his mind trying to figure out who might be there on a Monday morning, just before there was the sound of a key jiggling in a lock. The front door swung open. "Mom? You here? Whose car is . . ."

A solid-looking teenager with a shock of black hair and hints of a beard, wearing a gray hooded sweatshirt with a single pocket and a large purple *W* emblazoned on the front, under a navy down jacket. He looked just like the photos Aiden had been looking through. The only difference was he looked a little older, a little sturdier, and, of course, startled, his eyes going wide.

Aiden imagined he must've looked just as startled.

He was so intent on taking Kit in that he'd almost overlooked the man stepping in behind Kit. He looked about Aiden's age, with the kind of whipcord leanness that you saw in some of the older guys around the Falls . . . the leathery skin, the graying stubble. The guy had a baseball cap instead of a cowboy hat, but in his jeans, heavy work boots, and thick winter coat, the guy gave off mountain man vibes.

"Hi," Aiden said.

Kit blinked at him. "Um . . . hi?"

The bedroom door swept open, and Maggie all but sprinted out, sliding to a stop in her thick wool socks. "Kit!" She threw her arms around him, then pulled back. "I thought . . . you're not supposed to be here till Wednesday. I was going to pick you up at the airport!"

"I wanted to surprise you," he said, arching an eyebrow. "So . . . uh, surprise?"

She released him. "You're probably wondering . . ."

Then her words cut off as she, too, took in the guy behind Kit. Her eyes went so wide, it was like looking at a chibi version of her, distorted and overexaggerated. "Trev?"

*I knew it was going to be her ex-husband.* Because why wouldn't it? He quelled inappropriate laughter. Because all this week needed, really, was getting cut out of his family, finding a woman he wanted to have a future with, and then meeting her son and her son's dickhead father at the same time.

*Wonderful.*

"Pancakes?" he offered, deciding to go the "everything's cool" route and be polite. "I made a bunch, but I can mix up more batter pretty quick if you're hungry."

"We had breakfast," Kit said, turning his full attention on Aiden. "Who are you?"

Aiden stepped over, holding his hand out. "Aiden Bishop."

*"Aiden."* Kit shook his hand, suppressing a grin and shooting an assessing look at Maggie. "The healer?"

"Um . . . yes?" Aiden tried for a grin, even though this felt really uncomfortable. "In our *Blood Saga* guild."

"And you're here, making pancakes." Trev's voice wasn't loud, but it wasn't low either, and it certainly wasn't cheerful.

Aiden tried to parse what the guy was trying to say. He didn't sound thrilled. He couldn't possibly be jealous, could he? From everything Maggie had told him, the man had been no happier in the marriage than she'd been. Was it simply a matter of a favorite toy—if he couldn't have her, nobody else should? Or had he never moved on? She had said she'd kicked him out.

In the short time his brain processed the scene, Maggie's dark eyes gleamed and her chin jutted forward. "What are you doing here, Trev?"

"I picked up Kit at the airport." Trev shrugged. "He told me he was coming in early, and I told him I was planning on being in town for the week. His flight was really early, so we grabbed a sunrise breakfast, and then I drove him back."

The look of betrayal on Maggie's face was heartbreaking. She looked at Kit. "You told him? When did you talk to him?"

"We've been talking for a month or two," Kit admitted quickly. "I meant to— "

"I wanted to talk to him again," Trev cut in. "He's a grown man now, Mags. He doesn't need your permission to talk to me."

"You're making it sound like I *stopped* you from talking to him." Maggie's hackles were raised. "You could've called any time in the past five fucking years. Don't make me the villain in this little redemption story."

Trev sighed. "I didn't mean to . . . damn it, Maggie. I just wanted to get to know my son. Is that so much of a problem?"

Kit, Aiden noticed, looked hideously uncomfortable. "It's okay, Mom," Kit said. "I mean, I hung up on him the first few times he called, and then I yelled at him. But it's been better."

Maggie sent a look over to Aiden, one filled with pain, confusion, loss. He was at her side before he could consciously think about it, putting an arm around her shoulders and giving her a comforting squeeze.

"Why didn't you tell me?" she whispered.

Kit shrugged. "It's a long story —"

"Maybe it's better if we discuss this, just family," Trev interrupted, giving Aiden the smallest nod.

Aiden squeezed Maggie a little harder, looking down at her shell-shocked face. "You want me to stay?" he asked.

She swallowed hard.

Of course, that would be when his phone rang. He grabbed it to silence it, then saw it was Davy. Goddamn it. He ignored it.

When he looked back at Maggie, it was like she'd turned into a statue. Her eyes were dry, and her face was as blank as a TV that had been shut off.

"It's fine. I've got this," she said. "You probably want to find out what that is, anyway."

Dammit. Even if she hadn't figured out it was Davy, she knew he was constantly embroiled in family dramas. It would be reasonable for her to assume that he'd be off dealing with another one. Still, he didn't want to abandon her in the face of her own drama.

"Whatever. It can wait." He turned to her, unwittingly rubbing her arms. "I know you're upset—"

"I'm *fine*." Too sharp. She cleared her throat, as if she'd noticed her own overreaction.

"You have always been there for me," he said, disregarding their curious audience. "I want to be here for you now. Please. Let me."

"I don't need your help. I've got this." Her expression never changed. "Just *go*."

He swallowed. He knew what was happening. To accept his help was to admit she *needed* help. She was good at being a helper, a support, even with her token grumpiness. She was used to doing things for others.

She didn't know what it meant for someone to do something for her. The man currently standing in her living room had been her enemy for too long, making her doubt herself, making her protect herself. He could almost see her throwing on armor as quickly as possible, turning prickly.

Getting ready for battle.

"Please," she added, and he could see how the word cost her.

He wanted to kiss her, but he figured it wouldn't be welcome. He stroked her shoulder, and she glared at him.

He huffed out a breath, then nodded. "I'll call later," he said, even as he suspected she'd blow it off. "And if you need anything, I will be here as soon as I can. All right?"

"I know." She might as well have been carved out of stone.

*This* was Bogwitch.

This didn't feel good at all.

But he couldn't just ignore what she asked for, either, no matter how much he didn't think it was what she needed. He sighed. Then he pulled on his shoes and coat.

"Nice to meet you," he said with a nod, to Kit and Kit only. "Maggie . . ."

*I love you.*

Yeah, it might be kind of sudden, but it felt like all their months of friendship, and what they were doing now . . . he knew, in his gut. He loved this fierce, grumpy, adorable, wonderful woman.

But he couldn't say it, so he just looked at her, hoping she'd understand.

She nodded, then closed the door behind him.

He went out to his car, pulling his phone out and blindly dialing Davy. "What?" he snapped.

"I'm headed to the Falls in a few minutes," Davy said. "Just needed to drop the kids off with Sheryl's parents before we head to Mom's."

"Fuck's sake, *why*?"

"Mom called me this morning, all pissed off." Davy sounded at the end of his rope. "She said she's cutting you out of the will, and if I don't get her that new car *today*, she's cutting me out too. What the hell happened between you two? What did you *do*?"

Aiden gritted his teeth. He was *so* sick of this shit.

"Why are you bringing Sheryl?" Aiden said, then felt a chill in the pit of his stomach. "You're not . . . shit. Are you *actually* bringing her a new car?"

A split second's hesitation. "Well . . . at least it's safe. It's automatic. She shouldn't have a manual, and something a little . . ."

It was the straw that broke the camel's back.

"All right. Good luck with that."

Davy seemed taken aback. "Are you going to even talk to her?"

"No, I'm not."

"Dude!" Davy sounded pained. "I can't handle this all by myself! Just meet me at Mom's house, okay?"

Aiden gritted his teeth. "I will," he said. "But you're not going to like it when I do."

"Sure, sure." The relief was heavy in his voice. "I'll text you when I get there."

He hung up. Aiden rolled his shoulders, trying to get rid of the tension building there. He wasn't sure what was going to happen, but he knew one thing.

He was going to use every last zero-fucks-given lesson he'd learned from Bogwitch. It was long past time.

# CHAPTER 37

## DESPAIR EVENT HORIZON

Maggie wasn't quite sure how she felt. Hollow, for a start. Blindsided. Not even angry—well, anger was there, beneath the surface, but there was more of a sense of loss. All of it mixed with the previous day, when she'd slept with Aiden, and then made a pretense of watching something as they made out on the couch, and they'd had spicy ramen for lunch and then had sex again . . . She had been hopeful, and happy. She'd felt lighter than a dandelion seed, ready to almost float away. And as much as she loved Kit, it was always mixed with that ever-present *stress*, to protect and provide and most of all, to not screw up. Being with Aiden had been like flying—just joy, no expectations.

And . . . they appeared to be starting a relationship. Which meant even more of that gorgeous, wonderful feeling.

Only now, she had Kit *and* Trev, standing there, staring at her . . . Kit with bewilderment, Trev with a sneering judgment. Worse, Kit had *brought Trev here*, he'd been in contact with him for *months*, and he hadn't told her. She felt the biggest adrenaline drop of her life, hit with a feeling of utter, miserable exhaustion.

"Maybe you should go," Kit said to Trev, looking nervous. Kit had always been able to pick up on the tiniest emotions like a seismograph.

Reading the room was a survival skill he'd developed at a young age, one she was ashamed to have contributed to.

"Why did you come inside in the first place?" she asked Trev, hating how strained her voice sounded. She pushed harder, making herself colder.

"Kit was suspicious that there was a strange car by the carport," Trev replied, "so I wanted to check it out. Make sure you were all right." When she stared at him flatly, he huffed out a breath. "We might be divorced, but it doesn't mean I'd want you hurt. I still care."

It was so fucking textbook Trev. He had no problem with the idea of bursting in and wrestling with an armed intruder. That was brave, and tough, and dramatic.

Things like call his son over the past five years? That sort of thing didn't count. He'd take a bullet. He wouldn't pick up the fucking phone.

*And Kit just waltzed him in here.*

That was what hurt so much. She swallowed hard, ignoring it.

"I'm fine," she said. "You can go now."

"Who was that guy, anyway?" Trev asked. "Kit didn't say that you were dating again."

"Kit didn't say you two were talking," she said. "Guess we're both out of the fucking loop."

So much for staying cold.

Kit looked at her nervously. "Mom . . ."

"God damn it, Maggie, I'm not here to cause trouble," Trev said, an impatient edge to his voice. "I really don't care if you're seeing someone. It's been five years. I'm surprised you haven't before this, honestly. I did."

She wasn't surprised he didn't care, but he had to stick that little jab in anyway. She gritted her teeth. "What do you want, then?"

"I wanted to get to know my son better."

She looked at Kit, who nodded slowly.

"So you've been talking for . . . a few months," she said, trying to make it make sense.

"I know I screwed up, and it'd been on my mind for a while," Trev said. "I still had Kit's number. I figured he'd gone off to college, and I thought it wouldn't hurt to try reaching out."

She wanted to laugh. Or scream. Maybe both.

She ignored Trev, still staring at Kit. "And you decided not to tell me because . . . ?"

"I knew you'd be upset," Kit said, shifting his weight from one foot to the other, looking in that second like the six-year-old she remembered, when he'd done something bad but didn't want to admit it. Not that wanting to get to know his father was bad. She'd always hoped that Trev would finally show interest in their child, the one that he'd always judged. The one that he'd been sure she'd ruin with her lack of discipline, with her errors, with her softness.

She'd lost that softness and done everything she could to take care of that kid. She'd gone from the tender, quiet, desperately struggling woman to what she was now, raising her son as best she could and battling anyone who stood in her way.

Trev was here, as if nothing had happened. Like he'd never hurt her, hurt *them*. Like he had a fucking *right* to be here.

"I'm in town for the next two days," he said. "Then I'm back to Wyoming . . ."

"Dad . . . ," Kit warned.

". . . because I'm getting married."

She tilted her head, finally looking at him. He looked older, but that was to be expected. His hairline had receded, though it was hard to tell from his buzz cut. His short hair and the stubble on his still-granite jaw had more pewter than blond at this point, although his hair had always been light enough that it was hard to notice. He was still thin as a rail, ropy with lean muscle. He still had hazel eyes that she'd once hoped Kit would inherit, even as she realized that the Asian genes would probably come through. Just like Nana Birdie had hoped she'd have blue eyes like her father, but her mother's eyes stared back. It had been another disappointment for Trev, once upon a time.

He had a lot of disappointments.

So there had to be something he wanted. Something he was trying to do. Her brain whirred, conjectured. Something clicked.

"You want Kit to come to the wedding?" she surmised, after a long moment.

"I want Kit to be my best man. He's grown now, going to college." Trev let out a frustrated sigh. "I'd be proud to have him standing up for me."

Maggie went very still.

*You don't deserve him! You never fucking did!*

But the words wouldn't come out.

"Mom?" Kit's voice was anxious.

She swallowed hard. "Well, I'm glad you two are talking," she said. "I've always wanted you two to have a relationship, and if Kit wants to, then I'm okay with it."

Trev's mouth twisted in a smile. "Wow. That was easier than I thought. We used to argue about everything."

"Now get out."

His eyebrow quirked. "Ah. Here it is."

"This is my house, Trev," she said, her voice quiet but firm. Then she turned to Kit. "If you want to hang out with him, have a meal or two with him, you can absolutely do that. Just not in this house."

"Jesus, it's been five years," Trev grumbled, rolling his eyes. "I've let it go. Why can't you?"

"Dad!" Kit glared at him.

"What? You told me yourself: she's been living like a hermit. That's why you were worried when there was a strange car," Trev pointed out. "Hell, you've been jumping through hoops to get her to have a life and make some friends! That's not healthy, Mags, and it shouldn't be Kit's problem."

Maggie spun on Kit, who winced. "What? What is he talking about?"

Kit looked pale, his expression guilty.

"I know I made a lot of mistakes. I didn't think staying here would've made things any better for any of us, and I still believe that," Trev continued. "I wasn't in a good headspace. But I always knew he was a smart kid, and he turned out great. Better than I ever expected."

Kit looked stricken, and in that moment, she could've murdered Trev.

"But you should let him *be* a kid," Trev scolded. "Not have him worry about you and come up with crazy schemes to make you social. He's not the parent here. *You* are."

She felt like she was collapsing in on herself. She crossed her arms in front of her chest, which should've looked defiant, but felt more like she was hugging herself, trying to keep it together.

"Dad, you should definitely leave now," Kit said, his voice deep and sharp, brooking no argument. "I'll talk to you later."

Trev huffed. "Sorry," he finally said. "If I was, you know, harsh. I just feel like I've been out of the loop with Kit for so long. I don't want to see us make things worse, and this isn't good for him. You can't expect me to see something bad for my kid and hold back."

"You never did," she said. "Kit, why don't you go to your room for a second? I'm going to walk your father out to his truck."

"Oh, fuck," Kit muttered, and she shot a look at him. "Come on. Do you guys really have to do this? I'm sorry I brought him in, and I'm sorry I told him anything, but I'm eighteen years old, and I don't need to hear a fucking shouting match between my divorced parents!"

She closed her eyes. That had happened, years ago, when Trev had left. They'd had increasingly bitter fights, with lots of yelling on his part, lots of crying on hers. It had been a brutal stalemate, right up to him driving away and not coming back.

"I'm not going to yell at him," she replied, mentally reaching for the internal armor she'd built so meticulously. "Eat some pancakes if you want. Get a load of laundry started. I'll be back in a minute."

Kit's mouth twisted, shooting her a suspicious look.

"And then *we're* going to talk," she added firmly.

He sighed, then nodded. She gestured to Trev to follow her. The air was cold, even though it hadn't snowed, or at least it hadn't stuck. She should've put a jacket on, but she didn't feel the chill. Trev was driving a new black Ford F-150. He had always liked his vehicles.

"I really am trying with Kit," Trev said defensively. "He's a good kid."

"I know."

"I should've let him know that more," Trev finally said. "I should've done a lot of things differently. I see that now."

She shrugged.

"My girlfriend, Carleigh, is helping me see some of that."

"Was it her idea that you reach out to Kit?"

"No. That was my idea," he said. Then, reluctantly, he added, "After I saw the, uh, sonogram."

If Maggie's eyes went any wider, they'd pop out of her head. "She's *pregnant*?" she said. "That's why you're getting married? How old is she?"

Trev's expression pulled. "She's thirty."

"Wow." Twenty years' age difference. He was going to be fifty years old with a newborn. He hadn't even liked having a newborn when *he* was thirty.

She thought of a meme Mac had sent her. *It's called karma, and it's pronounced ha ha, fuck you.*

"Don't even start," Trev warned.

"Whatever. She's thirty, she's old enough to make her own decisions. And you're going to be a father again." The thought made her shudder. The idea of having a baby at this age, the sleep deprivation, juggling the strain of a new marriage and an infant . . .

God, she hoped this Carleigh was a stronger person than she had been.

"Kit really does worry about you," Trev said. No. *Lectured.* "He's been—"

She cut across his words. "I will deal with Kit momentarily. You've made it clear that you didn't think much of my parenting. You thought I was too soft on him. You just abandoned us when you decided that no matter what you did, my influence was going to be too strong, and you couldn't ever 'fix' the damage I'd done. Do you remember that?"

He looked a whole decade older. "I know I—"

"*Do you remember*?" she hissed. "Because I do. I took care of that kid. I helped him with homework and college applications, I was there when his first girlfriend broke his heart, I was there when his dog died. I might've been a bad wife, and maybe a bad mother. God knows that's been my biggest fear. But don't you fucking *dare* act like it's your place to call me out for it. You made your choices."

Trev's mouth pulled into a taut line, and he nodded.

"I'm warning you once: If you fuck this up, make Kit think that he's got a place in your life until your *new* son can be molded into the tough toxic masculine ideal you always wanted . . . I am not even kidding. I will kill you."

"I don't want to hurt Kit," Trev said. "I promise, Maggie. I mean it."

She looked at him. "I mean it too."

He sighed. "Not having another son, by the way," he muttered. "We're having a girl. And Carleigh's pretty determined we're going to be one and done."

She stared at him. God. Maybe that was why he was going to see Kit. He wasn't ever going to have another shot at this.

"Good for you," she said. "I'm going back inside. Kit'll get in contact with you, and you can pick him up if you want, or he'll drive to meet you. But either way, you're not stepping into this house again."

"Maggie?"

She looked over her shoulder. "What?"

"For what it's worth, I'm sorry," he said. "That I wasn't a better husband to you. It's not all your fault that we couldn't make it work."

She closed her eyes for a second. Then she laughed, the sound creaky and broken.

"Big of you," she whispered. Then she turned around and went back into the house.

# CHAPTER 38

## BEWARE THE IRON WOOBIE

As soon as Aiden got the text that Davy and Sheryl had arrived at his mother's house, he headed over. He'd spent the waiting time on *Blood Saga*, because, as Maggie would say, he felt like "killing shit." Unfortunately, school was out, and he found other members of the guild hanging out, so he quickly fled the hall and did a quick solo dungeon run just to leach some of the poisonous feelings out without needing to put on a friendly face with the other members of the guild. In that time, he felt his mind getting clearer, more focused.

By the time he walked into his mother's house, he felt preternaturally calm. Almost serene.

His mother was carping about him as he walked down the hallway toward the kitchen. Sheryl had her back to him, while Davy was standing and leaning against counters and nodding, looking pained. His expression shifted to relief. "Aiden," he said on an exhalation. "Listen . . ."

"What are you doing here?" his mother snapped, turning to him from her position at the kitchen table. "Because I meant what I said."

"I understand. You were very clear that if I didn't act the way you wanted, I wouldn't be your son anymore."

Davy looked ill. Sheryl turned to Aiden, her expression pinched.

"Did you see the new car Davy brought me?" his mother said, every word a barb. "*He* knows I can still drive. *He* isn't trying to take over my life. *He* doesn't embarrass me in front of family."

Aiden took a deep, cleansing breath. "I've worked in hospice, Mom. I've worked with the elderly. The last thing I want to do is infantilize you, or make you feel like you don't have autonomy."

She scoffed at his big words, rolling her eyes, but she still looked mollified. "I am an adult. You two are my kids, and you can't make my decisions for me."

"No, we can't," Aiden said. "But we're both adults too. And you can't tell us what to do at this point either."

Davy shot him a *why-are-you-bringing-me-into-this* look.

"And I already told *you*: I'm not going to stay in the closet just because you're afraid of what your church friends are going to say," he said. "Even if I'm dating Maggie. Just because I'm dating a woman doesn't make me any less bi."

*Or demi.* But he wasn't even going to try to explain that at this point. She couldn't even wrap her head around him being bi.

His mother was methodically tearing a paper napkin on the place mat in front of her, as if channeling her need to destroy something. "All right. You can keep seeing Maggie," she said, with obvious reluctance. "But nobody needs to know about . . . the other thing. We can keep it quiet. Sheryl, that means you too." She glared daggers at her daughter-in-law.

"That's not happening."

"Are you trying to make my life miserable?" Now her glare shifted to him. "You're just going to cause talk!"

"Well, maybe I can just leave town, then."

He hadn't meant to blurt that out. But it was a thought that had been turning around in his mind for a while. Of course, now he had Maggie to consider.

Hopefully, Maggie would still be open to being a consideration. He frowned.

When he refocused on the scene in front of him, he saw that all three of them were staring at him with shock. "You're moving?" Davy asked first.

"Figures you'd leave," his mother said, but her voice shook a little.

"What kind of son are you?" Sheryl added, her look venomous. "What kind of *person* are you?"

"I'm not leaving immediately, but it's been a long time coming." Aiden crossed his arms, surveying all of them in turn before zeroing in on Sheryl. "And why shouldn't I? What you're saying is, Mom can be a total biphobe and hypocrite . . . but I should stay here to take care of her despite it, no matter how she treats me. She can make choices, like driving a car despite having multiple accidents and incidents of dizziness and falling . . . but I need to be the one to deal with the consequences of her choices. Also, I need to deny who I am while I do that and ensure that she never hears gossip about me, which I can't even control."

Sheryl paled. His mother spluttered.

"Oh, and it's fine that you treat me like a monster in front of my nieces, telling them God knows what . . . while you two refuse to come out here and take care of Mom, because *I'm* here." He felt like he was drowning, but he kept his gaze firm. "Monster that I am."

Davy looked appalled. "Aiden, it's not like that."

Sheryl looked like she'd swallowed a lemon. "We have busy lives . . ."

"I love you," he said. "All of you—even though you might not believe it, Sheryl. But I'm not going to keep putting up with this shit. I'm not going to be punished when I haven't done anything wrong."

"Ha," Sheryl spat out, "you act like—" only to have his mother begin talking in the same moment.

"This is all your fault—" his mother started.

To Aiden's surprise, Davy actually cut across all of them. *"Quiet!"*

Sheryl stared at Davy, mouth agape. Even his mother looked surprised. Davy was the easygoing one, the charming one. Now, he looked older, almost stern. He rubbed at his eyes with the heels of his palms. "That Maggie lady was right, Sheryl. Do you have any idea how shitty I feel when you treat Aiden the way you do? The way you act *around* Aiden? *After all these years?*"

Sheryl looked stunned.

Davy looked at Aiden. "I knew that you . . . well, I mean, I thought you were gay," he said. "Sheryl said you were. But I didn't know that you were in a relationship. Hell, I didn't even think you *did* relationships." He rubbed his hand over his face, then turned his gaze back to Aiden. "I guess you've been hiding a lot."

"I didn't do relationships for a long time. I'm demisexual too," Aiden decided to throw in, since Davy seemed to actually be listening for the first time in forever. "Just figured that out, actually. In my case, that means I am attracted to people very rarely, although it can happen. So it's not like I've been in all these secret relationships or hooking up with people on the low or whatever. Honestly, I thought there was something wrong with me for a long time."

"I . . . don't know what demisexual means," Davy admitted, rubbing the back of his neck. "But I'll, um, learn."

"Get out," his mother said again, grabbing the coffee mug in front of her with a tight grip, like she was tempted to throw it at him.

Aiden sighed. Then he looked at Davy.

"I tried," Aiden said in a low voice. "But I'm not going to stay here, continuing to get kicked. Mom, you deserve to be treated with respect . . . but I deserve that too. And if you can't give that to me, then I guess we *are* done."

He turned, heading out the door, Davy hot on his heels.

"You can't just leave!"

"Why not?" Aiden asked. "I have felt like shit most of my life in this family. I had a college boyfriend who kept me hidden and made me feel ashamed for loving him. Then I was with Sheryl, who made me feel like my past was something I should hide, and who punished me when I was finally honest. My own mother wants me to let her do whatever the fuck she wants, including endangering herself and others . . . all the while hating what she knows about me and demanding I be less than I am. I'm surrounded by people who are supposed to love me, as long as I somehow become what they expect of me. And I'm done, okay? I. Am. Done."

Davy looked at him, and for a second, it was like when they were kids . . . Davy looking at him, his eyes soulful and rimmed with tears after a skinned knee, as Aiden bandaged him up because their parents were both at work. Davy, who wanted so desperately for Aiden to make him all better.

Davy, who was used to Aiden fixing things.

"I'll get Mom to calm down," Davy said. "And Sheryl and I are going to have a serious talk. This has gone on way too long, and I'm sorry I didn't deal with it sooner. It just seemed easier, especially since we didn't see you that often."

"You didn't see me that often," Aiden pointed out, "because Sheryl wouldn't let you."

Davy hung his head. "Shit. Yeah."

"And you're going to need to take care of Mom now," Aiden said, gentling his tone. "She's lucky, she has the church group that she's close to. She loves them, and they're like family. But things are going to start happening now. She's right, she's an adult, and it was perhaps wrong of me to try to force her. But I'm not going to sit here and act like it's fine that she ignores assigning power of attorney and advanced directives. I'm sure as hell not pretending it's awesome that she's driving when I'm afraid she's going to kill somebody. To top it all off, I can't sit here and do nothing while she treats me this way . . . then pretend it's all cool and that I'm going to take her to church and get her groceries and do all the things she claims not to want, as she bitches at me and . . ." He swallowed hard. "And hates me. I can't, Davy."

"I'll fix it," Davy said, sounding a little more panicked. "I'll get her to apologize."

"I need time," Aiden said, even as he thought *There is no fixing this.*

"Maybe she'll change her mind," Davy pressed. "Dad did."

"She was right. Dad was dying." Aiden shook his head. "But it did feel good there, for a while. The acceptance. Even if he didn't really understand."

They were quiet for a long moment. "Are you really leaving Fool's Falls?" Davy asked. "That's a big decision to make spur of the moment."

Aiden closed his eyes for a long second, thinking about it. "I need a little time on that too," he answered slowly. "I didn't mean to stay here this long, but it seemed like Mom needed me, and things just got worse, and I just . . . I don't know. Settled? Hid? It was nice to feel needed, and I guess I hoped things with Mom would change, but they didn't. I miss the west side. I mean, I had some trouble feeling like I belonged over there . . . but I fit in more."

"But what about Maggie?"

"I'm going to talk to Maggie," he said. "We're new, and I'll be honest: I want to be with her."

"Enough to stay?" Davy looked desperate.

That was the question, wasn't it?

"Enough to talk to her about it," he answered, then gave Davy a hug. "I'll call you next week, okay?"

Davy squeezed back, harder than he had in a long time. His eyes were shiny by the time they broke apart.

"Love you, Aiden," Davy said in a broken voice.

"Love you too."

Aiden drove home carefully, thoughtful as he navigated the familiar streets. The thought of moving was strangely exciting, freeing. He hoped things were going better with Maggie. And he hoped that she'd be open to listening to him—and not retreating into pain because of her asshole ex-husband's unexpected return.

# CHAPTER 39

## THE DOG WAS THE MASTERMIND

Kit was waiting for her, his hands stuffed so deep in his sweatshirt pocket that it tugged his neckline. In a different frame of mind, she'd tell him to stop, tease him for stretching out yet another collar. But now, she could barely talk to him.

"I'm sorry, Mom," Kit said, and the words tumbled out like rice from a broken bag. "I didn't want to upset you. Dad can still be a dick, but he seems to have turned around a little, and I . . ."

"What did he mean, you were scheming to get me a social life?"

He finally pulled a hand out of his pocket to tug at the roots of his hair, making it stick up like a cockatoo's crest. Ordinarily, she'd tease about that.

Not today.

"I . . . may not be as socially hopeless as I've let on," he said.

"Clarify, please." She was proud that her voice stayed even.

He reddened. "Um. Well. I wasn't lying, per se. I did have a rough start, and it was hard to get out and meet people. And I dragged my feet when it came to joining clubs and stuff, and I didn't meet anybody in my classes." He paused. "Until about a month in."

"Ah."

"But we had this RA that was a total douchebag," Kit said, his words picking up speed, all but tumbling out of his mouth. "Total power trip bullshit, and he'd try to punish us for doing stuff that was fine, like using the kitchen, and he got the microwave taken away, and it was this big pain in the ass. So I, um . . ."

She waited. Kit was the type that couldn't stand squirming in silence.

". . . I sort of started a bit of a revolt?"

She blinked.

"My roommate, Toby, is pretty cool, and he was complaining that they couldn't do that. So I figured, you know, we just needed to approach it with logic." Kit was shoving his hands in his pockets again, trying to look innocent and failing miserably.

She rubbed at her temples, even as she found a small glimmer of amusement. "Pranks, I take it?" She knew Kit's MO. When he'd had teachers who had been sexist or racist or just pricks, Kit figured out ways to torture them without getting anyone in trouble. She'd tended to turn a blind eye.

Sure enough, his flush deepened. "Just little ones," he quickly said. "We . . . may have sneaked into his room and done the zipper trick."

"Zipper . . . ?"

"Where you crimp two-thirds of his pants' zippers halfway with a pair of pliers," he clarified. "So they aren't able to zip or unzip completely or easily. But just a bit, so it's not noticeable and doesn't seem to be malicious."

She shook her head.

"A few other things too. Nothing horrible. Broke the filament in his lightbulbs, so it seemed like he couldn't keep a lamp lit. Got his personal email and signed him up for a bunch of stuff. Mostly annoying . . . and comprehensive. You know how I do." His grin was evil. "By the end of the semester, the guy was running around like he'd lost his mind."

She sighed, sitting down on the couch. Kit immediately sat next to her.

"I wouldn't have even gotten into it," he said, "but the guy was giving a really hard time to the girls across the hall from us, especially Dana."

There was a way he said Dana's name, a fondness, that she immediately clued into. "Girlfriend?" she asked.

He blushed. Kit looked like a tomato by this point. "Yeah," he said.

"How long?"

"Um . . . maybe two months?"

"Two months?" She looked at him, aghast. *"Dude."*

"I didn't mean to keep it a secret from you," he said. "But you were all gung ho about doing whatever you could to make sure I was getting the full social experience of school, while at the same time you were burying yourself in this tomb of a house. I swear to God, if you could hook yourself into the internet like they do in *The Matrix*, you would have."

"Damn it, Kit . . ."

"And I know you said you were fine," he continued earnestly. "But I worry, Mom."

She huffed out a breath. What to say, in the face of that? "I don't want you to worry," she said softly. "But even if you did . . . I'm the parent. Your father was right on that front."

He scowled. "I definitely didn't mean for Dad to give you shit. I shouldn't have told him, but . . . I don't know. It was nice to talk to him again. For him to listen."

She deflated. Yeah, she could see that.

"Still, I shouldn't have let him in the house."

"Why didn't you tell me you were talking to him, at least?"

Kit bit the corner of his lip. "Because I know how much you hate him."

She closed her eyes, sighing. It was fair. "I have been angry with him for a long time," she said. "Mostly because of how he treated you. He was hard on you when he was here, or he ignored you. Then he just ghosted you. I don't care how he treated me, but goddamn it, he'll treat you like shit over my dead body. I let him get away with too much for too long—"

"And this is why I didn't tell you." Kit looked mournful.

She took a deep breath, quelling the anger that had, indeed, welled as she started talking. "I'm sorry," she said. "I don't want you to feel like you can't talk to me."

He nodded. "You didn't tell me everything either," he pointed out. "How long have you been seeing the guy?"

"Who, Aiden?"

"Yeah. Healer guy." He grinned. "Pancake guy. Good pancakes, by the way."

She shrugged. "I didn't have a chance to eat any yet."

"He spent the night, I assume?" Kit looked a cross between amused and grossed out.

"I don't see that it's your business," she countered, "and we're not done talking about you yet."

Kit looked resigned. "In between all the pranks, we all managed to dig up the regulations and got proof of what the RA was doing that broke them. He's getting written up and won't be an RA next semester."

"Who's 'we'?"

Kit looked at the ceiling, as if mentally counting. "My roommate. Dana and her roomie, Naomi. Jesse and his boyfriend, Ty. Kirk from down the hall. And some of my friends from the library." He paused. "I got a job at the library, by the way."

"You got a job?" She was torn between being proud of him and distraught that she knew *none* of this. "Do you have time for that? Do you not have enough money?"

"I'm doing fine," he reassured her, with the easy confidence of an eighteen-year-old. "And it's an awesome job. I now know how to research *anything*, and I've met a lot of cool people."

She finally grinned. Then she startled when tears began to pour down her cheeks.

This was what she had wanted. Her son was independent, and brilliant, and no longer alone. And *happy*.

"Oh, God! Mom!" Kit quickly engulfed her in a hug. Even though he'd towered over her for several years now, she still felt a sharp pang as he cuddled her like she was a child. When had her baby gotten big enough to cuddle *her* completely? "What's wrong? I'm sorry! I should've told you everything. I just wanted you to not be alone."

"I know," she said. Well, sniffled. "But first: don't do that. Don't try to manipulate me just because you're concerned."

"Only okay when *you* do it, huh?"

"I didn't lie, my dude," she added sharply, and to his credit, Kit looked sheepish. "You could've told me you were doing all that stuff and then insisted that I do the same. You didn't have to lie, or use guilt. I hope to Christ I didn't teach you *that*."

The fear that she'd done exactly that made her sick to her stomach. She would've fucked up fairly significantly if that was the case. That *would* prove Trev right.

"No, this is my fault." He looked so miserable, she hugged him. "I'm sorry, Mom. I just wanted you to feel better, you know?"

"I know. But I also want to make sure you know this wasn't okay."

"I get it. I won't do it again."

"Damned right you won't," she muttered, then sighed.

"Sooooo . . . The guy?"

She huffed out a little laugh. "Aiden and I got together recently," she said. "Like, a day ago recent. But we've been good friends for months, and I value that. Nobody's rushing anything."

"You like him?"

*I love him.*

She wasn't ready to admit that quite yet, though. Probably.

"I like him," she agreed. "A lot."

"Well, I'll need to talk to him," Kit said, sounding so grumpy and ridiculous that she hugged him again.

"We'll see about that," she said, then got up. "All right. I'm having some of these pancakes."

# CHAPTER 40

## YOUR RESIGNATION IS NOT ACCEPTED

Aiden spent the better part of the day splitting wood for the fireplace, stress-cleaning his house (even though it didn't need it), and killing even more shit on *Blood Saga Online*. This time, he didn't avoid the other members of the guild. Ferocity, Gandalf, and Dork helped him demolish a dungeon, and if they noticed he was more subdued than usual on the chat, they didn't say anything.

As he mechanically went through the motions of annihilating cave demons and lichs, his brain turned over his current situation carefully. Even though his chest was sore over what he'd needed to do with his family, there was a feeling of lightness there too. A sheer relief, and a sense of unknown. It was like being in a huge open field, or out on the ocean, with nothing but possibility and the chance to go in any direction, the horizon just spread out endlessly. It was daunting and encouraging, both at once.

*Now, I just need to convince Maggie to be my girlfriend. How hard can that be?*

He sighed, feeling his forehead furrow.

First, having a "girlfriend" at fifty felt very weird. There had to be a better word for it.

Second . . . getting Maggie to do absolutely anything was a challenge. While she might've previously been amenable to the idea of being his girlfriend, she hadn't been smacked in the face with her ex-husband the asshole yet. After all these months, he knew that if anything would put her force fields up, it'd be that.

She liked being with him, at least. She was one of his best friends and favorite people, and he hoped she felt the same. And then there was the fact they'd been *together*. He wanted to do that again, as soon as possible. Not just the sex, although that was awesome, but spending the day together, sleeping next to each other. They'd hit that next level of intimacy.

She also had had no qualms about, say, jumping over a dining table to defend his honor. Which only made him love her more.

But she was skittish. He knew that. Add that to goddamned Trev's presence, and he was afraid she was going to retreat into herself like a turtle wearing Razor Ribbon. He was nervous he wasn't going to have a chance.

*No.* He wasn't going to let himself overthink this or psych himself out. He'd been letting other people call the shots most of his adult life. He wasn't going to ignore Maggie's wishes—he respected her. But that didn't mean he was going to just sit passively by and let her close herself off from a relationship with him because she didn't know how strongly he felt, or how committed he was to this, or because she was afraid that he'd judge her or criticize her. He was all in, and he loved her just the way she was. He needed her to know that.

But to do that, he had to . . . you know, *talk to her*.

It was eight o'clock at night. He'd texted her that afternoon, just as a check-in, but he hadn't heard back. The ball was firmly in her court.

He'd just heated up a cup of soup—from a batch he and Maggie had made together—when he saw the flash of headlights through his front curtains. Putting the bowl down on the coffee table, he opened the front door.

"Maggie?"

She gave him a scowling up-nod. "Can I come in?"

"Of course." He quickly made room for her to scoot around him. Her hands were stuffed deep in her thick fleece jacket. She was back to wearing no makeup, and her eyes looked a little red. Her hair was its usual crazed nimbus of waves and flyaways, and as she toed off her boots, he could see that they were a mess. Her jeans had a hole in the knee.

She looked wonderful, so good it made his heart hurt.

She was also in his house, with a serious expression, looking like she wanted . . . something. To talk?

Shit. That probably meant a "we need to talk" scenario. He was on borrowed time as it was. He was going to have to make the biggest pitch of his life . . . and he wasn't really what anyone would call persuasive. Davy had gotten all the charming genes.

He cleared his throat. "Can I get you anything? Something to drink? You hungry?" Anything that would keep her there a little longer, keep her occupied, while he sorted out his argument. Dammit, he should've done *that* today. Lord knows he'd thought enough about it!

She gave him a quick, curt shake of her head.

It *really* wasn't looking good.

He grimaced. Well, she had every right to not be interested. But he wasn't going to just assume, and he wasn't going to roll over and pretend. He had feelings, dammit. And he had the right to at least present his case.

"Why don't you have a seat," he said, surprising himself with how firm his voice was. "I think we probably need to talk."

She blinked at him, probably taken aback at his tone. She nodded, taking a seat on the couch, and he sat next to her . . . close enough to smell her coconut conditioner and that sweet, slightly spicy scent that was just her, but not so close that she felt crowded or uncomfortable. At least, he hoped not.

"Here's the thing," he said. "I talked to my family today—that is, my mom and Davy. Even Sheryl. And a few things became clear. First, I'm not going to keep getting treated like shit, and I said as much."

Her eyes went wide. "You did? Holy shit, that's fantastic!" She closed the difference, drawing him into a tight hug and nuzzling against his chest for a second. Then she pulled back. "I mean, it sucks too. But you deserve so much more than the way they've been treating you. I'm glad you stood up for yourself. And I hope they pull their heads out of their asses at some point soon."

He grinned, even though the pain was still pretty fresh. "Davy seems to have come around, which was a surprise," he said. "Sheryl was still pissy, but I don't care. As for my mom . . . well. We'll just see."

Maggie nodded. "That's still a hard decision," she said. "I remember that, from Nana Birdie. It's easy to feel guilty . . . and relieved."

"You understand." Of course she did. Maggie seemed to plug into him on a cellular level. She just *got* him. "Anyway . . . I never wanted to move back to Fool's Falls. I came back when my father was dying, and then wound up staying to make sure my mom was okay. But I'm seriously considering moving back to the west side."

Now her expression fell. "You're *leaving*?"

He took a deep breath. This was probably the wrong way to go about this, but now he'd stuck his foot in it, so it was too late. "Not necessarily," he said. "Here's the thing. I know we've only just started, well, whatever we have between us. We haven't labeled it. And I don't want you to feel pressured. We can go as slow as you like. But there's something there."

She was staring at him, still as a stone. But she was listening.

"I've gotten to know you over the past few months, and I hope it's obvious that I feel really close to you. I trust you." He swallowed, then went for it. "I think I fell for you before I knew what was happening."

Her eyes widened. Her breathing shallowed.

"I've been thinking of leaving the Falls for a while now," he admitted. "Didn't think I could, because of my family dynamics, but it's been a long time since I've considered it home here. Then I met you. I'm not ready to leave you."

She was still quiet. She didn't seem angry, and she would've probably said something if she was. Was she still processing? Trying to come up with an escape plan? Ready to grab one of his skillets and whack some sense into him?

What the heck was she *thinking*?

"My point is, I . . . um. Fell in love with you." He felt a stubborn bubble of hope. "That's kind of fast, but I don't care. I love you."

She blinked. Then he watched the delicate column of her throat work as she swallowed convulsively.

Then she tackled him.

He let out a surprised "oof" as she spread over him like a blanket, pushing him into the deep couch cushions. He let out a bark of startled laughter.

"I fell in love with you too," she grumbled, then kissed him. "And I drove here, *in the dark*, to tell you. And it's fast, and scary as fuck, but I don't care. You make me feel safe, and happy, and wanted."

She rested her chin on her hands, just below his chin, and surveyed him with long-lashed eyes.

"So I am keeping you," she added solemnly. "We're not in a hurry, right? We can figure all the other stuff out. But we can do that together."

He could feel his own wide smile as he kissed her back.

# CHAPTER 41

## I WAS TOLD THERE WOULD BE CAKE

Aiden couldn't remember the last Christmas he'd enjoyed this much. He was at Maggie's house, celebrating with her and Kit. After coming to the understanding that he and Maggie were an Official Couple, he was both excited and nervous to meet Kit under better circumstances. At least Trev had finally fucked off back to Wyoming. After what he'd heard from Maggie, he wasn't ready to pretend to be polite with that asshole.

He grinned. Maggie was *definitely* rubbing off on him.

She and Kit had set up a small artificial tree, adorned with mostly homemade ornaments. He'd driven to Spokane and braved the holiday crowds to get them presents, not wanting to show up empty handed. Based on what Maggie had told him Kit was interested in, he got Kit a few anime T-shirts from his favorite geek store. For Maggie, he got a box set of classic-movie DVDs since her streaming service could be spotty in the Upper Falls. He also got her a bunch of wool socks and a large, super-soft sweater. They seemed pedestrian, but he also knew that she'd hate things like jewelry or perfume. These gifts were comfy, for both her body and her mind. He hoped she liked them, anyway.

Now, after enjoying a delicious dinner of rib roast, buttery mashed potatoes, and green beans with slivered almonds, he was full and content and washing dishes while Kit did the drying, since Maggie had done the bulk of the cooking. (He had helped with mashing potatoes this time, something Kit had chuckled at, teasing her for being short.) Maggie was sitting in the living room, looking for Christmas music that "didn't drive her up a wall" on the TV's radio stations.

"So," Kit led, as he towel-dried and put away dishes with the speed of long practice, "you and my mom, huh?"

Aiden felt his cheeks heat, but he nodded. "Yeah."

"That's cool," Kit said. "I should let you know, though. If you do anything that hurts her, I will make your life incredibly, creatively, and unbelievably painful in the short time between my finding out and your body going mysteriously missing. Just so you know."

Aiden paused in scrubbing the roasting pan, staring at him. Then he started chuckling.

"Kit!" Maggie chastised from the living room. "I heard that!"

"Not sorry," Kit replied.

"You're right, Maggie," Aiden called out with a grin. "He couldn't be more your kid if you designed him in a lab."

The words seemed to make both of them happy.

By the time the dishes were done, it was evening, and the stars were out in the clear, pitch-black sky.

"C'mon, time for presents," Maggie said. "Then dessert."

Kit made a big show of mock solemnity. "I was told," he intoned, "that there would be cake?"

She rolled her eyes. "Yellow cake with chocolate fudge frosting, of course. And Aiden brought chocolate chip cookies."

Kit gave him an appraising look. "You bake, huh?"

"Kinda." Aiden smiled. "I'm okay."

"I'll be the judge of that," Kit said, but cracked a smile.

Before Aiden could answer, his phone started buzzing. He didn't expect anybody to call him—the fights had been too fresh, and he'd reconciled himself to that. He had a little ache of melancholy that things hadn't worked out better, but he was also in a good place about it.

But it wasn't his mother, or Davy.

It was Sheryl.

*Why the* fuck *is Sheryl calling me?*

He felt a stab of panic. "I'm sorry, I have to take this," he apologized to Maggie. "It's Sheryl. It might be . . . my mom's supposed to go there for Christmas, and . . ."

"No problem," Maggie said quickly, nudging him to her office and shutting the door behind him as he answered.

"Sheryl? Is Mom okay?"

"What?" Sheryl said. "Yes. She's okay. She's here, watching *Frozen* with the kids."

He frowned. "Is Davy okay?"

He heard her take a deep breath. "I have to assume he is."

Now his jaw dropped. "You don't know?"

"He's with Maria and Bug for Christmas."

*Holy shit.* "What happened?" he asked, then shook his head. "No, never mind. I don't care. Why are you calling me?"

She paused. "We got in a horrible fight," she said. "About you. About how I've treated you. And, um, him. I guess it's been bothering him for a while, and he finally just snapped."

Aiden thought of what Riley had once told him. *Sounds like a "you" problem, not a "me" problem.*

"Still not seeing what this has to do with me," Aiden said. "And I'm about to open presents with Maggie and her son, so I have to go."

Another pause. "I know I haven't treated you well."

His eyes widened. This was new.

"I told you," Sheryl said slowly, "when I went off to college . . . I got a little wild."

"The experimentation?"

"That. And, um, drugs. I didn't tell you about that." Her voice had lowered. "I went off the rails a bit. Almost flunked out, got in some bad situations."

"I'm sorry," he said. "But that—"

"My parents helped me out. I realized that all the freedom I wanted was more of a . . . trap. I needed to get my life back on track. I finally saw that even though they can be kind of overbearing, they genuinely care about me, and they had a point. So I cleaned up my act. Then I found you again, and it was like I was getting all my mistakes cleared off the board." Her voice was breaking with emotion. "I thought we had a second chance. I thought, finally, life was going my way. We could do it right this time."

He swallowed. "Then you found out I was bi, huh?"

"It just felt like I was being punished for my past," she said. "And I was so *angry*. Although I guess I should've been angrier at myself."

He shook his head. She'd been sweet, once. He'd loved her, and on some level, he really did still love her. "I'm going to go, Sheryl," he said, but with kindness.

"Please," she said. "Please tell Davy I apologized. I don't want to screw things up with him. Let him know I—"

"You're going to have to tell him yourself and see how that goes," he interjected. "Merry Christmas, Sheryl." He would've asked her to pass it along to his mom, but he knew there was no point. Then he hung up and shut off his phone.

He didn't know how things were going to go from here. Parts of this still stung . . . but he had hope. Things were different. With Maggie, he was happy. He was *himself*.

He was going to keep it that way.

He rejoined Maggie and Kit, out in the living room. Maggie looked at him with concern. "Everything okay?"

He nodded. He wasn't going to get into it tonight. Maggie was sitting on the couch, while Kit sat in the old recliner. She distributed the packages. He sat on the floor, leaning against the couch by Maggie's feet.

"Open yours first," she said, sounding strangely shy.

He did . . . and burst out laughing.

"A cast-iron skillet?"

"Building up your arsenal," she said, with a wink. Kit rolled his eyes. "You never know when a strange Asian woman is going to need something to arm herself with."

"You're not that strange," he said, leaning up and kissing her instinctively. She smiled against his lips.

"Ew, nobody wants to see that," Kit groaned. "Thanks for the T-shirts, Aiden."

Aiden nodded. Then he looked at Maggie. "Your turn."

She nodded, opening his lumpy, home-wrapped present. Her eyes widened. "*Auntie Mame*, *His Girl Friday*, the original *Sabrina*?" she said, her eyes shining. "And a new sweater? Wool socks!"

She was incandescent, and he felt his chest warm. She liked them. *Thank God.*

"You get her," Kit noted. "All right. You get the stamp of approval."

Aiden smiled broadly.

"For now," Kit temporized, and Maggie tossed a sock at him.

After they finished with their gift exchange and had the aforementioned cake, Kit left to have an all-night gaming session with Harrison, whose girlfriend had dumped him and moved out. There was going to be a bunch of the high school grads from Kit's class over. "Just make good decisions," Maggie admonished. Kit rolled his eyes, but gave her a big hug before leaving.

From there, Aiden took her back to bed. "Merry Christmas," he said, kissing her soundly. "I love you, Bogwitch."

She kissed him back, and it was soft and warm and just like he'd always imagined home felt like.

"Love you, too, Otter."

# EPILOGUE

## BATTLE COUPLE

***Three and a half years later . . .***

Maggie rushed through the front door of their house in Woodinville, a suburb that was . . . well, nowhere near Seattle, honestly, but was on the west side. "I know, I know!" she called, quickly putting the take-out bags she'd grabbed on the dining table. "Am I late?"

"Don't worry . . . the official run doesn't start for half an hour. Although the guys are talking shit," Aiden called back, humor evident in his voice. "Dork is saying you might be getting too old to play this late. Asking if it's senior hour at the community center."

"You tell Dork that I'll kick his ass," she answered as she walked into the spare bedroom. That's where Aiden's gaming computer was set up. She leaned down, giving him a quick kiss. Or at least, she tried to give him a quick kiss. He countered by taking his hands off the keyboard and tugging her onto his lap, giving her a much more thorough kiss. By the time he released her, she was breathless.

"We don't *have* to play tonight," she reminded him.

His gray eyes gleamed. "Yeah, we do. The new guy hasn't done the FireMiser quest, and it's all hands on deck for that. You know how hard it is, and we'll need your tank."

She sighed, standing back up. "Fine. But after we eat some dinner. I grabbed food from Ooba Tooba. You know how I feel about their carne asada."

He made a humming noise of food happiness before typing rapidly. "Sorry, guys, gonna have to hold off for a little bit," he narrated. He laughed. "DangerNoodle is saying that we'd better not be going off to have sex. We've been married for a year, and, I quote, 'you ought to be done with that shit.'"

"I am so teasing him about that," she said, with a laugh of her own. "C'mon. How was your day?"

He smiled, and she felt a feeling of quiet, all-encompassing *happiness*. "Good day," he rumbled, following her to where their delicious-smelling food was waiting. "The new guy at work has been a game changer. Malcolm and I wondered why we hadn't brought on a third partner when we started. Malcolm's wife is thrilled too."

She beamed at him. Ever since he'd bought back into the hospice business and they'd moved to the west side, he had focused much more on a work-life balance, something that Malcolm appreciated as well. They'd brought on a few more key employees, and they'd made sure to harmonize growth with their personal lives. She'd enjoyed getting to know Malcolm, his wife, their kids. They'd even been over to the house for barbecues, and met Kit a few times when he'd been home.

"How about you?" Aiden reciprocated, stroking her cheek.

"Finished the marketing-book edits and got a new high-fantasy project in the pipeline," she said, sitting next to him and opening packages, handing him his burrito, and grabbing her own soft tacos. "Also went out and grabbed a few books from the library, grabbed a few groceries. Ran into Janie—she wants us to have dinner with her and Richard, maybe next week?"

He nodded. "As long as it's not Thursday, should be fine." He took a bite, then groaned. "How are these so good?"

"I know, right?" She smiled at him.

They spent a little while like that, eating and talking.

She'd been with Aiden for six months before deciding that she wanted a change. Fool's Falls was a wonderful small town . . . but it wasn't *her* small town. She'd known that, but hadn't been ready to do anything about it, until Aiden. He gave her confidence, even while being patient.

She and Aiden had looked around frantically while her house was up for sale. They bought their current single-family house, and they'd moved in the Halloween of Kit's sophomore year. She'd gotten to know Malcolm and his family; they still connected with the *Blood Saga* guild. Kit was by once a month, mostly to do laundry and raid the fridge. She still texted Rosita and Mac regularly. She even emailed Klara, back at the Falls.

"Man," Aiden said, as they cleaned up the food. "I'm ready to food coma. I'm going to be slow as hell on this dungeon run."

She hugged him, straightening up to kiss him soundly. "You'll be fine, Otter."

He smiled against her lips, framing her face with his hands. "That's because I've got you . . . Bogwitch."

She grinned. This was acceptance. This was her small town. This was where her heart was.

This was home. *Aiden* was home.

"All right," she said, with one last firm kiss. "Let's kick some ass."

# Acknowledgments

I could not do what I do without the help of the amazing team at Montlake. Alison Dasho, Krista Stroever, Cheryl Weisman, Jillian Cline . . . you've all believed in my projects, no matter how weird (and let's face it, this one was bananapants).

Tricia Skinner at Fuse Literary, thank you for championing my work and talking me off metaphorical ledges when I am convinced my writing is trash. (Every! Single! Time! ☺)

Many thanks to the publicity team at Honey Magnolia, who have been amazing.

Finally, a big thank-you to my many writer friends, who have been a source of support and guidance.

Thank you all for being there for me.

# About the Author

Cathy Yardley is an award-winning author of romance, chick lit, and urban fantasy. She has sold more than 1.2 million books with publishers like St. Martin's Press, Avon Books, and Harlequin. She writes fun, geeky, and diverse characters who believe that underdogs can make good and that sometimes being a little wrong is just right. She likes writing about quirky, crazy adventures because she's had plenty of her own: she had her own army in the Society for Creative Anachronism, she's spent New Year's on a three-day solitary vision quest in the Mojave Desert, and she had VIP access to the Viper Room in Los Angeles. Now, she spends her time writing in the wilds of eastern Washington, trying to prevent her son from learning the truth about any of said adventures, and riding herd on her two dogs (and one husband).